KT-381-638

David Dickinson was born ??? ??? ??? ??? ???
degree in Classics from Cambridge, David Dickinson
joined the BBC, where he became editor of *Newsnight*
and *Panorama*, as well as series editor for *Monarchy*, a
three-part programme on the British royal family.

Titles in the series
(listed in order of publication)

Death of an Elgin Marble

DAVID DICKINSON

Constable • London

CONSTABLE

First published in the UK by C&R Crime,
an imprint of Constable & Robinson, 2014

This paperback edition published in Great Britain in 2017 by Constable

3 5 7 9 10 8 6 4 2

Copyright © David Dickinson, 2014

The moral right of the author has been asserted.

A CIP catalogue record for this book
is available from the British Library.

ISBN: 978-1-47210-866-1

Typeset in Palatino by Initial Typesetting Services, Edinburgh EH13 9PH
Printed and bound in Great Britain by CPI Group (UK) Ltd,
Croydon CR0 4YY

Papers used by Constable are from well-managed forests and other
responsible sources.

Constable
An imprint of
Little, Brown Book Group
Carmelite House
50 Victoria Embankment
London EC4Y 0DZ

An Hachette UK Company
www.hachette.co.uk

www.littlebrown.co.uk

For Max, who smiles a lot

PART ONE

THE ISLES OF GREECE

What I would prefer is that you should fix your eyes every day on the glory of Athens as she really is and fall in love with her. When you realize her greatness, then reflect that what made her great was men with a spirit of adventure, men who knew their duty . . . These men gave her their lives, to her and to all of us, and for their own selves they won praises that never grow old, the most splendid of sepulchres – not the sepulchre in which their bodies are laid but where their glory remains eternal in men's minds. For famous men have the whole earth as their memorial. It is not only the inscriptions on their graves in their own country that marks them out: no, in foreign lands also, not in any visible form but in people's hearts, their memory abides and grows.

Thucydides, Pericles' Funeral Speech,
The History of Peloponnesian War

1

It took the British Museum five days to realize that they had lost their Caryatid. In fact, if it hadn't been for the American, they might never have realized she was gone at all.

The Caryatid was part of the Elgin Marbles, a glittering treasure trove of ancient statuary that had once graced the walls of the Parthenon, the most prominent building on the High City, the Acropolis, of Athens, 2,400 years ago. All of the works had been seized by the British Ambassador to Turkey, Lord Elgin, at the beginning of the nineteenth century and carried back to Britain. For just over a century the Elgin Caryatid, tall, graceful and rather severe, had stood in her place in the Elgin Rooms to delight and entrance the population of London.

The Caryatid was a statue of a maiden or a young girl that took the place of one of six columns or pillars in the Erechtheion, a temple that had stood near the Parthenon. This Caryatid was the only one to have been taken by Lord Elgin – her sisters were not to be found in London. Seven feet six inches tall, the statue was wearing a floor-length sleeveless marble dress, carved like a tunic at the top and hanging in elaborate folds at her waist. She had a look of haughty pride on her face, as if only she and her five colleagues were fit to represent their city in its place of greater glory. Lord Elgin, hero or villain of the Marbles that bore his name, depending on your point of view, was in the habit of saying to his friends, 'That Caryatid filly, she looks rather a handful to me.' She had lived as a single Caryatid for over a hundred years since she came to London and was now about 2,300 years old. In the lifetime of the current generation of British Museum porters, always keen on some form of intimacy with their lifeless charges, the Caryatid had been known as Charlotte, or Charlie, Clare or Clary, Cristobel or Chrissie, Carmen or Carrie. The oldest porter on the staff had always thought that Carmen Caryatid had a good ring to it. The Head of Greek and Roman Antiquities called her Clytemnestra. The Director of the British Museum, more faithful perhaps to an English literary tradition, called her Clarissa, Clarissa the Caryatid.

The American was Stephen Lambert Lodge, a thirty-year-old lecturer in Architecture at Yale, one of the oldest and most distinguished universities in America. He was beginning a tour of the cities of Europe that held fragments of the Parthenon, for many cultural pirates apart from Lord Elgin had helped themselves to fragments of fallen statues or ripped them from the walls. From London and the British Museum he was travelling to the Louvre in Paris and on to Munich and finally to Athens itself. Lambert Lodge had arrived at the British Museum on the morning of his great discovery in a state of high excitement. He had been thinking about this trip for two years now and planning his itinerary for nine months

4

before he stepped off his liner in Southampton and onto the train for London. He was saving the Caryatid till near the end. As he stared at the battles between the Centaurs and the Lapiths and the procession of maidens and young men and the charioteers and the sacrifices from the Parthenon frieze, he felt a sense of exultation, that he had, in some strange way, come home at last in a city that was over three thousand miles from New Haven, Connecticut. He looked at the statue for a long time. He pulled a magnifying glass out of his pocket for a more detailed examination. Lambert Lodge spent nearly two hours with the Caryatid, walking round her, peering intently at the marble. He stroked the long robe with its delicate folds that flowed from the young lady's waist. It was the stroking that confirmed to the attendant on duty that this latest visitor was probably insane and certainly needing intercepting before he embraced the Caryatid and conducted intimate relations with her on the museum floor.

'Excuse me, sir,' said the attendant, who was called Philip Jones and came from Highbury, 'what exactly do you think you are doing?'

'I do beg your pardon, sir,' said Lambert Lodge, 'I know my behaviour must seem rather odd. My apologies. My card, sir.'

He drew a rather elaborate one from his waistcoat which carried the arms of Yale University and his name as lecturer in Architecture at the School of Fine Arts in a rather florid typeface.

'Forgive me, sir,' the young American went on, with the politeness inculcated from birth in the old families of Boston to which he belonged, 'are you an expert in Greek sculpture, by any chance?'

'I'm afraid I'm not, sir,' Jones replied, 'the missus says the only thing I am an expert in is the fixture list for Tottenham Hotspur and that's a fact.'

'I'm sure that's very valuable information,' said Lambert Lodge with a smile, 'but I do happen to be something of an expert on ancient statues and things like that. Do you think you could be very kind and show me the way to your director's office? I have something very important to discuss with him.'

'Of course, sir, seeing you're an academic gentleman, you'd be surprised how many of them we get in here, forgetting their documents and their umbrellas, most of them. I can't take you to the Director's office, since he's not here, and neither is the Head of Greek and Roman Antiquities, but the Deputy Director is in, sir, I saw him not half an hour ago. Would he do?'

'Splendid,' said Lambert Lodge. 'How very kind. Could you take me to him at once?'

Five minutes later the American was ushered into a large office looking out over the great steps and the front of the British Museum where the pilgrims milled about, smoking cigarettes and discussing the treasures they had seen before returning to the more mundane surroundings of omnibus and underground railway. A hundred and fifty yards behind him in the Reading Room young scholars were struggling with their theses and European revolutionaries were composing incendiary tracts far from the eyes of their country's secret police. The Deputy Director ushered Lodge to a chair on the left of the fireplace.

'This is indeed a pleasure, Mr Lodge,' he began. 'I have read one or two of your learned articles, I believe.'

'You are too kind, sir,' cried Lodge, stretching out his long legs. Theophilus Ragg, the Deputy Director, was a stooped man of average height in his early sixties with grey hair turning to white and a small, well-trimmed moustache. He was wearing a dark suit with a white shirt and a Balliol College tie. Inspecting him, Lodge thought he looked like a small town undertaker somewhere in the vast obscurity of the Midwest, waiting for retirement and fearful of more time with his family.

'What can I do for you this morning, Mr Lodge? The Director is in the Middle East and the Head of Greek and Roman Antiquities is with a party in the Alps, I fear.'

Lodge wondered if the ancient treasures of some long extinct tribe were going to be removed from the sands of Mesopotamia and brought back to join the other totems adorning the Bloomsbury museum.

'I'd like to ask you about the Caryatid in the Elgin Room, if I might, sir,' said Lodge, trying to sound as emollient as possible.

'Please do,' said Theophilus Ragg.

'I'm afraid what I'm about to say may come as something of a shock, Mr Ragg. I'm not absolutely sure, but I don't think your Caryatid is real. I don't think she's the real McCoy, if you'll forgive me. Let me explain. It may be there is a reason for this. Perhaps the real statue is away being cleaned or restored?'

'No, she's not,' said Ragg, pulling nervously at his moustache. 'Pray continue.'

'Believe me, Mr Ragg,' Lodge continued, 'I have no wish to cause trouble for you or your great museum here. My reason has to do with the marble. The real Caryatid, like all the statues here from the Acropolis, is carved out of Pentelic marble, brought to Athens from Mount Penteli in Attica all those years ago. Your Caryatid is made from Parian marble, very similar, but not quite the same. There

7

are many ancient works carved in the white marble from Paros, but the metopes and the frieze and the Caryatid from the Parthenon are not among them. The Building Research Program at Yale put on an exhibition three years ago of examples of the different sorts of marble used by the Greeks, the Romans and the great sculptors of the Renaissance. Maybe they hoped to encourage a new golden age in American sculpture, who knows. Anyway, Mr Ragg, I was able to touch and get the feel of all these different types of marble. Pentelic and Parian marble are similar, pure white and fine grained. But the Pentelic, from the Penteliko Mountain, is semi-translucent, the other one is not. Even after all this time you can just see the difference.' He paused.

The Deputy Director was writing very carefully in a large black notebook.

'I'm so sorry,' the young American concluded.

The Deputy Director stared into the middle distance, looking once more, Lodge thought, like the ageing Midwest undertaker, searching for a missing coffin perhaps, lost in the press of traffic between church and cemetery, the few mourners stamping their feet and peering down the yew trees that lined the drive.

'Maybe it's just a mistake,' he whispered, 'I expect she'll turn up in the end.'

'What can I do to help, sir? I am in London for about a week and could stay longer if that would be useful. I'm desperately sorry to have been the bearer of such bad news.'

Theophilus Ragg sighed. 'You have been most kind, Mr Lodge. Don't think I am not grateful. I'm just shocked, that's all. I shall have to conduct an inquiry to see if our experts agree with you and find out what has happened.

We need to know how long ago the switch happened, if it did, and what we would have to do to make sure it could never happen again.'

'Could I just ask you about the Head of Greek and Roman Antiquities, Mr Ragg? Will he be back soon? I should so like to meet him, you see. We have heard so much about him in New England.'

'Dr Tristram Stanhope, you mean?' Ragg replied, suddenly ceasing to doodle in his notebook. 'I think he should be back soon. He is still suffering from youth, you know, suffering rather badly, I should say.'

'Suffering from youth, sir? I'm not quite sure what you mean.'

'Forgive me, I may not have expressed myself very well. When you have lived in seats of learning like Oxford and the British Museum, you watch the rhythm of the passing generations. There are fresh drafts of the young every autumn, of course, the hope of youth coursing through their veins. But you look at the dons as they too grow older. By the time they reach middle age the hopes of youth have been replaced with some kind of accommodation with this complicated world. Stanhope is in his middle forties now. You would expect him to have passed through the hope and the optimism of youth. But no, he still behaves as if he were twenty-one years old. Never mind. We have more important things to think about now.'

The young American felt his time was up. 'I am staying at Brown's Hotel, Mr Ragg. Just leave a message if I am not there and I will come at any hour of day or night.'

Stephen Lambert Lodge bowed slightly as he left. As he made his way out towards the front door, he heard the plaintive cry once more. 'Maybe it's just a mistake, I expect she'll turn up in the end.'

The behaviour of the Deputy Director, left on his own, would have surprised Lodge. He shuffled next door into the Director's office and locked the door. He searched in the desk until he found a small, dark blue address book. He copied the phone numbers and the addresses given there for members of the Maecenas Club, a small but select group of the top museum directors in London: National Gallery, the Tate, Natural History Museum, the Science Museum, the Victoria and Albert. The institution was named after the great artistic impresario Maecenas who worked for the first Roman Emperor Augustus, persuading poets like Virgil to compose works that would add to the lustre of Rome and the glory of Augustus. Members met in a private room at the Athenaeum once every three months. In emergencies, special meetings or special assistance could be called at twenty-four hours' notice. This was what Theophilus Ragg proposed to do. He had to find a man who would bring his Caryatid back. He had no faith at all in the ability of the police to do it. One of these directors, surely, somewhere in their career must have needed a specialist who could solve a crime discreetly and without fuss. Money would be no object. The Maecenas members must help solve his problem. He gave no indication of what had happened when he wrote to the museum directors. He merely asked if, in the course of their professional lives, they had occasion to have recourse to a private investigator. The British Museum, he told them, needed the finest in the country and they needed him in the next twenty-four hours.

Few car salesmen have ever owned a house on the fashionable Old Mile at Ascot and maintained a stable of racehorses, thus keeping a foot, or hoof, in the quickest delivery of the oldest and the newest forms of human transportation at the same time. Octavius Stratton was also the sole representative of his tribe to ride to Ascot with the King in the Royal Landau. On this bright morning he was taking Lord Francis Powerscourt and his son Thomas for a drive in a new Daimler. Octavius, who really was the eighth child of his parents, was usually known as Eugene. He was a second cousin twice removed of Powerscourt's wife, the mother of Thomas Powerscourt, Lady Lucy. Stratton was confident that his family connections would help deliver what would, for him, be a profitable sale. The Daimler was the finest car in its class, he assured the Powerscourts. It might be unfashionable to say so, he virtually whispered at this point in case he was overheard at the northern end of Hampstead High Street, but German engineering would soon be recognized as the best in the world. He regaled his clients with accounts of the great speed the vehicle could attain, its record as a hill climber in the annual Shelsley Walsh Hill Climb in Worcestershire, and a barrage of statistics about brake horse power, transmission and engine size. Octavius might have been slightly alarmed had he seen Thomas Powerscourt in the back seat taking extensive notes on his shirt cuffs about the mechanical details. For the young man was one of the best mathematicians Westminster School had produced this century. He was the finest shot of his year in the public schools rifle shooting championships and fluent in both French and German. This was his last term at school, with the entrance exams for Cambridge a couple of months away. Thomas began staring very hard at the driver's back.

The cart was a nondescript sort of vehicle. It could have been carrying barrels of beer or crates of sausages.

Nobody would have looked at it twice. The two men were wearing the most nondescript clothes they could find, dark trousers, shirts that had once been white and boots that had seen better days. They might have been a couple of shepherds taking their wares to market. But in the back of the van there were no sheep. There was a long, heavy bundle swathed in blankets and other soft materials going to a place that was a long way from the British Museum. They were in the Welsh mountains now, making for their destination, a large house near a series of caves in the Black Mountains of the Brecon Beacons. The two men had no idea what their cargo was. For them, it was just another package. They spent most of their days moving packets and parcels of one sort or another from place to place.

Theophilus Ragg went to the stationery cupboard after he had despatched his letters. He took out a large new black notebook and wrote the day's date on the inside cover in red ink. He began a doodle on the opening page and stared out of his window. He had asked his experts for their views and he knew he had to wait for their report but he felt sure the young American was right. Where was the wretched Caryatid now? Was she still in one piece? Who on earth could have taken her? How on earth had they taken her? Where had they found a replacement? Had they made more than one?

Ragg had started his life after taking his degree at Oxford as a teacher of classics and junior housemaster at one of Britain's leading public schools. After three or four years he found the prevailing spirit of hearty athleticism tinged with what he privately termed 'the traditions of the philistines' more than he could bear.

He longed to hear eulogies of the odes of Pindar rather than of the triumphs of the football team and the military values of the combined cadet force. When a position was advertised as a Junior Fellow at one of the smaller Oxford Colleges, lecturing on textual criticism in the ancient Greek tragedians, Theophilus was accepted immediately. The conversation at the Shrewsbury College High Table, he told his parents, certainly took a turn for the better after the banalities of the school common room. Theophilus's talents as an organizer, if not of genius, then certainly of very remarkable powers, only came about by accident. The College Bursar, an expert in the poetry of Sir Philip Sidney, dropped dead of heart failure at four thirty one summer's day in the Fellows Garden, just as the dons in residence had assembled for afternoon tea. The Warden, a deeply impatient historian who regarded all his colleagues as ignorant fools, sought among his fellows for a replacement. Of newcomer Ragg he knew nothing at all. This was a virtue. He was appointed to the post immediately.

Like most great generals, Ragg moved slowly at first. He spent an entire term observing the working lives of the college staff, the cooks, the porters, those who waited at table and those who cleaned the young gentlemen's rooms. Their hours and their movements were all written down in his notebook. When the workers returned to Shrewsbury for the Hilary Term, their hours had been changed. There were fewer of them. Most were working slightly longer hours than before. All were better paid than in the past. The College made considerable savings. Over the years Ragg turned his attention to other questions of detail, the supply of food and drink to the College and its members, where he discovered a mass of swindles and petty corruption, to the costs of maintaining the ancient buildings where he replaced most outside contractors with permanent masons and carpenters employed directly by the College. Eventually, after fifteen years in post, he screwed up his courage and asked the Warden, now a genial theologian with a great weakness for Château Margaux, if he could take a look at the College investments and financial strategy. The usual progress, slow but well thought out, was followed. By now, Theophilus Ragg, who had originally been a figure of fun, taking detailed notes of the college laundry lists as his early critics maintained, was the hero of the hour, particularly among the better informed heads of Oxford houses who regarded him as a financial Clausewitz and tried to lure him away to their own establishments. Ragg turned down all positions of bursar or newer, even grander, titles invented specially for him, at Merton, Lincoln, Exeter and New College. Only one institution was able to lure him away, and that was, in part, because it was an old boy of his own college who made the offer.

Andrew Cronan had read Classics at Shrewsbury. Ragg had been his tutor and had treated him well. When he became Director of the British Museum, Cronan realized that the administration of his empire was in chaos with costs out of control and prima donnas and private satrapies rampant among the Hittites and the Assyrians. But he thought he needed a bait to draw Ragg down to London. The museum had, somewhere in its vast archive, a store of the manuscripts of ancient Greek philosophers and playwrights. Early editions of Aristotle and Aristophanes and Aeschylus were snuggled down in the basements beneath the pavements of Great Russell Street and the regular traffic of the Piccadilly Line. He asked Ragg to combine the roles of bursar and archivist at a salary rather greater than that of most of the heads of Oxford colleges. Cronar knew the high costs would be recouped many times over. And he enlisted an important ally, one whose very existence always brought on dark sighs of 'Who would have thought it?' or 'Well, I never,' or even 'I haven't heard of anything so remarkable this year or last.' Cronan's ally was the key factor in Ragg's decision to move. For, to the astonishment of his peers, he had, some years before, secured for himself a most beautiful wife who produced a small phalanx of equally beautiful children. Christabel Ragg was determined to conquer the larger field of literary London as she already had the academic communities of north Oxford. She would become, she told her husband proudly, the Zuleika Dobson of High Holborn and Sicilian Avenue.

After a quick trip up the Great North Road where the Daimler could show its paces, the little party returned to Markham Square. Octavius Stratton was hardly out of the Powerscourt front door when Thomas grasped his father firmly by the arm and made him promise not to buy the car. It was, Thomas assured his parent, a very bad investment. Octavius's parents might have been very successful in the numbers of children produced, but their eighth had no grasp of figures or of engineering principles. If the physical details of the Daimler's engine, as described by Stratton, were correct, said Thomas, shaking his light brown curls sadly as he spoke, the car would probably go backwards. Or possibly even sideways.

Powerscourt suddenly remembered the elation with which Thomas had greeted the arrival of the Rolls Royce Silver Ghost, the family's first motor car, several years before. He would huddle into the corner of the back seat, his cap firmly placed on his head, and wave at the passing pedestrians condemned to travel by foot and even at the cows and the sheep in the Home Counties countryside. Once Thomas had disappeared completely from the house in Markham Square. It was some hours before he was discovered, sitting happily on the back seat of the Silver Ghost, doing his homework.

Thomas was prepared to carry on about the Daimler for some time when his mother appeared and gave Powerscourt a small cream envelope. This requested him to present himself at the address at the top of the page as soon as possible. It was a matter of the greatest consequence. It could, the writer said, be described without exaggeration as a matter of the utmost national importance. The author looked forward to seeing Powerscourt within the hour. The signature was that of Theophilus Ragg, Deputy Director and Principal Librarian of the British Museum, Great Russell Street, London WC.

2

The old port in Corfu is guarded by an ancient fort, one of two that stand sentinel over the island's capital. The harbour front has the usual collection of cafés, bars, rundown tavernas and ship chandlers offering to sell you anything from fresh cordage to tinned food that will last for months in the hold of your vessel. And, hard by the oldest and most disreputable bar, the Hermes, stood a branch of the telegraph office. Sitting at a little table under the broken shade of the Hermes, a Greek sea captain was refilling his glass with ouzo and staring moodily out to sea. He was waiting for a message. He had been waiting for two days already but he knew he would wait as long as it took for the message to arrive. There was, he had been promised, a generous commission, a very generous commission awaiting him.

Captain Dimitri's vessel, in theory, was a seaborne circus, travelling with her entertainments back and forth through the Corinth Canal, across the island towns and cities of the Aegean and the Ionian Seas. Sometimes she carried things that had little to do with circuses.

The ship was old and dirty, the paintwork peeling with

age, the sails no longer white but flecked with streaks of grey. There was a mangy lion in a twisted cage by the main cabin, flanked by a couple of querulous monkeys. A pair of jugglers practised with dirty plates, specially hardened in taverna ovens so they would not break. A dark acrobat tumbled about in the rigging from time to time. All kinds of strange-looking packages went aboard the first day, amphorae, presumably filled with wine that might have been thousands of years old, tiny decorated vessels filled with honey that could have inspired a poet to write an ode to a Grecian urn. The Captain spat expertly into the oily waters of the little harbour and refilled his glass. The message had not come yet, but the ouzo was cheap, the taverna served a fine if rather greasy moussaka, and the waitress, daughter of the house, was of remarkable beauty. Captain Dimitri prepared himself for a long wait.

Theophilus Ragg, Deputy Director of the British Museum, led Powerscourt straight to the last known home of the missing Caryatid. He didn't let Powerscourt linger long by the replacement. He took him straight back to his office without saying a word. Only when he was sitting opposite his visitor on a long sofa in the centre of his office did Ragg speak. The Caryatid Powerscourt had just seen was a fake. British Museum staff had, with great reluctance, admitted to the Deputy Director that the American was correct. The original had been stolen, possibly during a fire alarm the week before. The only people who knew about it were the American scholar who had discovered the switch, now sworn to silence and awaiting instructions in Brown's Hotel, and the Deputy Director himself. The Director himself was out of contact in the

Middle East on a shopping expedition and not expected to return for some time. Would Powerscourt take on the case? Would he find the Caryatid? He would? Excellent. He, Deputy Director Ragg, would be happy to answer questions for the rest of the day, if need be.

Powerscourt began with the most obvious query. Why had the Director not sent for the police? Surely there must be stipulations in the insurance and so on? My decision and mine alone, the Deputy Director replied sadly. Men in uniform tramping through the museum would attract attention. The matter would appear in the newspapers. Publicity in a case as important as this could be ruinous. Other thieves might come calling for other treasures. The nation's cultural heritage was in danger. Lord Powerscourt should be aware that this Caryatid was the best preserved of her kind in the world. She was unique.

'Let me remind you, Lord Powerscourt, that it is only weeks now since the *Mona Lisa* was stolen from the Salon Carré in the Louvre. I do not know if you are aware of the tremendous outcry that has convulsed the city. The Parisian press have reports on the search for the criminal every day. Our own newspapers are also convulsed by the theft. The Director and staff of the Louvre have been vilified in a way France has not seen since the Dreyfus Affair. There is still no sign of the painting. Do you think we at the British Museum wish to be engulfed in such a firestorm? Our Caryatid may not be as famous as the *Mona Lisa* of Leonardo but she is still the finest example of her kind in the world.'

Powerscourt thought that the Museum Deputy Director was old and close to retirement. The prospect of a repeat of the controversy in Paris had turned his bones to water. He was a man of scholarship, not of the wider world

19

that swirled around outside the walls of his museum. Theophilus Ragg could not, for the moment, see beyond the scandal that could ruin his reputation and sully his last days in office beyond repair. It was to be over a week before Powerscourt realized, as he told Lady Lucy rather sadly later on, that Ragg was not a brittle tree, liable to fall in the first gales of winter, but an oak, a sturdy oak that would be left standing long after the storms had passed.

Powerscourt reminded the Deputy Director, as gently as he could, that the Metropolitan Police were perfectly capable of appearing in plain clothes and being discreet. His new employer seemed astonished to hear of the existence of a plain clothes policeman. Caryatids, said Powerscourt, wore long sleeveless dresses with great folds at the waist. Greek heroes on the Parthenon frieze wore short tunics with swords to kill their enemies. Some policemen went about in dark uniforms with helmets. Some did not. Each to his allotted station.

Treading carefully now, Powerscourt asked what seemed to him at this early stage the two most important questions. How much was the Greek lady worth? And who might want to steal her?

She was priceless, Ragg said after a long pause, staring down at his notebook. Neither the finest bursar in Oxford or Cambridge nor London's most experienced art auctioneer could put a price on a Caryatid. The Deputy Director could not imagine anybody wanting to steal such a rare and beautiful creature. Lord Elgin would surely be turning in his grave.

With great difficulty Powerscourt refrained from pointing out that the Caryatid had only reached Great Russell Street because Lord Elgin had stolen her in the first place. It was an hour and a half into the interview before

Powerscourt realized that he had one last card left to play. This, he thought, might be his last chance.

'Tell me, Mr Ragg,' he ventured in his most affable manner, 'have you met the present Commissioner of the Metropolitan Police?'

'Sir Edward Henry, isn't that his name?' replied Ragg. 'No, I have not.'

'Well, as a matter of fact, I know him quite well. I first met him years ago when he was Inspector General of the Bengal Police Force and we have kept in touch since. I feel sure that he would be happy to help and provide one of his most discreet and intelligent officers to lead a plain clothes team to look into the vanished Caryatid. I could ring him on your behalf, if you like, to effect an introduction. I can promise you would be in good hands.'

The Deputy Director of the British Museum might have appeared as mouse rather than man to the outside world, but he was damned if some upstart investigator was going to introduce him to London's senior police officer.

'That won't be necessary,' he snapped, 'I'm perfectly capable of ringing the man myself.'

'Of course, of course,' purred Powerscourt, 'sorry if I gave offence. It was not intentional, I can assure you. Tell me this, please, if you would, Mr Ragg, before I go.'

Powerscourt decided that retreat in the current climate might be the better part of discretion.

'Let us suppose that you were an art thief, one of the highest class, a Napoleon of crime. Let us suppose also that you stole the Caryatid with a view to selling her. Who would you approach? Which London firm would do the selling for you?'

'Every single one of them, I suspect,' replied the Deputy Director morosely. 'I'm sure all the major art dealers and auctioneers, the ones with international links, Linfords, Gonzagos, Whites, would all tell you at the front door that they could not possibly undertake such a business and then readmit you immediately via the rear entrance to discuss terms and percentages. I have no faith in any of them.'

'Thank you, Mr Ragg. As a matter of form I shall have to contact them all, but forewarned is forearmed. I am most grateful.'

Powerscourt was leaving a couple of calling cards on the Deputy Director's desk when Ragg looked up at him with a pleading look in his eye.

'Do tell me, Lord Powerscourt, you don't think it's all just a terrible mistake, do you? I mean you don't expect she'll turn up in the end?'

Powerscourt felt rather sorry for the man, plunged so suddenly into a world of which he knew so little.

'No, Mr Ragg.' He spoke as kindly as he could. 'I don't think it is just a terrible mistake. The Caryatid will only turn up when we find her.'

'Did you have the time to ask him about Tristram Stanhope, Francis?' Lady Lucy's first reaction on hearing of the assignation and the interview back in Markham Square was to enquire about her distant relative, the Head of Greek and Roman Antiquities at the British Museum.

'No, I didn't,' said Powerscourt rather stiffly, 'we were discussing the disappearance of one of the most valuable pieces of sculpture in Britain, not the current whereabouts of one of the darlings of Mayfair. Tell me, Lucy, why is everybody so obsessed with this man? What is so special about him?'

Lady Lucy felt that she might have made a tactical mistake.

'Of course, Francis, you are absolutely right. Please forgive me if I spoke out of turn. Tristram Stanhope? Why are people so obsessed with him, you ask. Maybe because that's how he wants the world to be, to be obsessed with him.'

'Can you give me some facts about the fellow?'

'Of course. Born into an old aristocratic family. Tristram Stanhope has classic English good looks, blue eyes, blond hair, a fine figure. He went to Eton and Christ Church and scored a hundred for his school against Harrow at Lord's. Elected to Pop and collected all the garlands of schoolboy glory. Our Tristram went to Oxford with the laurels of Victor Ludorum and all the rest. He took first-class honours in Greats as well as being a bulwark of the Bullingdon Club. They said he had the most glittering Eton and Oxford career since the young Rosebery at Christ Church a generation or two before. Then Stanhope went exploring in the Middle East and India for a couple of years after graduation. He was said to have discovered a previously unknown tribe speaking a previously unknown language somewhere at the back of the Hindu Kush. The language was thought to be very close to ancient Greek, so some scholars said it might have been left behind, as it were, by Alexander the Great.'

'Good God,' said Powerscourt, 'what did he do next? Walk on water? Bring down the walls of Jericho?'

Lady Lucy laughed. 'He might well have done both of those, Francis. You see, he went to work for the Foreign Office on a series of secret missions. When he finally resurfaced he had a slight scar on the left-hand side of his face which he refused to talk about.'

'Would I be right in supposing, Lucy, that the women found the mixture of athletic and academic success, spiced with a tempting dose of danger and secrecy, virtually irresistible?'

'You would, Francis, you certainly would. I've always remembered what one of my cousins said to me after a weekend spent in Tristram Stanhope's company at some grand country house party. She said he was a professional Adonis.'

'What did she mean?'

'She thought that the whole performance was a colossal display of male vanity. It was, she said, like watching a male peacock with those iridescent tails with the markings of blue, gold, red, and other colours. They use the large train in mating rituals and courtship displays. It can be arched, as you know, into a magnificent fan that reaches across the bird's back and touches the ground on either side. Females, believe it or not, are thought to choose their mates according to the size, colour and quality of these outrageous feather trains.'

'Really?' said Powerscourt, 'the females do that? You don't say, Lucy. And does your informant relate if the mating display was effective on this particular weekend?'

'Good point, Francis. I was told, I'm afraid, that not one, but two female peacocks, known as peahens, succumbed on the weekend in question.'

'God bless my soul,' said Lord Francis Powerscourt.

New York millionaires like to stick together. Who wants to share their piece of sidewalk with a nobody after all? And only in close proximity to their fellows can the millionaires indulge in one of their favourite sports, that of conspicuous consumption. What would be the point of banquets the Roman epicure and glutton Lucullus would have been proud of if nobody was there to see them and join the queue for the vomitarium? And when New York grew too crowded for truly vast construction projects, what would be the point of extravagant palaces, fit for a Persian emperor, in Newport or the Hamptons if nobody else could look at them and marvel at the expense?

But there were exceptions to the clubbing together of the wealthiest in the land. Wilbur Lincoln Mitchell was one of them. He was probably richer than most of your average millionaires but he chose to live in upstate New York, a couple of miles from the military academy at West Point, in a very large farmhouse built by his grandfather to house eleven children, expanded and extended ever since. Riverside, for that was what his ancestors had christened it, looked down on the great sweep of the Hudson as it made its way to the Atlantic. There was a large garden, big enough for small children to get lost, and a tennis court for the more athletic of the adults.

Wilbur Mitchell made his first fortune in railway tickets. He invented a family of machines that could manufacture tickets of any size or shape required for use on the railway systems of America. By the year 1905 he had cornered the market all along the Eastern seaboard. Four years later he had penetrated the West as far as the Atchison, Topeka and Santa Fe. His second fortune, even larger than the first, came several years later with a formula for cheap but effective soap, discovered by accident when searching for the perfect liquid to oil the ticket printing machines. In the meantime, he went to Europe. Mitchell spent a long time working out his own itinerary. He was not going to travel in some expensive touring party where everything was prepared for you and special guides were on hand in all countries to ensure you only had to speak English wherever you happened to be at the time.

After a leisurely tour of southern England, he moved to Italy where he marvelled at the canals in Venice and the austere masterpieces of the Uffizi in Florence. In Rome he fell in love. He discovered a previously unknown passion for ancient Greek and Roman sculpture and the early glories of the Renaissance. The twirling torsos of the Baroque and the Rococo left him cold. And he discovered something more important than love in his quest for ancient sculpture. For some reason he never knew, Wilbur Lincoln Mitchell could tell the fake from the genuine with an unerring facility. He was like a water diviner with an infallible touch. The three ancient statues he bought from Rome's most expensive dealer were, as their owner ruefully admitted after Mitchell had left, the only authentic pieces in his possession. He moved on to Greece. He watched the sun go down over Delphi, the colours fading fast from the peaks, the ancient force of the site pressing down upon him, the power of the gods numinous as the light faded and the mountains went dark against the sky. He climbed up to the Acropolis in Athens. He saw another sunset at Cape Sounion on the coast, the remains of Poseidon's temple clear and bright, the blue sea stretching far away, speckled with islands, a glowing golden sky above with a glittering ball of fire in the centre of the horizon. At Olympia he purchased his fourth and last piece on this tour, a statue of a charioteer with vine leaves in his hair. In time all four were delivered to him in upstate New York, where he built an orangery with great windows to house them, modelled on the one at the Royal Botanic Gardens in Kew, by the Thames in London. Here was the new home for the charioteer and Apollo from Mitylene, the Roman Emperor Hadrian and Athena from the first century AD. If they quarrelled or fought, if they went for walks or made love, they did so under cover of darkness.

Mitchell never left any of the European galleries or sculpture houses without leaving his card and without a request to let him know of any future treasures he might fancy. If these delights were genuine, he implied, he could well cross the Atlantic to see them and, who knows, to buy once more. So great was his wealth, and so great his reputation as a man with an eye for the fakes that filled the market, that the transatlantic cable was never used for the first few years after Mitchell's return to the United States. Then, in the summer of 1911, the year after the Philadelphia Athletics beat the Chicago Cubs to win the World Series, a slight whisper reached Riverside, high above the Hudson River. It came from a dealer Mitchell had heard of, but not met, in New Bond Street, London. It claimed that quite soon one of the most spectacular pieces of ancient sculpture ever to be offered for sale might become available, not to the highest offer at auction, but to the highest private bidder at the auction house. Nothing like this had come onto the market in over two thousand years. The piece had no name.

3

The letter from the Commissioner of the Metropolitan Police arrived at breakfast time in Markham Square. It was written in the clipped style Powerscourt remembered, as if Sir Edward Henry were sending a message from some remote mountain station where the telegraph was slow and unreliable, and the natives might come over the hill at any moment.

'Dear Powerscourt,' it began, 'took call yesterday from Ragg at British Museum. Some important old statue has gone missing. Panic among museum people. Have agreed to help. Ragg most insistent officers had to be discreet and intelligent. My inspector is well known for reading a lot, particularly modern novels. Has been seen with books by that man Forster who writes about rooms with views and the end of Howard. Have suggested he call on you this morning on his way to meeting with Ragg. Inspector Christopher Kingsley. Joined us after resigning from Army. Probably passed port wrong way. Regards, Henry.'

'Well,' said Powerscourt to Lady Lucy who was finishing a piece of toast and surreptitiously surveying a Georgian rectory in north Oxfordshire in the pages of *Country Life*.

'Well what, my love,' asked Lady Lucy, reluctant to tear herself away from the four reception rooms and the eighteenth-century pavilion in need of some refurbishment – was the thing actually falling down? she wondered.

'Well done, Theophilus Ragg, that's what I say,' her husband replied. 'I didn't think he'd do it.'

'Do what, Francis?'

'Sorry, Lucy, he's actually called in the police. I thought he'd never manage it. The Commissioner writes that the inspector in charge, fellow by the name of Kingsley, will be calling here on his way to the museum.'

'Is he interested in antiquities, do we know? Or is he a sportsman, forever playing for the Met Eleven at weekends?'

Lady Lucy had long maintained that in the police force, as with the Foreign Office, any private expertise, fluency in Spanish for example, or knowledge of burglary techniques, would guarantee that you were never employed in any capacity where that knowledge might come in useful, like the Embassy in Madrid or a campaign to lower the crime rate in the East End.

'The fellow reads modern novels, apparently. Commissioner believes he is well acquainted with the works of E. M. Forster.'

'My goodness,' said Lady Lucy who had not trodden very far through the pages of *Where Angels Fear to Tread* before giving up completely.

Ten minutes later a tall, slim young man in a dark grey suit that was well cut but had seen better days was shaking hands in the Powerscourt drawing room on the first floor. He was clean-shaven and had the most remarkable blue eyes Powerscourt had ever seen. He was reminded of the closing words of a biography of some long dead Scottish statesman: 'he had in his eye the look of a man searching for a far country'.

'Christopher Kingsley,' the Inspector said, bowing slightly to Powerscourt. 'I've heard so much about your time in India.'

'That's very civil of you,' said Powerscourt with a smile, 'it was a long time ago now.' He longed to ask about the policeman's service in the Army and his subsequent departure from the military, but felt a first introduction might not be the best time.

'Now then, perhaps you could tell us what you know of the affair of the missing Caryatid?'

'Well, my lord –' the Inspector had a light tenor voice that was most attractive and suggested that he should sing in a choir '– the most important thing, so far as I can work it out, is that nothing has happened. The official story is that there has been no theft, the Caryatid in place is the real one, we cannot question the people on the spot who might have noticed something unusual.'

'Have you been involved in a case like this before, Inspector?'

Christopher Kingsley smiled. 'As a matter of fact, I have. I suspect that's why I'm here. Late last year Sir William Sudburgh of Sudburgh, the chap who owns half the coal in Wales, had a painting stolen from his London home in Eaton Square. It was a half-length portrait by Sir Thomas Lawrence of one of his ancestors, dressed up in that bright red uniform they wore for the American Revolutionary Wars. Like the British Museum, Sir William wanted no publicity whatsoever. We couldn't talk to anybody at all except those on the periphery, as it were.'

'And?' Powerscourt cut in. 'Did you manage to apprehend the thief and recover the work?'

'We did,' Inspector Kingsley laughed, 'but it had nothing to do with us, really. The thief, poor man, was a junior footman and desperate for money, deep in hock to the moneylenders. He took the painting to the nearest shop with paintings in the window and asked how much it was worth. My men had already circulated all the antique dealers in central London with details of the picture. The antique dealer was quick on the uptake, I must say. He suggested that he could only give a proper opinion about the value by consulting an expert. Perhaps the footman could return at ten o'clock the following morning? He could? Splendid. The poor footman was arrested before the antique dealer's front door had closed when he went back. He's still in Wormwood Scrubs. I know. I visited him in there just before Easter.'

'Well done, all the same,' said Powerscourt, trying and failing to remember any policeman of his acquaintance who had been to see his victims in prison. 'I don't recall seeing anything of the affair in the newspapers.'

'No, it never got that far. Could I ask you a question, my lord? Do you think the Caryatid was stolen to order? That somebody had received part of the payment for the theft before it disappeared? You couldn't walk into an art dealer's like Linfords in New Bond Street and say I've got a Caryatid from the Acropolis outside, do you want to make me an offer?'

'The honest answer is that I just don't know. If you pressed me, I would say that is the most likely account of how the theft was organized, with a client or clients already in place and a price agreed.'

'I see. Can I ask you another question, my lord, if I may? How do you propose that we divide up the various tasks we can carry out without letting people know that we believe the Caryatid has been stolen? The Commissioner said he didn't think the four horsemen of the apocalypse would shift Mr Ragg from his obsession with secrecy. I shall, no doubt, be reminded of that when I see him later this morning.'

'Have you any suggestions about such a division of the spoils, as it were?'

'I have been thinking about that this morning, my lord. I think you should talk to the art dealers, the connoisseurs if you like. I think you should be our liaison point with the Deputy Director. He obviously thinks we policemen have mud on our boots and spend our time arresting minor criminals in the poorer parts of London. Well, let him think that. He will talk to you more freely than he would to me. I propose that we should put out feelers to our colleagues on the Continent and across the Atlantic, asking them to keep their eyes open, without specifying exactly what is missing. I think we should also talk to former employees who have left in the last couple of years. And I propose to find out all we can about the private circumstances of the leading figures in the museum. Somebody in that organization may have given information to the thieves after all. It seems highly likely that this was an inside job, or at least one where inside help was available. I haven't seen the actual statue yet, but one of my colleagues went to see it last year and he said that only people from the inside or profes-sional removal men could have taken one Caryatid out and put another one in. The job was too complicated for your common criminal.'

'Did you say all the leading figures in the museum, Inspector?'

'I did. And that includes the Deputy Director and the Director himself. Who knows who was short of money? Who knows whose private life could lead to blackmail? We shall, of course, be discreet.'

'Excellent,' said Powerscourt, thinking that the novels of this man Forster must encourage a suspicious mind. 'Could I just make one request? I was involved years ago in a case involving art fraud. My companion in arms, Johnny Fitzgerald, is at present returning from Sicily and will be with me tomorrow. On that earlier occasion he developed close relations with the porters of the leading art dealers. They even showed him the accounts on one occasion, though Johnny rather doubted if they knew what they were doing, so much drink had they consumed. I propose to ask Johnny to do the same thing in this case.'

'I'm sure that will be most helpful,' said the Inspector, checking his watch. 'Just one last thought before I report to the Deputy Director.'

'And that is?'

'I suggest we tell Ragg as little as possible about our investigations. Maybe he will become curious. Maybe we could say that we will tell him what we know when he lets us tell the world the Caryatid has been stolen. In the meantime let him stay in the dark with his ancient Egyptians and all those volumes ranged round that famous Reading Room. It'll be good for him in the end.'

'Very well. One last query, if I may,' said Powerscourt. 'Do the police have any inside intelligence about the theft of the *Mona Lisa* from the Louvre? I think that pushed Ragg into reluctance to have any publicity or to call in the police. Do you think there might be a link between the two crimes? Is there some international gang at work, stealing the world's most celebrated pieces of art?'

'We have had inquiries from the French police,' the Inspector admitted. 'But these were routine, asking us to contact the art dealers and so on and to report back if we saw anything suspicious. If the *Mona Lisa* and the famous smile are in London they're pretty well hidden. I don't know of any international gangs at work. Mind you, if they were any good we wouldn't have heard of them, would we? I did ask one or two people at the Yard who are meant to ask about these things and they hadn't heard of any gangs either.'

The man in the velvet smoking jacket was sitting at the writing desk by the window of his hotel room. He had a blank sheet of writing paper in front of him. The man began giggling quietly as he started his letter. He did not put an address at the top.

'Dear Mr Ragg,' it began, 'I am writing in connection with the missing Caryatid. I have the statue in my care. Today is Monday, 9 October. You have two days to follow my orders or the consequences will be severe. If you send us £100,000 by Wednesday, 11 October, you will receive instructions about where to collect the statue. Details of where and how to effect the payment will be sent to you once you have accepted this very generous offer. For every day you do not comply with these requests after that date, the payment will increase by £10,000. By Saturday, 21 October the figure will have risen to £200,000 and *The Times* and the *Morning Post* will have been informed about the theft. The news, and the details of your own role in the affair, will be all over the papers.'

The author paused and ran his fingers over his bald patch. The hair had not returned. When he started the next paragraph he was chuckling once again.

'We know where you live,' the letter went on, 'we know where your wife buys her clothes. We know where your children go to school.

'Any attempt to inform the authorities or to organize a payment supervised by the police will result in immediate action. That action will be violent.

'I look forward to hearing from you at the address below.

Friends of the British Museum. c/o The Ritz Hotel, Piccadilly W1.'

The man read the letter three times. He put it into a plain envelope and addressed it to Theophilus Ragg, Deputy Director, British Museum, Great Russell Street WC. As he popped it into the letter box in the crowded street outside his hotel, attentive passers-by might have heard a faint sound of mocking laughter.

'Atlas flycatchers! Black-winged stilts! Bar-tailed desert larks! Bonelli's eagles!'

There was a note of reverence, almost of worship, in the speaker's tone as he mentioned the birds he had seen on his latest trip, and he began circling round the furniture in the Markham Square drawing room as if he were a rare gull on some Mediterranean cliff high above the sea.

'Sicily, Lady Lucy, upon my word, Sicily, I've never seen a place like it for the wildlife. Fantastic, that's what it is!'

Johnny Fitzgerald, Powerscourt's companion in arms across India and in all his investigations since, had just come home from a research trip for his next book on birds of the Mediterranean. His mind was still on some hot Sicilian mountainside, his binoculars searching the skies. But the case of the vanishing Caryatid in the British Museum soon had all his attention.

'Tall female creature, rather snooty looking, holding a temple on her head, that the one?'

'Exactly so, Johnny.'

'And you are telling me, Francis, that the dry old stick in charge isn't letting the police interview anybody at all? The whole thing has to be hushed up?'

'Right again, Johnny,' said Powerscourt, 'we have to approach the thing from the side and the edges, as it were.'

Johnny Fitzgerald looked down at the carpet for a moment and then looked up at his friend with hooded eyes as if he were a bird of prey measuring the distance to its victim.

'I see, Francis, I see. Now I know why all those messages have been left for me to get in touch at once. Most immediate, they said. It's those auction house porters and the ones at the British Museum, isn't it? You're like some bloody elephant, Francis, you never forget. You've been thinking about that case years ago with Orlando the forger and that beautiful girl of his and the fake paintings up in Norfolk and me conducting negotiations with the art gallery porters all through the night in the Rat and Parrot at the back of New Bond Street.'

Powerscourt tried hard not to smile.

'Come to think of it,' Johnny went on, 'it wasn't the Rat and Parrot, was it? What was that bloody pub called? It had a name to do with animals, I'm sure of that.'

'Fox and Hounds?' offered Lady Lucy. 'Pig and Whistle?'

'Did you ever work out what the pig had to do with the

whistle, Lady Lucy? No, it's not that. Landlord came from Castlebar in County Mayo, I seem to remember, name of Cassidy and he had wooden legs. Slug and Lettuce? Three Horseshoes? Memory's going, you know, definitely going.'

'Spread Eagle? Red Lion? Green Dragon? Blue Boar?' Powerscourt tried his hand through the colours.

'No, no, you're confusing me now.'

Johnny Fitzgerald walked slowly over to the window. Nothing moved in Markham Square. Even the local birds seemed to have gone quiet. Johnny tapped quite loudly on the window.

'The Black Swan! The Black bloody Swan! That's what the pub was called! Thank God I've remembered it. I was beginning to feel quite flustered.'

There was a hesitant, almost an inquisitive knock at the door. Rhys, the Powerscourt butler, coughed apologetically and handed Powerscourt a letter.

'Just arrived, my lord. From the British Museum, my lord. Said to be very urgent. The porter person is below, my lord, waiting for a reply.'

Powerscourt opened the envelope and whistled quietly to himself.

'What is it, Francis?' asked Lady Lucy. 'Have the centaurs gone missing from the Parthenon frieze? The charioteers picked up their reins and walked?'

'Much worse than that,' her husband replied. 'That dry old stick, as Johnny referred to him, Deputy Director Ragg has had a blackmail letter, asking for one hundred to two hundred thousand pounds. And he and his family have been threatened. That bloody Caryatid may have been dead over two thousand years but she's still causing a lot of mischief.'

As Powerscourt and Johnny Fitzgerald clattered down the stairs, one to the British Museum, the other to the Black Swan, Powerscourt thought Johnny Fitzgerald was saying his prayers.

'Scopoli's shearwaters,' the murmur came, 'stone curlews, Heuglin's gulls, rock partridges, steppe grey shrikes . . .'

The birds of Sicily were making a reverse migration to Markham Square and the fleshly delights of the King's Road, Chelsea.

Leisure time at the Hellenic College near Amersham was always busy. The college was the only boarding school for Greek boys and girls in Britain, founded for the parents of Greek merchants in London and the Home Counties who might have to relocate abroad for years at a time. The Greek Orthodox Church, well used to running schools attached to its places of worship, was the principal mover in the school, and the chairman of the governors and a third of its membership were priests or archimandrites of the Orthodox faith. There was even a small Greek Orthodox church on the site with the most ornate iconostasis in the south of England.

The large estate had been built by one of the great devotees of Antiquity of the eighteenth century. He had filled his grounds with replica temples of every sort. There was a temple of Vesta by one of the three lakes, a temple of Apollo hidden in the woodland. A miniature Parthenon stood on top of a Chiltern hill and a tiny Pantheon by the side of the water. The house and the estate were a tribute to the eighteenth-century conceit that the classical world was superior to the present and the study of ancient Greece and Rome was the only path to a proper education. Stourhead and Stowe and Chiswick House outside London with their fabulous gardens were the templates for the Hellenic College.

Boys and girls studied all the usual subjects taught in the English public schools with special emphasis on ancient Greek language and culture. The eighteen girls, who lived in Penelope House, were taught weaving and dressmaking in the Greek style, the boys in Patroclus House learned carpentry and model-making. Every year Penelope House had to produce a new *peplos*, a garment originally designed for the goddess Athena. The boys had to make a working chariot and four of their number had to learn to drive it.

Powerscourt found Inspector Christopher Kingsley waiting for him on the steps of the British Museum.

'Thought it might be a good idea,' the Inspector said, 'if we went in together. Move about in pairs like Father Christmases in the East End where the natives are liable to regard them as airborne burglars and treat them accordingly. Have you seen the actual letter yet?'

'Not so far,' said Powerscourt cheerfully and led the way inside.

Deputy Director Ragg handed the letter over at once. Sitting side by side on the museum sofa, the detective and the policeman read it together.

'Thank you for showing this to us so promptly,' said Powerscourt.

'I presume it came in the morning post?' The Inspector was copying the letter into his notebook as he spoke.

'That's right,' said Ragg. 'It's a bloody outrage, that's what it is. Ridiculous blackmailing person, threatening me and my family, asking for hundreds of thousands of pounds. How are we to know he has got the Caryatid anyway? He could be a fraud and a chancer in some back room, making it all up.'

'How right you are, Mr Ragg.' Inspector Kingsley was still scribbling as he spoke. 'What would you like us to do about it?'

'I do not intend to take this lying down. This museum has an international reputation. It is respected the world over for the breadth of its collections and the depth of its scholarship. Whatever steps are necessary for the apprehension and incarceration of this blackmailing criminal should be taken. I and my family will cooperate in whatever way you suggest. I am more than happy to take a crash course in firearms and carry a pistol at all times. If I should meet the miscreant, believe me, I should not hesitate to shoot on sight.'

It was at this point that Powerscourt realized that he had underestimated Theophilus Ragg. Beached in the dusty backwaters of academe he may have been, but he had courage. He was like an earlier Queen before the coming of the Armada, who knew she had the body but of a weak and feeble woman; but she had the heart and stomach of a king.

'Let me tell you, Mr Deputy Director, what the Metropolitan Police can offer you at this time,' said Inspector Kingsley. 'We shall maintain a discreet twenty-four-hour watch over the post room at the Ritz Hotel, though I fear the villain, if he is genuine, may already have private arrangements in place to intercept any communication addressed to the Friends of the British Museum. We shall keep watch over your house at all hours of the day and night. Your wife and children will not be able to take a step outside your front door without being watched by one of our plain clothes officers. I propose to send the letter – if you would allow us to borrow it for a day or so – to a couple of graphologists the Yard has used in the past. We do not like to advertise our connections with these people, but they have sometimes been useful in earlier cases.'

'That all sounds very efficient, Inspector. I am more than grateful. But tell me, what do you gentlemen think I should do about the blackmail? Should I reply to this letter? Should I offer to make an appointment to meet with this person? Are the British Museum and its Deputy Director to be turned into a human honeypot to tempt a passing blackmailer? I do hope not. Lord Powerscourt?'

'I have to confess I have little experience of this sort of blackmail. If it were me, I should be happy to place myself in the hands of the police.'

'I too, Mr Deputy Director,' Inspector Kingsley added, 'have little experience of these negotiations, nor of sums as large as these. But I do know that the Commissioner believes it is always a mistake for those directly involved to negotiate with blackmailers.'

'I see. Thank you for that, both of you.' Theophilus Ragg smiled a wintry smile as if two undergraduate essays had just found favour with their tutor.

'And what, pray, do you make of the choice of the Ritz Hotel as headquarters?'

'Good choice, I believe,' Powerscourt replied. 'It's always busy, the pavements outside are always crowded, a man could operate happily from there without being noticed. I'm sure the Inspector here will check the guest list most carefully.'

'Of course.'

'Gentlemen, thank you for your advice. I shall follow

41

it to the letter and I am, as I said, most grateful for your assistance, Inspector. I suggest we meet again at four o'clock this afternoon. I have a meeting with the Sumerians in five minutes. Is there anything else you would like to say about the letter?'

'I hope we shall not keep the Sumerians waiting,' said Powerscourt, wondering if they were going to arrive in original costumes, 'but there is one thing that concerns me. It has to do with the publicity and the threat of exposure of the loss of the Caryatid.'

'Exactly so,' put in the Inspector, 'I too was going to mention the threat to tell *The Times*.'

'If you are both in agreement, then my guests may have to wait a moment or two. Please continue.'

Inspector Kingsley gestured to Powerscourt that the older man should pick up the baton.

'Consider the question of publicity, Mr Ragg. I'm sure the thieves thought there would be a great hue and cry once the loss was discovered. Headlines all over the newspapers, questions in Parliament from tame MPs, the usual sort of stuff. And all that, when you think about it, is to the thieves' advantage. Let's suppose that they had a buyer for the statue long before they stole it. The buyer will read the newspapers. I'm sure a story like this would find its way into the European and American papers too. For the buyer, the publicity acts as a kind of confirmation. He knows the Caryatid has gone. He believes it will come to him. All he has to do is wait.'

While Powerscourt paused, Inspector Kingsley picked up his train of thought. 'But suppose you are the man who has commissioned the thieves. There is no mention of it in the newspapers. As far as the real client knows, the Caryatid may still be in place. He may not believe the thieves when they tell him that she is gone, that she is in their possession.'

'Are you saying that the silence may promote suspicion and anger between the ultimate client and the thieves who actually took the Caryatid?'

'We are,' said Powerscourt. The Inspector nodded.

'Then surely we should keep quiet for as long as possible,' said Ragg firmly, closing his notebook with a flourish. 'By all means let us spread discord and mutual suspicion among our enemies.'

'Exactly,' said the Inspector.

'Indeed,' added Powerscourt.

As they made their way back to the street Inspector Kingsley stopped by the railings and looked back at the museum.

'I was so grateful, you know, my lord, when this investigation came along. I'd just looked after three murder cases in a row.'

'And you are not fond of murder cases, would that be right?'

'I loathe them. I absolutely loathe them,' Inspector Kingsley spoke quietly but with great force. 'But now I'm not so sure this Caryatid affair is going to be any better. This case is proving to be difficult and potentially dangerous.'

'But still preferable to murder inquiries?' asked Powerscourt.

'Oh yes.'

Neither man knew it at the time but they had not to wait long before the Case of the Missing Caryatid produced its first corpse.

4

Powerscourt went straight to Linfords in New Bond Street, one of London's leading firms of art auctioneers. They had been putting paintings, sculpture, tapestries, jewels of every sort under the hammer for nearly two hundred years. Their publicity claimed they could give you a quotation and a sale on everything from a Fragonard painting to a Fabergé egg. They cultivated an air of effortless grandeur, as if they were of a superior race to the people whose possessions they were selling. They were all, Powerscourt had decided long before, pretending to be patricians, patricians fallen on harder times perhaps, but still patricians sent down to earth to rule the waves and confound Britannia's enemies.

All these meetings with the art dealers and the auctioneers blurred into one after a time. He would be met in the reception area by a pretty girl, straight out of a grand country house in the Home Counties, and taken to the junior gatekeeper. The junior gatekeeper was usually aged between twenty-five and thirty and was already acquiring the superior patina that was the hallmark of the company. From this small but elegant room he would be taken to the senior partner's office three floors above with splendid views out over Mayfair.

'Lord Powerscourt, what a pleasure! So pleased you felt able to come and see us.'

The senior partner would then show him into a chair and offer coffee or perhaps a glass of champagne to set them both up for the day.

'Now then, Lord Powerscourt, how can we be of service to you this morning?'

It was this first opening up of the subject under discussion that Powerscourt found most difficult. He would begin with a display of modesty.

'Thank you so much for agreeing to see me. It's all rather difficult, actually. You see, I've been instructed to act as intermediary between a certain party and an auction house like yourselves about the possible sale of a possible work of art that has yet to come on the market. If you see what I mean. Please forgive the lack of definite information. My instructions are very definite and very limiting, I'm afraid.'

And at this point he would look rather helpless, as if pleading with the senior partner to extricate him from his difficulties. Lady Lucy always said that her husband was never more dangerous than when he affected this helpless look. About as helpless as a hungry tiger on the rampage, she would say.

'Well, Lord Powerscourt,' the senior partner would reply, 'this is certainly going to be an interesting commission! I can quite see that. Perhaps I could try for enlightenment point by point, if I may. You say you are acting as intermediary for a certain party. Could you perhaps fill in some of the details. An ancient family wishing to dispose of some assets? Death duties come to call in their usual

45

disagreeable way? Two deaths of an incumbent in quick succession perhaps? Always difficult, those cases. Always expensive too. A foreign gentleman perchance, wishing to retain his anonymity? The Government in some shape or form? A member of the Royal Family maybe? They have enough art after all to keep us in business till the end of the century!'

With that, the senior partner usually laughed loudly at his own witticism. Powerscourt would smile.

'I'm afraid I cannot be more precise at this point. Your list of possibilities is certainly comprehensive. Forgive me.'

'Of course, Lord Powerscourt, of course. Could I now ask about the object in question? A possible work of art that has yet to come on the market, you say. That could mean almost anything. Could I assume, for the sake of clarity, that we are talking about a painting or an Old Master drawing or a piece of sculpture, something that would come within the normal compass of activities for a firm like ours?'

Powerscourt would pause at this point and rub his hands together. 'I am going beyond my brief here,' he would announce finally, 'but you have been more than patient with this difficult enquiry. Yes, I can safely say that the work would fit into the categories you mention. But I dare not say any more. I am in breach of my undertakings already.'

'That is certainly helpful, Lord Powerscourt. Could I ask you this also? Would your client or clients like to sell the object or objects in open auction or would you prefer a private sale, something more discreet.'

'I am not an expert in these matters, Mr Senior Partner. What would your advice be?'

46

Now it was the turn of the man from the art dealers to pause. 'Well,' he would say, 'you could probably obtain the highest price at an open auction, well publicized, heavily advertised before the event. On the other hand there might be advantages to a private sale, details that could be kept out of the public domain, away from the prying eyes of the tax authorities and the perils of publicity about the export of works of art, selling off the nation's heritage, that sort of rubbish that always floods the newspapers when important works leave these shores.'

Powerscourt thought that a commission of ten per cent or more plus auctioneering expenses might be a sufficient compensation for temporary trial by newspaper.

'Would I be right in assuming, Mr Senior Partner, that your firm would be prepared to act in either case, public auction or private sale?'

'Why, of course. We are mere facilitators, the gears, if you like, which work to effect the connection of buyer and seller to mutual advantage. We would be delighted to offer our services.'

And that would be that. In one case the senior partner tried to obtain some more information about the object in question.

'Let me hazard a guess, Lord Powerscourt,' this managing director, considerably older than his colleagues, ventured, 'could it be that the revelation of the type of work would be such that it could have an impact on the future price? A lost Leonardo would cause a sensation to start with, but interest might die down after a while. Better to keep the identity of the work secret until the last possible moment perhaps? Fetch a higher price that way, what do you say?'

Powerscourt would smile to them all and set off on his

business. Two trains of thought would go with him on his walk back to Markham Square through some of London's richest streets. None of the leading art houses had, as yet, been approached by any thief. He felt sure that he could have told if they had been. The second train of thought never left him, day or night. Where was the Caryatid? How had the thieves got her out? How had they got the replacement in? Where was she now?

They built a special coffin for the statue, the sculptor, the carpenter and the undertaker in the little town on the edge of the Brecon Beacons. This was no ordinary coffin, just under eight feet long, twice the normal width and twice the normal height. The sculptor's eight-year-old son, who caught sight of it by accident one afternoon, thought his father was making a final resting place for a giant like Bendigeidfran fab Llyr, a mythological king of Britain in the time of legend, or Idris Gawr of the great mountain Cader Idris. Maybe it was a dragon, green or red perhaps, stretched out with the wings tucked in by her side.

The sculptor consulted the only book in the local library about Egyptian mummies. They decided to wrap her in linen sheets alternating with blankets and three rolls of canvas on top of those. The statue was secured to the floor and sides of the coffin and the bottom and sides of the casket were lined with tightly packed straw. This adaptation of ancient custom by the Nile with human remains to current Welsh practice with marble subjects by the Brecon Beacons would, they thought, keep her in one piece on her journey. For the statue was not being well preserved for a journey to eternal life in the next world, she was going on a journey across the seas to the New

World where a different kind of immortality awaited her. No cakes or ornaments were going with her.

The coffin was black, with handles along the side. The story concocted for the journey was complicated, but credible, largely the work of the local schoolteacher who was sworn into the conspiracy with a fistful of notes, a couple of bottles of whisky and a year's supply of tickets to the rugby internationals. The previous year, the legend went, a rich American had come home to visit his family and the tombs of his ancestors. On his journey he met a young sculptor who was his great-great-nephew on his mother's side. It was the rich American's special wish, before he went back to Baltimore, that the young man should carve something appropriate to adorn his tomb in the local cemetery after his death. The rich American only lasted three weeks after his return, for the journey must have taken more out of him than he realized. His funeral was held in his local church where he had been an elder for many years, the Third Presbyterian off Jefferson Drive in the wealthiest part of the city, and the body was duly interred in the cemetery. In the coffin was the offering from the young sculptor in Wales, a triumphant angel, wings furled, her arm aloft, pointing the way to heaven for the dead American relative. Surely she would see him to the last frontier and a better world.

A firm from Bristol were to organize transport to that city and the transhipment to America. They were one of the most experienced companies in the country at this sort of work. They watched the great lorry moving slowly down the mountain road, the sculptor, the carpenter, the undertaker and the schoolteacher, until it turned the corner by the railway bridge and vanished from sight, the noise of the engine the last link to fade away. They decided to hold a wake for their departed friend in the snug of the Green Dragon next to the undertaker's whose doors had only just opened for the day. How else could they mark the passing of a Caryatid, well over two thousand years old, on her journey of three thousand miles to a new home across the seas?

'I'm afraid I've had rather an unconventional thought,' said Inspector Christopher Kingsley, taking a cup of Earl Grey in the Powerscourt drawing room at about half past six in the evening. He now had a permanent invitation to call around this time.

Powerscourt looked at him keenly. Policemen, even ones in the habit of reading modern novels, were not usually supposed to harbour such thoughts.

'How unconventional?' asked Powerscourt with a smile.

'Well, I'm not actually ashamed of it, now I come to think about it,' the Inspector said, 'it could prove rather useful in our investigation.'

'Tell us more, please,' Lady Lucy chipped in.

'Well, I was talking about the Caryatid to my children yesterday evening. I should have been reading them a bedside story but my mind was so full of the marble lady with the long tunic that I told them all about her instead.'

'And what did they say?' asked Powerscourt.

'This is the interesting thing, my lord, Lady Lucy. James and Rosalind, he's seven and she's five, asked a whole lot of questions I don't think we would have thought of.'

'Out of the mouths of babes and sucklings,' said Lady Lucy, remembering the psalm and hoping the words could help bring forth victory, 'hast thou ordained strength because of thine enemies, that thou mightest still the enemy and the avenger.'

'Probably,' said the Inspector, slightly thrown by this display of biblical knowledge. 'Anyway, Rosalind wanted to know if the Caryatid had to have her face washed. And her hair, the little one added after a second's thought. James asked if she could talk to the other statues at night when all the people had gone away. Rosalind asked me if she had been a real person once. Did the sculptor copy a living lady to make his Caryatid? What sort of house would she have lived in? What sort of food would she have eaten? Would she be forced to have porridge for breakfast like everybody else? There were lots more queries along the same lines. I began to think I might have been better sticking to Toad's adventures in *The Wind in the Willows* after a while.'

'What interesting questions,' said Lady Lucy.

'I'm not sure I could have answered them all,' Powerscourt added. 'Forgive me, please, but I can't for the moment discern how they might help us in this inquiry.'

'That only came to me this morning, my lord. One of our problems, as you both know, is that we can't talk to any of the people in the museum. As far as they know, the Caryatid standing on her plinth is the real one. Nobody's told them or the public who come to see her anything different. Now consider this. If you are an academic, or a scholarly gentleman like the curators at the museum, there are learned articles you can look up about the Parthenon and the Elgin Marbles. I think they produce a catalogue of their sculpture holdings every few years, with considerably more footnotes than pages of text. That's fine if you've got a university degree and a pair of thick glasses but they're no earthly use to anybody else.'

Powerscourt smiled. He thought he could see where the Inspector was heading.

'Now then, my lord, who do you think are the most important clients of the British Museum? Not the middle-aged and the old, surely. Not even the younger people who flock there at the weekends. The most valuable visitors are the youngest, the ones who will be able to go back over and over again. There are children peering at the Parthenon frieze and the lapiths and the centaurs and the Caryatid all the time, depending on their teachers to be told what is going on.'

Inspector Kingsley paused and took another sip of his Earl Grey. Neither Powerscourt nor Lady Lucy would have dared to interrupt him now.

'I'm sure you can see what I am driving at,' he went on. 'The museum should produce a little pamphlet, a small book with lots of illustrations, aimed at eight- to ten-year-olds, that could be on sale for a few pence or given away free to young visitors. It would be a valuable contribution to the wider understanding of ancient Greece, surely.'

'Do you have an author in mind,' asked Powerscourt in the most innocent voice he could muster.

'Why, yes. I would write it.' The Inspector blushed a deep shade of red as he said this. 'For the real reason behind such a plan is that it would give us the perfect excuse to talk to people all over the museum. The porters would have to tell us how the Caryatid was cleaned and so on, how she was moved from place to place, the others would have to tell us how she fitted into the ancient world. But what a lot of questions we could ask! Anyway, I've always wanted to write something more interesting than police reports. This could be a start.'

'Splendid,' said Powerscourt, 'splendid. I'll speak to

Ragg in the morning. If he agrees, you could start work on the project immediately.'

Artemis Metaxas had never thought she would end up as a madame, a procurer of young girls for her clients. Certainly not at the tender age of twenty-seven. Her task, quite separate from her teaching duties at the school attached to the Greek Orthodox Cathedral of Santa Sophia in Notting Hill's Moscow Road, came round once a month. She was to collect a group of respectable young Greek girls under the age of twenty in London, and bring them on a Saturday afternoon to a secret address in the Home Counties. Half a dozen or so would suffice, but eight would be better. They were to be returned to the capital on the Sunday afternoon under the same conditions of extreme secrecy, darkened windows in the special train, closed carriages to bring them from the station to the remote garden door of the house in the country. Quite what happened to them in their secluded stay, Artemis never knew. She was put up in a cottage on the estate some distance from the house and not allowed to leave. She only met her charges again on the return journey. She knew the girls were well paid. She knew they were sworn to silence with some ancient oath of terrible power. And, whatever went on, Artemis was sure that what took place was not too dreadful. A number of the girls volunteered to go back over and over again.

Johnny Fitzgerald found only one regular at the Black Swan near the art dealers of Old Bond Street who remembered him from earlier times. This was a very old gentleman, universally known as Red Fred, widely believed to refer to a revolutionary period in his middle years, who had boasted only seven teeth when Johnny had first encountered him. Now he proudly pointed to his last remaining two, assuring Johnny, to Johnny's great delight, that there was food enough in the drink if you remembered to order the right stuff. But he was able to direct Johnny to the Cock and Whistle off Southampton Row where the porters from the British Museum took their refreshments at the end of a working day. Johnny was surprised at the number of Greek porters on the staff. There was a Yannis with a limp and a Kostas with an enormous beard, an Evangelos who doubled up as a card sharp in the evenings and a Stavros with immaculate English, all working alongside more conventional Londoners with more conventional names. Some of them, Johnny decided, might have been on duty the day the Caryatid was switched and the original disappeared. The Greek contingent, he discovered, felt more at home in a different pub called The Fox and Hounds near the Greek Cathedral on Moscow Road in Notting Hill. Here the landlord's brother-in-law was Greek and maintained a private drinking establishment in the basement serving a variety of Greek drinks, the aniseed-flavoured *ouzo* and *tsipouro*, *mastika* and *kitron*, a citrus-flavoured liquor from Naxos, and *tentura*, a lethal cinnamon-flavoured potion that came from Patras. On Saturday evenings his wife cooked a variety of Greek dishes, served with an assortment of wines from the homeland, which Johnny Fitzgerald believed produced the longest-lasting hangovers of any alcoholic liquid he had ever tasted.

But here, Johnny felt, was a place where he might be able to catch the hidden pulse of the Greek community in London, their secret hopes, their dreams of home, the things from Athens and Thessaly and the islands the exiles missed the most. Sometimes he felt so much of an outsider, speaking no Greek, unaware of the nature and origin of the drinks they so kindly pressed upon him, that he wanted to go home right away and never come back. But these exiles from the Aegean saw something of a kindred spirit in the Irishman, his lust for travel, his sense of adventure, his love of fun. They nicknamed him the Green Odysseus behind his back. He reminded them, he was told one evening, of a famous character, well known to all Greeks in London, Sokratis Papadopolous, ostensibly a former art dealer, but believed by his fellow countrymen to have been a smuggler of antiquities, and a pirate in his better days. He was believed to have seen the interior of prisons in France, Italy and England. The Greeks from the Fox and Hounds took Johnny to see him in the hospital where Sokratis was dying, his liver now a thing of the past, his other organs shutting down one after another like flowers closing at the fading of the light. Only one visitor was allowed at a time. Johnny asked the emaciated figure about the theft of the Caryatid. Johnny didn't think the man was in a position where he would be able to tell anybody anything ever again. An Irish nurse by the side of the bed was making clucking noises as if her patient should be left to die in peace.

The man was muttering to himself and thrashing about in the sheets. 'Remember the Riddle of the Sphinx, remember.' A pair of mad staring eyes bored into Johnny's skull. A violent coughing fit seized Sokratis at this point. Sometimes he shouted and pointed dramatically at the ceiling. Johnny knew some of the symptoms from the worst excesses of his own past, the voices in your head, the vivid flashes of lightning so intense you felt your head would burst, the spiders on the bedclothes crawling all over your skin, the rats hanging upside down from the ceiling above. Time had no meaning in this alcoholic half world, the only consistent feeling one of acute fear and terror. Sometimes the walls and the ceiling would start spinning round and continue even after you had closed your eyes. On one occasion, and even now Johnny was still ashamed of his younger self, he had to crawl to the bathroom with the decorations on the carpet and the pictures in the hall hurtling through his brain like a series of shooting stars. Sometimes Sokratis spoke in Greek. On other occasions a phrase would leap out and seem to hold some special meaning known only to the speaker. 'The Isles of Greece' occurred over and over again, spoken with a series of nods as if Sokratis expected his listeners to share his meaning. Fragments of poetry seemed to crop up time after time. 'I hear the Echoes through the mountains throng, The Winds come to me from the fields of sleep,' came five times in a row. It was followed by 'where is it now, the glory and the dream'. After that a short burst of weeping and then, raising himself up till he was semi-upright in his bed, he screamed, 'shades of the prison-house, shades of the prison-house,' and sank back on his bed. The breathing was shallow and very fast. Beads of perspiration glistened on his forehead and ran down the side of his face. The nurse continued to hold his left hand as if he were a small child in the middle of a nightmare. Now Sokratis looked as though he might pass out or pass away. Johnny had to lean forward to catch the next words, 'Got to go to the High City,' got to go to the High City, the High City.' Then he turned onto his side and spoke no more.

56

The nurse showed Johnny to the door as quickly and as quietly as she could. 'Let us all remember our God, whoever and wherever he is,' she whispered, 'now and in the hour of our death, amen.'

5

Inspector Kingsley had not yet heard of the Isles of Greece when he met with Deputy Director Ragg the following day to discuss the Booklet for the Young, as the policeman now referred to it.

'Capital idea, capital!' cried Ragg, rubbing his hands together. 'Why didn't we think of it ourselves? The Director will be so pleased, he's always keen to involve the next generation. Our Head of Greek and Roman Antiquities should be back from the Alps in a couple of days, he too will be delighted. I shall issue instructions for everybody to give you their full cooperation. Perhaps you could wait twenty-four hours before you embark on your enquiries? That would be splendid.'

'Thank you so much,' said Inspector Kingsley. 'I have some disappointing news, I fear, Mr Deputy Director. Not that I find it disappointing, for I had few hopes of success, but it does not take us any further forward.'

He paused and drew a couple of letters from his pocket. 'You will recall that my superiors wished to send the blackmail letter to a couple of so-called handwriting experts?' It sounded as though he thought his superiors should have been arrested immediately and locked up in Newgate for even harbouring such an idea.

'You will not be surprised to hear,' Kingsley went on, 'that their reports are totally without value.' He looked down at them distastefully. 'There's a whole lot of nonsense about pressure of downward strokes, upward inclination of the line indicating an optimistic temperament, decisive dottings of the i's and so on. The upshot, to conflate the two reports, is that the author is a middle-aged man, possibly with violent temperament, of determined and decisive character who may stop at nothing to get what he wants. Bravo, say I. Tom Thumb himself could have told us as much as that.'

'Never mind,' said Deputy Director Ragg, 'I thought it might be unprofitable. But tell me this, Inspector. Your men are patrolling my house and watching over my family day and night. I am most grateful. Today or tomorrow, by my calculations, we should hear from the blackmailer again even though the museum has followed your Commissioner's advice not to get in touch with him at all. Do you think I shall receive another letter? That the blackguard will write again?'

'I'm sure you'll hear from him again, Mr Ragg. Let's just hope a letter is all we get.'

Johnny Fitzgerald was rewarded with a large glass of Brunello di Montalcino, a new recommendation from Powerscourt's wine merchant, when he brought the news of the Isles of Greece and the other Delphic messages from Sokratis Papadopolous to Markham Square shortly after 6.30 on the evening of his trip to the hospital. Lady Lucy had observed to her husband only the day before that Johnny seemed to be drinking much less than usual.

She had heard a whisper from a distant outstation of her relatives in Warwickshire that Johnny was romantically involved with a rich and attractive widow resident in that county and in Flood Street, Chelsea, but no mention had been made of the putative love affair.

'What do you think it all means, Lady Lucy? Shades of the prison-house and the other stuff comes from a poem by Wordsworth as far as I know. The High City probably means Acropolis. Half the bloody cities in ancient Greece had their own acropolises, didn't they? I can't make any sense of either of those. But "The Isles of Greece", I mean, like the fellow said. What was he on about?'

'It could be anything, Johnny, he was a very strange man that Lord Byron who wrote it. Some long dead relation of mine was supposed to have been in love with the poet, you know,' said Lady Lucy. 'Your dying friend did say it was a riddle, didn't he? Like the Sphinx and what walks on four legs in the morning, two at midday and three in the evening.'

'Could be a pub, the Isles of Greece,' said Johnny hopefully, contemplating perhaps the long reconnaissance mission needed to identify such a place.

'Or a restaurant,' Powerscourt chipped in, 'roll up, roll up for the freshest seafood in London.'

'How about a nightclub?' asked Lady Lucy. 'Dusky Greek maidens dancing to the music of the lyre and the pipes of Pan perhaps?'

'Seven veils?' asked Johnny. 'Six? Eight? Ten?'

'That would depend on the time of the evening, I think, Johnny,' Lady Lucy replied. 'The later the hour, the fewer the number of veils, I imagine.'

'How late before the veils disappear down to zero?' asked Johnny.

'What about a shop?' suggested Lady Lucy, keen to escape from the veils. 'Posh sort of place in Knightsbridge perhaps, selling luxury produce from the Greek islands, olives from Rhodes, toy bull dancers from Crete, a better class of ouzo from Mykonos, warm jumpers for seafarers in the winter months, hand-knitted by Greek grandmas by the fire in their peasant cottages while the wind howls round the Aegean.'

'It could all have been a bluff, of course,' said Powerscourt. 'Maybe the fellow meant that the secret of the Caryatid's disappearance actually does have to do with the Greek Islands. It wasn't really a riddle at all.'

'There are a couple of verses at the end of "The Isles of Greece" about Samian wine,' said Lady Lucy. 'They might appeal to you, Johnny. I looked it up earlier. Here we are: "Fill high the bowl with Samian wine! Our virgins dance beneath the shade – Place me on Sunium's marbled steep, Where nothing, save the waves and I, May hear our mutual murmurs sweep; There, swanlike, let me sing and die: A land of slaves shall ne'er be mine – Dash down yon cup of Samian wine!"'

'Sounds good to me,' said Johnny, 'I bet those rogues at the Greek pub near the Orthodox cathedral have some Samian filth hidden in the cellar. Do you think I should go to Samos, Francis? Check out the wine and the veils and the maidens?'

'He said "The Isles of Greece", mind you,' said Powerscourt. 'Surely if he wanted to refer to Samos, he'd have said Samos, wouldn't he?'

'There must be hundreds and hundreds of Greek islands,' said Lady Lucy, feeling that the riddle wasn't going to yield up its secrets very easily.

'How long did it take that fellow Odysseus to get

home to his island from Troy?' Johnny Fitzgerald put his glass down and didn't help himself to a refill. Lady Lucy looked meaningfully at her husband. 'Ten years, wasn't it? Should have taken him a couple of months or so at the most. I reckon it could take you as long to check out all those bloody islands. I'm not usually averse to a glass or two, even of Greek if you twist my arm, and a spot of sun and sea air and a few birds. Normally I'd volunteer like a shot but I've got rather a lot on at the moment so you'll have to count me out of the expedition, I'm afraid.'

'It looks to me as though the riddle has won the first round,' said Powerscourt. 'The way things look at the moment, it's going to win the second and third rounds as well. Greeks with riddles are just as bad as the ones bearing gifts.'

The message from the Corfu telegram office down in the port was hand delivered by a barefooted ragamuffin who couldn't have been more than ten years old. The stones of the harbour were still cold on his feet at half past nine in the morning. Captain Dimitri was on his second glass of ouzo since breakfast. He was not yet tired of waiting for news. The taverna was still producing its rather greasy moussaka, served by the pretty daughter, and his small crew was kept entertained by the bars and bordellos of the city centre some six hundred yards away. His ship was swaying slightly at her mooring on the harbour, the mangy lion fast asleep, the querulous monkeys staring sadly out to sea.

The message was very brief. Thirty or thirty-first October, it said. Half past four in the afternoon. Brindisi railway station. So, the Captain said to himself, *I have six days to get from the Greek to the Italian side of the*

Mediterranean. If I take on stores today and leave first thing tomorrow I should have plenty of time. The Captain stared up at the sky with its wheeling gulls and decided that the weather would not trouble him on his journey. There was a widow he knew in Brindisi who ran a laundry in the town. Other services could be purchased for cash. Maybe she would be pleased to see him again.

Precisely what he was meant to pick up at the end of his journey, he did not know. All he knew was that it would be heavy and that he might have to hire a crane or a hoist of some kind to bring it aboard.

Over the next week Powerscourt and Lady Lucy opened relations with the upper layers of the Greek Establishment in London. They took morning coffee with the Greek Ambassador, Anastasias Papadikis, a former merchant who had made his fortune buying and selling new and second-hand boats of every description. Powerscourt's cover story was that his publishers had asked him to write a short guide book on the glories of ancient Greece. He brought with him as a gift to the Ambassador a presentation copy of his own first volume on the cathedrals of England. What advice would the Ambassador give to one about to embark on such a venture in his native land? Sipping his sugary coffee very noisily through his great black beard, the Ambassador gave Powerscourt his blessing.

'I don't need to tell a man of your education about the principal sites, Lord Powerscourt, you will know them as well as I do. And Greece will always be grateful to this country for British assistance in money and diplomacy in the long battle for the independence we enjoy today. But I could perhaps make a few small suggestions of my own? The site in Anatolia believed to be the location of the ancient city of Troy, Homer's Troy, is well worth a visit. But even you English know little of the key role played by an Englishman who advised the ghastly German Schliemann where to dig, and was a first-rate archaeologist in his own right. Calvert, Frank Calvert, is, or rather was, the man's name, as he died a couple of years ago. The Greek government sent a cabinet minister to represent the Greek nation at his funeral. Your fellow countrymen should know more about the man. And, of course, there is Missolonghi at the mouth of the Gulf of Patras where the poet Byron gave his life for Greek freedom. Maybe your readers would like to pay their respects?'

Powerscourt noted that there was a famous portrait of Lord Byron in Albanian dress above the fireplace, holding an Eastern sword and with a great storm about to break out behind him. The Ambassador informed him that this was on loan from the British Government Collections as a gesture of friendship to Greece from the British people. When asked if there were any points of disagreement, any areas of conflict between the two nations, one an empire of the past, the other an empire in the present, the Ambassador simply laughed.

'There are no disagreements at all, my dear Lord Powerscourt. Why do you think the post of Ambassador to the Court of St James is one of the most coveted posts in the Greek Prime Minister's gift? We have little to do here except attend official functions and represent our country on state occasions. It is a post for a lotus-eater rather than a real diplomat, I assure you!'

Powerscourt was anxious to meet with the Head of Greek and Roman Antiquities at the British Museum as soon as he returned from the mountains. He had remembered only the day before another account of Tristram Stanhope from his, Powerscourt's, brother-in-law, the banker William Burke, who had sat next to him at some grand dinner in Guildhall.

'There we all were, Francis, white tie and tails, course after course of French cuisine, decorations will be worn, the odd Victoria Cross on show amongst the baubles, and this fellow Stanhope beside me. He didn't look out of place at all, cufflinks and shoes all passed muster, that sort of thing. But he had this air about him. I couldn't put my finger on it for a long time. Then it came to me. Even there, in the beating heart of the City of London, Stanhope had the air of one forever looking to recover the dramatic excitement of some long forgotten sporting event like a cricket match. "There's a breathless hush in the Close tonight, Ten to make and the match to win." I rather had the impression he's been playing the game for most of his life.'

Powerscourt longed to talk to classical academics, art dealers, sculpture experts, modern Greek historians. If you were a serious thief, he would have asked after half an hour or so, what would you do with a Caryatid if you had stolen one? Copy it? If so, how many copies? Who might want to buy it? Greeks in Greece? Greeks in America? Greeks in London? How much would it be worth? Were there any examples of other works of major importance walking out of European museums apart from the *Mona Lisa*? Tristram Stanhope would have to answer for them all. Powerscourt thought about the links between the worlds of art, scholarship, Greek nationalism and crime. Somewhere, he felt sure, they intersected. If he could find that point, he might be able to solve the mystery. Once again Stanhope would be his guide.

> A bumping pitch and a blinding light,
> An hour to play and the last man in.

Theophilus Ragg, Deputy Director of the British Museum, thought he recognized the handwriting. The envelope too looked familiar. Feeling a great wave of anger sweep through him, he slid open the letter with an elaborately carved Japanese paper knife, a gift from the National Museum in Tokyo.

'Dear Ragg,' he read, 'you have dared to disobey my instructions. I have received no suggestions about the transfer of the monies mentioned in my earlier letter. The relevant sum is therefore going to increase by ten thousand pounds a day, starting today.'

Ragg felt that the anger coursing through him was growing stronger.

'Furthermore,' the writer continued, 'your pathetic attempts to secure your own safety and those of your family through the intervention of the Metropolitan Police have been noted. Their plain clothes policemen stand out on the streets of London like giants in a land of pygmies.

'As I said before, we know who you are. We know where you are. We have ways of making you pay and in ways you might not have thought of. Quite soon you will receive reminders that it is neither wise nor prudent to ignore our demands. It is not too late. Correspondence regarding the money transfers can still be sent to The Friends of the British Museum, Ritz Hotel, London W1.'

Ragg knew he ought to take a walk or read a Shakespeare sonnet or two, to calm himself down. Shakespeare sonnets, he had discovered some years before, were much more successful in assuaging his rages than any pill or potion. He remembered the last conversation with his doctor who had advised him that he should consider taking early retirement because of his health. His heart was not strong, the doctor said, and any strain or great upset could have severe consequences. But the wrath was upon him. He thought that if he had been younger and more martial he would have issued a demand for a duel. He grabbed a pen and wrote a reply:

'Dear Blackmailer,' he began. 'Yet again you have insulted me and my family and the Museum I represent. You are beneath contempt.

'"Rage – Goddess, sing the rage of Peleus' son Achilles" – these are the opening words of Homer's great epic of ancient warfare *The Iliad*, which tells the story of the battle for Troy. May it contain a lesson and a warning for you. "Would to god my rage," Achilles tells the Trojan hero Hector just before he kills him, "and my fury would drive me now to hack your flesh away and eat you raw, such agonies you have caused me."

'He then kills Hector, ties him to his chariot, and drags him behind it for a period of twelve days. I pray to the ancient gods of Achaea and the spirits of the Aegean that a latter-day Achilles may return from the dead and tear you into a thousand pieces.'

Ragg realized he was still shaking. He did not read his letter again. He called for a porter to take it immediately to the Ritz Hotel in Piccadilly.

He reached inside the top left-hand drawer of his desk

and pulled out a well-worn leather volume containing the sonnets of William Shakespeare.

Inspector Kingsley felt he was progressing well with his work for eight- to ten-year-olds about the Elgin Marbles and the Caryatid. He knew now that the Caryatid was cleaned in a mixture of mild soap and water once a week, and that she didn't seem to mind when her hair was washed. He learnt about the different time scales of the various pieces of statuary. The Parthenon frieze and the metopes that had been placed around the outer walls of the building were older than the Caryatid and had probably been created by a different generation of sculptors. The Parthenon, one of the young curators told him, was built at the height of Athens's glory, when she had an empire that spread out all over the Aegean Sea, and when her temples and public buildings were the glory of the city. The Caryatid, the young curator said, was created a generation later when the empire was lost, public life debased, and the city about to lose its thirty-year struggle with Sparta known as the Peloponnesian War. Athens had fallen from the height of glory into ignominious defeat, and the Caryatid, in a way, had marked the passing. Like Icarus, perhaps, Athens had dared to fly too close to the sun. The Athenians could always erect another temple, the Erechtheion, on the Acropolis, but they could not bring back the past.

The Inspector wrote down what he was told in a special blue notebook with his name on the inside, written in a large, childish hand by his son to remind him of his duty. He took a special interest in the routines of the museum, what happened after dark, what happened before the museum closed last thing at night. Above all, he was interested in the fire alarm that had occurred some time before. It was, people discovered afterwards, a trial run to test some new equipment, but the porters had hurried everybody out of the building into the forecourt in front of Great Russell Street as if their lives were in danger. One or two of the more punctilious curators were able to tell him that they had been left standing about for at least forty minutes. The Inspector decided it was time for another fire alarm. This time he and a couple of his men would be left hiding inside the museum to see how easy it would be to move things about or to replace one object with another. He would talk to Deputy Director Ragg that afternoon about arranging a date. He thought his children would probably approve of fire alarms with their promise of fire engines and ambulances rushing to the rescue with their sirens at full blast.

'I'm the bringer of bad news this evening, very bad.' Detective Inspector Kingsley had refused the customary cup of tea on his evening arrival in Markham Square and was sipping slowly at a glass of brandy. Powerscourt thought he looked very pale.

'It's Kostas,' he went on, 'one of the Greek porters at the museum. He's been killed, I'm afraid.'

'How?' asked Powerscourt.

'Well,' said Christopher Kingsley, 'the official story is, and will continue to be, that he was killed by a tube train. The usual story, too many people trying to get on in the rush hour, somebody slipped and then there was a body on the line waiting to be run over by God knows how many tons of Piccadilly Line train. There was an off-duty police sergeant several carriages down and he managed to keep all the passengers at the front of the train back until he spoke to them. The driver was weeping uncontrollably in the stationmaster's office. He'd only been in the job for two weeks and nobody had prepared him for anything like this. He kept saying that it was all his fault. The point is, the sergeant told his superiors that one of the passengers, a middle-aged woman in a fur coat, said she thought somebody was pushing the victim towards the front of the train, but she couldn't be sure. She's going to speak to us again in the morning when she's calmed down. You know how confusing and chaotic these situations can be, my lord. Very hard to make a sensible narrative of what's been happening.'

'What do we know of the dead man, Inspector?'

'Very little so far. Name of Kostas Manitakis, employed as a porter in the British Museum. Age, thirty-four, resident in a Greek boarding house, apparently, near their cathedral in Moscow Road in Notting Hill.'

'I wonder if Johnny Fitzgerald has come across him,' said Powerscourt. 'Maybe he drank in the basement of that pub down there with the ouzo and the unspeakable Greek wines.'

'I have made an appointment to go to his lodgings in the morning, my lord. I should be very happy if you would come with me. In the meantime, as a precaution, I have ordered his room to be sealed off and guarded and a watch kept on the house. All the other lodgers will be kept at home until they have spoken to us before they go off to work. The landlady is going to miss her normal cleaning duties in the cathedral.'

'It sounds as if you expect foul play, Inspector.'

'I do, and I don't. I happen to have worked before with the sergeant who was on the train and organized the passengers for questioning. He's a most reliable fellow.

He wouldn't have told us about the pushing if he didn't think there was something funny going on.'

Powerscourt looked closely at the Inspector and remembered what Christopher Kingsley had said about his dislike of murders. Now it looked as though he might have been plunged right into the middle of another one.

Number six Moscow Road was a three-storey terraced house with steps up to the front door, guarded by a large cat with fierce black eyes and half a tail. The landlady, Mrs Olga Henderson, was of Greek extraction but married to a man from Yorkshire. She greeted them nervously at the door, as Kingsley introduced his sergeant and Powerscourt.

'Come in, sir, my lord Powerscourt, Sergeant. Dear me, I never expected three of you all at once.'

'Don't worry, Mrs Henderson,' said the Inspector, 'nobody is suggesting anything illegal went on in this house.' Powerscourt's eyebrows rose a couple of inches at this point. 'We just want to ask everybody a few questions,' the Inspector continued, 'that's all. Perhaps we could begin with you and then you needn't worry any more. Is there somewhere quiet we could talk?'

'Yes, yes, come this way, please.' The front hall was adorned with pictures of Greek saints. She now showed them into what was clearly the front room, overlooking the street, obviously not used very much and entirely dominated by a large reproduction of a Byzantine Christ, gazing sadly at his earthly kingdom of a battered sofa and a glass cabinet filled with children's dolls.

'Perhaps you could begin by telling us how many residents you have here, Mrs Henderson.' Powerscourt was impressed by the way the Inspector avoided using the word 'lodgers'.

'Five at the moment,' Mrs Henderson replied. 'All my rooms are taken just now!' She brightened slightly at this point as if a full house was a guarantee of innocence.

'Perhaps we could begin with the late Mr Kostas, Mrs Henderson. How long had he been with you?'

'About a year and a half, he came with his brother Stavros just after Easter last year. They shared the little room at the back of the house at the top. Very good guests they were too.' Mrs Henderson looked as though she might be about to burst into tears at any moment.

'Tell us, if you would, Mrs Henderson, what sort of people they were, these two brothers, what they liked doing in their spare time, that sort of thing.'

'Well, it's hard to say when you get to know people, isn't it. They liked their work at the museum, I know that. They used to drink at that pub round the corner. Kostas liked playing football, there was some kind of informal Greek team that kicked a ball about in the park on Sunday afternoons.'

'Is the brother here at present?' asked Powerscourt. 'In the house, I mean?'

'No, Mr Stavros is away, he's been away a week or more now. I don't know where he's gone or how to get in touch with him, I'm afraid. There was some talk of a long journey, I think, but I'm not sure.'

There was a pause while Mrs Henderson dried her eyes on a large purple handkerchief that looked as though it belonged to her husband.

'Take your time,' said the Inspector kindly, in his best bedside manner, 'there's no hurry.'

Powerscourt looked up again at the huge mournful eyes of the Saviour above the mantelpiece. Lady Lucy had always maintained that it was the foreknowledge of their own death that made these Greek Orthodox Christs so sad. 'If you knew, Francis, that you were going to have a long and bloody death, stuck on top of a cross at the top of some hill with Roman soldiers abusing you, you'd look pretty miserable too.'

'Were they regular with the rent, that sort of thing?' asked the Inspector.

'Yes, they were, they never missed a rent day all the time they were here.'

'Were they religious, the brothers,' asked Powerscourt, 'living so close to the cathedral and so on?'

'Now you mention, they were very keen on the Church. There's another brother who's a monk in a monastery on a Greek island somewhere in the middle of the Aegean. Kostas always tried to get home early on Fridays for Vespers in the early evening and they both went to church on Sundays, regular.'

'Forgive me, Mrs Henderson, were there any women friends you were aware of?'

'Not that they ever brought any home, if that's what you mean. I always told them that if they were walking out with a nice respectable girl they were always welcome to bring her home to afternoon tea on Sundays. We have it in here, you know, with Greek cakes and a glass of wine before leaving. But nobody ever came.'

Powerscourt thought Mrs Henderson would have welcomed the chance to inspect these respectable young girls, but he said nothing.

'Were there any particular friends they went about with?' The Inspector was turning to a fresh page in his notebook.

'I don't think so,' Mrs Henderson replied, 'they were quite self contained and, of course, they were very friendly with my other Greek gentlemen. I have five altogether.'

'Perhaps,' said the Inspector, 'you could tell us a little about them?'

'Well, two of them, Maximos and Antonis, are also brothers and they work for a Greek bank with a branch in Notting Hill. There are a lot of Greeks living round here, as you know, with the cathedral and the school and so on. Very quiet boys.'

'And the last one?'

'Nikos,' said Mrs Henderson, 'he works in that big Greek store by the tube station, the one that sells Greek food and wine and newspapers and all sorts of things. He brings me olives and Greek cakes and pastries on Saturdays when he comes back from the shop. He's mad about football, Nikos, follows Arsenal home and away whenever he can.'

'Very good,' the Inspector said. 'That's all for now unless you can think of anything you want to tell us, any reason for his death perhaps? No? Then if I could talk to the other gentlemen one by one we'll let them go off to work. Lord Powerscourt here will have a look at the brothers' room, if you have no objections? Perhaps you could show him the way?'

The young police constable stepped aside as Powerscourt and Mrs Henderson came to the door of Kostas's quarters on the top floor. Mrs Henderson parked herself by the window and gave every appearance of intending to stay while her visitor searched the room.

'Thank you, Mrs Henderson, thank you very much. I'll see you on my way out.'

Mrs Henderson clattered noisily down her stairs. 'Well, Constable, is there anything to report up here?'

'I took over here at seven o'clock this morning, sir, my lord, seeing as how the Inspector wanted this room guarded twenty-four hours a day until you gentlemen had a chance to look at it. Not very much to guard, is there? I've checked under the beds and there's nothing funny about the floorboards, I can tell you that much.'

The room was small. The two beds were side by side at the window, divided by a small dresser with four drawers. There was a wardrobe in the corner by the door which revealed that the brothers had one suit each, three pairs of trousers and eight shirts between them and four pair of shoes. Powerscourt thought that brother Stavros would have taken some clothes on his journey.

'If there's anything here,' said Powerscourt, 'it's going to be in one of those drawers.'

'I could empty them out on the bed one by one if you like, my lord.'

'Thank you very much. Perhaps we could begin at the bottom.'

The bottom two yielded nothing but socks, underwear and sweaters. The Constable checked that there were no secret hiding places and put them back. The third drawer was full of letters, apparently stuffed in at random with no sign of a filing system at all.

'I'll bag these up for you, if you like, my lord, and you can take them away for translation,' the Constable said, after they had checked that every single page was written in Greek. But when they turned out the top drawer Powerscourt realized that there might have been a system after all. Everything here was in English for a start. It was as if one or both brothers had emptied their pockets into this drawer every evening. There were bus tickets, tube tickets, train tickets, some of them to and from Amersham, orders of service from the cathedral. There were rotas from the British Museum and the stubs of two pairs of theatre tickets at the Lyceum, both on Saturday afternoons. And there was a receipt from Thomas Cook for organizing the transportation of what must have been a large and obviously expensive package to be taken in a railway container from London Victoria to Italy. There was no date of travel and no precise information about what the package contained. Powerscourt showed the document to his new friend, the Constable.

'What do you think, young man?'

The policeman looked at it closely. 'I don't know, sir. Maybe Kostas and his brother didn't know how to organize the thing, so they asked Thomas Cook to sort it out for them? They'd have heard of Thomas Cook for sure, but maybe they felt uncertain about approaching one of the big removal companies themselves.'

'It's possible, it's certainly possible, thank you so much for your help,' said Powerscourt and took the stairs two at a time to confer with Inspector Kingsley on the ground floor.

Twenty minutes later Powerscourt was talking to a young man called Davies in the Holborn branch of Thomas Cook. Davies had a small, dark brown beard, well trimmed, and a pair of very thick spectacles as if the reading of multiple timetables, often in lamentably small type, had taken a toll of his eyesight.

'Why, yes,' he told Powerscourt, who told him that he was an investigator, 'I remember the two Greek gentlemen, of course I do. And I remember that receipt you have in your hand. They were very anxious and rather confused, I think, our Greek friends. They worked at the British Museum and they came to us for advice about transporting a very large package from here to Greece. They were anxious, for some reason, that the package should be picked up from Brindisi and make the final stretch of the voyage by boat.'

'And what did you tell them?' asked Powerscourt, feeling suddenly that he might be on the verge of making significant progress at last.

'I said that we didn't do packages like that ourselves. Whenever we're asked to provide that kind of transportation we place the matter in the hands of Rochfords, the furniture removal people. They've been moving stuff around Europe for decades. As a matter of fact I rang a friend of mine who works there and asked him to look after the brothers and their mysterious package. I did ask them, you see, what the package contained and they muttered something about a very large pipe needed for repair work in a big engineering project somewhere in Greece. I didn't quite believe them, actually. Anyway, the long and the short of it is that the package was booked to travel in a railway container from Victoria to Brindisi in southern Italy.'

The young man checked his papers. 'It is meant to arrive six days from now. I can ask my friend Wakefield over at Rochfords to provide all the paper documentation, the manifest, the customs clearance and so on if that would help. God knows where the wretched pipe is now; it's probably sitting in a siding somewhere like Lyon or Milan for all I know.'

'That would be most kind,' said Powerscourt, and handed over his card. 'Those details would be very helpful. Is there anything else you can tell me that might be helpful? Anything, however trivial it seems, could be useful.'

The young man took off his glasses and polished them vigorously on the end of his tie.

'I note,' he said, 'that although you introduced yourself as an investigator, Lord Powerscourt, you haven't told me exactly what you are investigating. I'm not asking you to tell me since it is obviously confidential. But there is one thing that might help you.'

'And what is that?'

'One of the Greek gentlemen decided on the spot that he should accompany their package. He too has a railway ticket from Victoria to Brindisi Central. But I doubt very much if he will be travelling on the same train. Stavros, that's your man, if you're thinking of joining him on his travels. I could probably book you a ticket on the same train if you like? I could do that right now.'

6

Inspector Kingsley came to Markham Square after he had finished his interviews with the Greek residents of the Moscow Road boarding house.

'I think you heard the most interesting bits from the landlady, my lord,' he said, 'but what did you discover at Thomas Cook?'

The Inspector whistled when Powerscourt told him the news. 'And Stavros has gone a wandering, has he, all the way to the boot of Italy. Well, well. What do you think we should do?'

'I don't think we have any choice, Inspector. Somebody has to go to Brindisi. Somebody has to be there, if at all possible, when this wretched container is unloaded from the train. We need to discover where on earth it is going after that, presumably on a boat if our friend at Thomas Cook is to be believed. I think you should continue your work at the museum talking to everybody about the daily life of a Caryatid. People might get suspicious if you suddenly disappeared. I shall go to Brindisi.'

'I think you should take Johnny with you,' Lady Lucy cut in. She always felt safer when her husband had his friend with him on a dangerous investigation. However colourful he might appear to the outside world, Johnny always brought his friend home safe and sound.

'I agree,' said the Inspector. 'I would not dream of going on such a mission without my sergeant. Two heads are better than one.'

'Very well. I shall telephone Leith immediately.'

Leith was Lord Rosebery's butler, a one man encyclopaedia of train timetables, railway buffets and station hotels right across Europe. He could tell you how to get to Vladivostok or Vitoria, he could recommend the fastest trains to Rome or Riga. His little office halfway down the basement stairs in Rosebery's town house in Belgrave Square was the finest private library in Europe of railway information across twenty countries and four different railway gauges. Powerscourt could see him now, the hair white, Leith himself as slim as a railway sleeper in his master's memorable phrase, a well-chewed pencil hovering over the pages of his sacred texts. Then the lights in his mind would go green, the signals would clack down, the points swing over, the steam would shoot up into the air with a great whoosh and a new journey plan would be born.

Rosebery maintained that Leith was now the best paid butler in the Western world.

'I do not believe even the American tycoons pay their fellows as much as I do,' Lord Rosebery would tell his friends. 'Leith just has to whisper "Thomas Cook" to me and I have to give him a rise to stop him deserting me. I couldn't travel anywhere without him now.'

'Brindisi in the tip of Italy, my lord?' Leith's gravelly voice sounded very close on the phone. 'To arrive by 31 October you say? I shall send you a telegram directly, my lord. Hard to remember details off these telephonic instruments I find. A very good morning to you.'

There was a great sense of relief at the British Museum. Those at the top sensed that something was amiss from the irregular behaviour of their Deputy Director, but there was great relief when the Head of Greek and Roman Antiquities returned to post from his mountaineering tour in the Alps. He left his climbing boots and a rather battered ice axe in his outer office and set off on a tour of his kingdom. He spoke to the porters, handing out praise and encouragement like sweets at a children's party. He conversed with his colleagues at the more scholarly end of the museum, regaling them with tales of his fifth successful attempt on the Matterhorn. 'Only the north-east route, mind you, not the most difficult,' he would say with his usual modesty. If he noticed anything amiss with the Caryatid, he did not say.

Leith's telegram reached Markham Square inside half an hour. It was couched in cryptic telegraph speak as if its paymaster, Lord Rosebery, was a poor man rather one of the richest peers in the country:

> Early train to Paris tomorrow, my lord. Seats
> booked on first two services. Essential to arrive
> before 18.30 sleeper from Paris Bercy to Bologna,
> Florence and Rome. Have reserved first class
> dinner and sleeper tickets for two on this con-
> veyance. Informants report excellent service
> from new French chef on board. Arrive Bologna
> 19.30 in the evening, my lord. Have made reser-
> vations at Hotel Cellini in Via Garibaldi to the

left of the main entrance to the station, my lord. Pasta and lamb dishes come highly recommended. Further sleeper following day, my lord. Depart Bologna 15.30. Service quite slow. Stops at Ancona, Pescara Centrale, Foggia, Bari Centrale. Provision of meals and refreshments ceases at Foggia, my lord. Brindisi station on Piazza Francesco Crispo. Few reports from this far south, my lord, but Hotel Mazzini highly recommended for cleanliness. Simple food prepared by proprietor's mother. Have booked suitable accommodation. I await instructions on the return journey, my lord. Leith.'

Powerscourt spent the journey rereading Thucydides' account of the Peloponnesian War. He remembered reading some of it one hot summer in Ireland, lying by the side of the great fountain at the bottom of the steps in the Powerscourt House garden, the sparkle and the gurgling of the water a relief from the austere and rather difficult prose of the ancient Greek historian. He marvelled again at the extraordinary claim Thucydides had made at the beginning of his great work, that it would not be a mere trifle to be picked up and put down lightly, but a possession for ever. He wondered if the historian had ever imagined that people would still be reading his words over two thousand years after his death, hurtling across the plains of northern Italy. Johnny worked on his bird book, staring out of the window for long stretches of time, then writing furiously in an enormous notebook.

Three days after their departure Powerscourt and Johnny Fitzgerald were standing on the balcony of Powerscourt's enormous suite at the Hotel Mazzini. In the centre of the square was a huge statue of King Victor Emmanuel the Second, first king of a united Italy fifty years before. Powerscourt wondered how many people down here in Puglia had even heard of Victor's original kingdom of Piedmont far to the north at the time of independence and how many of them spoke his language. In front of them was the square, populated by a couple of mangy dogs and a bar with broken chairs on the pavement outside. Way over to their left, out of sight from their position, was the port.

Powerscourt's halting Italian had discovered from the hotel reception that goods that came by train were kept in a siding overnight and moved to the port or other destinations first thing in the morning. He was shown the single-line track that led from the back of the station in the direction of the harbour. Reception did not think that proceedings would begin before eleven o'clock at the earliest. People had to have time for breakfast after all. By that time Johnny Fitzgerald was sipping a large glass of Greek brandy in the café by the quays. Powerscourt watched as an old horse drew a pallet containing one battered railway container down the tracks in the general direction of the harbour. He sprinted off through the side streets, dodging a couple of cats and a flock of skeletal chickens on the way. He joined Johnny at the bar and ordered a glass of ouzo.

Captain Dimitri, the ship's captain, watched the two men carefully from a chair on the deck of his vessel. Strangers were common in Brindisi, but they were usually sailors or railway workers or refugees from the countryside looking for work. These men were foreigners, rich foreigners.

The single-track railway line stopped opposite the ship

and about a hundred yards from the water. Between it and the ship there appeared an ancient crane that must have been painted dark green in its youth but was now a rather dirty black. Its driver sat in his coach with a bottle of retsina in front of him. A couple of dockers appeared and made a great fuss of attaching the cables of the crane to the container. A space appeared to have been cleared on the deck of Captain Dimitri's craft to receive the visitor. By now it was almost one o'clock. There was a heated conversation between the Captain and the crane driver. Powerscourt suspected it might have to do with the time to stop for lunch, the Captain anxious to get the container on board as soon as possible. A handful of notes changed hands. There was a great roar as the crane's engines began to lift the container off the ground. Shortly after that Johnny Fitzgerald grabbed Powerscourt firmly by the arm.

'For God's sake, Francis! There's something wrong with that bloody crane!'

The container was well aloft now, twenty to thirty feet above the ground. The driver began to turn his load towards the ship. Then disaster struck. Whether it was a mechanical malfunction, or the retsina, or the driver was having a fit or a heart attack, the crane began throwing the container higher and higher in the air in a series of great loops, rising further and further from the ground every time. Powerscourt and Johnny could see the driver struggling desperately with the controls. A flock of seagulls that had been sitting quietly on a couple of bollards further round the quay took off in search of safety. The monkeys on deck, blessed perhaps with some form of second sight, set up a terrible squawking. The humans, the barman, the Captain and a couple of members of his crew were frozen, staring at the great box that might come crashing down on their heads at any moment. Higher and higher went the container. It was now swinging like a trapeze artist way above the quay. Then one of the cables snapped. Still it swung, but listing now like a drunken man going home on a Saturday night. Inside the cabin the driver had fallen forward, collapsed over his controls. The waitress from the café came out on to the pavement and screamed when she saw the great rectangle swinging erratically above their heads. Johnny maintained ever after, he could never say how or why, that the screams were responsible for the other cable breaking. The container seemed to hang in the air for a fraction of a second. Then it fell and landed on the hard stone of the quay with a terrible crack. The sides caved in and splinters of wood shot around the little harbour. The actual cargo inside broke into pieces before their eyes. Powerscourt saw an elegant marble head that might have come from the start of the fifth century before Christ. There were two sections of dress flowing in elegant lines. There was what might have been a marble knee, protruding slightly from the bulk of the statue. Shards of marble joined the wooden fragments from the container, shooting round the wreckage. Then all the pieces toppled slowly into the water. There was a mighty splash, but after a few minutes the waters had closed over the remains of the cargo that had left Victoria station a few days before. Small fish, which had disappeared with the noise, gradually reappeared and circled the great muddy space on the water where the remains had fallen.

'God in Heaven, Francis,' whispered Johnny Fitzgerald. 'Do you think that was the Caryatid from the bloody museum?'

'Yes, I do. The only question is was it the Caryatid, or a

Caryatid. Real or copy? False or original? Made in Greece or made in Britain? We'd need a team of divers to bring up the statue before we could know the answer. But I tell you one thing, Johnny. Here on this forgotten quay, surrounded now by splinters of broken wood and shards of broken marble, we have just witnessed the Death of an Elgin Marble.'

Before Johnny could answer, they were being prodded heavily in their backs. Two men, swarthy and unkempt, pushed them towards the boat, shouting at them in Greek to move along.

'Such a pity I can't remember much of my ancient Greek, Johnny,' said Powerscourt, 'I always knew I should have paid more attention in class. How was I to know it might come in useful one day?'

The two men were marched onto the boat across a plank that Powerscourt thought looked rather precarious. They were shoved onto a couple of chairs opposite the Captain and a young man in a suit who gave his name as Euripidis. Powerscourt wanted to ask him if he wrote plays in his spare time but thought better of it.

The Captain spat out a torrent of Greek abuse. Off to their left a series of bubbles was breaking through the surface of the water where the Caryatid had fallen, as if she were sending a last message to the faithful.

'What are you doing here, the Captain wants to know?' Euripidis spoke English with a strong American accent.

'What are you doing here, we might ask?' said Powerscourt indignantly, going onto the offensive. 'We are simple tourists, just come from London, staying at the Hotel Mazzini. We came to take a look at the harbour, that's all.'

Euripidis translated. The lion was watching them

carefully from its cage on deck, rubbing its face with a great paw from time to time.

'The Captain wants to know why you have come to see the Caryatid, why you are here this morning.'

'Caryatid?' said Powerscourt. 'Caryatid? What's a Caryatid for heaven's sake? I think we have one of them in some museum in London and there's half a dozen on permanent duty at St Pancras Church in Camden, but I've never set eyes on any of them. Was that thing that fell into the water one of these Carry things? I must tell my children when I get home. They're very fond of Greek statues and stuff like that.'

As he spoke, Powerscourt could see the translator scribbling furiously and handing a message to the Captain. Then there was a further volley in staccato Greek.

'Well, the Captain says to forget all about that. He thought you were somebody else, that's all.'

'Well,' said Powerscourt, 'I'm sorry you seem to have lost your container. Very bad luck. Now, if you'll excuse us, Johnny and I have to be getting back to our hotel. We're still tired out from our journey.'

They waited once more. 'The Captain wishes to know when you are going back to London, please. He would like to offer you a little cruise in his boat if you have time before you go.'

'We'd be delighted, please thank him very much. Tomorrow perhaps? The day after?'

'The day after would suit admirably. Eleven o'clock? Down here by the café?'

They all shook hands. The lion looked on, growling slightly as it watched the visitors leave.

'By God, Francis,' said Johnny Fitzgerald, 'that was a close shave. Do you really think he thought we were different people altogether? And why did you say yes to the cruise?'

'Don't walk so fast, Johnny. We don't want them to think we're running away. I would love to know what the translator said to make the Captain change his mind. Did the Captain know we were coming? If he did, how the hell did he find out? And I've no intention of showing up for the cruise. I think we'd end up as food for the fishes. Or maybe the lion if the Captain was in a bad mood.'

'Where is Stavros, Kostas's brother?' said Johnny Fitzgerald. 'He had a ticket to bloody Brindisi, didn't he?'

'God knows. Davy Jones's locker perhaps? Maybe he offended the bloody lion.'

'There is one good thing, Francis. We've found the Caryatid, or, as you said before, maybe a Caryatid, one of a family of sisters perhaps, numbers unknown.'

They were passing the last known resting place of the marble lady who might have come from the Acropolis. The deep muddy pool that marked her fall had disappeared. The surface of the water was covered with its usual oily sheen and fragments of floating refuse. Down below in a watery grave, the fragments of the Caryatid waited for redemption and resurrection.

'It's good we've seen her, Johnny, even if it was only for a moment. There's one other thing. My spoken Greek may be down there with the minnows, but I could just work out the name of the Captain's ship. I'll give you one guess as to what it is.'

'*The Greek Maiden*?' replied Johnny. '*The Girl from Athens*? *Face of the Acropolis*?'

'Good try, very good try.' Powerscourt grinned. 'Nearly but not quite. We've solved one of Sokratis's riddles at any rate. The Captain's ship is called *The Isles of Greece*.'

PART TWO

MORTLAKE TERRACE, SUMMER'S EVENING

Our love of beauty does not lead to extravagance: our love of the things of the mind does not make us soft. We regard wealth as something to be properly used, rather than as something to boast about. As for poverty, no one need be ashamed to admit it: the real shame is in not taking practical measures to escape from it. Here each individual is interested not only in his own affairs but in the affairs of state as well ... we do not say that a man who takes no interest in politics is a man who minds his own business; we say he has no business here at all.

Thucydides, Pericles' Funeral Speech,
The History of Peloponnesian War

7

They left the Hotel Mazzini at half past one in the morning, tiptoeing down a rickety fire escape in their socks. Powerscourt and Johnny had kept a watch on the square all afternoon and evening. There was nothing obvious to be seen, but a series of idlers and loafers, all keeping a close eye on the hotel, had paraded past their windows at regular intervals. Powerscourt only left the building once. In the late afternoon he took himself to the offices of the local newspaper where he secured the services of the paper's youngest reporter for a large handful of Italian banknotes. Antonio Paravacini, an eighteen-year-old veteran of Brindisi journalism, was to report any further comings and goings of *The Isles of Greece* and anything else that struck him as relevant to the recent happenings at the harbour. The banknotes should be sufficient to pay for a whole series of telegrams to London.

Powerscourt had paid for their rooms for two days in advance, a precaution he had been following for years in foreign hotels where a quick escape might be the order of the day. Just after three o'clock a slow train bound for Taranto pulled slowly out of the station. There were two passenger compartments and two goods vans, and an engine that Johnny Fitzgerald claimed must have pulled Garibaldi across Italy on one of his interminable marches.

'When we get to Taranto,' Powerscourt explained, waving an Italian train timetable liberated from the Brindisi waiting room, 'we can go home a different way, up the Mediterranean coast through Naples rather than the way we came down the Adriatic coast.'

Johnny stretched himself out across an entire bench and went to sleep. Powerscourt stared out of the window into the Italian night. He remembered another early escape, in a mail train from Perugia nearly twenty years before in his investigation into the death of Prince Eddy, eldest son of the Prince of Wales. He had been escorted to his compartment long before the dawn by Captain Ferrante of the Perugia police and guarded by two of his officers all the way to Calais and the Dover boat. Dawn, he remembered, had come in slivers through the slits of the carriages, black sacks of Italian mail piled up at his feet.

Three-quarters of an hour out of Brindisi the train stopped in the middle of nowhere. Peering back at the goods vans Powerscourt saw a number of milk containers being loaded and a man who might have been a shepherd with a couple of sheep going to market.

The journey from Taranto to Naples took seven and a half hours. Johnny began snoring at Metaponto, continued through a long stop at Potenza Centrale and only stopped on the outskirts of Battipaglia, south of Salerno.

'I bet your man Leith hasn't been on this bloody train, Francis. I can't see Rosebery careering through southern Italy on this line. Even the man who built it would see it's totally out of date now.'

Powerscourt laughed. He had been thinking about their

reception aboard *The Isles of Greece*. The more he thought about it, the more certain he became that the Captain knew they were coming. And if he did, how did he know? Had Kostas's brother told him? And where was Kostas's brother? There had been no sighting of him on the ship or at the railway station. Had he too been taken for a cruise on the circus ship and tossed into the sea by the acrobats or served as lunch for the lion? Had he been asked to escort the container all the way to Brindisi, only to be disposed of when he arrived? For if he had disappeared, two of the porters at the British Museum, intimately involved with the Caryatid, had both vanished. One body under the Piccadilly Line train might be an accident, but two disappeared brothers was unlikely to be a coincidence. More and more, Powerscourt was convinced that this was an inside job. Who might have suborned the two porters he had no idea.

It was only in the late afternoon that Powerscourt caught sight of a southern Italian newspaper in Bologna railway station. *Inferno a Hotel Mazzini*, said the headline. He could just make out the main points of the story. A huge fire had enveloped the hotel shortly after two o'clock in the morning. The staff of the Mazzini and all the guests save two had been evacuated safely. Two English tourists were still missing. Their rooms had been at the very epicentre of the blaze. The local fire chief gave it as his opinion that their bodies would be unrecognizable, so fierce had been the blaze. The local mayor, who prided himself for being a reformer in one of the most conservative parts of Italy, speculated that the fire was the work of the local Mafia.

The huge coffin dispatched from South Wales arrived safely in New York. The crossing had been peaceful, without any storms that might have disturbed the cargo. The passengers had all disembarked when a couple of men in shiny suits and with large hats pulled down over their eyes made their way aboard. They demanded to see the records of all freight carried on the voyage. Then they removed all mentions of the coffin from Bristol, details of its size, weight, length and general appearance. The vessel's clerk was initially reluctant to carry out their instructions, maintaining that falsification of documents was a sackable offence. Two stilettos, one under each ear, persuaded him of his folly. When the men in the shiny suits had finished their work on the great ledger where the records were kept, it was as if the funeral statue, so carefully dispatched from the Welsh mountains, had never existed.

The visitors went below to supervise the unloading of the coffin. It was transferred to the back of a nondescript lorry which drove off in the direction of New Jersey.

Powerscourt told Lady Lucy on his return that he had rather enjoyed being a dead man walking. The terrible fire in the Hotel Mazzini was not reported in the British newspapers, fires and other disasters being regarded as part of the natural order of things in the unruly lands on the far side of the Channel. Now he was going to meet the Head of Greek and Roman Antiquities who had invited him to lunch at a fashionable restaurant near the British Museum, a place where people went to be seen as much as for the quality of the food.

'A glass of prosecco, Lord Powerscourt?' Tristram Stanhope was wearing a dark pinstripe suit with a cream shirt and the scarlet and gold MCC tie. 'I always think champagne has grown rather vulgar nowadays. Every

Tom, Dick and Harry seems to be drinking it.' They were in a private room, the dark red walls lined with prints of famous actors and actresses from the past. Powerscourt examined Tristram Stanhope very carefully. Here at last was the man he had heard so much about. Here was a man who could answer many of the questions about the Caryatid that tormented him day and night. He thought the early halo of glamour that had marked Tristram Stanhope's career – elected to a fellowship at All Souls at the age of twenty-three, winner of the Newdigate Prize, a famous Alpinist renowned for his easy grace on the high rock faces – was beginning to fade. Even the golden hair now had streaks of grey at the temples.

'That would be very kind,' replied Powerscourt, 'I've always had a weak spot for prosecco. Tell me – forgive me for plunging into the middle of things, in medias res as it were, but I have a lot of questions for you – how do you find things at the museum on your return?' Powerscourt remembered that Ragg's obsession with secrecy meant he had not told Stanhope about the plain clothes policemen at the British Museum.

Stanhope smiled the kind of patronizing smile he might have worn if some opposing bowler had just sent him a no ball. 'Well, let me be perfectly frank with you, Lord Powerscourt, things are bad, in my view, if not catastrophic!'

'What makes you say that?'

'Far be it from me to cast doubt on my colleagues' abilities,' he said, and Powerscourt was sure that, as night follows day, Stanhope was about to do just that. 'It's Ragg,' he went on, 'perfectly competent administrator, but he's a hopeless leader, absolutely hopeless. He's made the wrong decision. How do you expect to get the Caryatid back? You are among the most distinguished practitioners of your profession in London, Lord Powerscourt, but forgive me if I say your resources are limited. We need to be working with the police. We need publicity. We need articles in the newspapers. We want eminent scholars like myself writing for the general public about her place in Greek culture and religion, where she fits into the long narrative of Athenian history. We want people coming forward with information every day until she is found. What do we have instead? A wall of silence. The clarion call not of the trumpet but of a broken reed. How on earth Ragg ever imagines the Museum will bring her home I know not. Is she supposed to acquire the power of movement after all these years and walk back into Great Russell Street of her own accord?'

He paused briefly while the waiter brought a dish of oysters to their table. 'Only four for me,' Stanhope said with a winning smile. 'Six would be too many. Nothing to excess as our Greek friends used to say.'

'If you had been here, Mr Stanhope, would you have called in the police from the very start?'

'I most certainly would, Lord Powerscourt.' Stanhope paused to brush the remains of his blond hair away from his forehead. 'I tell you what the whole thing reminds me of. Years ago now I was due to play for Oxford against an MCC side at the Parks, our home ground in the city. It was important because an England selector was believed to be watching, looking for talent. On the day in question I was delayed by an accident on the Woodstock Road and was an hour late for the start of play. They should have waited for me, of course, but the MCC man was a stickler for the rules. Anyway, when I arrived our score was thirty-one for seven. The fool of a captain who had replaced me decided to bat first when even one of the college gargoyles could have told him that the wicket would be very difficult at first but would calm down later.'

'So what happened?' asked Powerscourt. 'Were you too late?'

Tristram Stanhope coughed slightly and sipped delicately at his hock. 'As it happens, I was able to make a contribution,' he said. 'I managed to make a hundred and thirty-seven not out and our score mounted to two hundred and fifteen all out. It was no good, of course. The MCC knocked our bowlers all over the place and won easily. But don't you see, it all goes back to the fool of an acting captain's decision to bat first. It's the same with Ragg. He's lost the match before it even started. I doubt we'll ever get the Caryatid back now. I'm compiling a report for the Director when he gets back. Maybe then Theophilus Ragg too will be removed from his pedestal and sent into outer darkness. Rather like the Caryatid, don't you know. I've been here before.'

'What do you mean you've been here before?'

'It was only a couple of years ago, actually. I was still at Oxford then – I'm just a Visiting Fellow now. But the old Provost died rather suddenly. There was a terrible battle over the succession between two factions, one for the redhead, the other for the bald man. The redhead was an English professor, full of high ideals and windy rhetoric. He wanted the College to move with the times, press for more modern subjects, chemistry, I suppose, biology, that sort of thing. He claimed we had to keep up with the Germans, science and all that. The bald one was a classicist of the old school, no need to change, keep things as they are. The battle grew so fierce that the two sides used to sit at opposite ends of High Table, not even speaking to each other. Then the Dean proposed a compromise candidate. Man by the name of Weightman, Albert Weightman. Theologian. World-famous scholar, could talk for hours about the Coptic Gospels, you know the sort of stuff. Quiet sort of chap, our theologian. Used to take most of his meals in his rooms. Came from a humble background, father a docker in Liverpool with eleven children. Our man had all the brains. When it came to the vote the theologian came through the middle and won by six votes.'

'And they all lived happily ever after?'

'Not so. Not only was the Coptic person from a poor background, he had no idea of the social airs and graces. Couldn't tell a claret from a chianti. Barely able to handle a knife and fork according to his enemies. He surpassed himself at a College Feast, lots and lots of courses, enough wines to sink a battleship, you know the form. The theologian asked for HP sauce to put on his venison. That was it. I was prevailed upon to organize a petition to the College Visitor, sort of Super Chairman of the Board of Governors who arbitrates on disputes. Our visitor was the Bishop of Gloucester, possibly because the College still owns half of Gloucester for heaven's sake. The Bishop suggests the theologian has to go. And the Bishop organizes his removal to the Chair of Theology at Durham. Very efficiently done I must say. Weightman was never seen in Oxford again. That's what's going to happen to that man Ragg if I have anything to do with it.'

The waiter came back to take away the remains of the oysters and refill their glasses. Powerscourt noticed that Stanhope never spoke of business when anybody else was in the room, as if he felt there might be listeners everywhere, possibly working for an unknown enemy.

'I would welcome your opinion on this question, Mr Stanhope,' he said, and turning to the waiter, 'Those oysters were delicious, quite delicious.'

The waiter bowed slightly and departed.

'Obviously the statue could have been taken by a madman, a lone maniac following the messages in his head. But I don't think so. What do you think? Do you believe, as I think I do but without any great conviction, that she was stolen to order? That the thieves had a buyer long before they committed the crime?'

'Even ancient historians,' said Stanhope with a patronizing smile, 'with the limited amount of original evidence available to them, are taught not to produce theories that cannot be substantiated by the facts, Lord Powerscourt. So I could not subscribe entirely to that theory. But it does have some merit.'

A Dover sole, gleaming with butter and glazed onions, appeared for Stanhope, roast lamb with a sweet-smelling mint sauce for Powerscourt. The hock was replaced with a bottle of wine.

'Not many people know about this wine from Quincy, Powerscourt. I discovered it en route to the Jungfrau some years ago and recommended it to my friend, the proprietor here. I should welcome your opinion.'

'Perfect,' said Powerscourt taking a small sip, 'a sauvignon blanc to challenge sancerre and pouilly-fumé, I should say.'

Stanhope smiled. 'To your question, Lord Powerscourt. I have thought about this a good deal. People like to dismiss the possibility of rich collectors prepared to spend hundreds of thousands of pounds on something they can only look at under cover of darkness in the depths of their cellars.'

Stanhope took a deep draught of his wine. Powerscourt thought the man was drinking too fast.

'However,' the Head of Greek and Roman Antiquities went on, 'the key question is this. Let us suppose that you are a rich German industrialist who has made his fortune in engines for motor cars or turbines for dreadnoughts. It has long been a dream of yours to own a genuine ancient statue. You have a passion for antiquity – interest in the classics always increases when countries turn into empires or want to turn into empires. When you're on the way up, so to speak, you concentrate on the rise of Athens in the fifth century BC. On the way down you become obsessed with the fall of the Roman Empire. Be that as it may, our rich German friend pays a great deal of money to the criminals who steal the Caryatid and deliver it to his schloss. But what do you say when the authorities come to call and ask you how you got it ? They might be the local police or the British Museum or the man from the Louvre. How did you come by this Caryatid hidden in the bowels of your great castle? This is where it gets interesting, Lord Powerscourt. Remember, there is no longer a Caryatid from London for the authorities to look at, no original for them to inspect and pronounce on the authenticity of your Caryatid one way or the other. The ones left behind in Athens have all deteriorated badly. You bought her on the Grand Tour in Rome some years ago, you say. This Caryatid has been here for years, you are talking nonsense, Mr Policeman, please leave my house at once. It would be very difficult to prove that the one supposedly bought on the Grand Tour is not the real thing when you no longer know, apart from photographs, what the real thing actually looked like.'

'That's most interesting, Mr Stanhope. How well you put it.'

'If the Museum ever tells the truth and lets the world know that the Caryatid has been stolen I intend to give a series of lectures about the subject at the Methodist Central Hall. I have had the good fortune to speak there on a number of previous occasions.'

Stanhope refilled his glass again. Powerscourt wondered if the vanity might be forced even further to the surface by larger and larger helpings of quincy.

'There's another explanation our German millionaire could offer to the authorities. He could say he bought the statue in Athens or Corinth or Olympia. It had been found by divers at some wreck and brought to the surface because the fishermen knew how much money these things could fetch from rich foreigners. There are a fair number of famous pieces of Greek sculpture that have been brought up from the seabed. They're remarkably well preserved. The marble may get dirty but it doesn't disintegrate. Why, ten years ago or so, they discovered some strange artefact in a shipwreck off the island of Antikythera with dozens of gears. That should appeal to our German friend in his schloss. Earlier versions of his machinery perhaps. He could say that he found the Caryatid for sale in Corinth or wherever it was brought to the mainland. Receipts, you say? Receipts? It was years ago, Inspector. Written records in the shop or the art dealers where you bought it? Don't be silly. And don't even think of suggesting that the Greeks might have kept the details of the transactions. Greeks? You must be joking. So, you see, Lord Powerscourt, there is another very plausible excuse. How can you prove that the thing has not been on the seabed for all those centuries? You may

101

be sure it will have been cleaned and recleaned by the most sophisticated machinery the Germans can provide.'

'I see,' said Powerscourt, as the waiter poured a final round of wine. The restaurant behind the private room was growing quiet now, as the diners departed to their various afternoons. 'I'm sure you can answer my next question, Mr Stanhope. You mention our friend the German in his castle, rich from his engineering triumphs. There must be others who have the same love of Greek antiquities. Americans perhaps? Modern Greeks? Englishmen? What is the secret behind their affection for ancient Greece? Why do they love it so much? Why is it their favourite period in history?'

Tristram Stanhope pushed his plate away.

'Philhellenes all? I must confess I am among their number. I always have been. Tell me, Lord Powerscourt, do you not have a favourite place in the past? A time when you would rather have been alive than in the present?'

Powerscourt laughed. 'Well, I've never really thought about it. I'm very fond of the old Greeks, you know. But if I had to choose, I think I'd rather go back to Renaissance Florence. The first sight of Brunelleschi's Dome perhaps? Michelangelo's *David* on display in the Piazza? Those divine Botticelli Madonnas gracing the altars and the side chapels of the churches? Or maybe late-eighteenth-century England? I could have gone to the impeachment of Warren Hastings and listened to Edmund Burke denouncing the evils of the French Revolution in the House of Commons.'

'Believe me, there are more of us Philhellenes than you might imagine, Lord Powerscourt. Remember how many generations of English public schoolboys have been brought up on the Classics. Think too of the Americans who populate the novels of Henry James, captivated by Florence and Venice, of course, but also of the tribute they paid to the ancient Greeks. It was, after all, the rediscovery of many ancient manuscripts that led to the birth of the Renaissance. For many, the Classics will have been the drudgery of the declensions, the horrors of the Greek optative mood or the terror of the Latin unseen. But for others their eyes will have been opened. The contribution of the Greeks to Western thought – the playwrights, the philosophers, the historians are supreme. They invented most of those disciplines after all. Think of the Grand Tour, an orgy of wine, women and song for many, of course, but for others it will have been a labour of love, travelling the ancient world, often for years, collecting Greek and Roman statues to bring home to their great houses like the Cokes in Holkham Hall up in Norfolk, its tribune elegantly adorned with the sculptures of antiquity. Then there is the light, so clear, so perfect on a summer's day, so intense yet so delicate. England, by comparison, is a land in shadow. Think of the beauty of those ancient statues. Nobody has surpassed the grace and the glory of Praxiteles' statue of Hermes at Olympia. You mention the late eighteenth century, Lord Powerscourt. If I had been alive then, I would have built a garden like the ones at Stowe or Stourhead, festooned with temples to the ancient gods, and adorned my house with ancient statues like those in the Antique Passage and all over the grounds at Castle Howard.'

Stanhope spoke with rare passion. Powerscourt felt sure it wasn't just the quincy.

'Fanatics, Mr Stanhope? Would that be a fair description of you Philhellenes?'

The Head of Greek and Roman Antiquities finished

his glass. 'Maybe I could put it slightly differently, Lord Powerscourt. Maybe it's like an illness. Being a Philhellene is rather like catching a very severe dose of a virus called love of ancient Greece, Phil-Hellenism in its ancient form. At its most extreme, yes, I suppose you could call us fanatics.'

'One last question, please,' said Powerscourt as the waiters cleared away the remains of their lunch. 'How difficult would it be to move the Caryatid and replace her with the substitute one currently on show?'

'Well,' said Stanhope, checking the bottom of his glass rather sadly, 'it's easier than you might think. Those porters are moving statues about all the time, many of them bigger and heavier than the Caryatid. Some of the Egyptians on parade are far heavier but they still get taken away for cleaning and things when required. Some of the porters are called in by outside firms who have to move great lumps of sculpture from place to place. They're highly skilled. Occasionally they ask for outside help if they're not sure how to shift something. So I don't think moving them would be much of a problem.'

8

Early the following morning Powerscourt was greeted by Leith, Rosebery's train-obsessed butler, as he called on his master in Belgrave Square.

'Good morning, Leith, I trust you are keeping well? And thank you for your recent assistance with the Italian trip. Much obliged.'

'Only sorry, my lord, that I was unable to provide the relevant information for the return journey. My apologies.'

Leith glided away like a train going downhill to his lair halfway down the basement stairs where his records were kept and the train timetables of Europe sat in neat rows on his shelves.

Rosebery was a former Foreign Secretary and Prime Minister, his political career marred by a fondness for resigning that was almost greater than his love of high office. He was famous for having fulfilled the three ambitions he had set himself as a young man: to marry an heiress, to become Prime Minister and to own a horse that won the Derby. Many said he had reached his objectives too early, though few would have doubted that his life was severely damaged by the early death of his wife, the heiress Hannah

Rothschild. Rosebery had been a friend of the Powerscourt family for years, with a paternal interest in Lady Lucy.

'I'm trying to sell a horse, Powerscourt. Only thing is, nobody seems to want to buy the bloody thing.' Rosebery was waving a report from his bloodstock agent in Newmarket in the air.

'Animal too expensive, Rosebery? Price not right perhaps?'

'To hell with the price, Powerscourt, the beast is too slow, that's the problem. Entered in seven races, never placed higher than seventh. You'd think that with a name like Imperial Spirit the creature could do better than that. Never mind. How can I be of assistance this morning? Your note said you would welcome the benefit of my wisdom, such as it is.'

'Thank you for seeing me so promptly. I am grateful. Perhaps I could ask you a question to start with. How many statues do you own?'

'How many statues? Venus with no clothes on? Julius Caesar wearing a garland on the day of his triumph, that sort of thing?'

'Exactly.'

'Well, I don't really know. I've never actually counted them.'

'Put it another way, how many houses do you own?'

'You are being difficult this morning, Powerscourt. How many houses do I own? I don't think I've ever counted them either, now I think about it.'

'Try.'

Rosebery stared at a Winterhalter portrait of Queen Victoria and her children above his mantelpiece. 'Twelve,' he said finally, 'that's if you count the hunting lodge in Scotland and the villa in Italy.'

'And how many of those houses have statues?'

'Look here,' said Rosebery, 'why don't you tell me the reason for these questions? I can't believe you want to carry out an inventory of the statues in my houses, it would take too long. I'm not sure I could count the number of marble Greeks and Romans – well, they're supposed to be Greeks and Romans – in my place in Italy. I picked them up for a song from a museum in Naples that was going bankrupt. There are loads and loads in Mentmore, as you well know. You've been to stay there plenty of times.'

Powerscourt told him about the missing Caryatid at the British Museum and the refusal to call in the police, about the various possible explanations for her disappearance, about his trip to Italy.

'Tried to burn you out in Brindisi, did they? Thank your stars those boys don't travel very much. I'm still not sure why you are asking me these questions, my friend. The British Museum has lost a Caryatid. I don't own any Caryatids, more's the pity, but I do have a large enough collection of Aphrodites, Artemises, Hephaistos with his fire, Hermes with his bloody messages like an ancient telegraph boy, innumerable Roman emperors ranging from the virtuous to the deranged. What, pray, is the connection?'

'Rosebery, I'm sorry. I've explained things very badly. I've got so used to having conversations where I'm not allowed to mention the fact that the Caryatid is missing I end up tying myself in knots. What we don't know, and would dearly like to find out, is how the fake Caryatid arrived at the British Museum and how the real one was spirited away. Precise removal and installation details if you like. Of the two porters closely involved in looking after her, one was run over by a tube train and the other was last heard of buying a ticket to Brindisi from where, as far as we can establish, he has not returned. Don't look so impatient, I'm coming to the point. I would like to borrow some of your statues. I would like to place an advertisement in *The Times* and the *Morning Post* asking for expert removal firms to bid for the transfer of a number of statues from Mentmore to your house in Scotland.'

'How many?'

'Six would probably do it.'

'Any particular size?'

'Two or three should be about the same size as the Caryatid.'

'From memory, I should say she was a little over seven feet tall, slightly larger than life size. Am I right?'

'You are. Seven feet and six inches more or less. Marble.'

'Marble I can certainly do. I have one or two famous pieces up there in Mentmore of about the right size. The Sounion Apollo from the late fifth century BC must be about the same age as the lady from the British Museum. I could throw in my famous bronze charioteer which I've always liked, and three or four more. But tell me this. Do you actually want me to move them?'

'Certainly not. Just to advertise the fact that they are going to move house and invite bids for their transfer to Dalmeny.'

'I shall speak to my man of business, Powerscourt. I shall do that this afternoon. I have never known you not to be in a hurry on one of your investigations. Perhaps we could place the advertisement the day after tomorrow? If you like, I could have a word with the editor of *The Times* about a brief news story in the paper. Famous Rosebery statues on the move, that sort of thing?'

'Please do,' said Powerscourt.

'I would like to sit in on the interviews if I might. Add a touch of verisimilitude to the proceedings. I'd better bring my man of business too. Do you know, I've always been touched by the fact that people in your profession place great hope in the results of advertisements placed in the newspapers. It's as if you all believe that the criminal classes, to a man, read *The Times* over breakfast every morning.'

Johnny Fitzgerald was tucked up in bed in a Powerscourt guest room, dressed in one of his host's finest pairs of pyjamas. He had been taken ill on the journey home, reeling from frequent trips to the bathroom and gradually losing all colour, his face changing from a light brown to a chalky white and an emaciated pale yellow by the time they reached Victoria station. Since then the attacks had continued, his strength so weakened on the third day that he could no longer walk, only crawl. In his lucid moments he would complain, not about the disease, but about its causes.

'Maybe it was those bloody prawns in Brindisi, Francis. I thought they tasted funny at the time. Or the squid. It looked pretty cross at being cooked and eaten, that squid. How about the oysters? I must have been mad, eating oysters in a place like that. Never again. You know those bloody people called vegetarians? Only eat carrots and broccoli God help them? I'm going to become a carnivore. Only meat. No more bloody fish for me.'

So Inspector Kingsley found that only Powerscourt and Lady Lucy were fit for active service on his evening visit to Markham Square. Powerscourt reported the fruits of his trip to Italy, the meeting with the Captain, the fire at the hotel, the disappearance of the other Greek porter. The Inspector was especially interested in the forthcoming advertisement about the removal of the Rosebery statues.

'Excellent news,' he said. 'That could yield some important clues. There are a number of possible conclusions from your Italian affair, my lord. If the Captain knew you were coming, as you say, who told him? Is there a secret channel of communication between London and Brindisi? Then there's the fire. I suspect the people who wanted to get rid of you simply hired another lot to burn the place down. They probably intended to frighten you rather than incinerate you. It was only when there weren't any bodies found that they thought you'd been cremated in the Mazzini. We know very little about those local gangsters apart from a totally unpronounceable name, but I can't see them stealing works of art from the British Museum.'

''Ndrangheta,' said Lady Lucy, 'that's the name of those gangsters down there. The word means courage or loyalty.'

'That's very impressive. How on earth do you know that, Lucy?' asked Powerscourt.

'Rosebery told me last year, Francis. He was complaining about the thugs near Naples. They're called the Camorra. They were asking him to pay protection money for his villa. He said they were as bad as the gangsters in Sicily. He said Calabria had another lot, the 'Ndrangheta. It's quite easy to pronounce once you've said it a few times.' She smiled at her two gentlemen.

'This has only just occurred to me, my lord.' The Inspector was drinking a glass of chablis very slowly. 'What kind of people would want to steal a Caryatid? You'd think they'd have some artistic inclinations even to know about the thing in the first place. Your average London criminal doesn't know what or where the British Museum is, let alone what's inside it. That might be one sort of person. But are they the same sort of citizens as the ones who push people in front of trains or burn down hotels in the middle of the night? I'm not so sure.'

Inspector Kingsley stopped suddenly and slapped himself violently on the knee.

'I'm a bad policeman! Really bad! Rampant speculation! If there's one thing the Metropolitan Police drum into their inspectors it's that you shouldn't speculate. You should never, they tell you over and over again, speculate in advance of the facts.'

'Never mind,' said Powerscourt cheerfully. 'We forgive you. Nothing wrong with some well-founded speculation if you ask me. But still, what news of the museum?'

'Precious few facts available there, my lord. I sent my sergeant to make enquiries about the late Kostas. He didn't come up with anything we didn't already know. I can't be seen there as the author of a booklet for children one day and Inspector Kingsley the next. I do have one thing to report, my lord. The fire alarm is going to go off tomorrow morning, shortly after eleven o'clock. That, so far as we can work it out, seems to have been the time when the alarm went off before. Everybody should be out of the building for at least forty minutes. Neither Ragg nor Stanhope knows anything about it. I've brought along a few plans of the building, my lord. I hope you'll be able to join us.'

'I wish I could come too,' said Lady Lucy. 'There is one thing that occurs to me, however. You always say, Francis, that, when you know how, you are well on the way to knowing who. Maybe after the Rosebery advert and the alarm we shall be a little clearer. But I do wonder about that container, the one that went all the way to Brindisi and broke into pieces on the quayside. It came from Victoria, I think you said, Inspector. But how did it get to Victoria? There must be a record of its arrival at the station, surely. Where did it come from? There can't be that many firms who send containers shooting round about the place like children playing tiddlywinks, can there?'

'Good point, Lady Powerscourt, very good point. I shall put my people onto it. Trailing through official records is the perfect occupation for policemen. No time for speculation there. There is one thing I forgot to tell you both. You remember I said I was going to look into the financial records of the people at the museum? Well, some of them will take a very long time. They can involve complicated negotiations with the Bank of England and the tax people, so help me God. But we have established that two members of the museum staff recently received very large payments into bank accounts specially set up for the purpose.'

'Who are they?' asked Powerscourt. 'I think I could make a good guess.'

'Have a go,' replied the Inspector.

'I should say the recipients were Kostas and his brother. And – this is pure speculation, Inspector – I should hazard a guess that the bank in question was the Greek one with a branch in Notting Hill?'

'God bless my soul,' said the Inspector, 'I shall never complain about speculation again. You are right on both counts, my lord, absolutely right.'

Brother Andreas had been a monk for nearly ten years. He was part of the Orthodox community of St John the

Divine on the Greek island of Kythnos in the Cyclades. The monks were now the only residents of Kythnos. Their monastery started on the little quayside and climbed back up the hill. There were olive trees to nurture and vines on the lower slopes. Twenty monks were resident here, a life alternating between work and prayer. The little church had remarkable frescoes, miraculously preserved, and even now, visitors sometimes came from the mainland in the summer time to wonder at them. The monastery had a series of deep caves below the surface, some converted into chapels with paintings of the saints on the walls. Every monk on this island had his own special role to make the community prosper: the baker, the tailor, the gardener, the cook, the icon painter. Andreas was the boatman, responsible for maintaining the small sailing vessel and a couple of rowing boats. Part of his duty was to provide the fish that was served on feast days. If supplies or stores were needed from the mainland, it was his responsibility to bring them back safely.

The lives of the monks were regulated by the different bells that summoned them to services during the day and night. They prayed together by the icons of centuries past on the chapel walls. In their cells they prostrated themselves time after time, a symbolic act that represented the path from sin to forgiveness, from the darkness of sin to the light of redemption. When they died their bodies were placed in the earth higher up the hill. There they rested for three years before their remains were taken out and replaced by a brother who had just died. The bones were transferred to the charnel house, the air made sweet by mountain flowers.

The monks of the monastery of St John, like the clergy of the Orthodox Church, had always been patriotic

Greeks. Their efforts had helped keep Greek identity alive during the long years of the Turkish occupation. It was well known that the monks from a monastery on the mainland had blessed the first revolutionaries at the very beginning of their struggle for Greek Independence and consecrated their weapons to God. That spirit still lived on, with the wider community of Orthodox monks in favour of the Greek Diaspora, the greater Greece which would encompass all the places where Greek was spoken across southern Europe.

Every morning and evening now after prayers Brother Andreas would stand at the edge of the sea and look out for a ship. They had promised him that one would come, his two brothers in London. They had assured Andreas that he would be told what to do with the cargo. But as the sun rose and fell on the blue waters, the ship did not come. Brother Andreas was worried. His eldest brother Kostas had never let him down. Why should he start now? Where was the ship?

'What's the matter with this jacket, Lucy?' Lord Francis Powerscourt was struggling to climb into a special uniform in Markham Square on the morning of the fire alarm in the British Museum. 'I can't seem to make it sit properly.' Lady Lucy came and pulled quite hard at the sections at the back and sides of the garment. She pulled the hem at the rear down as hard as she could. There was a grunt from her husband.

'Steady on, Lucy, you make me feel as though I'm being trussed up ready for market.'

His wife gave one final heave. 'I wonder if it isn't too small, this thing,' she said, standing back to inspect her work. 'But I think it'll do now.'

She smiled at her creation. Sergeant Powerscourt of the Metropolitan Police stood before her, shifting from foot to foot as if the boots were too small as well. It had been Inspector Kingsley's suggestion. 'Only a small disguise, my lord, but I don't think we want any staff in the British Museum recognizing you. Once you're a sergeant you've got freedom of movement. You'll be able to go wherever you want without any questions being asked. It'll be an independent command. I look forward to seeing our latest recruit. You don't have to salute your Inspector every time you meet him, my lord.'

'It's a pity the twins have just gone off to school,' said Powerscourt. 'I wonder if I could have arrested them without being recognized.'

Forty-five minutes later he was waiting with the Inspector and a couple of constables in a police car behind the British Museum. 'You do look the part, my lord,' the Inspector said cheerfully, 'ten or twelve years' service, I should say, at the very least. Now then. We would normally be called in by the fire brigade whenever there is a major alert like the one we're about to have here.' Kingsley peered out into the street. 'The starting pistol should go off any minute.'

A few moments later the British Museum fire alarm sounded. Powerscourt thought it sounded as loud as an artillery salvo at the start of a battle. Even the ancient statues, thousands of years old, must have felt a faint tremor passing through their limbs. The inmates of the museum fled out into the front of the building. Nobody emerged from the exits at the rear. Powerscourt's first concern, once they were inside, was to find the shortest route between the Caryatid and the loading bays in the basement. The basement was a huge area with enormous doors for the arrival and departure of ancient artefacts great and small. The thieves must surely have been waiting for the alarm in a side street close to the back entrance and then brought their replacement in here once the building was empty. A series of ramps led to the Elgin Rooms on the upper floor where the Caryatid lived along with her brothers and sisters from the metopes and the Parthenon frieze. Powerscourt and the Inspector commandeered a large trolley and set off. It took six minutes from the basement to the statue. Powerscourt stood very still for five minutes beside the Athenian maiden, then they retraced their steps. Powerscourt thought it must have taken twenty minutes, maybe half an hour, to wheel the fake Caryatid in from the basement and take the original out, assuming the thieves were nimble at the business of taking one marble woman, seven and a half feet tall, down from her place on the porch and slotting another one in. All that must, as the Inspector pointed out on the return journey, have taken a great deal of experience and expertise. Once they were back in the basement, the two men looked around. They were surrounded by a host of strange equipment, with ropes of every size, hoists, small cranes, trolleys great and small lying about in no particular order. Over to one side was a great variety boxes, packing cases and, to Powerscourt's great delight, a cluster of wooden railway containers, all of them empty, as if they had already given up their booty. Powerscourt pointed at them, still panting slightly from their exertions with the trolley.

'That must have been how they did it, Inspector, another bloody container.'

'Don't suppose this one came all the way from Brindisi,' the Inspector muttered, 'somewhere closer to home, I'm sure.' He looked at his watch once more. 'I think you should go back to the car, my lord. I'll head out through the museum and tell the fire people to sound the all clear. You'd better be out of here before they come back.'

As the Museum staff, porters, scholars, secretaries and admission staff made their way back into the building nobody took any notice of a nondescript man in dark overalls in the front of the crowd. He made his way directly to the Deputy Director's office and deposited a plain envelope on the secretary's desk. It was addressed in a familiar handwriting: Theophilus Ragg, Deputy Director, British Museum, Great Russell Street. The dark overalls slipped away with a giggle to be lost in the crowds of Holborn.

9

It was late afternoon when the plain van climbed up the final ascent to Wilbur Lincoln Mitchell's great house high up in the Hudson Valley in upper New York State. The four men who got out had no markings on their overalls and made no identification to their hosts.

'We've brought the package,' was all they said, as they began manoeuvring the outsize black coffin out of the vehicle and along the passageways to the orangery in the garden. With much swearing and a great chewing of gum, they unpacked their cargo and placed it at the far end of the great room. They checked with Mitchell that it was in the right place. He gave them a generous tip and waved them off down the road back to the city. Then, one by one, he turned on the powerful lights he had installed in this great hall. The first light illuminated the statue of Apollo from Mitylene, one of the most famous statues of the Greek world. Then the Charioteer from Zakynthos, then the Roman Emperor Hadrian who had been responsible for the Pantheon in Rome and the Athena from the first century AD. He paused before he turned on the last two lights. Standing proudly on her plinth stood a

118

Greek maiden who looked as though she was carrying something on her head. A Caryatid from late fifth-century BC Athens had come to her new home in the New World. Wilbur Lincoln Mitchell gazed at her in wonder for a long time. Tears began to flow down his cheeks and into his well-trimmed moustache. He wondered if he should build a whole porch to make her feel at home.

No spasm of rage shook Theophilus Ragg as he opened his latest letter from the blackmailer. This one was shorter than before.

'Very well,' it began. 'You have chosen to ignore our requests. Tomorrow morning the full details of the disappearance of the Caryatid will appear in *The Times* and the *Morning Post*. Your role in refusing to tell the police and the public will be made very clear. *Fiat justitia ruat caelum*! Vengeance is mine.'

Ruat Caelum, indeed, Ragg said to himself. Let justice be done even though the heavens fall. He felt a great sense of determination. Let the newspapers say what they would, he would defend his museum to the last breath in his body. He helped himself to a small glass of malt whisky from the Director's inner cabinet and prepared to defend his conduct. *Theophilus*, he said to himself, *the end of my career may be near, it may even be nearer now than it was this morning, but I shall go down fighting to the last breath in my body. Bloody blackmailer*. The man from *The Times* was due in a quarter of an hour.

Late that evening Inspector Kingsley brought an early edition of *The Times* round to Markham Square. 'Picked it up at King's Cross,' he said, 'it was on the way to Scotland.'

The story was prominently displayed. 'British Museum

119

Caryatid Stolen!' the headline said in enormous type. 'Replaced with fake in daring raid! Theft concealed from the public!' There was considerable detail about the robbery, none of it fresh to Powerscourt or the Inspector. Beside the article was an interview with the Deputy Director of the museum, Theophilus Ragg, described as 'the official at the centre of this sad story of deceit and humiliation'. The readers were directed to a leading article where the editor wondered if the British Museum had failed in its duty to keep this most special statue safe in England. 'It has long been the contention of Lord Elgin and his apologists,' the paper thundered, 'that the Elgin Marbles, of which the Caryatid from the Erechtheion is such a distinguished member, would be safer in London than they would have been in Athens, liable to pillaging and theft from any passing antiquary. Now the theft has indeed occurred, but in the heart of the imperial capital. This is a black day indeed for Lord Elgin and the British Museum. Let us hope it is not also a black day for Britain and the Empire.'

Ragg, Powerscourt thought, was making a pretty good fist of things, playing well with a bad hand. 'Why did you keep it secret?' demanded *The Times*. 'Why were the police not called in?'

'There have been a number of similar incidents across the world,' Ragg had replied, 'where the missing object is quickly returned once the thieves discover it is almost impossible to sell it. Publicity and policemen, in my judgement, would make such a course less likely.'

'Were there any negotiations about the return of the maiden to the museum?'

'Certainly not,' had been Ragg's reply. Technically right perhaps, Powerscourt said to himself, because Ragg had refused them, but an offer, however unreliable, had certainly been made.

'Do you think the same thieves were at work here as in Paris with the theft of the *Mona Lisa* from the Louvre? Shouldn't that have been a warning to you to take extra precautions?'

Powerscourt felt rather proud of Ragg for his next answer. 'Of course,' the Deputy Director had said, 'how silly of me,' and you could almost hear the sarcasm in his voice, 'I should have realized that the two were obviously linked. You could pick the *Mona Lisa* off the wall and walk out of the Louvre with it under your coat and nobody would be any the wiser. The Caryatid is over seven feet high, made of marble, unable to walk on her own two feet. Only a giant of a size and strength not, alas, equalled in any of the museum's vast collection of statuary from across the known world would be able to walk out of the British Museum with her under his arm. Apart from that, of course, the similarities between events in London and Paris are self-evident.'

The final question drew another firm response.

'Are you able to reassure our readers and the wider population that you will now be taking all possible measures to secure the return of the statue? Perhaps you could tell us your plans?'

'Certainly not,' Ragg retorted, 'you have accused me of incompetence and inactivity. That is your right as gentlemen of the press. But if you think for one second that I am going to share with you or your readers, however distinguished they might be, our plans to secure the return of the Caryatid, you are very much mistaken. Perhaps you would like me to write an open letter to the thieves outlining all our plans?'

'Well,' said Lady Lucy, 'I think Mr Ragg did jolly well. It can't be very nice having those horrid reporters firing questions at you, implying you're completely hopeless.'

'There may be another, even more unpleasant, helping tomorrow,' said the Inspector.

'What do you mean?' asked Lady Lucy.

'It's the *Daily Mail*,' replied the Inspector, 'and all the rest of the newspapers. They'll all want to dip their hands in the blood. But on this sort of form Ragg should be able to survive. The Commissioner has asked me to appear with him tomorrow when he talks to the other journalists. I'll just have to pretend I haven't known about things before today.'

Lady Lucy made a final cup of tea after the Inspector left.

'I'm too wound up to sleep, Francis,' she said. Her husband was still deep in the pages of *The Times*. 'Is there another article in there about the theft?'

'Not that I can find. But there is a short story on page nine about Lord Rosebery's plans to move a very large number of his statues from Mentmore to Dalmeny, his house outside Edinburgh. The writer says that with all that beauty on the move it will truly be a Pilgrimage of Grace. And the advertisement, asking for bids for the removal work, is prominently displayed on the front page, next to the London property sales.'

'Francis, I know it's very late, but I've had an idea.'

'Inspiration or even genius can strike at any time of the day or night, my love. Carry on, please.'

'Well, I don't think I've thought it through very carefully. But you know the theory that the theft may have been carried out to order, that the thieves may even have received part of their payment before the robbery took place and before they delivered the Caryatid to its new owners?'

'I do, Lucy. I have to tell you that it does not meet with total favour from your friend of the peacock fan, the Head of Greek and Roman Antiquities at the British Museum.'

'Why not?'

'He muttered something about not theorizing ahead of the evidence. But what are you driving at?'

'Do you think, if you were going to embark on such a high-profile theft, that this would be your first time, as it were? Wouldn't you have had a few practice runs before the big one? Entered your horse, if you like, for a few preliminary gallops at the minor racecourses like Lincoln or Salisbury before the St Leger or the Derby?'

'Do you mean that the thieves would have stolen some minor artefact from Great Russell Street as a sort of trial run?'

'No, I don't mean that at all. Let me try again.' Lady Lucy sipped her tea quietly for a moment. 'Look,' she said, 'suppose you're a big-time criminal in the world of art and museums, or you want to be a big-time criminal in the world of art and museums. You probably don't go round wearing knuckle dusters or a balaclava and you don't beat your enemies to a pulp if they cross you. This criminal probably looks like you, Francis. Well dressed, well spoken, butter wouldn't melt in his mouth. So, he wants to play with the big boys. He's not interested in knocking off a couple of family portraits by unknown persons on the wall of the vicarage, that sort of thing. He knows how difficult it has been for his brothers in Christ in the criminal world to sell on a famous painting after you've stolen it. Eureka! Whether he has the idea in the bath or not I don't know, but this is his fresh contribution to the annals of crime. Surely, if you want to steal something as audacious as the Elgin Caryatid, you would have had a rehearsal or two? Suppose you stole a Constable, one of those Constables with carts going through the water in the sunshine and a lot of haystacks, a few cows and a couple of peasants. You would have learnt how to negotiate beforehand with the buyer you have in mind. You'd have worked out how to handle such people better next time. Perhaps there have been one or two or even three such trial runs by now.'

'That's very plausible, Lucy. Extremely convincing, if I may say. But how do we turn this to our advantage?'

'That's the easy bit. So far we have only talked about the criminal. We shouldn't forget the victim. He wakes up one morning or he comes back after his holiday and his Constable has gone. Maybe it's just one of his Constables. He might have three or four, a whole garage full of carts and haywains. Our man may or may not like Constables, though he would certainly not say so in public, even if he never looks at the thing from one year's end to the next. It'll be part of the family heritage. Not quite bought on the Grand Tour – even the Venetian art dealers would think twice before selling a British visitor a Constable – but maybe picked up by an ancestor at one of those great sales like the Marlborough or the Beckford. Anyway, our victim gets very cross. How dare they? An Englishman's home should be sacrosanct! If he'd have been at home when the thieves called, he'd have horsewhipped them himself, that sort of thing. But there is one thing he more or less has to do. He has to tell the police. Otherwise people may think the owner himself had something to do with it. The insurance people will insist on it.'

'This is all sounding very plausible, Lucy. I have to tell

you, you have developed a very suspicious mind. I fear you may have been married to me for too long. But carry on, please.'

'I would rather like to go on being married to you, Francis, if that's all right with you. But there's not a lot left to say. The police arrive. They plod round the doors and windows. They question all the servants. They may even arrest one or two of them if they're foreigners and don't speak English very well. They put the word out among the artistic salesmen and the auctioneers of New Bond Street and King Street and so on. But they don't know that the criminal has simply bypassed all those normal routes. The Constable goes straight to the man who paid the money. Nobody else hears anything about it, not even a whisper. The Constable, effectively, disappears. No records, no receipts, not even a crumb for the taxman. But, Francis, and now we must surely go to bed in a moment, the police must have records of the theft. It may have gone down in their books as an unsolved crime but it stays on the books. There must be names and addresses.'

'Just one last question, Lucy. Do you think the master criminal carries out the crime himself? That he breaks into the house with his jemmy and his accomplice to carry the Constable away? Is he mastermind and chief operator?'

'The honest answer is I just don't know. I would guess that he is not likely to break the windows or slip the catches himself. He will hire other people to do it for him. Maybe by now he has a regular team who always do the dirty work. Perhaps the people who stole and replace the Caryatid are the same ones who carried the Constable away across the lawn in the middle of the night.'

'If you're right, Lucy, and you may well be, our next course is simple. We just have to ask the Inspector to

125

send word to the police forces of England and request the records of all unsolved major art thefts over the past two or three years. Then I go a-calling.'

'That's it,' said Lady Lucy. 'You're absolutely right.'

It took Johnny Fitzgerald five days to rise from his bed after the Brindisi food poisoning. To the end he had inveighed against the sea creatures of the Adriatic.

'I'm still not sure, Lady Lucy,' he said on the morning of his return, sipping a cup of coffee rather suspiciously in the Powerscourt drawing room. 'I can still see that horrid little squid with its nasty eyes. I can still feel those ghastly oysters slivering their way down my throat to cause havoc in my innards, damn them all to hell.'

Once they knew Johnny was on the road to recovery the Powerscourt twins, Christopher and Juliet, eight years old, had found pictures in their books of various fish and other sea creatures. They would rush into Johnny's bedroom, shrieking 'I'm a squid, I'm a squid!' or even worse, 'Look at me, look at me, I'm an oyster, fiddle de dee!' and waving the appropriate illustrations in the air. Johnny would retreat beneath the bedclothes and groan loudly until the children went away.

Powerscourt was at the British Museum with the Inspector. Lady Lucy brought Johnny up to date.

'I see, I see,' he mused. 'So where do you think my talents could best be employed at this time? Francis no doubt has marked me down in his mind as the boon companion of those Greek porters from the museum, but there don't seem to be any of those left alive just at the moment. Anyway, Lady Lucy, I could happily go to my grave without another glass of ouzo or the filthy Greek island wine at that place near the cathedral. There should be a ban on importing the stuff if you ask me. People should be asking questions in Parliament.'

'Where do you think you should go, Johnny? Where do you see yourself being most useful?'

'Well,' said Johnny Fitzgerald, 'you know about that fielding position in cricket called longstop? You don't? It's passed you by? Dear me, Lady Lucy, dear me. Longstop is a fielder placed between the wicketkeeper and the boundary, usually closer to the boundary. You only need a longstop if your wicketkeeper is hopeless, liable to miss every other ball that passes the bat. Longstop's job is to stop the ball going to the boundary for four runs. That's why he's called longstop. You with me so far, Lady Lucy?'

'I am, Johnny. I do believe I may have seen a cricketer in the position you describe. But I don't see how this fits in with Francis and your investigations.'

'I am a sort of longstop, Lady Lucy. It's as if Francis is the wicketkeeper. I try to discover things Francis can't or hasn't got the time to find out. You and I can see him doing many admirable things but drinking all night with museum porters and the low life of the auction houses isn't one of them. This is what I think I'm going to do. If your theory about the criminal is true, that he knows the world of art and the people in it very well, then it should be possible to catch a sniff of him or narrow the field down to three or four likely characters. I'm going to buy lunch for a man I know who works on the *Burlington Magazine*. Come to think of it I believe he actually owns the *Burlington Magazine*. That's always full of the latest gossip.'

'That sounds excellent to me, Johnny. I'll let Francis know when he comes back. Just one thing, though.'

'What's that?'

'Keep well clear of the fish.'

When the first visitors arrived at the British Museum the following morning the Caryatid had gone. The marble lady had vanished from her plinth and been taken to a secret place in a corner of the basement, referred to by those in the know as the Room of the Doubtful. In here were kept some of the frauds that had deceived earlier curators, statues of Hermes supposed to be from first-century ancient Corinth that turned out to have been manufactured in late-nineteenth-century Birmingham, fraudulent Aphrodites and at least three busts of Roman emperors that had been born in Munich rather than the Roman Empire. The fake Caryatid joined this bizarre conclave of the unreliable and the unloved. On the plinth a notice announced that the real Caryatid had been stolen. The museum was doing all it could to secure its safe return.

Powerscourt had gone to the British Museum with Inspector Kingsley. On his arrival he was hustled straight to the Deputy Director's office.

'Ah, Powerscourt, good to see you. I've got the man from the *Daily Mail* coming to talk to me in a few moments. I propose to tell them that not only do we have the services of the Metropolitan Police Force at our disposal, but that we have employed one of London's top investigators to assist us and work alongside the officers of the law. That's you. I take it you have no objection, my lord? I think it will give the appearance that we have the matter well in hand.'

Ragg paused to read a telegram his secretary had brought in.

'We're both for it,' the Inspector whispered to Powerscourt. 'If we fail, the press and the politicians will be baying for our blood. Hung drawn and quartered, I shouldn't wonder. Heads impaled on pikes on Tower Bridge for a month like Thomas More.'

'What's that? What's going on?' Ragg looked up from his telegram. 'This is from the British Ambassador in Istanbul. The Foreign Office wired him yesterday to see if his people could find and recall our Director, believed to be somewhere in ancient Mesopotamia. The Ambassador has no news about the Director's whereabouts. He has sent messages to various local leaders but has little hope of a quick outcome. The people who might know where he is, Ambassador Henderson says, are not likely to read telegrams. They probably travel by camel.'

Before the Inspector had time to explain his whispers the man from the *Daily Mail* was shown in. Matthew Dawson was an aggressive young man of about thirty years with bright red hair and wearing a suit of doubtful cut. Dawson came straight to the point.

'When are you going to resign, Mr Ragg? Today? Tomorrow?'

'I have no intention of resigning, thank you. Allow me to introduce Lord Francis Powerscourt, one of London's top investigators, who is helping us in the quest for the Caryatid. His appointment is further demonstration that the museum authorities have the matter well in hand.'

'Pleased to meet you, I'm sure,' snarled the man from the *Mail*, 'another one for the chop if the statue isn't found.'

The exchange continued in this bad-tempered fashion for some time until Theophilus Ragg moved into a different gear.

'Look here,' he said, glowering at the red-headed

reporter, 'this handing out of blame isn't going to help anybody. It's all very well implying that I and the police and Lord Powerscourt are incompetent fools who should all resign at once. That won't bring her back. I have a responsibility in my position, to the Trustees of this great museum and, ultimately, to Parliament. If they tell me to go, I shall go. But that is their responsibility, not yours. The *Daily Mail* too has responsibilities, Mr Dawson. You have hundreds of thousands of readers out there. One or two, or maybe more, will have seen something that could help us find the Caryatid. Somebody must have seen her go. Somebody may know where she is now. Appeal to your readers! Launch a crusade! Let's find the Caryatid together! Think of the fame and glory that would attend upon your newspaper if it solved or helped to solve the mystery. *Daily Mail* praised in the House of Commons! My word, that would make a change! Being constructive is much more positive than being critical, carping for ever on the sidelines. Think about it, Mr Dawson. I suggest you return to your offices and lay the matter before your editor. I am sure he will know which way his duty lies. And now, I wish you a very good day.' With a gesture to his companions Theophilus Ragg led his forces from the field. The reporter picked up his hat and his notebook and stared after the Deputy Director.

'Christ,' he muttered to himself, 'they told me he was a little mouse of a man. No spirit, they said. Dried out like a human walnut. The chief sub editor offered me a pound if I could actually make him cry. No chance of that, no chance at all.'

130

10

Powerscourt was walking along the north bank of the Thames beyond Hammersmith Bridge in the direction of Chiswick. To his left the river was a twinkling blue in the afternoon sunlight. To his right he had passed the ancient pubs of the Blue Anchor and the Dove that had borne witness to the river life of London for centuries. He was heading for a grand house near the church of St Nicholas called Norfolk House. There, Inspector Kingsley's men checking the details of London's unsolved art crimes reported, lived a family called Wilson, proud possessors until the previous year of a Turner, said to have been one of the most beautiful Turners still in private hands.

Other police forces across the Home Counties were conducting similar searches for thefts of works of art that were never solved. Powerscourt wondered if it would be like calling on the bereaved.

Norfolk House was a late Georgian villa with great bay windows. An ancient gardener was sweeping busily in the front lawn that looked out over the river. Autumn leaves, the dead golds, the lifeless browns, the pale greens, the anaemic reds with the colours drained out

131

of them always made Powerscourt think of death. Only a few months before these leaves had the sap of life in them. Now it was gone.

He was shown into a large drawing room with a spectacular view of the Thames. A couple of barges, travelling towards the Port of London, hooted as they passed. An inquisitive seagull was perched on the patio outside the double doors into the garden. Its friends and relations were squawking noisily around the church spire.

'Lord Powerscourt?' said an old and tired-sounding voice, 'how kind of you to come. My name is Alice Wilson. Won't you sit down?'

Mrs Wilson looked like the archetype of a perfect grandmother, white hair, a kindly face that looked as though she smiled a lot, hands with wrinkled skin like parchment and a dark blue dress that looked as though it had been a part of her wardrobe for years. A very faint trace of mothballs still hung in the air.

'Mr Wilson is not at home this afternoon?' said Powerscourt, and halfway through the sentence, looking at the old lady's face, he knew he had made a mistake.

'No, I'm afraid Mr Wilson is not at home this afternoon. Mr Wilson isn't here any more, Lord Powerscourt. He's in the cemetery behind the church now, between a man who won the Victoria Cross at Rorke's Drift and the tomb of that American painter James McNeill Whistler. It's turning green, whatever they put Whistler in, Lord Powerscourt, some kind of great box that's going bad.'

'Please forgive me,' said Powerscourt, 'I'm so sorry. I do apologize. I had no idea Mr Wilson has passed away. The records only refer to a Mr and Mrs Wilson.'

'You weren't to know my Horace had left us, were you, Lord Powerscourt. It was all quite sudden. Three months after the theft he was working in the back garden one morning. The heart attack must have caught him just outside the shed where he kept his tools. He was dead when the ambulance came, quite dead. I've often wondered if the robbery didn't finish him off. He wasn't that old, you know. He was only sixty-eight when he was taken from us. I thought we'd be able to watch the sunsets over the river together until we were seventy-five or eighty. Two old people with their memories and the view. Now that's all gone. There's just me.'

Mrs Wilson paused and rang the bell for tea. 'You'll have some tea, Lord Powerscourt? My housekeeper makes the most delicious scones. I've brought down my diary that covered the period of the robbery. That might help. I understand there have been developments in the case. I'm not sure I want to know any details, I'd only worry, you see, but I'm happy to help in any way I can.'

'Let me tell you what I know, Mrs Wilson, and perhaps we can take it from there.'

'Of course.'

'I believe the painting was taken about eighteen months ago. The thieves took it from a wall in this room some time during the night of Thursday eighteenth of March.'

Mrs Wilson poured tea and proffered a buttered scone. 'That is correct. When we came down in the morning, it was gone. And, do you know, to this day we don't know how the thieves got into the house. None of the doors and windows were forced, as far as we could tell. Our housekeeper – I'm still saying we, how stupid of me – lives in a cottage round the corner and her keys had not been touched.'

'These scones are quite delicious,' said Powerscourt, brushing a few crumbs off his waistcoat. 'Please send my compliments to your housekeeper. The police records also say that they have no idea how entrance was effected. But perhaps you could tell me about the painting itself, Mrs Wilson. The police are good at writing down and recording many things but I don't suppose any of the great auction houses would think of employing them to describe their offerings to the public.'

Powerscourt suddenly remembered his suspicion on the way that it might be like talking to the bereaved. Mrs Wilson seemed to be as upset at the loss of the Turner as she was by the loss of Horace.

'You're obviously a man of the world, Lord Powerscourt. I'm sure you know what it must feel like to lose a painting that's been in your family for a long time. It's like losing a child in some ways. What was it like, our Turner? Well, it wasn't one of those Sturm und Drang Turners, if you know what I mean, terrible storms at sea with the waves whipped into a shape like a corkscrew, helpless humans and frail boats hanging on for dear life. You know how they talk in the Bible about people being possessed by the Holy Spirit, speaking in tongues, that sort of thing? I've always thought Turner painted those awful seascapes in a frenzy, scarcely aware of what he was doing. But our picture, *Mortlake Terrace, Summer's Evening*, was completely different. He painted it by the Thames in Mortlake, obviously, about a mile or so to the west on the other side of the river from where we are sitting now. There's a fine house that belonged to a man called Moffatt, – the house is still there by the way – a peaceful view of the Thames looking towards Chiswick, a fraction of garden, an avenue of limes. It's serene, it's so beautiful it's perfect. Horace used to say it changed slightly with the weather, looking less peaceful in a storm, but I never thought that.

Turner painted a couple of pictures from more or less the same place. I believe the other one has been sold to a rich American in New York for a great deal of money. We wouldn't have sold ours, you know, not ever, however much people offered.'

Mrs Wilson sighed and then managed a wan smile. Turners can cross the Atlantic, Powerscourt said to himself. They go to New York, to Fricks or Carnegies or Mellons. Could Caryatids cross the Atlantic? Could they swim that far, weighed down with their girdle and all that marble? How would you send one to the New World? If you were a first-class passenger on a transatlantic liner, could you take one with you? Could she have her own cabin? Could you disguise her as a monstrous piece of luggage, stowed safely and securely in the hold until the Statue of Liberty and Ellis Island welcomed the two of you on the other side?

'Thank you so much for that, Mrs Wilson, I am touched by what you say. And are the police records right again when they say that you have not heard a word about your Turner since it was taken? Not even a whisper?'

'That is right, Lord Powerscourt. The seagulls may know where it has gone, we certainly don't. Every leading art dealer and every leading auction house here and abroad was contacted by the police. All promised to let Scotland Yard know the minute they heard of anything. They've heard nothing, nothing at all, not a word. It's as if the painting has disappeared into thin air. It was never very big, mind you. It would be easy to hide.'

Powerscourt looked at the rectangular gap above the fireplace. The picture hooks were still there. Surely a painting must have hung there until fairly recently, as the colour of the wall was different. He thought it better not to ask.

'Can you remember the painting leaving your house at all? In the months before it was taken, I mean? Or any strange people coming to look at it?'

Mrs Wilson opened a dark blue diary. 'A man came from the insurance people in January,' she said, turning pack the pages. 'That was normal. What wasn't usual was that a second insurance man, rather older than the usual and very well spoken, came a week later. Just to double check, he said. Maybe he liked paintings.'

Mrs Wilson stopped and looked through her diary from the year before. 'The only other thing I can think of happened the previous December. The tenth, it was, a Friday.'

She looked up at Powerscourt as if expecting praise for the accuracy of her memories. 'We both belonged, I still do, to a local club called the Chiswick Literary Society. They organize talks from visiting speakers, that sort of thing, and sometimes they broaden the subject to include the visual arts as well as the written word. Horace organized a meeting here so the members could look at the painting. He gave a little talk. Our housekeeper baked a couple of cakes for the gathering, her special chocolate and a fancy sponge she hadn't made before. They went down very well.'

'And had you seen all the visitors before, Mrs Wilson?'

'Goodness me, you're not suggesting that the thief disguised himself as a member of the Chiswick Literary Society to come and work out how to steal our Turner? That would be very wicked.'

'Did you know them all?'

'Sorry, Lord Powerscourt, I didn't answer your question. I knew them all apart from maybe three or four I didn't think I'd seen before. But they all seemed very respectable, proper Chiswick inhabitants if you know

136

what I mean. I know you're going to ask me if I can remember any of the strangers. I can't. You see, I didn't think it was important at the time.'

'Of course you didn't, Mrs Wilson, nobody could have expected you to remember that.'

'You don't think it's my age, Lord Powerscourt? I forget things so much these days. I'm sure it must be because I'm getting old.'

'Nonsense,' said Powerscourt with a smile, 'if anybody asked me who came to my house, even for chocolate and fancy sponge cake, six or eight months ago, I wouldn't have a clue.'

Powerscourt looked out across the Thames once more to the other side. He wondered what kind of easel Turner had carried to the spot where he painted the views. Maybe he only made sketches there and finished the works off in his studio. He looked again at the empty space on the walls, left as a reminder of what had been there before.

'Mrs Wilson,' he began, 'it has been a great pleasure talking to you. Now I must leave you in peace. You must get in touch at once if anything occurs to you. Thank you so much.'

'I've almost enjoyed it, Lord Powerscourt, thank you for being so patient. I don't often have a proper conversation these days.'

Powerscourt waved goodbye at the gate. A couple of horses from the brewery round the corner from Norfolk House were pulling a cart laden with beer barrels towards Hammersmith. As he walked back along the river he thought once more of Lord Rosebery's train-obsessed butler. William Leith also had an encyclopaedic knowledge of the great transatlantic shipping lines like Cunard and the White Star and their French and German equivalents. He could tell you which one had the best cotton sheets, which one served the best food, the finest wines. He would also know how much luggage you could take. Looking back at Mrs Wilson's house and the church of St Nicholas where her husband was buried, Powerscourt remembered Inspector Kingsley's account of visiting a man he had helped convict serving his sentence in Wormwood Scrubs prison. He thought he too should begin a programme of visiting, not necessarily those in prison, but a mission to the unhappy and the bereaved. He could start with Mrs Alice Wilson in Norfolk House.

The builders were late arriving at the Hellenic College outside Amersham. They were all Greek, fit, young and under thirty, led by a small, stocky man called Maximos who called on the Headmaster to make his apologies in person.

'You were meant to be here five weeks ago,' said the Head.

'I know, I know, I'm so sorry, sir.' Maximos reckoned that everybody else round here would call the Head 'sir'. When in Rome or the Hellenic College, follow the local customs. 'You know how it is, sir. We had to do that work for the cathedral down in Moscow Road. They wouldn't let us go till it was finished. There was more damp there than anybody expected. I've brought extra workers to make up for it, mind you.'

'How many?'

'We originally said we'd bring three. Now we've brought eight. I'm not saying we'll catch up on the original timetable, but we'll take less time than we said before.

138

Is it still all right for us to sleep in the barns and the stables?'

The Headmaster nodded. 'I'll arrange for a dining room to be set up for you over there. Just let me know when you want to eat.'

The Headmaster did not say that he wished to keep these young men as far away as possible from the teenage girls in his charge, but they both knew what he meant.

The girls of the Hellenic College looked out of the windows of their classrooms as the young men began their work, digging out the foundations for the new building. It was to be at the end of a long glade that led to the small Parthenon, built perfectly to scale at the end of the eighteenth century. When it grew dark the men worked on under great lights they had brought with them from London. When his men had gone to bed later that evening, Maximos took out the drawings for the project. He stared at the plans very carefully. Years before, Maximos had been taken to meet the members of his extended family in Italy and in all corners of the Greek world. He had only been twelve years old, but he still had vivid memories of his relations and the places he had seen. Looking at the architect's work laid out on the table, he knew he had seen it somewhere before. But he was unable to recall exactly where. Rome? Sicily? Corinth? Athens? Olympia? He simply couldn't remember.

Detective Constable Peter Smithson was in his third year in the Metropolitan Police. He had been hand-picked by Inspector Kingsley to work as one of the extra members of the team investigating the disappearance of the Caryatid from the British Museum. Kingsley liked the fact that Smithson was obviously highly intelligent but didn't flaunt it. And he understood money, he wasn't frightened by it. Kingsley had encouraged the young man to go to evening classes in finance and accounting. So it was that Detective Constable Smithson, who looked more like an altar boy than a policeman with his blue eyes and curly light brown hair, reported early one morning to the freight offices of the Great Western Railway, hidden well away from the trains and the platforms of Isambard Kingdom Brunel at Paddington station.

He was instructed to climb three sets of stairs and knock on a black door opposite the top. This was the entry point into the warren of attic rooms where the records were kept.

'Keep going straight through this room and the one after, then turn left onto a little corridor. The room you want is at the end.' The receptionist was an elderly man, bent almost double with back pain or lumbago. Smithson wondered if he had sustained his injuries in a life of lifting as a porter at the station. When he reached his destination there was nobody there at first. There were great ledgers, all with dates stamped on the front running right round the room from floor to ceiling. Even up there an ingenious system of boxes fixed to the joists provided yet more storage space. Looking out of the small grimy window Smithson saw a vast flotilla of forgotten or disused railway carriages. Some of them, he thought, must have been over fifty years old. You could almost trace the evolution of the differing styles and fashions in train comfort across the decades.

'You the policeman?'

An elderly receptionist was leaning heavily on a stout stick by the doorway.

'Yes, I am.'

140

'Why didn't you say so? Freight records, that's what you want to look at, isn't it? The last five years start at the bottom shelf right by this door. Then they carry on towards the roof. Most recent entries in the ceiling, I'm afraid. We're running out of space. Begin wherever you want.'

'Thank you very much. I'm obliged to you, sir.'

'Don't come asking me for any help now. This isn't my patch. Man who looks after it is off sick. He's been off sick for months now. Don't know if he's ever coming back. Count yourself lucky in one area, mind you.'

The young policeman took a quick look at his surroundings and found it hard to see where he might have struck it lucky.

'Why is that?'

'You've just got the records of all the shipments in here. The actual receipts, invoices and all the rest of them are stored further up the corridor.'

'Really?'

'Really. The last time anyone counted them, there were thirty-eight cardboard boxes full of the stuff. And they're not sorted by date. And that's just the last three years. A very good morning to you.'

Knightsbridge Barracks lies about three-quarters of a mile from Buckingham Palace. In the event of an armed insurrection or a serious disturbance at the palace, the First Life Guards or other branches of the Household Cavalry could be on the scene in a matter of minutes. But it was not their proximity to the throne that brought Lord Francis Powerscourt there this wet and windy afternoon. Nor was it their long and distinguished history, going back to the Restoration of Charles II. Inspector Kingsley's researchers reported that, like Mrs Wilson of Norfolk House on the Thames, the Life Guards had been the victims of a robbery that was never solved and the treasure never recovered.

'Colonel Erskine is waiting for you, sir! This way please, sir!'

Boots echoed down the corridor. Powerscourt was shown into a small library with a view out over the park. Leather-bound books marched in regimental order across the shelves. Powerscourt wondered how long it was since anyone had actually read any of them.

'My name is Erskine! Delighted to meet you, Lord Powerscourt!'

Everything about the Colonel spoke of military perfection. His boots were so well polished that he could have shaved in them and trimmed his elegant moustache. His red jacket looked as though it had been cut by one of London's more fashionable tailors. Under his arm he carried a swagger stick of polished black with a silver tip. He was standing at ease by the window, arms folded behind his back in the correct military stance.

'Fellow said you had come about the robbery a year or so back,' he boomed.

'That is correct, Colonel.'

'I should say at once that the bloody silver has nothing to do with me. Most of the chaps here wouldn't know the difference between a cruet and a candlestick. My family have a certain amount of the stuff so the top brass put me in charge.'

'Could you tell me a little about the silver collection, Colonel? I'm afraid I didn't know the regiment had such a thing.'

'Not many people do. Stuff's so valuable it wouldn't

142

do to advertise it to any thieves or art dealers passing through Knightsbridge, don't you know.'

The Colonel stopped suddenly and placed a monocle carefully in his right eye. He leant over to inspect Powerscourt as if he were a badly turned out lieutenant on parade.

'I've heard of you, dammit, man, I'm sure I've heard of you! Wait a minute. Aren't you the fellow who reorganized Army Intelligence in the Boer War? Didn't you have a sidekick called Johnny who could drink a depot dry?'

'I'm afraid I am,' Powerscourt replied. 'My companion in arms Johnny Fitzgerald is a reformed character now. He only starts drinking before lunch rather than before breakfast. There are rumours of a rich widow in Warwickshire.'

'Are there, by God. Heaven help the widow!' The Colonel began pumping Powerscourt's hand in a bone-crushing embrace, beaming from ear to ear.

'You're one of us! You're one of us!' he said, throwing his swagger stick and his monocle onto a chair and loosening the buttons at the top of his jacket. 'Let's sit down and put our feet up for God's sake! I only do this swagger stick, formal Life Guards officer routine because I've had to represent the regiment in talks with the War Office. Bastards tried to amalgamate us with some damned peasants in the West Country. Nothing against peasants, myself, plenty of them good workers at our little place in Shropshire, but we don't want to join the buggers.'

The Colonel leant back and pressed a bell. 'Claret please, Corporal! Two glasses if you would! One of our better bottles if you will, not that rotgut you served up the other evening. I think we should drink your health, Powerscourt, and to your temporary return to the military fold!'

The Colonel had now kicked his boots off and was sprawling in an armchair with his feet up on a small stool. 'We'd better go back to the bloody silver, I suppose,' he said.

'It would be helpful, Colonel, if you could tell me something of its background, how the regiment came to acquire it, that sort of thing.'

'That's part of the trouble,' said Colonel Erskine, indicating to the Corporal that he should put the claret on the round table by the window, 'nobody thinks it would be very sensible to have people asking where we got it.' He poured two very full glasses of claret and peered at the label. 'This looks more like it. Your health, welcome back to the Army, Lord Powerscourt!'

Powerscourt nodded his appreciation of the wine. 'Forgive me, Colonel, why would it not be very sensible to have people asking how you got the silver?'

'Damn it, man, you worked out how to find the bloody Boer in South Africa, I'm sure you can work out the answer to that one!'

'I wonder,' said Powerscourt with a smile. 'I really do. Spoils of war? Booty from the battlefield? Houses of the rich ransacked after a siege? How about that, Colonel?'

'You've got it in one, Lord Powerscourt. The regimental silver collection dates back to the late seventeenth century so I suppose they must have started making off with the stuff right from the start. They got an enormous haul after the battle of Vitoria near the end of the Peninsular War when Napoleon's brother, acting King of Spain, was foolish enough to bring a great deal of material with him in his baggage train, paintings, silver, valuables of every sort. There's quite a lot of that baggage train in

144

Wellington's Apsley House by the way. They bring out heaps of Vitoria silver every year for the Waterloo Dinner.'

'So what exactly have you got? In general terms, obviously.'

'Don't ask me for a full inventory, for God's sake. I should say that if it exists in silver we've got it. We've got cruets and salt cellars and any number of combinations of those. We've got enough candlesticks to light the Albert Hall and have lots left over. We've got plate and cups and goblets of every shape and size, decorated wine coolers and ornamental chamber pots, we've got an elaborate rococo epergne, sort of multi-purpose holder for condiments, matching sugar casters and salt cellars that would have stood on its branches. God knows where we stole that from. Better not ask.'

'Could you tell me about the theft, Colonel?' Powerscourt had been warned that this might be a tricky subject.

'Ah yes, well, that's all rather embarrassing really.' The Colonel drained his wine glass and poured himself a refill.

'Never mind,' he continued, 'orders must be obeyed by all ranks, time to advance, Steady the Buffs! It was the Regimental Feast, you see. That's what did the damage.'

The Colonel paused again. He stared at an ornate pair of silver candlesticks on the mantelpiece. Powerscourt waited.

'Once a year, at the beginning of September, we have a Regimental Feast or Dinner, if you prefer. We dine by candlelight off silver plate. The wine is served in ornate silver goblets, the ones for white slightly smaller than the ones for red. There are silver cruets and silver salt cellars, enormous silver wine coolers, everything silver to do with food is on display and used as its original owners intended. The fancy epergne thing stands in the centre of the top table where the generals are. In the centre of the tables, and ranged round the edges, are the pick of the remaining pieces, Communion vessels, more goblets, ewers, the pick of the collection.'

'So what happened exactly?' said Powerscourt.

'This is the embarrassing bit, my friend. As you can imagine, the wine on these occasions flows like nectar in paradise. We used to have a very fine wine cellar, by the way, also liberated from the nation's enemies, but that's all been drunk by now. Well before the coffee and liqueurs there were officers passed out on the floor. By the time the last Life Guards finally left, every man jack present was drunk, very very drunk. There are records of an earlier Regimental Dinner in the 1800s, Lord Powerscourt, where the average consumption per man was two and a half bottles each, not counting liqueurs. This time it was worse, much worse.'

'What about the theft?'

'I'm coming to that. It was early afternoon the next day when the steward and his people realized some of the silver was missing. They have to check everything in and out from an enormous list, you see. A number of pieces weren't there. But – and this is the really embarrassing bit – when the adjutant, who wasn't at the dinner, being, if not actually teetotal, a puritan kind of a man who doesn't like being surrounded by the totally inebriate, began asking questions, nobody could remember anything. Most of those present had difficulty recalling their own names. Nobody had seen anything untoward. Nobody had seen a thief come or go. Nobody had watched the

146

stuff walk out of the door of its own accord. Nobody could remember a thing.'

'What about the servants? Couldn't they help?'

'Help? They were even more helpless than the officers. Five of them were still stretched out on the scullery floor at nine o'clock the next morning. They have a tradition on these occasions – all the wines have to be tasted by the staff before they are served. At least a glass at a time. No wonder they were all laid out.'

'So what exactly was taken?'

'Four ornate silver plates, early 1700s, French. A pair of exquisite candlesticks believed to have come from the high altar of the cathedral in Badajoz, Spanish, late 1700s. Very beautiful silver wine cooler, English, early nineteenth century. Oh, I nearly forgot, a tiny silver salt cellar, believed to have belonged to Mr Samuel Pepys. God knows how we got hold of that.'

'What did the police say? I presume the thing was reported.'

'Funny you should mention that, my friend. Two policemen came, summoned in to see Officer Commanding, asked me what was gone and then they vanished. Rather like the bloody Boer in that damned war, disappearing into the veldt all the time.'

'And you never heard of the stolen silver again? No blackmail notes arrived, suggesting a rendezvous and a handover and a pay-off?'

'I'd like to see the villain who tried to blackmail the Life Guards. No, nothing like that. It's been as silent as the grave ever since. The police never came back with any news. They just write to us every three months and say inquiries are progressing but there's nothing new to report. Do you know what's happened to our silver, Lord Powerscourt?'

Powerscourt did not reply.

'Never mind,' said the Colonel, 'don't expect you could say even if you did know.' He raised himself once more in the direction of the claret. 'Better finish this off while you're here. Stuff never tastes the same after you've put a bloody cork in halfway down. Don't suppose you can tell me what this is all about? Fellows like yourself don't come poking about unless there's something fishy going on.'

Powerscourt assured the Colonel that he was right in his assumptions but that, just for the moment, he could not speak about it. He was sure the Colonel would understand.

'Of course, of course, my friend. Drink up, drink up! Any time you need a little help with your inquiries, show of muscle here, discreet disposal of your enemies there, let me know. Erskine and the Life Guards will be there for you, have no fear!'

11

Another one engaged! That was the third or the fourth this year! There couldn't be many of them left, surely. One of Lady Lucy's innumerable cousins was holding a drinks party in honour of her daughter Hermione's engagement to a young solicitor called James Wentworth. Powerscourt reckoned that there must be over a hundred people in the room, most of whom must be related to him in some way or other but whom he did not recognize. He had belonged to this enormous extended family for years now. He still did not feel part of it. The record turnout for one of these huge family assemblies had been the christening of the Powerscourt twins in Chelsea Old Church some years before when he had counted a grand total of 127 in-laws.

He took refuge in a small sitting room with his brother-in-law William Burke. Burke was a noted financier in the City of London who now collected directorships as he once collected old volumes of Wisden.

'Bloody noisy in there, Francis,' said Burke, clipping the end of a large Havana.

'Much better in here,' agreed Powerscourt.

'How's business? They tell me you've been looking into the missing Caryatid at the British Museum. That so?'

'Afraid it is. I'm not having much success so far.'

'I took our youngest, Miranda, the one you stood godparent for, to see that Caryatid when Miranda was little. I always remember her telling me she was going to be a Caryatid when she grew up. She liked the girdle, apparently, something like that. Oddly enough, I've had a lot of dealing with those wretched Greeks this week.' Burke looked rather troubled at this point. 'The modern ones, I mean, not the ones who went around all day talking philosophy and putting Socrates to death.'

'Is all not well in Plato's cave, William?'

'You're bloody well right, all is not well in Plato's cave. They need a wizard in money and finance rather than philosophy. Whole bloody country's pickled in debt, Francis, pickled. I've never seen anything like it.'

'Really? I don't recall seeing anything about it in the papers.'

Burke laughed bitterly. 'Plenty of people have been taking plenty of trouble to keep it out of the papers. It's been going on for years now. Some so-called friends in the City of London advanced the rebels a lot of money to fund the sacred cause of Greek independence. Bonds. Plenty of money up front, plenty of interest to pay ever after. Our Greek friends had trouble paying those bonds so they borrowed some more. Then their main export collapsed about twenty years ago so the money dried up. Sorry, Francis, do you know what the main Greek export was?'

'Not a clue.'

'Currants, would you believe it, currants. Then they lost a war with the Turks and had to pay a huge indemnity. Guess how they decided to pay that off? You've guessed it, Francis. Another bloody loan. So now all Greek loans are supervised by an international consortium of six leading countries. I'm one of the British representatives on this Tower of banking Babel, so help me God.'

'Do you think this is any use to me, William, investigating the theft of a Greek statue from the British Museum?'

'Can't see how it is. Just one thing, though, Francis.'

'What's that?'

'It's that old saying about don't trust Greeks bearing gifts. Be even more suspicious than usual. Chances are the buggers won't be able to pay for anything. Not for a long while.'

The lecture hall close to the British Museum was almost full. Londoners were crowding in to hear a lecture called 'Some Reflections on the Lost Caryatid', by Dr Tristram Stanhope, former Fellow of St Luke's College, Oxford, Head of Greek and Roman Antiquities at the British Museum. The event was being staged by a new body calling themselves the Caryatid Committee. Powerscourt and Lady Lucy were seated on the side near the back. The principal players were already on stage. There was a bishop in his finest purple with a silver cross prominent round his neck. He was attended by a humbler man of the Church, clad in plain black, possibly his chaplain. A harassed-looking man sat beside him, checking his notes. There were a couple of substantial citizens who looked as though they might be important players in the City. Of the principal speaker, there was, as yet, no sign.

'Do you think our friend with the peacock feathers is going to be late, Francis?' whispered Lady Lucy. 'And who is that bishop?'

'I shouldn't be at all surprised if Stanhope is late. He's

probably been here for some time, just dying to make a dramatic entrance. The worried chap is that Liberal MP from Bristol who always supports the latest fashionable craze. The purple Bishop is called Jeffreys, bishop of Oxford. They believe they're closer to God in Oxford, the bishops, always have.'

Lady Lucy looked sharply at her husband, but he pretended to be fiddling with his shoelaces. One floor above, latecomers were being ushered into the last available seats at the back of the balcony. The Bishop began to look rather anxious. Outside the bells of a nearby church were striking seven o'clock. The lecture was due to begin. Powerscourt watched carefully as the Bishop closed his eyes, possibly in prayer. At last, a curtain at the back was flung open. Tristram Stanhope strode dramatically to the centre of the stage and took his seat. He was wearing a long smoking jacket in dark blue velvet with a cream cravat and a yellow carnation in his buttonhole.

'That's the peacock feather equivalent, Lucy,' Powerscourt muttered. 'Wait for the bloody carnation to expand into an ornamental tail halfway through the lecture.'

'Ladies and gentlemen.' The MP was on his feet at the lectern now. 'For those who do not know me, my name is Archibald Street, Member of Parliament for the City of Westminster. It is my great pleasure here this evening to welcome one of the most distinguished classicists of his generation, Dr Tristram Stanhope of the British Museum. Dr Stanhope.'

The Head of Greek and Roman Antiquities made his way to the rostrum quite slowly. He spread his arms out over the sides and waited until his audience was completely quiet. Then he waited a moment or two longer.

'Ladies and gentlemen,' he began. 'It's good to be back here so soon! Less than a year ago I was honoured to be chosen to give one of the Lipton Classical Lectures in this very room on the Roman Idea of Virtue. I am glad to be able to report that on that occasion, as on this one, the hall was full to overflowing!'

He paused. Lady Lucy poked her husband gently in the ribs.

'This evening is a sombre occasion for all of us concerned with the study and scholarship of the classical world in this country. As you all know, a Caryatid, *the* Caryatid as we like to call her, has been ripped from her place in the British Museum and replaced with a forgery.'

There was a long pause while Stanhope adjusted his notes and fiddled with his glasses.

'I want you to picture a column or a pillar,' he went on, 'slender, graceful, taller than a man, adorned with the marks of the Ionic or the Doric or the Corinthian orders. Now I want you to imagine your column standing beside other columns in a row of six or eight or twelve. Your column may be standing to attention as part of the front of a building – it could be the Bank of England or the Royal Exchange here in London, it could be the front of the Pantheon in Rome, it could be the front of one of Andrea Palladio's churches in Venice. Your column might be on display inside a Renaissance church – it was the masterstroke of the architects of that time to turn the classical order inside out. In ancient Greece or Rome, the columns or the pillars were on the outside, the brick building contained within them was on the inside. Brunelleschi and his colleagues turned it round, with the brick walls on the outside and the columns on the inside. Think of your column in all those places and then go back to the beginning, to the building on top of the Acropolis in Athens, the building that now serves as a visual shorthand for Greece itself, the Parthenon and its rich panoply of columns. The history of our columns is a key part of the history of Western architecture and of Western culture.

'The Parthenon and the Acropolis are also a key part of the Caryatid's story. Above all else, Athens is the city of the goddess Athena. A giant statue of her, eighteen feet tall, adorned with gold and jewels was the centrepiece of the building contained within the inner Parthenon walls. The Acropolis is a memorial to the days of Athens's glory in the wars against the Persians. The unlikely victories at Marathon and Salamis are all woven into the story of the buildings on Athens High City. Each year there was a great festival to Athena, the PanAthenaica, and we believe that the people taking part in the procession to the Acropolis, the soldiers, the horsemen, the maidens who made the new cloak for the goddess every year, the animals for sacrifice, the charioteers, are all shown on the Parthenon frieze we have in the British Museum.

'Our Caryatid was a human pillar, a human column. She and her five sisters took the place of columns in another temple on the top, the Erechtheion, built about 406 BC. The Caryatid was part of the continuing story of the myth of Athena, patroness of Athens and her Acropolis. Erechtheus, to whom the temple was dedicated, was a former ruler of Athens in years gone by and the building may have replaced an earlier one, dedicated to Athena Polias, Athena of the city, that was destroyed by the Persians seventy years before.

'People often ask me lots of questions about our Caryatid. Was she based on a real person or did the sculptor simply invent her? We do not know the answer, of course, but it was the custom for the sculptors of the time to use models in their work. So the man who made the statue may have met the Caryatid, made a drawing of her perhaps to help him in his task. The more discerning ask at this point: how or where would the sculptor have met the model? Ladies of the night might have wandered round the streets of Athens but well-born young women – and scholars are unanimous in saying that our young lady was well born, if not actually from a noble family – the respectable kept themselves behind closed doors, rarely venturing out into public view. Our Caryatid has kept her great presence, her air of suppressed authority, a slight hint of feeling herself to be better than others across the centuries since her birth. The most interesting theory – and I have to confess here that it is my own – is that the Caryatid may have been based on one of the aristocratic women involved in the priestly rites surrounding the goddess Athena. Maybe the sculptor asked the priestesses for help in his work on the Caryatids for the new temple.

'The final question may be the most intriguing of all. Was she married? Was there, as it were, a Mr Caryatid? Little Caryatids perhaps, waiting in the wings to weave the robes of the future? Once again, we just don't know. But we do know that it was the custom for the young women involved in the cult of Athena to be married. Children, who knows. But it was one of the principal duties of Athenian womanhood to produce the warriors of the future, the beautiful young men who would serve in her armies or her navies and bring glory to the city of Athena.'

The audience were entranced, except the Bishop. Powerscourt observed that he seemed to be nodding off, only for the black-clad chaplain to nudge him in the ribs with increasing vigour as the lecture went on.

'So let me, in conclusion, ask another question. Why does this Caryatid matter so much? Why should we care about the statue of a marble girl born 2,300 years ago? I will tell you. We care because we took her in the first place. The British Government bought the Elgin Marbles, of which the Caryatid is such a distinguished member, that they should be safe in London, in better care than they would receive if they had been abandoned on some Greek hillside. Care, ladies and gentlemen, does not include theft. We care because, of all the statues that make up the Elgin Marbles in the Elgin Room, the Caryatid is the most complete. Not to put too fine a point on it, she has a head, a body, two legs and most of her arms but not her hands. That amounts to more than the goddesses and the charioteers on the frieze. But we should care for her not just because she is so nearly complete. We should care because she stands at the end of an Athenian century, the fifth century before Christ. She looks back to a glorious past and forward to a less glamorous future. Her grandparents might have fought with Miltiades at Marathon or sailed with Themistocles at Salamis. Her parents may have been present at the high point and finest definition of Athens's glory, Pericles' Funeral Speech over the fallen at the end of the first year of the Peloponnesian War. Members of her family will have watched the plays of Sophocles and Euripides. They will have marvelled at the work of Phidias and his sculptors on the Parthenon. They may have come across the philosophy of Plato. They could have argued with Socrates in the public spaces of the city. The Caryatid speaks to us from that long distant past. She speaks to us of the best civilization man has yet aspired to, one that has been a beacon and a model to past generations as it is for us today and will be again in the future. The Caryatid speaks to all of us of the better selves we might yet become.'

Tristram Stanhope stared at the back of the balcony as he finished his peroration. He waited for the applause. As it came rolling out, and the audience rose to their feet, he raised his arms aloft like a victorious boxer. He was drinking in the applause, storing it up perhaps for inspiration in quieter, less eventful days ahead.

'My goodness me,' Lady Lucy whispered to her husband, 'we certainly got the whole peacock tail on display this evening.'

'Look at the man,' Powerscourt replied, 'I do believe he is getting bigger with all the applause. Maybe he's going to end up twice his normal size like Toad in *The Wind in the Willows*.'

The Bishop was now at the lectern, one hand raised to bring peace to the multitude. He conveyed all their thanks to the speaker.

'And,' he continued, 'I have another happy task to perform this evening. It has fallen to me to act as the Chairman of the newly constituted Caryatid Committee. As of this afternoon, this is a legal entity, thanks to the activities of my two colleagues, Mr Hugo Findlayson of the solicitors Slaughter and May, and Mr William Finch of Finch's Bank.' The two substantial citizens rose to their feet and bowed to the audience.

'The purpose of the committee is to raise funds to act as a reward for information leading to the recovery of the Caryatid. The cathedral authorities of the Greek Orthodox Cathedral in Moscow Road have indicated that they will be happy to join the Committee, as has the

Commissioner of the Metropolitan Police. We pray that the Lord will look kindly on our efforts. After hearing the words of Dr Stanhope I do not have to tell you how important this work is. Stewards will be waiting to take any contributions you may feel able to offer the fund as you leave the hall this evening. Or you can approach the banker or the solicitor here about other forms of payment. And now, ladies and gentlemen, I suggest we close our evening with the National Anthem.'

'Damn, damn, damn!' said Lord Francis Powerscourt. 'Why is everything going wrong this afternoon?' The news had not been good that day in Markham Square. Lord Rosebery had reported in some irritation that nobody at all had replied to his advertisement asking for tenders to move a lot of his statues from one of his homes at Mentmore in Buckinghamshire to another one outside Edinburgh. Did Powerscourt regard this as an accident or a conspiracy? And, Rosebery's note concluded, what did Powerscourt want him to do now?

Lord Rosebery's butler, Leith, had replied to Powerscourt's query about the possibility of sending a Caryatid to America in a transatlantic liner. There were, his note said, dozens of ways in which the statue could have been sent by ship to New York, especially if she was travelling first class.

Inspector Kingsley had called on his way to the British Museum to reveal that they were no further forward with their inquiries into the death of Kostas, the Greek porter at the British Museum who had been run over by a train. The witness who had originally claimed that she thought he was pushed changed her mind later on and said she could not be certain about anything that had happened on the platform any more. She was confused. She did not wish to speak about it again or she would become even more confused. And Inspector Kingsley's bright young Constable Smithson, working his way through the freight records in an obscure outpost of the Great Western Railway at Paddington station, was pessimistic. There were records of the freight containers, hundreds if not thousands of them. But they were never specific about the content. The only entry in that respect was 'Household Goods', nothing more. And that, as the Constable pointed out, could cover a multitude of sins. He told his Inspector that you could have sent the body of the risen Christ through Paddington station in a railway container and nobody would have been any the wiser.

There was a cough at the door. Coughs at the door in Markham Square usually meant only one thing. Rhys, the Powerscourt butler who had served with his master in India, had something to say.

'Gentleman to see you, my lord. He claims to have met you before. The gentleman is waiting in the hall below, my lord. Name of Hudson, John Hudson, representing the *New York Times*.'

Powerscourt looked across at Lady Lucy. 'Hudson?' he asked. '*New York Times*? Ring any bells?' Lady Lucy shook her head.

'Never mind,' said Powerscourt, 'better show him up.'

A well-dressed young man in his early thirties strode into the room and shook hands.

'I can see you don't remember me, Lord Powerscourt. Well, it was some time ago. You came to ask my advice about some paintings of Irish aristocrats that had been stolen from their houses. The ancestors of the Anglo-Irish patricians, to be precise. The pictures seemed to have walked off the walls. I was working for a little gallery off Bond Street at the time.'

'Of course I remember you now,' said Powerscourt, wondering if he himself had changed as little over the years as John Hudson. He rather doubted it. 'How nice to see you again. Have you abandoned the galleries altogether? What made you change jobs to the *New York Times*?'

'Well,' said Hudson, 'I don't think the change is all that great. I've always wanted to write a book about the Renaissance, you see. The gallery took up too much of my time. I thought I would make more progress if I left.'

'And did you?' asked Lady Lucy. 'Are we to see the book in Hatchards quite soon?'

The young man laughed. 'I'm afraid not, Lady Powerscourt. The book is as far from being finished as ever.'

'And what is your role on the *New York Times*, Mr Hudson?' Powerscourt asked. 'Are you one of their London correspondents?'

'Well, I suppose I am.' John Hudson grinned. 'I have this wonderful job title which always impresses people. I'm called European Arts correspondent.'

'That sounds frightfully grand, Mr Hudson,' said Lady Lucy. 'What do you have to do for that?'

'Well, most of the time I stay in London. When there's a major exhibition in Paris or Berlin or Rome I travel there to see them and send back one or two reports. That depends on how I rate the show. It's much cheaper than sending somebody over from New York one exhibition at a time. Mostly I write about what's happening here in London. Rich Americans who read the *New York Times* are always keen to know what's going on in London's art market, who's up, who's down, that sort of thing. One or two of them come to visit me when they're here and ask who or what they should buy.'

'And what do you tell them?' said Powerscourt.

'I make a point of never giving any advice at all. Suppose I told them all to buy French Impressionists and then the market collapsed. I'd have a lot of angry Americans on my doorstep. No thanks.' John Hudson laughed. 'I'm sure you know why I'm here this afternoon, Lord Powerscourt. I've come about the Caryatid, the one missing from the British Museum. I believe you're trying to find her.'

'Ah yes, the Caryatid. I am trying to find her, as you put it.' Powerscourt nodded. 'How very proper, how can I help?'

'Let me put it like this, Lord Powerscourt. I have read some extraordinary things about this damned statue in recent days. They can't all be true. She's been stolen by the same gang of thieves who took the *Mona Lisa* in Paris. The *Rokeby Venus*, possibly the only other work of art the crime correspondents have heard of, probably because she has no clothes on, may be next. The thieves are actually working for a museum in Germany. They've got lots of ancient artefacts over there in Munich and Berlin but can't stand the fact that the British seem to have more and better examples. Envy and jealousy about colonies in Africa transferred in the German mind to that enormous museum in Great Russell Street. Some psychic with Greek connections has brought her back to life and she walked out of the door in the middle of the night of her own accord. Honestly, Lord Powerscourt, I can't send any of that nonsense to the *New York Times*. I'd be fired within the hour.'

'I can see that your readers would not be receptive to

those theories, Mr Hudson. Perhaps they would go down better in the Midwest?'

'Kansas more credulous than Connecticut, Lord Powerscourt? It's perfectly possible. Let me put my position in another way, if I may. We're not meant to have opinions on the *New York Times*, unless we write the leading, articles, and even then it's frowned upon. But I want to see the Caryatid back home in the museum. I want her back as much as you do. Is there anything I can put in my paper that would really help your investigation? I can't print a pack of lies, obviously, but is there something I can do?'

Powerscourt smiled at the young man. His enthusiasm was infectious. Powerscourt had liked him a lot the first time they had met. He had been helpful and discreet in the Irish investigation.

'Let me propose a bargain, if I may, Mr Hudson. Not a bargain like that of Mephistopheles and Faust, but a bargain nonetheless. I will tell you now how the investigation is progressing, on condition that you give me your word that you will never tell a soul, not even your editors in New York, where the information came from. In return, I would ask that you carry out, or ask your colleagues to carry out, a little investigation for me, probably in New York, but certainly on the Eastern seaboard. And that, once again, you would not reveal where the request for the information came from.'

John Hudson didn't hesitate for a second. He rose and offered Powerscourt his hand. 'I'll shake hands on that, Lord Powerscourt. Maybe I'm out of my mind to agree to such a deal before I know what it is, but I'm sure you'll play fair.'

'Let me offer you first of all an account of how the

investigation is going, Mr Hudson. The short answer is that the inquiry, as of this moment, is going absolutely nowhere. We have no idea who took the statue or why. I am working very closely with the police, of course. There are a number of theories, as you would expect, more plausible certainly than the ones you mentioned earlier, but theories nonetheless. Was it a disgruntled member of staff? Or a former member of staff? Did the thieves have a buyer before they carried out the robbery? Was it theft by mail order, as it were? If so, who did the ordering? Were they English or American or French? We have no idea. There is one titbit I can offer you to establish your credentials on this story if you like. Please don't say where the information came from. Are you happy with that?'

'I am, Lord Powerscourt, perfectly happy. I can always say I heard it from a police source. All newspaper editors believe you can buy information from the police for money; not all that much money, usually.'

'What a wicked world it is!' said Powerscourt with a smile. 'Now then. There is, or was, a porter at the British Museum, whose duties and responsibilities will have included the care and observation of the Caryatid. He has disappeared. He was run over by a tube train. It could, of course, have been an accident.'

Powerscourt decided not to mention the large amount of money in the savings account, or the brother who also seemed to have vanished, possibly head first into the Adriatic. Those facts could be brought into play later on.

'Really, I say, that is most interesting,' said John Hudson, whipping out an expensive-looking leather-bound notebook and taking notes very fast. 'I don't believe anybody else has that part of the story. Could I ask you a question, Lord Powerscourt?'

'Of course.'

'Those lines of inquiry you mentioned earlier, disgruntled former members of staff and so forth. I would propose mentioning them without attribution. In other words I could put them down to informed opinion, or sources close to the museum, or close to the authorities – that could be anybody right up to Prime Minister Asquith, for heaven's sake – if that's alright with you?'

'Absolutely fine. Nobody's going to complain about that.'

'Thank you, Lord Powerscourt. Now what can I do to keep my side of the bargain?'

Powerscourt was looking at his most innocent at this moment. He's dangerous just now, Lady Lucy said to herself, extremely dangerous. Watch your step, Mr Hudson. Mind how you go.

'My proposal is this, Mr Hudson. I mentioned before the possibility that the theft was carried out to order, that there was a customer waiting for the Caryatid long before she was stolen.'

'You did.'

'Could that customer be American? By that I mean, a great collector, one of those who buys European paintings or First Folio Shakespeares, or ancient sculptures, you know the sort of man I mean.'

John Hudson whistled softly.

'I see,' he said. 'You think one of these millionaires, never too scrupulous in the business dealings that brought them their millions in the first place, broke one or two more rules to get their hands on the Caryatid? Money no object, obviously, as the European art dealers have been fleecing those people for years.'

John Hudson stared into the fire for a long time. He

began writing names in his pocket book, a list of suspects, perhaps. 'Is it possible?' he asked finally. 'Of course it's possible. I've been sure long before the *Mona Lisa* walked off the wall in the Louvre that something like this might be going on. I tell you what I'll do when I get back to the office, Lord Powerscourt. It's only eleven o'clock in the morning on the East Coast. I'll send a cable to my colleague who covers the arts for the paper in New York. I'll say there's a rumour that a rich American collector has recently spent a fortune buying some top piece of European art. I won't mention a specific painting or sculpture, no Caryatid or anything like that. I doubt if even my friend Franklin will make the connection. If that doesn't work, I can try something else.'

Mephistopheles Powerscourt smiled at the young man. 'That sounds an excellent plan,' he said. 'Welcome aboard, Mr Hudson. I can't tell you our destination but I can certainly promise you an interesting ride!'

12

Johnny Fitzgerald was tired of drinking. Well, that wasn't absolutely true, but he was certainly tired of drinking with the porters and the doormen and the clerks of the London art world. He felt that they had nothing more to tell him about the death of Kostas the porter from the British Museum. All he had gathered in his nights in the taverns and the private taverna off Moscow Road was that Kostas had been unusually generous in recent weeks. Before he had always stood his round, but he had been careful. Just before his disappearance he had been more than generous, on one occasion buying everyone an entire bottle rather than just a glass. Beyond that, there was, in Johnny's view, nothing more to learn.

He had been thinking about his visit to Sokratis, the dying Greek with no liver left, and some of the last words he had spoken, 'shades of the prison-house'. He had looked up Wordsworth's poem in a battered book of verse left over from his schooldays. Johnny remembered his English teacher saying that the poem was a lament for the loss of innocence, that children have a heightened and more acute sense of the world, a special vision which passes as they grow older.

> Our birth is but a sleep and a forgetting:
> But trailing clouds of glory do we come
> From God, who is our home:
> Heaven lies about us in our infancy!
> Shades of the prison-house begin to close
> Upon the growing Boy,

Johnny did not think that the late Sokratis would have been a believer in Wordsworth's theory about the death of innocence. Sokratis knew far too many other causes for the loss of innocence in a grown-up world. Johnny felt sure that the phrase ringing in that twirling kaleidoscope of Sokratis's brain was shades of the prison-house. Which prison-house? Who was inside the prison-house? Where was the prison-house? Had Sokratis himself been locked away at some stage of his career?

He packed the book of poetry into his bag. Johnny was going out of London for a few days. Warwickshire, he thought, there should be some fine birds to watch up there, even at this time of year. He dropped a note to Powerscourt saying he was going to the country for a few days. He did not think there was much more to be gained from his drinking activities. He was, however, working on another line of inquiry. He would, of course, tell Powerscourt and Lady Lucy all about it on his return.

Inspector Kingsley had given Powerscourt a list of five unsolved robberies involving major works of art, going back over the past two years. He had now visited two of the victims, Mrs Wilson by the Thames and the Life Guards with their disappearing silver in the Knightsbridge Barracks. He had an appointment the following day in Chiswick, with the Secretary of the Chiswick Literary Society who had organized the visit to the Turner in Norfolk House. Now he was on the last lap of another visit to another house that had been robbed. This time the lost items were pieces of sculpture. Powerscourt wondered if this theft had been a rehearsal for the removal of the Caryatid in the British Museum.

The drive from the main road to Harcourt House, the cabbie informed him, was just over five miles long and one of the grandest in the British Isles. The road twisted and turned through beech and lime trees. As it rose and fell he caught glimpses of strange buildings, outriders perhaps to the main house. Over to his left he could see the round top of what the driver told him was a mausoleum, and behind it the top of an obelisk and what might have been the upper part of a pyramid. On his right a Greek temple sat on top of a lake and a round tower perched on the crest of a little hill. The buildings came in and out of sight, as if in a dream, and then, almost straight ahead through a break in the trees, Harcourt House itself, a giant in English Baroque with a central block flanked by two projecting wings and an enormous dome on top. Xanadu, Powerscourt thought, the stately pleasure dome had come to rest in the county of Oxfordshire in twice five miles of fertile ground.

Simon Cook, eighth Earl of Harcourt, was waiting for him in the red drawing room. Busts of two very different Roman emperors kept watch above the fireplace, the virtuous Marcus Aurelius on the left, the bloodthirsty tyrant Caracalla on the right. The Earl was in his sixties with a few wisps of white hair on his head and a drooping moustache. Everything about the man drooped a little, Powerscourt thought, for he sat slumped in his chair and leant forward at an angle when he walked as if he might fall over at any point.

'Good of you to come, Powerscourt,' he said, rising very slowly to shake his visitor by the hand, 'you're here about the statues, I gather. Just the latest in the long line of things and people that have gone.'

'I don't understand,' said Powerscourt. 'Have there been more robberies, a whole series of break-ins here?'

'No, no, it's not like that really.' The Earl sank further back in his chair. Powerscourt had been warned that the man was eccentric but he had no idea what to expect.

'Wife's gone. Two years ago next Thursday, that was.'

'I'm so sorry.'

'Oh, she's not dead. Not by any means. My bankers keep reassuring me that she's alive and drawing money out of my accounts. She just cleared off and left me. Said she couldn't stand being stuck out here in the middle of nowhere so she pushed off to Antibes. Plenty of people there, I expect. Probably speaking French, mind you.'

'I see.'

'Then there was Magnus.'

'Magnus?' Powerscourt didn't think there had been any Roman emperors called Magnus but he wasn't sure.

'He did die, actually. Last Thursday, that was. He was only sixteen.'

'How very upsetting for you, Lord Harcourt. Life has obviously been difficult. Let us hope things improve from now on.'

'I really loved Magnus, you know. Finest hunter I ever had. I used to have long talks with him in the afternoon.'

Was Magnus a horse? Better wait and see. The Earl

looked up and peered out through his great windows to his parkland beyond. There were a couple of deer in the distance, standing beside a Greek temple.

'Goodness me, Powerscourt.' The Earl seemed to move into a different gear. 'Here am I rambling on about a horse and all you want to know about are the missing statues. Come this way, we'll go through the Great Hall, everybody likes looking at that.'

This was an enormous space, rising seventy feet into the air with a lantern and a gallery at the top with light flooding in through the windows. Mighty columns, heavily decorated, rose up from the four corners and the whole space was painted with scenes of ancient mythology. It was one of the most dramatic rooms Powerscourt had ever seen, a triumph of swagger and style over the more sober conventions of English architecture. The Earl took no notice of his astonishing room. He passed no comment at all as he led the way to a long corridor lined with ancient busts.

'My brother used to call this the Rogues Gallery. God knows why my ancestors wanted to cart all this lot back from Rome or wherever they bought it. They're quite friendly, really, these ancients. Sometimes I spend the morning talking to them. They're good company.'

Powerscourt wondered if the old man lived here entirely alone, except for the trophies of his ancestors and the livestock in his stables. The only people to talk to were the marble gods and dead statesmen lining this corridor and his four-legged friends behind the great house.

'What about the ones that were stolen?' said Powerscourt softly, feeling rather oppressed by the grandeur of the house and the madness of its owner.

'Ah yes,' said the Earl, tottering slowly down the

passage. 'They were side by side, just here. Bacchus, the god of wine, and his helper Silenus who had vine leaves in his hair. My steward said they left because the cellars are almost empty now. We've drunk almost all the wine there was left. Maybe that's why they went.'

'Could one man have carried them both? Both busts, I mean?'

'If he was very strong, he could. But the police thought there must have been at least two of them. Let me show you the other statue that's gone. It was rather bigger than these two.'

The Earl led the way outside to the South Front where a fountain in the lake was sending great shoots of water high into the air. A copy of the sculpture depicting Laocoön and his sons wrestling for their lives sat in the middle of the lake, Laocoön the Trojan priest who warned against accepting the gift of the wooden horse, being strangled by sea serpents that had turned green in the Oxfordshire air.

'There's a sort of sculpture gallery at the very end of this building,' the Earl said, moving very slowly now. 'The thieves came in through a window just ahead of us.'

The gallery stretched along the side of the house, past seven tall windows. Inside were full-length Roman and Greek gods and goddesses, Apollo and Juno, Ceres and Aphrodite. It was Artemis who had gone.

'Seven feet tall she was, Carrara marble, bow in one hand, arrows in a sling over her back, rather beautiful if you like your women as warriors. The thieves must have brought some lifting equipment with them to get her out.'

So, Powerscourt said to himself, could this have been a rehearsal for the British Museum? Were the two busts a blind, a diversionary tactic designed to draw attention from the larger statue, one close to the Caryatid in size? The Earl appeared to be having a long conversation with the Emperor Tiberius.

'Sorry to interrupt, Lord Harcourt, but did the thieves and their equipment and the statue leave through the window?'

'That's what the police thought, Lord Powerscourt. That's about all the thought they did manage, mind you. They have no idea who the thieves might have been. They have no idea where the missing busts and statue are. A couple of properly trained Roman centurions could have done better.'

The Earl gestured to Powerscourt to join him on a small settee at the end of the gallery. 'Tell me this, Powerscourt, why are you here? I know you said you were interested in the thefts, but I don't believe that's the only reason you've come.'

'What makes you think that, Lord Harcourt?'

'Well, if there had been any developments, the police would have come to tell me about them. But they haven't. You have. A fancy investigator come all the way from London? For a minor burglary that happened just over a year ago?'

'So what do you think has brought me here today?'

The old man stroked the thigh of the goddess Hera, one of the losers in the Judgement of Paris. Powerscourt thought his host dipped in and out of normality like an old watch that stops and starts for no apparent reason.

'It's that Caryatid, isn't it,' he said, 'the one that was taken from the British Museum. You've come to see if the robbery here was the same sort of thing.'

'You're absolutely right, Lord Harcourt. I'm most impressed by your insight. Tell me this, did any unusual

172

people come to visit the house in the months before the robbery?'

'Unusual people come to visit this house all the time, Lord Powerscourt. I sometimes think this place acts as a magnet for the unusual from all over the world. Architecture students, they call themselves, some of them. Then there are the self-styled lovers of classical antiquity, they're often quite mad.'

Coming from the Earl, Powerscourt thought they must have been quite remarkable people, these lovers of classical antiquity.

'Then there are the ones who like visiting other people's houses. They tell you that your lake isn't as good as the lake at Blenheim or the North Front isn't a patch on Chatsworth. They probably come from humble semi-detached houses, four small rooms and an outside privy by the railway lines, these people, but they live out fantasy lives in what's left of our stately homes.'

'Would you say any of them might have been thieves, or acting for thieves? That they had come to take a good look at the place and make their plans?'

'God knows, Lord Powerscourt. I had a great lecture from the local Chief Inspector about security here. He seemed to think the place should be like the Tower of London, Beefeaters certainly, ravens maybe, locks, bolts, bells all over the place. People always assume you've got plenty of money if you live in a home like this. It'd probably be cheaper to stay in a permanent suite at the Savoy than here, roofs leaking, plaster falling off the walls, taxes going up all the time, death duties waiting for you round the last corner.'

'There wasn't anybody who seemed to take a particular

interest in the statues that have been stolen, was there? Somebody who lingered over Artemis, maybe?'

'I'd be damned careful about lingering over that Artemis myself. The short answer is I simply don't know. You don't imagine that I loiter about the corridors, waiting to engage the visitors in conversation, do you? I retire to my private apartments when the invasion starts and I don't come out until the housekeeper rings the bell to tell me the coast is clear. Imagine having to talk to those people! It would be too dreadful.'

'And your housekeeper didn't mention anything?'

'Certainly not.'

Powerscourt felt he had outlived his welcome. Maybe the Earl would disappear any moment and retire to his private apartments.

'This has been most useful, Lord Harcourt. I'm most grateful to you and I have enjoyed seeing your beautiful house. I shall, of course, let you know if anything comes up.'

'You won't find the bloody Caryatid here I tell you. I wish you God speed in your quest, Lord Powerscourt.'

As he made his way along the South Front back to the main entrance, the Earl appeared to be engaged in another conversation, this time with Aphrodite. Powerscourt felt she might be more interesting than the Emperor Tiberius. And, like her fellow goddess and contestant in the Judgement of Paris, Hera, the Oxfordshire Aphrodite was showing a great deal of thigh.

The schoolteacher in the little village on the edge of the Brecon Beacons knew that things were not going his way. Ever since he had helped concoct the cover story for the statue that was taken away to Bristol his luck had run out. The money had been useful, of course, but that had long gone. He had been forced to sell the tickets for the rugby internationals to the highest bidder in the Green Dragon late one Saturday night. He had wept on his way home. Wales had only lost 8–0 to England the year before and there were high hopes for greater success this season.

Part of the problem was that he was the root cause of his own misfortunes. The schoolmaster knew that he was fortunate in his position. Thirty or forty miles to the south the only jobs to be had were down the mines, one of the worst paid and most dangerous jobs in the country. Carwyn did not come home with his clothes and features stained black with dust. His lungs were not being damaged by years of working underground. His trouble was that he could not keep hold of money. It slipped through his fingers. It poured out of his hands. He was generous to his wife, he was generous to his children, he was generous to his parents. Sometimes he felt that his debts would simply overwhelm him and he would be swept away on a sea of bankruptcy. Every New Year he made resolutions, of keeping weekly accounts of everything spent, of setting strict limits on his expenditure, but it was no good. By the middle of January he was back where he started.

English papers did not reach the valleys on a regular basis. Sometimes the local library in the nearest town would have old copies of *The Times* but the supplies were not regular. One day Carwyn saw a story about the disappearance of the Caryatid from the British Museum. This particular report gave details of the reward for information to be given by the newly formed Caryatid Committee and an account of the speech given by Tristram Stanhope. As he walked up the hill to his little cottage he suddenly remembered the statue that had been sent off to Bristol. He recalled the secrecy that had attended its departure, with the undertaker telling him firmly to keep his mouth shut at the wake in the Green Dragon. He wondered if the authorities knew what had been going on here in the Brecon Beacons, the strange hammering noises that had come from the cave and the huge barns, the rumour that there were foreigners living in the caves where they could not be seen until they too disappeared. He wondered what they would say if he told them. It was in the morning break at school the next day that the idea came to him. There might not be any money to be made from telling the authorities what he knew. That would be his civic duty. But would there be money to be made from threatening to tell the authorities? Blackmail was not a word that appealed to the schoolteacher. He preferred to think of it as tribute, monies due to him for services rendered, services that might as well consist of staying silent as any other form of duty.

The undertaker, he had been the principal figure in the affair of the statue for the New World. The undertaker, had, after all, invited him to join the conspiracy and paid over the money and the other bribes. Carwyn's letter was quite short. He did not say that he was short of funds. The undertaker would probably know that already, as he would certainly know that the schoolteacher's wife was pregnant again. Carwyn Jones's main point was contained in a question. Could it be that the statue in the coffin was actually the Caryatid stolen from the British Museum? And would he be right in thinking that the elaborate legend he had helped to concoct was totally false, a cover for the export of a national treasure? Would the undertaker and his colleagues make it worth his while to remain silent on this point? If not, he would have to take his concerns to the police. Sergeant Prosser in Ebbw Vale, after all, was his first cousin, twice removed.

13

The secretary of the Chiswick Literary Society did not actually live in Chiswick. Martin Boyd's home was a small late Victorian house in the streets off Brackenbury Road in Hammersmith. But he worked in Chiswick, as an English teacher in the local secondary school. Shakespeare, he informed Powerscourt, was the great love of his life. His own wife, he admitted, as he showed his visitor into the little sitting room on the ground floor, claimed that he loved the Bard more than he loved her.

'Never mind Shakespeare for now,' he said, 'you said in your note you wanted to talk to me about the Society's visit to Mrs Wilson's house eighteen months or so ago. The place with the Turner? Is that right?'

'That is correct, Mr Boyd. There are certain questions arising from the theft of the painting which took place some months after your visit. Do you remember how many people went to Norfolk House?'

'I have thought about that, Lord Powerscourt. I have here the little book where I keep notes of the Society's events. I have to write a report on our activities for the members at the end of the year, you see.'

'And what do your records tell us?'

The page was already marked. The secretary obviously believed in doing his homework. 'There were fifteen of us, including the hosts,' he said. 'Mr Wilson gave a most illuminating talk about the picture. Mrs Wilson gave us tea, it says here, with some splendid cake. We left about a quarter to five. The Turner was so peaceful and it was good to see it so close to where it was painted.'

'Forgive me, Mr Boyd, were all the people who went to the Wilsons' house known to you?'

The teacher consulted his book once more. 'Williams was there, Cook, Ferguson, Smith, the other Smith with the spectacles, Richards, Hall, Peters, O'Malley, Cameron, I knew all of those quite well. Most of them have been members of the society longer than I have.'

'And the other two? I think you said there were fifteen altogether.'

'Well, I have made a note of them too, I see. One of them is described as the thin young man from the bookshop. We have a very good bookshop in Chiswick. The thin young man is still there.'

'And the other one?'

'I have put him down as the bald man with the posh voice. That's all I've got. No name, I'm afraid.'

'Can you recall how he came to be there? How did he know you were going to see the Turner?'

'I remember now, he said he'd heard of it from a friend of his who is also a member but couldn't make the visit to Norfolk House. Do you know, I don't think he gave me the name of his friend at all. You don't suppose he was making it up, do you, Lord Powerscourt?'

'Your guess is as good as mine, Mr Boyd. Could you describe him at all?'

178

Boyd paused and stared at the lines of Shakespeare plays that sat on his bookshelves. Powerscourt thought they had been arranged in order of composition but he couldn't be sure. Boyd scratched the back of his head.

'Average height, bald, as I said. He was wearing a dark blue suit, I think. I can't remember anything about the shirt or the tie, I'm afraid. Black shoes, well polished, I remember that for some reason.'

'And his voice? Was there anything remarkable about that?'

'He was well spoken, Lord Powerscourt. I would have said that he enjoyed a position of some authority, if you know what I mean. He didn't sound like "the whining school-boy, with his satchel And shining morning face, creeping like snail Unwillingly to school." He was more like a man of the world.'

Boyd looked at his Shakespeares once more. 'I know what he sounded like, Lord Powerscourt. He sounded like a man who would be at home in clubland, leaning on the fireplace in the Garrick, taking port with his friends in the Carlton, that sort of man.'

'I see,' said Powerscourt. 'And tell me, how did he behave in Norfolk House with the Wilsons? Was there anything remarkable there?'

'Nothing at all, except that he seemed very knowledge-able about the Turner. He asked Mr Wilson if it was a companion piece to the Mortlake Terrace view in New York. I remember wondering how on earth he knew that. Unless—' Boyd looked as he had been visited by a flash of inspiration '—unless he knew all about art; maybe he was a critic or a connoisseur.'

Or a thief, Powerscourt said to himself. Here in Hammersmith there were lumps of pure gold.

'Anything else you can remember, Mr Boyd? Your information is most useful, I must say.'

'Thank you, thank you very much, Lord Powerscourt. I don't think there is anything else. His hands were rough, unlike the rest of him which was very smooth, if you see what I mean. As if he'd been doing a lot of gardening or digging in his spare time. It's probably nothing.'

'You've been more than helpful, Mr Boyd. May I wish you and your society every good fortune in future. I am most grateful to you.'

As he headed back towards Chelsea, Powerscourt wondered about a bald man who might have come from the art world with roughened hands. Martin Boyd wondered why he had forgotten to ask the one question all the members had urged on him. Why had Powerscourt come? Why the interest in a visit to a painting that had been stolen so long ago? Had it been found at last?

A bald man, well spoken, who knew a lot about art. Powerscourt asked himself how many of those were walking the streets of London? A dead man who might have been pushed under a tube train. Got to go to the High City. A broken statue in the waters of a Greek harbour which might or might not have been the Caryatid. The Isles of Greece. Shades of the prison-house. The Caryatid connection was proving elusive, to say the least. Powerscourt was on his way to see a painter who might help him identify the bald man. Lord Rosebery had effected the introduction and the appointment.

'He knows everybody in the London art world, Francis. He knows all the rich patrons – he's painted portraits of most of them and many of their wives and mistresses for God's sake. He's even done a portrait of me. He studied in Paris in his younger days so he's probably well aware of the latest developments in the theft of the *Mona Lisa*. And he travels regularly to his native country of America so his expertise straddles the Atlantic. I can't think of a better brain to pick than that of Josiah Wills Baker.'

The great artist lived in a huge house in Eaton Square with a studio running the entire length of the first floor. He greeted Powerscourt in his drawing room one floor below, the walls lined with some of his earlier compositions. He was in his seventies now, the hair and beard that had been such a distinctive feature in his younger days now snow white.

'Good of you to come and see an old wreck like me, Lord Powerscourt. Any friend of Rosebery's is welcome here. Forgive me if I remain seated. It's my eyes, they're going. They've nearly gone, come to think about it. So I might be able to get up but I'm not sure about sitting down again. I might miss the chair and end up on the floor.'

'I'm sorry to hear about your eyes, Mr Baker. And I'm most grateful to you for sparing me your time this morning.'

'Time,' said Baker with a bitter laugh, 'time is the one property in this world of which I have a surfeit. If you can't see, you can't paint. If you can't paint, after a lifetime devoted to the study and practice of art, your reason for living seems to have gone away. And there are no signs that it will come back. However, let there be no self-pity in my house. Rosebery tells me you are investigating the theft of the Caryatid from the British Museum. How can I be of service?'

Powerscourt gave the old man a brief history of his involvement, the Greek porters at the British Museum, one killed under a train, the other one vanished in the Adriatic, the fallen statue in the harbour at Brindisi, his visits to the houses with the unsolved thefts and the mysterious visitor to the Turner in Norfolk House, described as bald and well spoken by the Secretary of the Chiswick Literary Society.

Josiah Wills Baker's sight might have been fading fast. His mental powers were not.

'Would I be right in thinking that you suspect this bald person may have been conducting a reconnaissance on the painting? Collecting information that would enable him or his associates to steal it?'

'You would be right, Mr Baker. Absolutely right. One of the things I would like to ask you about is this. I know it is a very long shot. Have you any idea who this bald man, age about forty, might be? Even a list of possibilities would be useful.'

'I fear that's rather a tall order, Lord Powerscourt. I've painted a couple of bald men in my time, both too old for your purposes, I fear. Far too old. It's always difficult to get the light right on the bald patch itself. It's like painting a boiled egg in a spotlight.'

The old man looked round at the paintings lining his walls. Delightful young girls played in a garden with flowers. Important statesmen stared out of the frame with an air of great authority. Grand patricians stood in front of their pillared halls resplendent in the Order of the Bath or the Order of the Garter. Groups of children were draped around an empty living room in tribute to Velasquez's *Las Meninas*. Rosebery had told him that Wills Baker held the record for the most portraits painted of members of one family. He had produced twelve separate portraits, man, wife and all ten children for a leading London art dealer.

Powerscourt suddenly realized that the old man couldn't see any of his own work hanging in this room any more. They must be mere blurs on what was left of his sight. *Sic transit gloria mundi.*

'We know he was never seen again at any meeting of the Chiswick Literary Society. Nor has he been seen again in Chiswick itself.'

'Maybe we could look at the thing in another way, Lord Powerscourt. Why would anybody want to steal the Caryatid? Insanity? A rather special kind of insanity would be needed to work out the organization and logistics of such a theft. They rather suggest to me a logical criminal with a definite plan, not some strange eccentric with visions and voices in his head.'

'Could you sell her? Who would want to buy a statue you could never display? Surely all the art galleries in the world would report you to the British Museum immediately?'

'They would, they would indeed. But they aren't the only people who might want her. Let's try to think of the collectors who might be happy to part with their money for a Caryatid. Years ago now I painted a couple of portraits for a lord and a lady with a fifty-room mansion in Berkeley Square. Fifty rooms! Think of it! But that was just the start. Their house in Yorkshire, sitting right on top of a coalfield, had 365 rooms, one for every day of the year. And a man whose full-time job it was to circumnavigate this place every day winding the clocks when their time came, once a week or a fortnight. That took him all day every day of the week. You could hide any number of Caryatids in there. Or in any of the other great houses with more rooms than people.'

'But what would you charge? Surely you couldn't ask

for a lot of money for something you couldn't even show to your friends?'

'You might be right and you might be wrong there, Lord Powerscourt. I rather suspect you're wrong. Pretend I'm the salesman, and you're the buyer. Not only am I offering you a rare example of a classical Greek statue, among the most famous in the world, but think of this. You are the only person in the country who will be able to look at her. She is yours, yours alone, to adore, to wonder at, to fall in love with, who knows. There's just you with that special privilege, like the lovers who want to lock their lady away so that nobody else can even see her. That's worth a penny or two.'

'Dollars?' asked Powerscourt. 'Dollars too?'

Wills Baker smiled. Powerscourt saw that his teeth, like his eyesight, were almost gone. 'I should say. Many of these millionaires are pretty secretive fellows, as you know. I've painted enough of them, God knows. They pay very badly, did you know that? They all try to get the lowest possible rate and then you almost have to send for the bailiffs to get the money out of them when you've finished. I've often thought of writing an article about it for the art magazines. But I can just see some of them lapping up the secrecy, deriving a great deal of pleasure from it. Not only can you see her, but none of your fellow millionaires can. They're losers. You're not. You've got the Caryatid all to yourself.'

'How much money are we talking about?'

'God knows, Powerscourt. A lot of money. A Caryatid, like the stolen *Mona Lisa* from the Louvre, is priceless.'

'What else do you think might have happened to her, Mr Baker?'

'Ransom perhaps? That's a possibility. She could be

a hostage. Even then she would be worth a great deal of money. Think of the crowds flocking to see her when you announce she's come home again! I know the British Museum doesn't charge for admission as a rule, but I'm sure it could get round that. Put the Caryatid in a special section with lots of security men. Say the cost of guarding her is so high you have to make a small charge for people to come and see her. Exceptional circumstances for an exceptional work of art. You and I could write the announcement in five minutes.'

Powerscourt wondered if it was time to go. The old man was looking tired, as if the discussion about the Caryatid had worn him out. The eyes looked blanker than when he had arrived.

'Could I ask one last favour, Mr Baker?'

'Of course.'

'I'd like you to think about this affair. Not only who the bald man could be, but the whole question of who might want to buy the Caryatid. Could you do that? I could come back at the same time next week, if that would suit.'

'I'd be delighted to help. It'll be a change to think I've got something to do. I've just got one word of advice for you, as you go about your business.'

'What's that, Mr Baker?'

'It's this. However unlikely your conclusions are in this affair, don't be concerned. The art world is capable of the most extraordinary surprises. Things happen that you could not possibly imagine. I look forward to seeing you next week.'

The twins liked trains. They liked sitting by the window and watching the world go past. They liked trams too. Sometimes when they had nothing better to do, they would take the top floor of the number 27 up to Trafalgar Square and back, just for the ride.

Richard and Robert Haskins were identical. You could have swapped the dark brown hair and the grey eyes and the thick legs over and nobody would have noticed the difference. People said that their trouble must have started at birth. Some people claimed that they had been born with some sections of their brains missing. Others said they had been cursed in their cradle. The God-fearing and the teetotal believed their troubles stemmed from the fact that both of their parents drank more gin and whisky than was good for them.

School did not suit the twins. They learnt to read and write with great difficulty. They were never likely to find a job in insurance or banking where numbers counted for so much. For a time they worked as building labourers, but that work didn't suit their temperament. They were bored too easily. Walls or windows that were meant to be completed by the end of the day were left unfinished. They tried to join the Army but the military wouldn't have them. 'Mentally defective' was the comment scribbled on the side of an assessment form by the recruitment staff.

Richard and Robert found their true vocation by accident. Even as small boys they were always fighting, not each other, but against anybody who crossed their path. As they grew older their reputation grew so that people all over Deptford knew that it didn't pay to interfere with the Haskins twins. In that part of London it was inevitable that they would come into contact with the criminal underworld one day. During a particularly brutal episode of gang warfare one of the leaders appointed them as his private bodyguard. He paid quite well. Then he realized that the twins might be more use to him in an offensive rather than a defensive capacity. He sent them out to do battle with his enemies. One broken nose, one bruised wrist later, the twins returned from the field, their foes nursing broken bones, broken teeth, broken arms. The gang leader realized what nobody else had seen before. The twins liked violence. They enjoyed inflicting pain like other people enjoyed chocolate or roast beef. As the gangster prospered and became respectable, his income from protection rackets and gambling houses growing ever larger, the twins prospered with him. After one particularly horrible beating nobody refused to pay for a year and half.

The train was well out of London now, passing through the bare countryside on its route to the West Country. The twins were happy to wait. They knew that their final destination was somewhere in South Wales. They had been given the name of the station and the time they were due to arrive there. They had been told they would be met at the station.

'It's really quite remarkable, Lucy, I never knew it until today.' Lord Francis Powerscourt was sitting in his favourite armchair by the fire in the drawing room in Markham Square, inspecting an old catalogue from one of London's leading art auctioneers that had arrived in the post that morning.

'Knew what, my love? I don't understand.' Lady Lucy was reading a long letter from one of her great-aunts who was housebound now in her cottage in the Peak District and spent her time composing longer and longer letters to her relations.

'Why, paintings have records, rather like houses. When

you buy a house you may end up with the legal titles of all those who had it before. Turner's *Mortlake Terrace, Early Summer Morning*, the twin of the Hammersmith Turner, has a pedigree like a racehorse. I wondered if any of the details might help us in our inquiries. I know it's a long shot, but we could do with one or two long shots at the moment. Twelve years after Turner painted it, *Mortlake Terrace* was sold for eighty-four pounds to somebody or some firm called Allnutt, who were probably dealers of some sort. Allnutt mean anything to you, Lucy?'

'Nothing at all. Eighty-four pounds doesn't seem very much money. Don't paintings start to grow more valuable the older they are? My aunt who claimed to know about art told me that Old Masters cost so much precisely because they were old. Who ever heard of a Young Master, she used to say. Turner was still alive in 1838, wasn't he? How long before the *Terrace* was sold again?'

'It says here in brackets, as if they're not quite sure, that the picture belonged to a painter called Fripp. At any rate it was sold in 1864 and ended up with Agnews the art dealers. That's no use to us at all.'

'How much did it sell for this time?'

'Well, it's really begun to take off now. It went for £1,102 10s, then it doubled in price in ten years and was sold to a man or firm called Price for £2,200 ten years later. Do you have any thoughts on the Price person, Lucy? Price relatives in rural seats?'

'None that I can think of, I'm afraid. Didn't you say that the painting is now in New York, Francis?'

'I did. It went through a New York dealer called Knoedler for £13,230 three years ago and ended up with a rich industrialist called Frick, Henry Clay Frick.'

'Can people go and see it? Could some thief have

passed by one day and realized that the sister painting would be worth a fortune?'

'I don't think so. Not unless he was a friend or relation of Mr Frick's. And Mr Frick himself is so rich that he could afford to buy the sister painting for an enormous sum and hardly notice. He's one of the richest millionaires in New York, but I can't see him organizing a break-in at the house in Hammersmith, I really can't. It's all very interesting, the life and times of *Mortlake Terrace*, but I can't see how it helps us. There is one interesting fact, mind you.'

'What's that?'

'Well,' said Powerscourt proudly, 'if you had held on to the painting all the time, from 1838 to 1908, your investment would have gone up by a factor of 157. That's your one pound seventy-four years ago turned into one hundred and fifty-seven pounds today.'

Lady Lucy looked at her husband suspiciously. 'Did you work that out yourself, Francis?'

'Work what out?'

'All that one hundred and something times whatever it was. I don't think you did, I really don't.'

'Oh ye of little faith,' said Powerscourt, 'how sharper than a serpent's tooth to have a thankless wife.'

'But you didn't, did you?'

'Didn't do the arithmetic, you mean? Well, no I didn't, actually, now you come to mention it. Thomas did it for me, before he went out this morning. It seemed to take him about three seconds, scribbling on the back of an envelope.'

14

'Please don't tell anybody this, not even your wife. You mustn't tell a soul.'

One hour after the 157 times tables Powerscourt was being rushed to an emergency meeting at the British Museum. Inspector Kingsley looked as though he hadn't slept properly for days. He hadn't yet told Powerscourt the reason for their journey, driven at top speed across the capital by one of the Inspector's sergeants.

'Very well, Inspector. You have my silence. Does what you want to say have to do with the Caryatid?'

'Not directly, no.'

'What do you mean, not directly?'

'I'm going to resign, that's what I mean. I've decided.'

'What do you mean? Today? Tomorrow? Next week?'

'Oh, I'm not going to do anything as drastic as that. Once this case is over I'm going to leave and start afresh. I'm going to write my letter of resignation this evening and hand it in later. I've talked it through with the wife.'

'Could I ask about the reasons, if they're not too private?'

'You can, of course you can. I feel I've failed in this

case. That's just the start. I can't help thinking about that poor Greek man smashed to bits under the train. If I'd solved the case, maybe that wouldn't have happened. I'm sure there are going to be more deaths before the end of this affair. I can feel it in my bones. I don't care about everyday crimes, burglary, fraud, gangland fights. It's the deaths I can't stand.'

Powerscourt remembered the despair in Inspector Kingsley's voice when he had talked about the strain of conducting three murder inquiries in a row. He felt that a diversion might be the best course for now.

'I'm sure we could talk about your resignation later this evening. Perhaps we could have dinner together. But just for now could you explain why we are going at Derbywinner speed across London to the British Museum?'

'Sorry, my lord, of course. I have been too wrapped up in my own affairs. It's Deputy Director Ragg. He's running out of patience. He may be running out of sense. You remember we advised him not to go and meet that man who might or might not have been a blackmailer? The one who claimed he wrote his letters from the Ritz?'

'I certainly do. Has the man from the hotel turned up? Carrying a large Gladstone bag to put the fifty-pound notes in?'

'Not quite. It's still pretty bad though. Ragg wants to set up a meeting.'

'With the blackmailer?'

'With the blackmailer.'

'God in heaven! Has he lost his wits?'

'We're just about to find out, Lord Powerscourt. Unless I am very much mistaken, the next turning leads us into Great Russell Street and the British Museum. Ragg is

191

waiting for us. If we cannot persuade him otherwise, he says he will send a note to the Ritz first thing after lunch and suggest a meeting this evening.'

'God help us all, Inspector. That's all I can say. God help us all.'

The Deputy Director of the British Museum, Theophilus Ragg, did not look like a man who had lost his wits. He looked as though he had been wrestling with a thorny problem for a long time. Now he has found his answer and the decision has set him free.

'Good of you to come, Lord Powerscourt. I thought our friend the Inspector would bring some reinforcements. I know I am going against your advice. Would you like me to go through the reasons for my decision? I presume you know what it is? Good. I have to tell you, my mind is quite made up.'

'I'd be honoured to hear your reasons, Mr Ragg,' said Powerscourt. 'Please carry on.'

'Thank you. I think it would be useful if I touched on the different responsibilities the three of us face in this matter. For you, Inspector, this is a matter of professional pride, a case to solve, a theft to be cleared up and taken off the books of the Metropolitan Police. For you, Lord Powerscourt, you have very kindly agreed to investigate this robbery for a fee. That is perfectly proper. Securing the return of the Caryatid for you is a matter of honour, a badge of success. Like the Royal Canadian Mounted Police, I believe, you both like to say that you always get your man. Success for both of you is the same. But failure is, I suggest, rather different for the two of you than it is for me. The public will forget the theft of the statue in a couple of months. It will be replaced in the newspapers and the popular imagination by another set of stories and scandals we do not yet know. You will be at work on other cases, solving other crimes. A few people may remember that the Caryatid was never recovered, but you both have long and successful careers behind you. This affair will be just a pause in a long trajectory of professional achievement. After all, who can recall the names of the detectives who failed to catch Jack the Ripper? Do you follow me so far, gentlemen?'

'Perfectly,' said the Inspector.

'Clear as day,' added Powerscourt.

'Good,' said Ragg, smiling a wintry smile at his visitors. Powerscourt had been watching Ragg's right hand, twirling a fountain pen round and round as he talked. 'But for me, I think, the position is rather different. You both come from institutions quite separate from the British Museum. I am, for the moment, in charge of this ancient body. It is my responsibility to bring the Caryatid home. By that yardstick I shall be judged, in this life at any rate, if not in the next. As long as ships sail the oceans people will remember that the Captain of the *Titanic* was called Edward Smith. If the Caryatid does not come home future generations will always remember me as Ragg, the man who lost the Elgin Marble and couldn't get her back.'

The Deputy Director paused to take a pinch of snuff. 'I know that you two gentlemen think little of this purported blackmailer.'

Powerscourt smiled to himself at the words 'purported blackmailer'. It was good, very good. He would tell Lucy about it later.

'You both believe,' Ragg went on, 'that it would be unwise and unhelpful to open negotiations with him. I have to tell you that I have given the matter considerable thought and I disagree with you, I disagree with you very strongly. It is my responsibility to do everything I can to bring the Caryatid back. I would be failing in my duty if I did not do whatever I think is necessary to secure her return. I know your objections, gentlemen. I reject them. My mind is made up.'

With that, Theophilus Ragg put his cap on his pen and leaned back in his chair.

'Surely you must realize—' Inspector Kingsley sounded as if he were talking to a small child '—that we have no way of knowing if the man from the Ritz is the real thief or not? That he could be just a common blackmailer? And what are you going to do when he asks you for £150,000 or whatever figure comes into his head?'

'I do not regard the question of money as relevant at this point,' Ragg replied. 'My first duty is to make contact with this man. I hope his address remains the same.'

Powerscourt thought the Deputy Director's statement about the money not being relevant was strange, to say the least. What could be more relevant, in this mercenary age, than £150,000? Then a thought struck him with the force and speed of a lightning bolt. Perhaps the money didn't matter because the Deputy Director knew where he could get his hands on it.

'Mr Ragg,' Powerscourt began, choosing his words carefully and looking Ragg directly in the eye. His gaze was not to leave the Deputy Director's face during the rest of the conversation. 'Let me put a suggestion to you, if I may. The money always seemed to be an obstacle, a very considerable obstacle, when we talked about this in the past. Now your position seems to have changed somewhat. The money, you say, is not relevant. Is that because you have found a way of putting your hands on £150,000 at short notice? There are, in my view, only two ways you could have secured a guarantee of such a considerable sum. One would be a very rich benefactor. I rather doubt that, myself. Rich benefactors might put up a great deal of money to buy another Caryatid, one that could take physical shape in the museum here in a special room named after the benefactor. I doubt they would hazard their wealth on the gambler's throw of meeting a man who might have nothing in the foyer of the Ritz.'

Theophilus Ragg was looking slightly uncomfortable now. The top was off his pen once more and he was drawing lines on his blotter.

'I put it to you, Mr Ragg. You have been to the Government. An acting director of the British Museum always has access to the Prime Minister in Number Ten Downing Street. Come to that, he also has access to the Chancellor of the Exchequer in Number Eleven Downing Street. In this case maybe he has a meeting with both of those gentlemen. They say the Government will pay the blackmailer, however much that takes. The true figure may never be disclosed, of course, it will be smuggled away in the Treasury accounts for years to come, but the Government will foot the bill. How's that, Mr Ragg?'

The Deputy Director looked carefully at the crooked lines on his blotter. He blinked a couple of times. Powerscourt thought the man was too honest to tell lies about such a delicate subject.

'Very well. I shall not insult your intelligence by fobbing you off with a pack of lies. Whatever financial and fiduciary arrangements the British Museum enters into with His Majesty's Treasury must remain confidential, and rightly so. But it would be fair to say that such an undertaking has been given, that the Government will underwrite any subventions necessary to secure the return of the Caryatid. I propose to write to the Ritz Hotel – I am not familiar with the building, but I am given to understand that it is situated on Piccadilly, not far from Fortnum and Mason – immediately after lunch today. Do you follow me, gentlemen?'

'Yes,' said Powerscourt.

'Could I ask if you intend to proceed to any such meeting alone? If you do, I have to tell you that the Metropolitan Police cannot guarantee your safety. We have a duty to protect the citizens of the capital. Our duty lapses if the citizens disregard the advice they are given about their own security. Goodness, man, we have had people watching after the safety of your wife and children twenty-four hours a day since the start of this affair. Are you going to throw all that away? Surely it would make more sense to go to a meeting if you must, but one where we can take reasonable steps to keep you safe and, if possible, to apprehend the blackmailer?'

'We shall have to see what demands the blackmailer may wish to place on any rendezvous. From our earlier correspondence I would presume that he will take every step to secure his own future. If you think about it, gentlemen, the blackmailer needs to keep me alive after our first meeting. Otherwise how is anybody to know when and where the exchange of specie for the Caryatid is to take place?'

'I don't like it one little bit,' said Inspector Kingsley, 'I cannot give such a plan my blessing. I shall have to seek an urgent meeting with the Commissioner. I expect he will be in touch with you this afternoon.'

'I can't say I like it either, Mr Ragg,' said Powerscourt. 'But I do respect your courage, although I agree with the Inspector about being unable to approve your plans. I think they are rash, and likely to lead to more problems.'

'Thank you both for listening so carefully, and for your advice. Now, if you will forgive me, I have a lunch appointment with the Egyptians. They tell me Rameses the Second needs some care and attention.'

A scowling Inspector Kingsley set off for Scotland Yard. Lord Francis Powerscourt took himself to the foyer of the Ritz Hotel in Piccadilly. Seated inconspicuously behind an enormous vase, his face largely hidden by the pages of *The Times* and an enormous plant, he spent the early part of the afternoon in reconnaissance. That, after all, he reminded himself from his days with the military, was often half the battle.

The twins' first evening in Wales began well enough. The undertaker brought them to the Green Dragon where the schoolteacher Carwyn Jones was waiting. The local beer was stronger than the stuff served in the twins' local, the Highwayman, off Deptford High Street. Though the visitors from London seemed not to know very much about rugby, they seemed to be fitting in very well, even if most of the locals had reverted to speaking in Welsh once the strangers arrived. It was when the twins announced that they wanted a word with Carwyn in private that things began to go wrong.

The undertaker took them to a long outbuilding at the back of his premises where he stored his coffins and other odds and ends. There was one bare light bulb in the ceiling and a couple of wooden chairs left beside the door. The undertaker left them half a dozen bottles of beer and announced he needed to go back to the pub to buy some more supplies. The twins strapped Carwyn Jones into one of the chairs with some rope.

'You've been writing very naughty letters,' said Richard, shaking his head.

'Very naughty letters. Letters that should never have been sent,' Robert agreed.

'I don't know what you're talking about,' Carwyn replied.

'Come, come. We know you've been sending these naughty letters. Why don't you just admit it?'

'No, I haven't,' said Carwyn defiantly. 'I tell you, I don't know what you're talking about.'

'You don't want to make things difficult for yourself now, do you,' said Richard, punching Carwyn's head so he sat slumped sideways in his chair. 'Did you write these letters or not? We wouldn't want to make life even more painful for you, would we, Robert?'

'That would never do,' his brother replied. There was no answer from the chair.

Richard delivered a force eight blow to Carwyn's stomach.

'Next time it'll be your face and all those lovely white teeth you've got.'

There was another deeper groan. Robert pushed the teacher's face back into the upright position.

'All right,' Carwyn said between howls of pain, 'I did write a letter. Just one letter. No more.'

'Is that so? You admit you wrote a naughty letter, do you? Who else did you tell about it?'

'What do you mean?'

Richard punched him quite lightly in the mouth. 'That's just for starters, my little Welsh friend. Next time I'm going to knock your teeth out. I'm just beginning to enjoy myself now. Are you enjoying yourself, Robert?'

'I am indeed. What do you say, schoolteacher?'

'I didn't tell anybody else. That's the truth. Honest.'

'Don't believe you. You'll have to do better than that.'

Carwyn Jones felt he was doomed. This was an East End version of Morton's Fork where you paid your taxes or the King came to stay and ate you out of house and home. If he said yes, they'd beat him up even more. If he said no, they'd beat him up until he said yes.

'I know what, Robert,' said Richard. 'Let's have a cigarette and think things over.'

'Good idea.'

The twins smoked the Pall Mall brand, named after the street with the showroom of the parent company, Rothmans.

'I don't think we're going to offer you one, Mr Jones the schoolteacher,' said Robert, waving his cigarette close to Carwyn's face. 'Naughty boys who write naughty letters don't deserve them, do they?'

'Look at it another way,' said Richard, laughing loudly, 'they could get a cigarette, but not how they expected it.' He stabbed the lighted end into Carwyn's arm. Twice. Carwyn screamed. He kicked out blindly, for although his arms were tied, his legs were not. Quite by accident his boot landed on Richard's leg, on the bony section just below the knee.

The twins lost their tempers at exactly the same time. They threw their cigarettes to the ground and threw the chair over. Both began kicking Jones as hard in the head as they could. Then they took turns to stamp on his face and his private parts. All the while they made a crooning noise, a terrible mixture of anger and pleasure. Jones passed out. He was unconscious long before he died. As they looked at the corpse they had just created, the twins shook hands. They always did that after a murder. They had another cigarette.

'What are we going to do with him now?'

'I know. Let's pop him into one of these coffins lying about the place. Then he won't have far to go.' They began to laugh.

The next morning the twins left very early on the milk train to Cardiff. The undertaker found that his first client of the day was already in place.

200

PART THREE

SHADES OF THE PRISON-HOUSE

A great city, whose image dwells in the memory of man, is the type of some great idea. Rome represents conquest; Faith hovers over the towers of Jerusalem; and Athens embodies the pre-eminent quality of the antique world, Art.

Benjamin Disraeli

15

'Nice of them to leave us a bottle of champagne, don't you think?' Inspector Christopher Kingsley was standing at the tall window of room 107 on the first floor of the Ritz Hotel overlooking Piccadilly. Lord Francis Powerscourt was pacing up and down the room. It was the evening after Deputy Director Ragg sent his dispatch to the blackmailer. Ragg was due to come to the hotel reception in an hour and ten minutes' time to meet the man who might or might not have the Caryatid. The time and the place was all Ragg would tell them, and even that had caused a row, with Inspector Kingsley accusing the Deputy Director of placing his own vanity and reputation above the prospects for the safe return of the statue. Ragg had refused all offers of protection. He insisted that he be allowed to go to the meeting alone and that no policemen should be on duty at the time of his arrival. He had refused to show Powerscourt and the Inspector either his original letter or the blackmailer's reply. The Head of Scotland Yard had been emphatic.

'I don't care how you do it, Kingsley, I couldn't care less really. But we've got to have a presence there. We've got to arrest this blackmailer if we can. And we can't let anything happen to Ragg. Bloody fool must think he's performing heroics at the Siege of Troy or some damned thing. It's bad enough losing a bloody Caryatid for God's sake. To lose a Deputy Director as well would be a catastrophe!'

Less than an hour to go now. Powerscourt was not happy. 'Tell me again, Inspector, if you would, the full disposition of our forces.'

'What you have to remember, my friend, is that there are no policemen here this evening. I felt we had to let Ragg think that he was coming alone. I don't think he'd be a very good liar. Let me see now. There are a number of guests at the hotel, dressed in plain clothes, their Sunday best most of them. There's a sergeant and a constable one floor up, two constables on the third floor and another five spread out all over the upper floors. There's another inspector and a sergeant in a room right at the back in case they try to go out the back way through Green Park. Some clever chap here at the hotel offered to fix up a system of bells like they have in all the rooms here. He said he could even make me a little control panel show-ing which bell was ringing at any given time. I said no in the end because we couldn't work out a system for what one, two or three rings might mean. The chap thought we might get confused. They've put a trainee footman, young and quick, on every floor to carry messages.'

Kingsley peered out through the gap in his curtains once more. 'No sign of Ragg yet. I bet he'll be early but not this early. That's just the guests, my lord. In the lobby there are three police footmen, there's a pair of police waiters in the dining room and an assistant sommelier from Marylebone Police Station who knows as much about wine as I do about the Mohammedans. There are more officers deployed up and down the street and two police cars with drivers who know London well lurking in the side streets. And, I nearly forgot, there are a couple of cyclists hidden away in the streets opposite the hotel.'

One of the young footmen knocked on the door. He came from the third floor. What, the young man panted, were they to do if Ragg and the blackmailer went into one of the rooms on their level? 'Watch and wait,' Inspector Kingsley replied. 'Send immediately for reinforcements. If you do anything rash Ragg might end up dead.'

The ornate French clock by the side of the fireplace said it was a quarter past seven. Fifteen minutes left.

Powerscourt tiptoed to the other great window looking out over the street and stared out through the curtains. It had started to rain. The pavements were glistening in the street lights. The citizens of London pulled their coats tight around themselves and continued their journeys home. Powerscourt thought that action seemed to have revived the Inspector. The urge to resign seemed to have been conquered by a passion for logistics and organization. He hoped it would last.

'I'm very impressed,' said Powerscourt, pulling back from his window. 'It's like being back in the Army hatching plans for a secret night attack. Mind you, I'm still worried that this may all be a waste of time.'

The Inspector checked his watch. 'Ten minutes to go now,' he said, taking up his position by the window. 'I know it could all be a waste of time. But we can't take that chance, can we?'

Powerscourt returned to his sentry station by the other window. Anybody looking at the Ritz very carefully from the other side of the street would have noticed tiny gaps in the curtains all the way up the front of the great hotel. Every floor had its own tiny sliver of light. Down below the rain was falling faster now. It rattled off the street and onto the pavement of the arcade that ran between the front of the hotel and the reception. The porters had greatcoats on now, buttoned up to the throat.

Five minutes to go. 'Damn, damn and damn again!' cried the Inspector. A forest of black umbrellas, adorned with the crest of the Ritz, a lion with an orb in its paw, had shot up, raised aloft by the porters anxious to preserve the health of their guests. All Powerscourt and the policemen on the higher floors could see were the umbrellas outside the front of the building.

'You could commit murder down there and we'd be none the wiser!' The Inspector was kicking the leg of a Louis XIV table very hard. A tinkle from the clock said it was now half past seven. The rain showed no signs of abating.

'Christ, Powerscourt! You must have been in these kinds of situation before! What do you think we should do? Should we all rush downstairs?'

There was another knock at the door. The footman was panting this time.

'Message from the fourth floor, sir. "Can't see for the bloody umbrellas. Please advise."'

'Tell them to sit tight and wait for news,' replied the Inspector.

'You've got men in the lobby, haven't you?' said Powerscourt. 'And all across the ground floor? Charging downstairs like the Light Brigade at Balaclava won't do any good. The blackmailer will take to his heels and run.'

Down below the ritual pavane continued on the pavement outside the Ritz. Taxis would draw up. The porters

206

would rush forward to shelter the guests under their umbrellas. Distinguished visitors would receive an even more obsequious greeting from the Head Porter. People leaving the hotel would be escorted to the waiting taxis or, occasionally, lent an umbrella from the supply held for the purpose in a stand behind the double doors that led into the great entrance hall. Staring down, Powerscourt counted nine Ritz lions on top of the umbrellas dancing about in the half-light. The rain was still spluttering onto the pavement by the arcade and running down the gutters, discreetly tucked into the facade of the building.

At seven thirty-five, according to the later testimony of the porters, a middle-aged man of average height, wearing a dark overcoat and a hat with a very wide brim, made his way out of the hotel and into a passing taxi. The driver, one of the porters reported, seemed to be expecting him. Another man was just visible on the back seat. There was a brief greeting and the taxi drove away. Behind it a black hearse appeared to be having some difficulty. The steering seemed to have gone awry. The vehicle slewed across the road and came to a halt at an angle of forty-five degrees across Piccadilly. A bus, following behind, could not get past. The driver of the hearse climbed out of his seat and ran into the hotel, looking for assistance. Black smoke began to ooze out from the engine, as if some serious mechanical problem was under way. Behind the bus, other drivers and other buses began hooting their horns. After a couple of minutes the traffic jam extended right back to Piccadilly Circus with tributary blockages in the side streets leading onto the main thoroughfare. Further up on the opposite side towards Piccadilly Circus, the Royal Academy, packed with masterpieces of British art, could only watch as the seizure gradually spread to the other side of the street.

It was many hours later in Markham Square before Powerscourt and Inspector Kingsley understood what had happened. The porters were only asked to report on what they had seen at ten o'clock.

'I should have seen it coming, Inspector! God knows, I've planned enough engagements where the trick was to attack from the direction the enemy least expected.'

'You've got to hand it to the blackmailer, I suppose,' admitted the Inspector. 'He had us all looking the wrong way. We thought Ragg would disappear into the hotel, like a rabbit down a hole, and we could catch them in flagrante, as it were. Instead he walks out of the front door and into the taxi he must have sent to collect Ragg. All our plans went up in smoke. Plain clothes men disguised as hotel guests on every floor, waste of time! Police waiters, police footmen, police sommeliers, useless and redundant every one! Half the cars and the cyclists stuck in the traffic jam! Why didn't we think it might all work the other way?'

'You mustn't reproach yourself. I'm as much to blame as you are.' Powerscourt poured the Inspector another glass of whisky. 'I don't suppose your people have told you any news about Ragg? Is he all right, that sort of thing?'

'Sorry. I should have told you. He didn't go back to the Ritz. He didn't go back to the museum. A taxi dropped him off at home shortly after nine o'clock. My man on duty at the house said that there seemed to be a second man in the cab, travelling with Ragg.' Inspector Kingsley checked his notebook. 'Just one thing about the passenger. Nondescript sort of fellow, apparently. Took his hat off as Ragg was getting out. My man thinks, but he's not sure because of the light and the rain, that the fellow was completely bald.'

'The Commissioner of the Metropolitan Police for you, Prime Minister.'

Sir Edward Henry, Britain's most senior policeman, was trying hard to conceal his irritation. He was not cross with the Prime Minister or his Government. He was cross with his own subordinates and most of all with himself for not keeping a tighter watch on events. Kingsley's behaviour he could not condone but the man was young, with a brilliant track record and a reputation as one of the most original detectives in the Force. That was why he had been assigned to the British Museum case in the first place. But the Head of Scotland Yard? What had the man been thinking of? He might not have given his blessing to the Piccadilly operation, but he had not forbidden it and he had not reported it upwards as he was duty bound to do. In a lifetime dealing with the maintenance of rules, of drawing up rules for the behaviour of his men, of suggesting or advising on rules or laws for regulating the behaviour of the general public, Sir Edward had always been sceptical about complete success in these difficult areas. Rules and laws were all very well, he had once told a conference of chief constables, but human frailty would always get through in the end.

The Prime Minister smiled at the policeman. Coffee and biscuits were being served.

'You asked to see me, Sir Edward, on a matter of great urgency. How can I help?'

'The matter is delicate, Prime Minister. It has to do

with the theft of the Caryatid from the British Museum. I believe you know some of the details of the case?'

'That is correct. I have been informed about the matter.'

Sir Edward Henry had a reputation for blunt speaking when he felt it was appropriate. He had always maintained in domestic negotiations with his wife that there were times when it was better to run the risk of offending the person you were speaking to, rather than dodging the issue and hiding in the long grass. This was such a time.

'Forgive me if I have been misinformed, Prime Minister—' there was no hostility in his voice at all '—but I was given to understand that you and the Chancellor of the Exchequer had given your blessing to some preposterous scheme to pay blackmail to secure the return of the British Museum Caryatid. Is that true?'

'What a lot of trouble that elegant young woman has caused us all! It might have been better if Lord Elgin had left her where she was. Don't you think so? Yes, you are quite right, Commissioner. The Chancellor and I did come to such an understanding, let me call it that.'

'I'm sorry, Prime Minister, forgive me, but I believe that was the wrong decision.'

'You may be right, of course you may.' The Prime Minister was famed for his ability to disarm his critics. 'If I can be allowed to speak off the record, as it were, and for your ears only, it was a political calculation. Leave things as they are and the Caryatid may never be returned. God alone knows where the wretched statue is now. But it would be a continual reproach to this administration that prides itself on keeping a firm grip on questions of law and order, as the wretched newspapers keep referring to it. How can the electors feel safe in their beds when the Government cannot even recover a Greek statue seven and a half feet tall? If, on the other hand, the statue were recovered, then the question of how the return was effected will be drowned out in the general rejoicing. Nobody is going to quibble once she is back on her plinth or whatever she stands on in the British Museum. By the way, Commissioner, I have not yet been informed what happened when Deputy Director Ragg had his meeting yesterday evening. I believe you may have some news on that?'

'I have very little to report, Prime Minister. The two men met. They managed to avoid my officers who were disguised as hotel guests and hotel staff in the Ritz Hotel. Both are safe and well. I have, as yet, no knowledge of what was said. Deputy Director Ragg is having a meeting with my inspector early this afternoon. But let me come to the point, Prime Minister. As the senior policeman in the capital, I am asking you to take steps to ensure that the discussions about paying a ransom are closed down, and that there will be no more meetings like the one last night.'

'That is rather a lot to ask for all in one go, Commissioner. Might I ask why?'

'Of course, Prime Minister. We have had a policy in the force for some years now of never paying blackmail. Let me explain. We believe – and the experience of some other European countries bears me out here – that paying blackmail becomes like a virus. Once you start, it is very hard to stop. Consider, if you would, the likely reaction in the criminal fraternity to the news that the return of the Caryatid was secured for £100,000. The thieves who traffic in these kinds of crime are not stupid, not by any means. Word will leak out, it always does. Soon they will have a sort of stock exchange in their minds of the monies the authorities are likely to pay out to redeem some work of art or public figure they may have kidnapped for ransom. Fifteen thousand pounds for a Constable? Forty thousand for a Raphael? Fifty for a Leonardo? Eighty for a real duchess? The National Gallery will be denuded of masterpieces; not all at once for that would bring the prices down, but over time. One a year, perhaps? The knowledge may spread lower down the ranks of the criminal fraternity. Robbery could become a popular pastime, not because the thieves want the furniture or the precious stones, but because they know they can get ready cash to hand it back. You could end up, Prime Minister, having to pay to have your stolen spoons returned.'

'Surely it cannot be as bad as that?'

'I exaggerate, of course, but only to make the point. Once you start paying up for blackmail the road is slippery, the path treacherous. Who knows where it may lead? Refuse to pay and the thieves may still steal – what else are they there for, after all – but they will not think it worth their while to go in for blackmail.'

'Are you sure that it would become known in the criminal fraternity that we had paid a ransom? What happens if the whole business is conducted through an intermediary, somebody whose name neither you nor I need ever know of? Surely that would meet your objections?'

'My objections, Prime Minister, are to do with the paying of blackmail. Whether it is paid by the Chancellor of the Exchequer or the Garter King of Arms or the Archbishop of Canterbury is immaterial. The results will be the same.'

'I see,' said the Prime Minister. 'I am most grateful to you for bringing the matter to my attention. I shall consult with colleagues and let you know what we have decided.'

Instant defeat, instant capitulation, the Prime Minister had decided, would never do. It would be like giving in to the blackmailers. He would disguise his retreat behind the matador's cloak of consultation with his Cabinet. Not that he had any intention of speaking to a single one of them.

'Of course, Prime Minister, I am most grateful for your time.' The Commissioner had played this game often enough to know that an orderly retreat was the most likely course to bring success. Further argument would be futile. He did, however, have one last card to play.

'If I could just make one final point, Prime Minister. I would remind you that Deputy Director Ragg is due to meet my Inspector immediately after lunch.'

'Of course, my dear Commissioner. I haven't forgotten.'

The Headmaster thought his colleague looked quite peaceful. He had heard the details of Carwyn Jones's death from the police and shuddered. As the attendant in the hospital morgue began to pull back the sheet he thought he was going to be sick. But the face he saw was not the battered and bloodied wreck he expected. Somebody must have cleaned him up. Thank God for that, the Headmaster said to himself.

'Yes.' He nodded to the senior policeman. 'Yes, that's Carwyn Jones. I'd know him anywhere.'

Illtyd Williams walked slowly back to his school. He had been a teacher and then head teacher here for nearly forty years. The nearest he had come to violence in all his time there did not have to do with his pupils. The violence came from the terrible accidents at the mines further down the valley where so many of his children had uncles and cousins working. Illtyd could still see the faces of the women standing at the pithead, waiting to see if their man would be the next body brought up to the surface from the killer coal hundreds of feet below.

He knew there was a letter waiting for him in his office. Mrs John the cleaning lady had told him. She also informed him that there was no stamp on it, so it must have been hand delivered, and she thought she recognized the handwriting as that of his deceased colleague Carwyn Jones. Mrs John was waiting for him when he returned and hovering around with her best duster. He knew she was waiting to be told what was in the letter. Illtyd thanked her for her good work and showed her the door.

'Dear Illtyd,' the letter began. 'I think I may have made a terrible mistake.' Carwyn went on to describe his role in providing the cover story for the enormous coffin sent off to Bristol months before. He mentioned the rumours, of men working through the night in the lonely barn beside the entrance to the caves, of extra food being purchased by the undertaker when he had no guests staying in his house. He mentioned his suspicions after reading the London paper that events in the Brecon Beacons might have had something to do with the Caryatid stolen from the British Museum. He mentioned his financial problems, the rugby tickets sold, the roof in need of repair, the extra mouth or mouths soon to arrive, for his wife's family had a long history of giving birth to twins. He confessed that he had written to the undertaker asking for more money to keep his mouth shut. He even mentioned his threat to go to his cousin the policeman in Ebbw Vale and tell him the whole story. Now, in his final sentence, he told his headmaster that he was due to meet the undertaker and a couple of his friends specially come from London to talk things over with him in the Green Dragon in an hour's time.

There was no mention in the letter of what Carwyn expected him to do. Was he supposed to go immediately to the police and hand over the letter? The policeman who told him about Carwyn's death had left little out of his account of the last minutes of his colleague's life, the cigarette burns on the arms, the savage kicking, the stamping on his face. The policeman was sure the two men responsible had gone back to London. What if they came back? When he was a boy, like everybody else, he had been forced to play rugby. Being in the centre or out on the wing he didn't mind so much. It was cold and sometimes you had to stop people getting past you. But then somebody had suggested putting him in the scrum as a second row forward. Illtyd could still remember his fear and the sheer discomfort of sticking your head into the gap between the faces of the front row, other forwards leaning into you from the side and the back, and pushing for all he was worth. Not long afterwards he gave up rugby altogether. He walked over to the window and stared out at the mountains beyond the playground. He thought of Carwyn in his happier days, tramping across the hills, climbing to the top of Cader Idris on a summer's day and exulting in the view of Cardigan Bay stretched out beneath them like an enormous map. He thought of the broken body down in the hospital morgue, kicked to death by killers from another country. He shivered slightly. For the moment, he decided, he would do nothing. He would keep quiet about the letter. He wasn't even going to tell his wife or their children. Maybe, he said to himself, things will be clearer after the inquest.

Theophilus Ragg, Deputy Director of the British Museum, was late for his meeting with Inspector Kingsley and

215

Powerscourt. It was half an hour after the appointed time when he walked slowly into his office and threw his hat and coat onto a chair.

'My apologies, gentlemen. I would have left word if I could. I didn't know I was to be summoned to see the Home Secretary at very short notice.'

Powerscourt thought Ragg sounded tired. He looked like a beaten man. He made it sound as if being summoned to see the Home Secretary was an ordeal like being called upon to meet one's maker, frightening at best, possibly terminal.

'Might I ask what he had to say?' Inspector Kingsley too had an appointment to keep that afternoon, with the Commissioner himself at five o'clock.

'You may indeed, Inspector. You may indeed. I am more annoyed than I can say. Who, after all, is meant to run this museum? The Director and his deputy and their staff? Or the Home Secretary, a man with no experience of running artistic establishments at all? I doubt if he has ever stepped inside this building, now I come to think about it. But this former newsagent dares to tell me what I may and may not do in the course of my duties! It is disgraceful! It's worse than disgraceful! It's probably unconstitutional!'

'Perhaps you could tell us,' Powerscourt asked in his most emollient tones, 'what it is that you may or may not do? Is the Home Secretary proposing to come and reorganize the seating arrangements in the Reading Room? Change some of the galleries round perhaps? Send the Hittites to Assyria and the Assyrians to the basement?'

'Would that he were, Lord Powerscourt. It's not as simple as that. The Home Secretary, speaking, he assured me, on behalf of the Cabinet, told me that it is Government policy never to give in to blackmail. Therefore all negotiations with the purported blackmailer must cease. Therefore our best chance of recovering the Caryatid is gone, swamped by the Home Secretary and his newspapers. It's monstrous!'

'It does seem a little steep to me,' said Inspector Kingsley, 'the Government taking such a high and mighty line on blackmail. It only takes about fifty backbenchers to leap up and down and threaten to withdraw their support for them to change their minds, or commission a policy review as they usually call it. However, I'm not a politician. Ours not to reason why.'

'I can fully understand your irritation, Mr Ragg,' said Powerscourt. 'You have my sympathy. Did the Home Secretary give any idea what caused the change of heart? There were no objections from the Head of Scotland Yard to the meeting at the Ritz yesterday, after all.'

'Nobody said anything, but I rather gathered the shift came from the very top, from the Prime Minister.'

'This only goes to reinforce my feelings about what we were talking about the other day, my lord.' Inspector Kingsley was shaking his head. 'Why should I stay when my actions are rejected by my superiors? I am virtually certain that it was the Commissioner himself who persuaded the Prime Minister.'

Powerscourt thought the meeting was in danger of getting out of control. 'I don't think there is anything we can do about this decision now. I can't see the Prime Minister changing his mind. But I am sure we still have much to learn from the meeting yesterday evening. In our haste to vent our wrath on the Government we have rather forgotten about the Caryatid and the blackmailer. Mr Ragg, could you tell us what happened yesterday evening? Starting perhaps with your collection by the taxi?'

Theophilus Ragg put his head in his hands. He leant forward on his desk. Powerscourt thought he might be going to cry. After a moment or two there was a rustling noise as the Deputy Director searched in his pockets for his snuff. He took a very large pinch and stared sadly at his visitors.

'Forgive me, please, this is all rather difficult.' Ragg took another, smaller, dose of snuff, and stared at his bookshelves. 'Let me tell you something about myself, gentlemen. In my early days I made my reputation in Oxford as an administrator. I was known for my ability to control costs. This involved such life-threatening decisions as whether the cleaning staff should start work at nine or half past, and whether it would be cheaper to have four porters working overtime or to have six on normal hours. On such pillars did my reputation rest. I came here to this great institution where the same skills were required. Should we have separate departments for all the Middle Eastern holdings, or should they all be parcelled up into a single body with one head rather than seven? Should the museum be prepared to lend some of its treasures to other similar institutions? But now, I don't have to tell you gentlemen, I am plunged into high politics. The Government changes its mind about what I believe might be the best course of action. I am confronted with blackmailers. Nothing has prepared me for this, nothing. It is as if a junior officer in the commissariat has been lifted up to field marshal's rank and told to run the entire campaign. I am not fit for this level of responsibility. I am not the right man to have to carry out the necessary actions.'

Powerscourt felt sorry for the Deputy Director. But he knew from his time in the military that the reluctant are often called and that fate does not always wait for the right man to come along.

'When I served in the Army in India, Mr Ragg, I spent a lot of time with a man who went on to become a most distinguished general. He was a colonel then, a colonel of artillery, a gunner. By accident he found himself in charge of a large detachment of foot about to be assailed by a much larger enemy force. I always remember what he said to us before the battle. "We are where we are," he said, "we are who we are, and, a gunner in charge of infantry or no, I am going to do my damnedest to win this fight." And he did. One of his junior officers said to him afterwards, "You are who you are, sir, and you've just won a bloody great victory." Just because you have sailed in calmer waters in the past doesn't mean that you're not fit to command in a storm.'

'Think of those two at Rorke's Drift,' said Inspector Kingsley, 'two young officers, Chard and Bromhead, who'd never fought in a battle. Yet they organized their defence so well with their 150 men that they were able to hold off thousands of Zulu warriors.'

'Come, Mr Ragg, you are who you are and you are where you are. Tell us, if you would, what transpired yesterday evening with the blackmailer.'

They were not out of the woods yet. Ragg put his head in his hands once more. 'I promised the man,' he said finally, 'that I wouldn't tell anybody what had happened between us. I wouldn't say what he looked like or anything like that. I swore. I gave him my word.'

Inspector Kingsley muttered under his breath. He looked as though he were about to fire a salvo or two of his own. Powerscourt thought he might make the point more gently.

219

'My dear Ragg,' he said as mildly as he could. 'Let us consider the facts. We are all engaged on the recovery of the Caryatid. That is the only priority. There was a meeting with the blackmailer. The Prime Minister, we believe, has forbidden any further negotiations with this person. So you are not going to meet him again. It is our duty, your duty, to do everything in your power to further the cause of recovering the statue. That includes knowing all we can about the man who may or may not be a thief or part of a gang of thieves. I suggest you tell us all you know. We wouldn't want another directive from Number Ten Downing Street so soon after the last one.'

Ragg stared at Powerscourt for quite a long time. 'May God forgive me,' he began.

'I'm sure he will,' put in the Inspector.

'There's not very much to say,' Ragg continued. 'He never told me his name. I never saw what he looked like. We didn't go anywhere, you see, not to a house or anything like that. We drove round in that cab until he dropped me back at my house.'

'What did you talk about?' asked Powerscourt.

'He tried to persuade me that he really did have the Caryatid. He said he wasn't going to give me any details of handing over the money until I agreed to do so. He said the statue would be returned the day after the ransom had been collected.'

'But no details of when or where the transfer was to take place?' Inspector Kingsley, practical policeman to the last, planning ambushes and surprise attacks.

'None. You see, I think he was suspicious. He kept his hat on all the time. He kept looking round a lot and checking in the mirror.'

'What was his voice like?' Powerscourt felt the details

were sketchy. He wondered if Ragg was telling them the whole truth.

'Well spoken. He sounded like one of us, really.' Clever criminals always did, Powerscourt thought bitterly.

'And that's it, Mr Ragg, is it? You drove round in a cab, you promised not to tell anybody anything and the man said he would let you know about dropping off the ransom? Nothing more?'

'No,' said Ragg. 'I would you tell you more if there was any, I promise.'

'Two last queries,' said Powerscourt. 'The policeman on duty by your house thought he got a glimpse of the blackmailer as you got out of the cab. He thought the man was completely bald. He raised his hat as you got out, apparently. Good manners and all that. Did you see that?'

'No,' said Ragg rather sadly. 'I didn't. Sorry to be such an inadequate witness. And the other thing?'

'The other thing, Mr Ragg, is this. Did you think the blackmailer was genuine? By which I mean, did you think he had the Caryatid? That he wasn't bluffing?'

'As a matter of fact,' Ragg replied, 'I did think he had the Caryatid or that he knew how to get his hands on her. I was quite sure about that.'

16

Johnny Fitzgerald had arranged to meet the art world veteran porter known as Red Fred in the Admiral Collingwood close to Fred's old stamping grounds of New Bond Street. Johnny was on the trail of one of Sokratis's riddles. He remembered the emaciated face, the body writhing in torment in his last illness, raising himself up till he was semi-upright in his bed, screaming, 'Shades of the prison-house, shades of the prison-house.' Who, Johnny wanted to find out, might have been the other residents of the prison-house?

They settled in a small booth at the back of the Saloon with frosted glass walls and a wooden door rather like a closed pew in an Anglican church. Johnny had first met the old man years before when he was looking into a case that involved forgery and corruption in the art world. Fred had always been a reliable, if thirsty, witness.

'How have you been, Fred?' Johnny was looking well after his stay in Warwickshire, which had turned out to be rather more abstemious than he would have liked. He proposed to make amends.

'Good, all things considered. Can't complain. Wife's

not too good though. Arthritis they call it. Dolores can hardly move.'

'I'm sorry to hear that,' said Johnny. 'Please send her my best wishes for a speedy recovery.'

'I'll do that, so I will.' Red Fred took an enormous draught of his beer. 'You said you wanted to pick what's left of my brains, Mr Fitzgerald.'

Johnny had never told his companion that he was a member of the Irish peerage, and not, strictly speaking, a Mr at all.

'I did and I do,' said Johnny. 'As you know, my friends and I are looking into the disappearance of the Caryatid from the British Museum.'

'Not surprised she went,' said Red Fred, downing another huge mouthful, 'none of us who worked on the street were surprised. They had no idea of security in that damned museum, no idea at all. Too busy writing learned papers nobody will ever read to think about the safety of their treasures. Some of them would be bloody hard to move, mind you, if you think about it. God knows how they ever got some of those huge statues here in the first place. Big bastards they are, some of them.'

Johnny remembered that Red Fred's favourite technique when being plied with drink in exchange for information was to produce a small shoal of diversions at every available opportunity. That way the conversation was longer, the drinks more plentiful.

'I've got a very particular request for you, Fred, and I'm not quite sure how to put it.'

Fred coughed and pointed at his empty glass. Johnny departed in search of refills.

'It's vague, Fred, very vague. I'm ashamed it's so vague, so I am. I'm looking for a man from the art world who was sent to jail some time in the last ten or fifteen years. He's out now, mind you.'

'Armed robbery? Attempted murder? Grievous bodily harm?'

'Sorry, Fred. I don't think it was any of those things, though I could be wrong. Fraud, I would have said, much more likely. Robbery, maybe, forgery, whatever the charge for forgery is. One of those.'

'Art world's full of people who should have gone down for all of those, Mr Fitzgerald. Let me have a think.'

Red Fred stared closely at the loops and curving lines etched into the glass on the side of their little cubicle.

'Chap from Contarini's, the fine art dealers, he went down, I remember. I'm not sure I can remember when he was a guest of His Majesty, he might even have been a guest of Her Majesty, begging the late Queen's pardon, I'm sure. He used to hang out a lot at the Travellers Club. I only know that because I had a cousin who worked in the kitchens. Our man had these big dinners there every now and again. They said he used to drive a four-in-hand round his country place at the weekend. One of the best drivers in the south of England apparently.'

'Name, Fred? Any chance of a name? And the nature of his criminal activities?'

Fred looked blank. His glass was nearly empty. Then it was empty.

'Would you like something stronger, Fred? Port? Whisky perhaps? They say they have a fine selection of malts here.'

'I'll stick with the beer, if that's all right with you, Mr Fitzgerald. Port gives me terrible wind and that's a fact. Dolores always complains about it.'

'Very good,' said Johnny, heading back to the bar.

'I've got it,' Fred announced as his fresh glass came into view, 'at least I've got part of it.'

'Which part?' asked Johnny as Fred introduced himself properly to his new drink.

'What he was done for, Mr Fitzgerald. Forging old ladies' wills, that's what sent him down. Eighteen months? Two years?'

'Rich old ladies?'

'Well, nobody would bother locking you up if you fixed some wills of the poor, two or three mouldy dresses and a couple of pairs of sheets, would they? Only thing is I can't remember the man's name. It's as if the thought of those horses has driven it right out of my mind.'

'Did he go back to the art world after he was released? Can you recall how old he was when he went down?'

'Ah,' said Fred, 'you're wondering if he might still be around now, aren't you? I don't remember any fresh sightings of him after his time in the Scrubs. Maybe he turned over a new leaf. Age? How old was the bugger? I would say he wasn't more than thirty-five when he departed.'

'Did he have a full head of hair, Fred?'

'Great God, Mr Fitzgerald, what will you think of next. I have no idea about his hair. I heard a lot about this man, so I did, but I only saw him once in the flesh and then I was on the top deck of a bus for God's sake.'

'Sorry, Fred,' said Johnny and pushed over an open pack of cigarettes. 'Any more suspects?'

'Yes,' said Fred, drawing deeply on his cigarette, 'there's two more I can think of now my brain is moving into something approaching full working order.' He downed another large gulp of his beer.

'There was a man from Linfords, the auctioneers. Must

225

have been about five years or so ago. I think he was done for fraud of some sort, don't ask me what. They said he made the police really cross, that he treated them as if they were idiots and beneath contempt. The Inspector in charge of the case took his revenge, mind you. Blakeway, that was the name of the fellow, he used to conduct a lot of the auctions himself. There he was one fine morning, selling away for all he's worth. Six policemen come in and make their way to the front. The second Blakeway has finished with the last lot, they move in. He was arrested in front of his own customers. Going, going, gone, you might say.'

'Is he out now, Fred? Any reports on that?'

'I heard he'd moved out of London, Mr Fitzgerald. Opened an antique place in the Cotswolds. Burford? Steeple Aston? Stow on the Wold? Somewhere like that. Hold on a minute. I remember now. Burford, that's where it is, Burford.'

It was time for another refill. There was not long to go now till closing time. Fred, Johnny thought, looked as though he could keep the bar staff fully occupied for another couple of hours.

'Last man,' said Fred. 'Only three or four years ago now. Isn't it strange how you remember the least about the one that's the most recent.'

Johnny waited as Fred lit another cigarette. 'Hand in the till, that's what he was up to.' Fred took an enormous swig of his latest pint of beer.

'Whose hand, Fred? Which till?'

'Hand belonged to a chap called Kennedy, Mr Fitzgerald, Michael Moloney Kennedy. The till belonged to Brotherhood's, the other big auctioneers. Kennedy's hand was supposed to have been busy in the till for years.

226

Only caught when the firm changed their accountants. The judge took exception to the thing. Warbled on about the prisoner betraying a position of trust in one of our most trusted and trustworthy businesses. Two years in Wormwood Scrubs if you please. Auctioneers? Trusted? Trustworthy? I ask you. New Bond Street laughed about it all for a fortnight. And no, I can't remember if he has come back to the art world or not. Probably not directly, I would think. They were calling him Trustworthy Kennedy the day he was sent down. I don't think people would have forgotten.'

Johnny Fitzgerald walked home, muttering to himself. Shades of the prison-house indeed, shades of the prison-house.

'What news from New York?' said Powerscourt. John Hudson, the young Englishman employed by the *New York Times* as European art correspondent, was back in the Powerscourt drawing room in Markham Square.

'Well, my lord, on one level the news is rather disappointing. But another door has opened, only slightly, and the room within may be empty. Or it may not.'

'You sound as though you have been taking lessons from the Delphic oracle, Mr Hudson. Could you be a little clearer? The *New York Times* is famous for the clarity of its writing after all.'

John Hudson smiled. 'My apologies, my lord. My friend and colleague Franklin tells me that he is sure the Caryatid is not in New York City. He would not, however, swear to that in a court of law. His reasons may surprise you. He says that if one of the millionaires had got their hands on the Caryatid, it would have been the ultimate symbol of one-upmanship in the most competitive city on earth. The holder of the Caryatid would have outsmarted all his rivals. Franklin says he cannot imagine one of this selective club not boasting about it. It would not be enough to have the thing, you see. Everybody else would have to know you had it too.'

'That sounds probable. Your friend Franklin will go far. And he is sure of his theory?'

'There has not been a whisper about Greek statues, Parthenon marbles or anything like that. Apparently the millionaires are all wondering if they will be summoned to a reception by one of their rivals and arrive to find the *Mona Lisa* on the wall.'

'That would cause a sensation, even in New York,' said Powerscourt. 'You mentioned a possible source of good news elsewhere, Mr Hudson.'

'I did. It all comes back to Franklin's knowledge of the American art business, my lord. He says that the most knowledgeable man in America about classical sculpture does not live in New York at all. He has some enormous mansion there with a vast ballroom of course, the usual thing, but he lives in upstate New York.'

'In what way is he the most knowledgeable man in America?'

'They say he can spot a fake at five hundred yards distance. The man has a gallery attached to his house, apparently, populated entirely by ancient statuary. Years ago he went to Greece and Rome and came back with stuff that was all genuine. For some reason even he couldn't describe, he could tell the fake from the real thing without fail. He bought a couple of pieces from the top people in Rome that were the only originals they had in the entire place.'

'Great God!' said Powerscourt. 'Does he rent himself

out? The big galleries would pay fortunes for such knowledge, surely.'

'I'm not sure about that, my lord, I'm not sure at all. Think about it. If the big galleries and the great auction houses were only to offer genuine works of art their business would collapse. The number of objects coming through would drop like a stone. So would their income.'

Powerscourt laughed. 'Does our American friend have a name? And where does he live if he's not in New York?'

'The great collector is called Wilbur Lincoln Mitchell, my lord. His parents were devoted to the assassinated President and gave their only son his middle name. He lives in upstate New York in a wild and beautiful spot looking out over the Hudson River. It's not far from the military academy at West Point.'

'Isn't that the place where they trained up General Custer for the last stand?' asked Powerscourt.

'They did, my lord. They also trained Robert E. Lee and future President Ulysses S. Grant. They trained everybody. There is no indication, mind you, that Mr Mitchell has any links with the military. But my friend Franklin has an idea.'

'What's that, Mr Hudson?'

'He says it came to him when he was reading about the Caryatid in the New York Public Library. Lost Greek statues are in the news. All the East Coast papers carry reports on her disappearance and the efforts to find her. What could be a better time for an article on the man who has one of the finest collections of Greek and Roman statues in America? Some of the museums have more, of course, but Lincoln Mitchell's are all of the finest quality, paid for by the fruits of private enterprise. Franklin proposes, with your approval of course, to write to Mr

229

Mitchell and request an interview. The lost Caryatid would make it highly topical and of great interest to the *Times*'s readers.'

'Of course I give him my blessing,' said Powerscourt. 'I only wish I was going too.'

The population of Wales are known for many things. Love of their native land, a weakness for myth and poetry, devotion to their local culture and a certain insularity of outlook. These traits were as common in the police force as they were in the population at large. England and Wales do not have a national police force that can investigate crimes from Carlisle to Land's End. Each county has its own. The police force covering the Black Mountains and the Brecon Beacons were as competent as their fellows in other parts of the country. But they did have a certain suspicion of foreigners and a very great suspicion of London which their preachers told them was a human cesspit waiting for the flames of God's judgement. When the local inspector discovered that the visitors who seemed to have been responsible for Carwyn Jones's death came from London, he became even more cautious than usual. It was the custom with crimes involving people under the jurisdiction of other forces to write and let the other police force know what had happened. So a letter was sent to the Metropolitan Police Liaison Unit with details of the crime. They spared their colleagues in the capital nothing – the kicks to the head, the stamping on the body, the cigarette burns on the victim's arms. They did not, however, mention the fact that the two men were known as the Twins, because they did not know that. The undertaker had been given no names when he met the men at the station. London might never have heard the full story had it not been for the growing reach and growing success of the Caryatid Committee.

After the meeting near the British Museum and the high levels of contribution delivered there by the public, many would have rested on their laurels. Not Tristram Stanhope. A man fond of the sound of his own voice will always welcome another opportunity to listen to it again. Tristram set out on a national tour, taking time off from the British Museum with the approval of Theophilus Ragg and the other heads of department. He purchased a couple of flamboyant waistcoats and a Regency full-length jacket in a colour his supporters' club described as imperial purple. He delivered the speech he had made in London with a number of variations. He had three interchangeable paragraphs about each of the ancient Greek dramatists, choosing the one he thought most appropriate to the location he was in. Aeschylus, he discovered, played well in Bristol. They liked Sophocles in Norwich. Birmingham was devoted to Euripides. When he grew weary of fifth-century BC Athens and the glories of Plato and Pericles, Tristram replaced the disappointments of democracy with the glory of conquest and spoke instead of Alexander the Great. No general in history, he told his audience, not Caesar, not Charlemagne, not even Napoleon, conquered as much of the globe as the young warrior from Macedon, tutored by the philosopher Aristotle himself. Packed houses came to hear him in all the great cities. In Newcastle they gave him a standing ovation that went on, he told his admirers later, for five minutes thirty-seven seconds. In Liverpool they carried him off the stage in triumph. Tristram always closed with the London peroration about the appeal of the Caryatid. The money flowed in.

And that was not all. Tristram Stanhope enlisted the help of the classic departments in all the leading public schools and the top grammar schools. They were urged to send their most eloquent speakers to give lectures on Caryatids and ancient Greece in their nearest towns. When Lady Lucy Powerscourt heard the news she said that the principal peacock had enlisted a whole flock of subsidiary peacocks to help in his campaign. More money flooded in. Regular announcements of the progress of the fund were placed in the newspapers. When the total reached £5,000 the cynics said that you could get more money for the return of the Caryatid than you could earn in twenty years as a skilled workman.

The provincial newspapers reported the story of the Caryatid and the reward. Illtyd Williams, the man who knew the secrets of Carwyn Jones's death, earned about the same as head teacher of a small primary school in Wales as an experienced craftsman would make in a great city. He decided that his information could indeed provide a lot of help to the authorities. Indeed, he began to feel, as he contemplated the £5,000, that his information would be the principal factor in the recovery and return of the statue. With the £5,000 he could buy a new house. He could have better holidays. Maybe he could buy a motor car. So he wrote, with the full details of what he knew and what he suspected, to the address supplied in the *Western Daily Mail*, The Caryatid Appeal, c/o Finch's Bank, Moorgate, London EC.

Powerscourt had written to the old artist, Josiah Wills Baker, with details of two of the three members of the art community in London believed to have served time in prison. He said that he proposed to call on Bacon the following day to seek his counsel. He gave such details as he had from Johnny Fitzgerald about the man with no name who forged the old ladies' wills, Blakeway the fraudster now believed to be running an antique shop in Burford, and Michael Moloney Kennedy, the man with his hand in the till at one of the great auctioneers.

Once again the old painter did not rise from his seat to greet his visitor. He waved him to a chair just a few feet away.

'Powerscourt,' he said, 'good to see you again. Please forgive this forced intimacy with the seating, it gives me a chance to see you, or rather, to see the shape I know to be you. Now then, let's talk of the prisoners at the bar.'

He leant back in his chair and peered at his visitor through eyes that were now cloudy. 'I have a young man from the National Gallery who comes in to help me from time to time, Lord Powerscourt. I asked him to look up various records of mine to see how I could be of assistance with these gentlemen. Have you ever thought, by the way, how certain occupations give rise to suspicions of criminality almost automatically; bookmakers perhaps, door-to-door salesmen, pawnbrokers, while others, bankers, solicitors, clergymen, give off an air of probity and respectability? We artists are aligned with the bankers, I feel, though it must be a near thing. The attribution of paintings, a very limited profession numerically, must be one of the most suspect occupations in the kingdom. I digress. The young man from the National Gallery is always most patient when I wander off the subject but even he starts to cough loudly and significantly after ten minutes or so.'

A very pretty maid in a very correct uniform brought in a tray with a couple of glasses of champagne. 'Thank you, my dear. Your health, Lord Powerscourt. I often take a glass of something at this time of day. It brightens up the rest of the afternoon.'

The clock on the mantelpiece said a quarter to four. Powerscourt wondered if the old man was a kindred spirit of Johnny Fitzgerald who had expended quite a lot of treasure on the beer to lubricate the memory of Red Fred.

'Blakeway, Nicholas George Blakeway, late of Linfords the auctioneers, believed to be involved with an antique business in Burford. I remember him as an auctioneer, Powerscourt, many years ago. He had a great talent for it, you know. He could play on his audience like one of the great violinists. His particular calling card came with paintings sent up from the provinces to be sold as part of an estate, that sort of thing. In the gap between arriving at Linfords and standing on the easel at the auction they would be transformed from a copy of a Parmigianino Madonna into an early Raphael. The price went through a similar transformation. Some wily provincial solicitor worked out what was going on and that was the end of Blakeway. I don't think he's working at the shop in Burford any more. It sells second-hand books as well, by the way. I'm told Blakeway retains his financial interest but employs a young man to run the shop for him. Where he is now, I'm afraid, nobody knows.'

'That's very helpful, very helpful indeed. I shall take a day trip to Burford and see what I can find. What of the others?'

'I can tell you a little about Michael Moloney Kennedy, the one with his hand in the till,' the old man said.

'He's gone abroad. France, I think? Italy perhaps? Some wealthy relation died while he was in prison and left him a great deal of money. By the time the cash escaped from probate and the lawyers he was out of Wormwood Scrubs and ready to spend it. I'm told it's doubtful he will ever come back to live in this country. Not that living abroad necessarily rules him out of your business with the Caryatid. You could have planned the thing from anywhere in Europe with the right trips to the right capitals and the right contacts with the right criminals. I'm sure of that.'

'And what of the other fellow, the one with no name who went to prison for forging old ladies' wills? Do you have any news of him?'

Josiah Wills Baker stared myopically round the walls of his Eaton Square drawing room, lined with paintings he could no longer see.

'I have a name for you. Easton, William Tyndale Easton. That's almost all I know about the fellow. I know nothing of what became of him after his time as a guest of His Majesty. But this much I do know. I'm afraid it's not what you would want to hear. Of the three who were caught – and heaven knows how many more were up to similar tricks but got away with it – William Tyndale Easton is the most formidable, the cleverest, the one with the most original mind. When I discussed him with one of my colleagues yesterday, the friend said that he was perfectly capable of organizing the theft of the Caryatid. And also perfectly capable of getting away with it.'

17

The members of the Caryatid Committee had originally expected a small response to their appeal for funds to pay for a reward for the recovery of the marble lady. She was only a statue, after all. Not that many people had been to see her at the British Museum. The citizens would have other things on their minds. But as Tristram Stanhope's travelling lecture tour and the other talks organized by the schools took off, so did the appeal. Letters poured in from all over the country. The police representatives on the Caryatid Committee insisted that all correspondence had to be checked by a responsible party. At first they installed a retired detective inspector with long experience of major crimes in a small back room in the offices of Finch and Company, Bankers. Then the detective inspector became a detective inspector with two sergeants, seconded from the police station at Charing Cross, and they were transferred to an empty suite of offices on the top floor of the building. The two sergeants weeded out the weird and the fanciful. Anything that looked more serious was sent through to the inspector next door.

There was plenty of the weird and the fanciful and

the downright mad in the correspondence. A letter from the West Country claimed that the theft had been organized by the Freemasons as part of their campaign for world domination. Another, from Melton Constable in Norfolk, alleged that the Caryatid had been stolen by a group of pagans who wanted her to represent the Earth Mother in their ceremonies. If the authorities wished to send a representative to the spot called the Devil's Hallow, three miles north of Swaffham, at the time of the next full moon, they would find the Caryatid there, her neck festooned with garlands. The author enclosed a stamped addressed envelope for the reward. Three people from different parts of the country maintained that the Caryatid had been taken under cover of darkness to an embarkation point in the Thames Estuary. There, she had been placed aboard a German submarine, before being transferred to a German dreadnought. The Caryatid was now in a private room in the Kaiser's New Palace at Sans Souci Park in Potsdam.

Another correspondent claimed that the Tsar's chief minister was responsible for the theft. The Caryatid had been taken in a sealed train to St Petersburg and would never be discovered as it was concealed in the depths of the Winter Palace, a place full of unrecorded rooms and corridors nobody ever visited. From these secret quarters the Tsar and his wife could bring her out for private viewings in the dark watches of the night. Alexandra, wife of the Tsar, was said to believe that the Caryatid had special powers relating to fertility and haemophilia.

The police had insisted right from the start that all correspondence should be assessed within forty-eight hours of receipt. The rejects were preserved in large filing cabinets provided by the bank. The more interesting, even

237

the doubtful, went through to the detective inspector whose workload was less arduous but more responsible than his colleagues. Illtyd Williams's letter fell into the doubtful category.

'What do you think of this one here,' the first sergeant said to the second sergeant, 'big barns in Wales and hammering heard in the night? Enormous coffins being sent away to Bristol for transit to God knows where. Man beaten to death at the end. Throw it in the bin, do you think?'

'Let's have a look,' said the second sergeant who was an avid, if secret, consumer of the wilder reaches of detective fiction. 'God knows,' he said after a moment, 'could be true, mind you. Anything might happen in Wales. Let's send it through.'

Burford, Powerscourt thought, is really one very long main street running downhill to a fine old church at the bottom. There were a few people about at eleven o'clock in the morning: a vicar walking his dog, a publican bringing barrels out of his cellar, a couple of old ladies armed with wide hats and shopping baskets. Powerscourt thought the place could stand for the essence of England. Even the pubs that lined the main street and the little roads running off it had names resonant with history. There was a Royal Oak and a Highway Inn, a Bull, a Lamb and a Mermaid. In the churchyard at the bottom the dead of England had slept for centuries, Coopers and Farmers and Smiths, some of them lying here since the turmoil of the Civil War. Powerscourt wondered what the Caryatid would make of Burford with its quaint rituals, its weekly market and the fluctuating fortunes of the village cricket team on the village green. She came from a more tumultuous world, not one where the potential extremes of religion and belief had been tamed and watered down into the lowest common denominator of the Authorized Version and the Book of Common Prayer. You could have mysteries involving a descent into Hades, sacred boxes and sacred baskets, mind-altering drugs a key part of the ritual, secrets so secret that disclosure meant death, in Eleusis, but not in Burford. You could have oracles in Delos or Epirus but not in Banbury. The orgy on the island, sacred to the god Dionysus, where Ariadne reeled down the mountain drunk, disorderly and holding something revolting, could happen on Naxos. It couldn't happen in Oxfordshire, not even in Kingston Bagpuize.

The antique shop had no doubt of its identity. Burford Antiques occupied a prime position halfway down the High Street. Old books filled one of the windows, an elegant Pembroke table the other. Powerscourt was welcomed by a young man who must have been the thinnest individual he had seen in his life. He seemed so skeletal that you wondered if he ever ate anything at all. His nose was long and thin, like its owner, and he had a mop of unruly brown hair.

'How can I help you, sir?'

Powerscourt resisted the temptation to say that the best thing the young man could do to help would be to have a large meal at once. 'I was looking for Mr Blakeway, actually. Is he here today?'

The thin young man shook his head. 'No, he's not here today, sir. He usually drops in once or twice a week, normally on Saturday afternoons.'

'Do you have an address where I could find him, by any chance?'

The thin young man sighed, as if he was asked this question more often than he would have liked. Was Powerscourt just another debt collector or a man yet to be paid for his antiques? Did Mr Blakeway still consort with his former fellow inmates in Wormwood Scrubs?

'I'm afraid not, sir.'

'Surely you must be able to contact him in an emergency?'

'I could,' said the young man defiantly, 'but that doesn't mean I'm to hand the address to any Tom, Dick or Harry who comes along.'

Powerscourt thought this was the first time in his life he had been compared to any Tom, Dick or Harry who came along. It was a whole new experience. He thought he rather liked it. But he didn't want to make a scene that might be reported back to the elusive Mr Blakeway.

'Never mind,' he said, 'another time perhaps. A very good morning to you.'

The landlords at the Royal Oak next door and the Lamb across the street had no memories of Mr Blakeway. Neither had their companions in arms at the Bull or the Mermaid. Maybe Mr Blakeway was teetotal. Powerscourt caught up with the vicar, the Reverend Matthew Carey, and his dog just as he was going back in to his Old Rectory with the River Windrush meandering along the bottom of his garden. The vicar's wife provided coffee and home-made cake.

'Please forgive me for taking your time, Vicar, I am an investigator, I'm afraid, employed by the British Museum, to look into the disappearance of the Caryatid.'

'Goodness gracious,' said the vicar, 'you don't think she's here, do you, here in Burford?' He looked around him suddenly as if the statue might be hiding behind a bookcase.

'Certainly not,' said Powerscourt with a smile. 'But I was rather hoping to talk to your Mr Blakeway, the man who owns the antiques shop halfway up the High Street.'

'That Mr Blakeway,' said the vicar with a sigh, 'I didn't think we'd heard the last of him, even when he went away.'

'Were you suspicious of him in some way?'

'Well, no, not exactly. He came to church fairly often when he first arrived, but I never felt his heart was in it. I don't think he was a believer, if you know what I mean.'

'So why do you think he came to your services then?'

'I never worked that out. My wife saw him once when I was reading the prayers with his eyes wide open, staring at the stained glass. I don't think that is normal behaviour.'

'No, indeed,' said Powerscourt reflecting on the innocence of a world where a man could be marked out for keeping his eyes open during prayers. 'Do you think he came to make friends? He must have been a newcomer to Burford at that time, surely?'

'I don't think that was the case. We have a number of social gatherings, mainly for the old and the lonely, though we're not meant to say that, but he was never seen at any of those.'

The vicar went over and stood by his window, watching the birds on the lawn. A swan floated by with that irritating air of complete superiority.

'May I ask you a question, Lord Powerscourt?'

'Of course.'

'Is Mr Blakeway a suspect in some way for the theft of

the Caryatid? It seems scarcely possible that such a crime could be conceived here in Burford.'

'No, I wouldn't say he was a suspect,' said Powerscourt, but something in his tone did not convince the Reverend Carey.

'But he is, isn't he? You're just being prudent, and quite rightly so. Goodness me, a master criminal here in Oxfordshire, it doesn't bear thinking about!'

'Not so fast, vicar, you're running away with yourself.'

'I'm sure you're right, Lord Powerscourt. Martha always tells me I mustn't rush to judgement. But thinking about crime and Mr Blakeway in the same sentence does give me another idea. I wonder if it's correct, it might well be.'

'What is this idea, vicar?'

'Suppose Mr Blakeway is a man with a past, a record, as I believe people in your profession refer to it. He comes to Burford, because it is so peaceful. He goes to church because that's what he thinks people here do. But it was all a cover; he was trying to persuade us he was one sort of man when in fact he was somebody completely different. We were cover, matins, Holy Communion, evensong, all used for a purpose totally different from what the church fathers intended. What do you think of that?'

'I think you might well be right,' said Powerscourt, and he did.

Inspector Jack Hegarty was enjoying his return to active service on the top floor of Finch's Bank in Finsbury Circus between Moorgate and Liverpool Street station. During his time with the Met he had served all over London, ending up in the crime-filled quarters of Catford and Rotherhithe. His wife was, if anything, even more pleased than her husband about his return to the colours. Having grown accustomed over many decades to Jack's irregular hours, frequent absences, sometimes not returning home until three or four in the morning, and general unpredictable behaviour, she found his regular appearances at meal times, as regular as the clock he had been given as a retirement present, rather a strain.

The Inspector had lost count of the number of letters he had read claiming the reward for the recovery of the lost Caryatid. Privately he felt certain that good police work rather than the efforts of a pack of amateurs, many of them, in his view, clinically insane, would secure the return of the statue. He was nearing the end of a four-page missive from Crewe in which its author claimed that the most likely means of transportation for the missing Athenian lady would be a railway container. His correspondent helpfully provided a number of diagrams of the things, and lists showing the various dimensions of different sorts of container. There were a lot of exclamation marks, and in a number of key places the conclusions were underlined with bright red ink. In spite of all that, the Inspector added it to a small pile he was going to discuss with his colleague Christopher Kingsley later that day. The man probably works on the bloody railways if he lives in Crewe, he said to himself. His next letter came from Wales. There were no drawings and no underlinings in red ink. One section fascinated him. He read it three times. It spoke of a man kicked to death, stamped on, cigarette burns on his arms. Bells were ringing in the Inspector's brain. It took him a moment to remember why this account stirred his memory. One of his many protégés, a young inspector called Ferguson, was now working in Deptford.

He had horrific stories of the exploits of some violent gangsters called the Twins who specialized in gangland punishments and executions, including cigarette burns. There was no mention in Illtyd Williams's letter of any twins, but there was a reference to two people who came from London.

Inspector Hegarty ran down the stairs at top speed to the telephone exchange where the police had been given priority. 'This is very urgent,' he said to the girl. 'I need to speak to the police based in Brecon in South Wales. Just put me through to the police station. And after that, can you get me Inspector Billy Ferguson on the line? You will find him at the police station on Deptford High Street.'

Artemis Metaxas was still escorting a number of Greek girls to the College near Amersham every weekend. The money was good. Artemis was putting most of it aside to pay for her wedding dress the following spring. She noticed that the girls were always the same now. Eight of them made the journey on the train with the blacked-out windows. And though they were careful not to talk about what went on during their country outings, Artemis suspected that there was a major event being planned at the College. Artemis's charges were going to take part. And they were very excited about it.

Six men were crowded round the little table on the top floor of Finch's Bank in Finsbury Circus. Inspector Hegarty and his two sergeants had their backs to the street, Inspector Kingsley, Powerscourt and the police-man from Deptford, Inspector Ferguson, had a view of the rooftops of the City. Billy Ferguson was in his late thirties, a cheerful soul with ruddy cheeks and jet black hair. He finished reading the note from Wales and passed it back to Jack Hegarty.

'I don't like the sound of this, Jack. Do we know anything about the writer, apart from the fact that he says he's a head teacher? Do we know that he really is a head teacher? The people who write these kinds of letters often think they're the Pope or Queen Victoria or H. G. Wells.'

'I've spoken to the police station down there,' said Hegarty. 'The man who looked into the murder is not on duty today. He's going to call me first thing in the morning. But they did confirm that Illtyd Williams runs the local school and that the murdered man was on the staff there. That's all I've got at the moment.'

'Could you tell us, Inspector,' said Powerscourt, 'what concerns you about the letter from Wales? What exactly don't you like the sound of?'

Inspector Ferguson sighed. 'It's all tenuous so far. I'm going to put two and two together and come up with an answer that's more than four, if you'll permit me. The letter only speaks of two men. It speaks of another man kicked to death, trampled on and with cigarette burns on his arms. It's the cigarette burns that send all my alarm bells ringing. All kinds of murderers have been known to kick people to death, as we are all aware. But the cigarette burns are almost a trademark, a calling card for a particularly violent couple of criminals in my patch known as the Twins. They're well known for torturing people with cigarette burns among other horrible things. I believe they really are twins, by the way. They act as enforcers, as the muscle behind the throne, if you like, for the gangster who runs Deptford and half of Rotherhithe, Carver Wilkins.'

'He wasn't christened Carver, surely?' Inspector Kingsley asked.

'No, he wasn't. I've no idea what his real name is, actually. His nickname was originally Carving Knife because he used to carry one around in his coat pocket and pull it out at appropriate moments like Billy the Kid drawing his gun. Then it got shortened to Carver. They say he still walks round with the carving knife in his coat pocket.'

'What sort of criminal is our friend Carver?'

'There are a lot of robberies, we believe, almost all of them outside the borough so we don't get to hear a lot about them. His main activity is protection rackets. We think most of the local shops pay up, maybe some of the more affluent householders, who knows? Obviously all the pubs shell out and the few restaurants in the place. Even the undertaker has to pay his way. If you don't pay, you get a visit from the Twins. That often means a couple of weeks in hospital for repairs. They collect the money once a week and bring it back to Carver. Most of the prostitutes in Deptford are on the payroll, and the pawnbrokers and the moneylenders. Carver is like a human leech, sucking the lifeblood of the community. And I don't have to tell you gentlemen that prosecution is virtually impossible. You need witnesses. Once you are known to be appearing as a witness you too have a visit from the Twins and your face is beaten in.'

'And what, Inspector Ferguson, do you suppose the link might be between Deptford and a sleepy little place in South Wales?' Powerscourt had been trying to imagine what form such a link might take and failed.

'I don't know and I won't pretend to know, my lord,' Ferguson replied, 'but I'm going to find out. I'm going to speak to my governor when I get back to the station and suggest that I and a couple of my men take a little trip to the valleys. Fresh air will be a welcome change from Deptford.'

'I wish you luck with the Welsh,' said Inspector Kingsley. 'They're so suspicious of outsiders. I hope they won't clam up on you just because you don't sound like you come from the next valley.'

'I've had dealings with the bloody-minded Welsh before,' said Inspector Ferguson, and it sounded from his tone as if the memories were not happy ones. 'That's why I want to take two others with me. We can interview the policeman, the schoolteacher and the schoolteacher's wife all at the same time. They won't have a chance to get together and cook up some pack of lies then.'

'I think that's an excellent plan, this expedition to the Land of My Fathers,' said Powerscourt. 'I wish it God speed and good luck.'

'We'll keep going with the letters, so we will,' said Inspector Hegarty, 'we might find some more gold dust, who knows?'

On the way to the underground at Liverpool Street Inspector Kingsley threw in another piece of information. 'Our Greek friend, my lord, Kostas, we've been looking into his past, as you know.'

'You mean the late Kostas? The man under the train?'

'The same. It transpires that before he worked for the British Museum he did similar work for a place called the Hellenic College near Amersham. Do you know anything of it?'

'Not yet,' said Powerscourt.

One thought troubled him on his way home. He wondered as he always did on his own about the whereabouts of the Caryatid. Where was she now? It was becoming like losing a daughter, he said to himself. What troubled him was the link, if there was one, between gangsters in Deptford and the murder of a schoolteacher in the Brecon

Beacons. And how on earth could those two events be linked to the theft from the British Museum? And, last but not least, was there a link between Deptford, South Wales and the urbane man, possibly bald, who drove Deputy Director Ragg round the streets of London in a taxi?

18

Inspector Ferguson laid his plans carefully on the train to Wales. He himself would speak to his opposite number who had looked into the death of Carwyn Jones. Sergeant Bennett had the advantage of being Welsh. His family had left the principality when he was sixteen to look for work in London. He had told Inspector Ferguson that he could still understand the language. His mother, he said, spoke to him in Welsh every time he went home for the weekend. Bennett's task was to speak to the other policemen who had been involved with the death at the undertaker's, well away from their superior officer. The third man in his command, Sergeant Broome, was to speak to the widow and see what news he could find. Broome was always being teased in all the stations he had ever worked in about his looks. At one point it looked as though he was going to be stuck with the nickname Sergeant Adonis, but the usage faded when most people using it realized that they had no idea who the original Adonis bloke actually was.

Initially, all three were to have a disappointing day. Sergeant Broome used all his charms on Megan, the widow of Carwyn Jones. He managed to make her smile, something she had rarely done since her bereavement. But he realized that she knew very little about what her husband had been doing. She didn't even know that he had been going to meet two men from London in the Green Dragon on the day he died. She thought, she told the Sergeant, that there were money troubles, but Carwyn never bothered her with those kinds of worries. Broome was convinced she was telling the truth. When he asked if there was anything else she would like to tell him, she shook her head sadly. 'He was a good man, my Carwyn, whatever people might say. He didn't deserve to end up like that.' When pressed about whatever people might say, she just repeated that he was a good man.

Sergeant Bennett found it virtually impossible to get the sergeant and the constable who had been called to the undertaker's where Carwyn Jones's body was already lying in a coffin to talk. They had found him, they said. They had made out their reports. There was very little else to say. To the Londoner's disgust they didn't even speak in Welsh.

Inspector Ferguson found a common interest with his Welsh colleague in mountains. They both liked walking in the highest places they could find. The Brecon Beacons, Inspector Davies assured Inspector Ferguson, afforded some of the finest mountain walking in the kingdom. And Davies performed one other service for his visitor. He took him to meet the head teacher who had written to the Caryatid Committee and left the two of them alone together, reasoning that the teacher might be more forthcoming to a stranger from the capital than he would be to a man who lived two streets away.

'Now then, Mr Williams,' said the Inspector, 'perhaps

you could tell us a little more about what you mentioned in your letter to the Caryatid Committee?'

'That's all there is. I have nothing to add. It didn't say on the appeal that the police were going to read the applications.'

'Come, come, Mr Williams. You must have realized that the only people authorized to catch the thieves would be the police, so the police were the only people who could judge which piece or pieces of information might be the most useful.'

'Did you say pieces of information plural? Do you mean that the reward might be chopped up into pieces, that there could be two or even three winners?' Illtyd Williams could see his reward shrinking before his eyes.

'I don't know the answer to that, I'm afraid. It's possible but we just don't know yet. I come back to my original question. Could you please tell me more about your letter?'

'I've told you. I've got nothing to add.'

'I am assuming that some, if not all, of the information came from the dead teacher at your school, Mr Jones. Would that be right? Did you have a conversation with him before he died?'

'Inspector Ferguson, I'm tired of telling you, I've got nothing to add.'

The policeman from Deptford was as tough as any other Inspector in the Metropolitan Police. But he had another side to him. He had a passionate hatred of injustice, of unfairness, of cruelty, even though he met some if not all of those qualities every day of his working life. There was a look in the head teacher's eyes he had seen all too often before. Small shopkeepers on Deptford High Street, honest landlords who ran public houses filled with the dishonest in his borough looked at him like that. They were afraid. Illtyd Williams was very afraid. Thinking of the description of the corpse in the undertaker's, Inspector Ferguson could understand only too well what they were afraid of. Boots in their faces. Vicious kicks to the head. Cigarette burns all over their bodies.

He knew most of his colleagues would turn tough and start talking about obstructing the course of justice, of the penalties for refusing to cooperate with the police, of possible time in a prison cell. Inspector Ferguson didn't think that would work. Whatever he said, the head teacher would be more frightened of the violence brought by the Twins than he would be of the police. In any terror contest, the villains would win. His only hope was to persuade Illtyd Williams that he could help secure the arrest and trial of the criminals who had beaten his colleague to death. That way the threat to his own safety and his own limbs would be removed.

'Mr Williams,' he began, 'let me take you into my confidence. I would ask you not to repeat what I am about to say. We think, we are not sure yet, but we think we know who these men from London are. They have criminal records going back many years. Our problem is that nobody is prepared to give evidence against them. Let me ask you a question. Did you actually see the two men who came on the train?'

'I did not, as a matter of fact.'

'Well, that's good news for you. If you didn't see them, they didn't see you. They will have no idea who our informants are. They don't know we're here, the villains in London. If you didn't see them, you couldn't identify them. That means you are safe from their violence because they don't even know you exist.'

Illtyd Williams didn't look any happier. But the Inspector thought some of the terror might have gone from his eyes.

'With your help, Mr Williams, we can put these people away. If the two men can be convicted of the murder they will hang. They will be out of your life for good. Now then, I come back to where I started. What else can you tell me about what you wrote in your letter to the Committee?'

Illtyd Williams stared at the policeman from London for a long time.

'It's quite simple really,' he said, and Billy Ferguson knew he had crossed into new territory. 'Carwyn wrote me a letter before he died. I think he must have done it when he knew these people were coming down from London to talk to him. He'd started the whole thing off, you see.'

'What do you mean, Mr Williams, he'd started the whole thing off?'

'He was short of money, see. Once he heard about the missing Caryatid he thought it might have had something to do with what was going on here some time ago. Lucas Ringer the undertaker knew a lot about it. Carwyn wrote to him, asking for more money or he'd tell his cousin in the police force. Ringer sent the letter off to London. You know the rest.'

'I know some of it. You spoke in your letter of big barns in Wales and hammering heard in the night, enormous coffins being sent away to Bristol for transit to God knows where. What else do you know, Mr Williams?'

'I only know what Carwyn said in his letter. That's all.'

'Very well,' said Inspector Ferguson, 'could I ask you for a favour? Could you bring me to meet this Lucas Ringer? Right now?'

'Of course.'

'Let me assure you of one thing before we leave your house, Mr Williams. Before I leave South Wales I'm going to arrange with the local police for a guard, a watch, to be put on certain people in this town. Knowing what I do now, I don't think for a moment that you are in any danger. But I propose to put your name on the list. I hope that will help set your mind at rest. I don't think it will be for very long.'

Ringer and Sons, the local undertakers, had a discreet office in the High Street opposite the Methodist Chapel. The ring on the door was answered by a spotty young man with filthy brown hair who looked as though he hadn't washed for a week. Inspector Ferguson thought he was not the best advertisement for the firm.

'Now then, young Gareth, is your father at home?' Inspector Davies began. 'This gentleman here would like to speak to him.'

Billy Ferguson smiled at the boy. 'Just a matter of routine,' he said.

'Well, you can't,' said Gareth Ringer, 'speak to him, I mean. He's not here.'

'Has he just popped out to see a client perhaps? Are you expecting him back soon?'

'He's not here,' the young Ringer replied triumphantly, 'he's gone away. He's gone away on business, so he said. He didn't say when he would be back.'

'And you have no idea where he's gone, I suppose?' Inspector Ferguson often wished he had a pound for all the people he wished to speak to who had been called away on business. The world was a very busy place. They didn't always come back.

254

'I have no idea at all.'

'No,' said Inspector Davies sadly, 'I don't suppose you do.'

'Could I speak to Mrs Ringer, please? Is she still at home?' Inspector Ferguson had little hope of succour from the temporarily abandoned wife, but the formalities had to be gone through.

'She's just next door. I can't stop you speaking to her,' said the boy in a tone that implied he wished he could.

'And while Inspector Ferguson is next door with your mother perhaps you could show me the company records for the last three months.' Inspector Davies headed off towards the back room where the records were kept. He didn't mention what he was looking for but he hoped to find further details of certain transactions with a firm in Bristol some time before.

Half an hour later the two Inspectors met up again outside the undertakers.

'I hope you had more joy than I did,' said Inspector Ferguson. 'That bloody woman managed to say nothing at all for well over twenty minutes. I don't think she knows enough to be frightened, not of nasty people coming down from London anyway. Maybe she's frightened of the undertaker she's married to. But however he did it, he's certainly managed to shut her up good and proper. What about you?'

'Well,' said Inspector Davies, 'it's more bad news, I'm afraid. I had a good look at those records. I never thought about it before but there's a remarkable amount of traffic in corpses going round South Wales all the time. A lot of people don't die in their beds as they're supposed to. They die on a visit to their relations, or on business, or on their holidays. Our friend Lucas Ringer was forever

255

sending bodies off to Cardiff or Bridgend and waiting for his own dead to come home from wherever they'd passed away.'

'Giants' coffins?' asked Inspector Ferguson. 'In transit to Bristol perhaps?'

'There's the interesting thing.' Inspector Davies checked his notes carefully. 'For a period of two weeks a couple of months ago the records have disappeared. They've been cut out of the ledger with a sharp knife, I should say. There is no record here of any traffic with Bristol or anywhere else for that time. All the written records have vanished.'

'Francis, I think you'd better stop reading that boring newspaper and pay attention. You're going to love this.'

'Love what? Love whom, Lucy?' Powerscourt put down his copy of *The Times* and looked across at his wife. It was breakfast time in Markham Square. The children had all gone off to be educated. He saw that she had an official-looking document in her hands. He was well used to mysterious packages, sent under plain cover from provincial estate agents with details of desirable properties in the West Country or in the remoter parts of Norfolk. These were always carefully filed in one of Lady Lucy's plain folders with the boring name 'House Improvements' on the spine for further inspection when her husband was out.

'You remember telling me,' Lady Lucy began, 'that the poor dead porter from the British Museum, the man run over by a train or something, used to work at a place near Amersham called the Hellenic College?'

'I do,' Powerscourt replied.

'Well,' Lady Lucy went on, 'I rang them up yesterday

and asked them to send me some information about the place. This—' she waved a brochure over the remains of the toast '—is what they sent. It's full of useful facts about the school. Situated, apparently, on the edge of a great park full of statues and reproductions of ancient temples like they have at Stowe. There's a scale model of the Parthenon, apparently. And the College themselves are building a replica of that later temple on the Acropolis called the Erechtheion. That's nearly finished, it says here. They have close links with the Greek Orthodox Church, compulsory Sunday school with the bearded Fathers, and do everything in their power to re-create the atmosphere and values of Greece in a different culture.'

'Did you say they were building an Erechtheion, my love? That's where the Caryatid came from, as you know. Any word of marble maidens holding up the porch, that sort of thing?'

'Not yet, but you never know.'

'I think I should go and see this place,' said Powerscourt. 'I would dearly like to know why they are embarking on this building programme.'

'Maybe I should go, Francis. I could be a devoted mother looking for a place for her children. Greek husband is away on business much of the year and insists his wife goes with him. What sort of Greek husband would you like to be, my love? Banker? Shipping magnate with interests all over Greece and the Near East? Raisin importer?'

'I think I'll be an import export merchant, if that's all right with you, Lucy. Maybe I could have a chain of shops in the Greek districts like that one near Moscow Road.'

'Very good,' said Lady Lucy happily, 'but I haven't told you the best bit.'

'What's that?' said Powerscourt.

'Well, you've got to look at the staff list quite carefully. After Mr Avramopoulos and Mr Livieratos and Mr Roupakitosis we have an English name. The person is described as Senior Educational Consultant in Greek and Roman studies.'

'And who might this lucky fellow be?'

'Why, Francis,' Lady Lucy put her brochure on the table next to the teapot, 'he is none other than the Head of Greek and Roman Antiquities at the British Museum, Dr Tristram Stanhope.'

'Five feet ten inches tall. Broad chested. Built like barrels rather than humans if you see what I mean. One of them has a scar on his left cheek. Otherwise they're identical.'

Inspector Ferguson was giving a description of the Twins to Eli Postgate, landlord of the Green Dragon where the visitors from London had met with Carwyn Jones on the last day of his life.

'Does that ring any bells, Mr Postgate?'

'I don't remember the visitors very well. I seem to remember they sat in a corner. They didn't come near the bar at all.'

Inspector Ferguson nodded. The Twins always stayed in the background. Nobody would be keen to identify them anyway. And if they were virtually invisible, so much the better.

'I have to ask you this, Mr Postgate. Would you be prepared to swear that the Twins were the two visitors from London who came to your bar with the undertaker and the teacher all those weeks ago?'

'No, I couldn't do that,' said Postgate, and Inspector Ferguson felt that the normal cloud of uncertainty and reluctance to bear witness had followed him all the way from Deptford to South Wales. 'I didn't know they came from London, see. I didn't hear them speak. They could have come from Talybont as far as I knew. Or Timbuktu for that matter.'

'Never mind, Mr Postgate, you've been very helpful.' Inspector Ferguson stared at the publican's back as he made his way to attend to his other customers in the public bar. In spite of all the problems, he felt that his trip to the valleys had been worthwhile. The Twins had indeed come to Brecon. They had, almost certainly, killed Carwyn Jones, though he had no witnesses and could never bring them to trial.

'Gentlemen,' he said to his two colleagues and the three local policemen, 'let the Met buy you a drink before I ask for your further assistance.'

A couple of minutes later, with six pints on the table, Inspector Ferguson made his requests.

'I think we need to keep a close eye on one or two of the locals, if you don't mind,' he began. 'That school teacher fellow for a start. He's scared out of his wits already by the death of his colleague, and though I tried to persuade him that he's perfectly safe, I'm sure he'd sleep better if he felt the police were keeping an eye out for him. Then there's the undertaker person, Lucas Ringer. Have any of you gentlemen any idea where he might have gone? Relations or family in other parts of Wales perhaps?'

'Don't you worry. We'll put the word out for you,' said Inspector Davies. 'Nobody goes missing in Wales for very long. Mind you, we've had our eyes on Mr Ringer for some time.'

'And why is that, might I ask?'

'We suspect he's been involved in criminal behaviour,

handling stolen goods, acting as a courier or providing transport for the big boys from Cardiff and Bristol. It's amazing what you can hide inside a coffin. Nobody's going to be in a hurry to look inside, are they. It was no surprise to hear he'd been mixed up in these stories of bangings in the night and so on.'

'Really,' said Inspector Ferguson, before taking a long drink from his glass. 'Who knows? Who knows indeed? Maybe our friend Mr Lucas Ringer has got a little out of his depth.'

Years later, in the comfort of his retirement in a pretty cottage in the Cotswolds, Theophilus Ragg would look back on this time of the Lost Caryatid as the worst period in his life.

The days passed. Policemen came to talk to him. Reporters pestered him for more quotations on the steps of his building. He felt, he knew, that hostile rumours were already flying around the corridors of the museum. Any building that housed the remains and the statues of so many tyrants and human monsters was bound to contain some hidden residue of venom, of poison leaching from the stone and marble past into the present. Rumour, he remembered Virgil's lines from *The Aeneid*, is of all pests the swiftest. They said that the theft of the Caryatid was his fault, that he should have taken more trouble with the security. He was too old. He should be sacked. If only, the whispers went, the place was run by a man with real vision like the Head of Greek and Roman Antiquities, this would never have happened. Ragg was certain that this particular untruth originated from Tristram Stanhope himself.

Towards closing time, when the museum was nearly

empty, the Deputy Director haunted the plinth where the Caryatid had stood. His curators told him that more people were now coming to look at the empty space where the statue had stood than came to see her when she was at home in her glory and her hauteur. He also haunted the foyer and the reception rooms of the Ritz Hotel in Piccadilly, searching for a sight of the man who had driven him round London in the dark. Sometimes he would start and move rapidly towards a figure disappearing out of a distant door but he never found the person he sought. At night he prayed for deliverance.

'I've got some interesting news, my lord.' John Hudson, the young man who worked for the *New York Times*, was taking off his gloves in the Powerscourt drawing room. 'It comes from my colleague and friend Franklin in New York.'

'It must concern the millionaire with the eye for a fake, Lincoln Mitchell, was that his name?'

'Correct, my lord, well remembered. Now then, Franklin thought of writing to the man and asking for an interview. That is the normal practice on the *Times*. It usually works. But something told him that he might be fobbed off. So he decided to call at Mitchell's house on the pretext that he was on his way back to the city after visiting a friend who was studying at West Point. It would be on the off chance that the great collector would be at home, nothing important.'

Hudson paused and checked a letter in his hand.

'So what happened? Was the Caryatid hiding in the attics?'

'We don't know. She could have been standing to

261

attention in the hall or taking tea with the millionaire in the drawing room or posing in the gallery attached to the house. Franklin never got past the front door. A rather flustered butler – Franklin's own words – greeted him and reported that Mr Mitchell was suffering from an infectious disease which made it impossible for him to receive visitors. Mr Mitchell was very sorry. He would be more than happy to welcome Franklin another day.'

'And did your friend Franklin believe the story?'

'No, my lord. The story was plausible, the butler's delivery was not. He sounded, my friend reported, like a man who has been told that telling lies is a sin from a very early age and is, therefore, hopeless at telling them. There is more, however.'

John Hudson turned to another page of his letter. 'We reporters are curious people by nature, my lord. That's probably one reason why we become reporters in the first place. Anyway, Franklin spent some time ferreting about in the village near the millionaire's mansion. The *New York Times*, he reported, was happy to dispense generous hospitality to the clients of the Red Fox Inn. Thirsty folk, these country people apparently, but two pieces of gossip emerged which Franklin thought worth passing on across the Atlantic. The first was that an extension had recently been built to the great gallery attached to the house where Mr Mitchell deploys his finest works. And the second concerned a van driver from New York City who had asked in the Red Fox for directions to the Mitchell establishment. The porter who helped him on his way was of the opinion that this must be a fairly bulky delivery because the van was large and, unusually, had no names written on the side. It was, apparently, Franklin said, an anonymous van. Most of them have displays of the owners' names and businesses in huge letters on the sides and at the back. Not this one.'

'Did the porter have a theory? Does Franklin have a theory?'

'Neither of them does, my lord. Franklin merely thought it might be significant. Then again, it could mean nothing at all.'

'Interesting,' said Powerscourt, 'very interesting. I wonder if I could enlist your help on another related matter.'

'Of course.'

Powerscourt told the young man about the three people with links to the art world who had been sent to prison: Easton, the man who forged the old ladies' wills, Blakeway the fraudster now believed to be running an antique shop in Burford, and Michael Moloney Kennedy, the man with his hand in the till at one of the great auctioneers.

'You'd like me to see if I can get on their scent, run them to earth maybe, is that it?'

'Absolutely,' Powerscourt replied.

'I'll do what I can, my lord. Delighted to be able to help. There is one other thing that might interest you.'

'What's that?'

The young man pulled a newspaper article from the inside pocket of his jacket. 'This is the piece I wrote for the *New York Times* about the Caryatid Appeal. My masters really liked it. They want a follow-up story.'

'Good. I look forward to reading it.'

'There's more, my lord. The readers were so enthused they began sending in their own contributions. You know how devoted rich Americans are to charity. I've always thought the millionaires are convinced that the charitable donations will atone for their sins. The *Times* has arranged for the money to be sent to a Wall Street bank with close links to Finch's here in London. The total has already passed one thousand dollars.'

'God bless my soul,' said Lord Francis Powerscourt.

19

Lady Lucy could see a great obelisk way over to her left. In front of her was a Palladian bridge across the lower part of a lake. Everywhere you looked, often appearing without warning round a bend in the road, hiding behind a clump of trees, were temples of Venus, temples of Artemis, classical pavilions and Chinese pagodas. There was a rotunda with a perfect reflection in the water and a tiny pantheon by the side of a river.

'Bloody temples, bloody statues, bloody useless, all of them.' The cabbie driving her to the Hellenic College looked as though he might have been about the same age as the buildings he criticized.

'Why couldn't they build something useful, like homes for people to live in?' the driver demanded, negotiating a great pothole in the road and opening up a view of another patch of higher ground with a scale copy of the Parthenon sitting happily on top of its Home Counties Acropolis.

'Perhaps they built some of those too,' said Lady Lucy, reluctant to enter into argument with the cabbie.

The driver snorted. 'They say,' he observed, spitting

vigorously into the side of the road, 'that some of the people in this college you're going to come out late in the evenings in the summer and dance round these bloody temple things. Do it in winter too, when the moon is full. All dressed in white, the girls, like bridesmaids at some bloody wedding. Bloody pagans if you ask me. Who would have thought Amersham could be a centre for devil worship?'

They had now drawn up at the front of the College, another neo-classical building with fine columns at the front.

'Thank you kindly, madam,' said the cabbie. 'I'll come back for you in an hour.'

The Headmaster was a tall man in his late forties with that air of authority men acquire through years of telling children what to do. Through the window behind his desk Lady Lucy could see the workmen finishing off the construction of their very own Erechtheion, a companion structure for the Parthenon round the corner. She could see the beginning of the porch, but there didn't seem to be anybody at home.

'Welcome to the College, Mrs Stamatis, welcome indeed. Some Greek coffee after your journey perhaps?'

Richard Doganis rang a bell and placed his order. 'You said in your letter that you were looking for places for your two boys, thirteen and fifteen, is that right?'

'It is indeed,' said Lady Lucy, 'my boys Robert and Thomas are currently at the day school attached to the Cathedral in London, but my husband is going to have to move abroad quite soon.'

The coffee arrived, sweet and sickly.

'Forgive me, Mrs Stamatis, your husband is a Greek gentleman?'

'My Panos?' Mrs Stamatis smiled at the Headmaster. 'He most certainly is. We have an agreement, you see, Headmaster. I got to give my boys English Christian names, but he has the dominant say in their education. He's very proud of being Greek, my husband, and he wants his boys to be brought up in the Greek tradition. The only concession he is prepared to make to English ways is that he wants them to play cricket. He's quite determined about that.'

Lady Lucy Stamatis thought Francis would have approved of the comments about cricket.

'And is the good Mr Stamatis in business, might I ask?'

'How silly of me, Mr Doganis, I should have said. My husband is one of the leading Greek import–export merchants in Europe. His firm want him to travel all over the Continent in the next couple of years, searching out new business opportunities. He wants me to go with him.'

'I'm sure he will be as successful in future as he has been in the past. Now then, Mrs Stamatis, I believe in letting our potential parents see round the school before I give my little talk about our traditions and our policies. So, the Bursar will take you round the living quarters and the dormitories where your boys would sleep. She'll show you the kitchens where—' the Headmaster checked his watch carefully '—lunch should be in preparation and then she'll show you one or two classrooms. I look forward to welcoming you back on your return.'

The Headmaster rose from his desk and bowed to his visitor. The Bursar, a formidable woman in her early forties who looked, Lady Lucy thought, like the matron of a hospital or maybe a Mother Superior, took her round the practical side of the school, the dormitories, the washrooms, the common rooms. Then they peeped into a mathematics class where younger children seemed to be reciting their mathematical tables in Greek to a sing-song beat conducted vigorously by the young teacher. The room next door was filled with older pupils. They were reading from their English books. The first reader was a boy of about sixteen with bright red hair.

'"But most the modern Pict's ignoble boast, To rive what Goth, and Turk, and Time hath spared: Cold as the crags upon his native coast, His mind as barren and his heart as hard, Is he whose head conceived, whose hand prepared, Aught to displace Athena's poor remains: Her sons too weak the sacred shrine to guard, Yet felt some portion of their mother's pains, And never knew, till then, the weight of Despot's chains."'

'We're reading Byron's *Childe Harold*,' the teacher informed his visitors. 'The modern Pict is a reference to Lord Elgin, the man who brought the Parthenon Marbles to London. It would be fair to say that Byron was not a devotee of the former Ambassador to the Sublime Porte, also known as the Ottoman Empire.'

He nodded to a blond lad at the back who carried on.

'"Cold is the heart, fair Greece! that looks on thee, Nor feels as lovers o'er the dust they loved; Dull is the eye that will not weep to see Thy walls defaced, thy mouldering shrines removed By British hands, which it had best behoved To guard those relics ne'er to be restored. Curst be the hour when from their isle they roved, And once again thy hapless bosom gored, And snatched thy shrinking gods to northern climes abhorr'd!"'

'Very good, Konstantin,' said the teacher, a middle-aged man beginning to go bald. The Bursar took her visitor back to the Headmaster. He told her about the academic curriculum, the religious devotions supervised by the Greek Orthodox Church, the various festivals and ceremonies conducted throughout the year. He pressed more information onto Mrs Stamatis, about fees, about sport, which included cricket, Mrs Stamatis was pleased to hear, and the history of the school and its links with other academies in Greece itself and on the Continent.

'This is all very impressive, Mr Doganis. I must speak to my husband. Could I just ask you one question? Panos and I went to hear a lecture in London recently given by the Head of Greek and Roman Antiquities at the British Museum, Dr Tristram Stanhope. I believe he has some links with the College here?'

The Headmaster nodded vigorously. 'Indeed he does,' he said. 'He is one of our most valuable consultants. You heard the pupils reading from Byron this morning, I believe? The teacher, Mr Blakeway, is a protégé of Dr Stanhope's. It was the good doctor who brought him to us.'

PART FOUR

THE PARTHENON PROCESSION

Who are these coming to the sacrifice?
To what green altar, O mysterious priest,
Lead'st thou that heifer lowing at the skies,
And all her silken flanks with garlands
    drest?
What little town by river or sea-shore,
Or mountain-built with peaceful citadel,
Is emptied of this folk, this pious morn?
And, little town, thy streets for evermore
Will silent be; and not a soul to tell
Why thou art desolate, can e'er return.

O Attic shape! fair attitude! with brede
Of marble men and maidens overwrought,
With forest branches and the trodden
    weed;
Thou, silent form! dost tease us out of
    thought
As doth eternity. Cold Pastoral!
When old age shall this generation waste,
Thou shalt remain, in midst of other woe

Than ours, a friend to man, to whom thou
    say'st,
'Beauty is truth, truth beauty,—that is all
Ye know on earth, and all ye need to
    know.'

John Keats, 'Ode on a Grecian Urn'

20

Lady Lucy's wrinkled cabbie was driving her back to the station, muttering something inaudible as he drove them past the porticoes and the pillars that adorned the great estate. Lady Lucy was satisfied with her morning's work. She had found the elusive Mr Blakeway. Francis would be pleased with her. And as they reached the station there was some other connection with Amersham she had heard of in this investigation. She chased it in her memory all the way back to London but she couldn't find it. Maybe Francis would know.

As Lady Lucy's train was leaving, her husband was walking past the display windows of the great auctioneers Linfords. He was wondering yet again about the whereabouts of the missing Caryatid and hoping the lady was not being mistreated. He had gone right past the picture before he realized what it was. He turned back and stared through the glass. There, beautifully displayed and discreetly lit, was a painting. It showed the garden of a handsome house on the Thames. The river, bathed in sunlight, is curving away towards the west. Shafts of light from the last of the sun are falling in stripes between the lime trees. A large boat, the Lord Mayor's barge, is making its way along the river. A small dog is barking at the vessel from the wall by the river. The artist was recorded as Joseph Mallord William Turner 1775–1851. Powerscourt felt certain that this was *Mortlake Terrace, Summer's Evening*, the painting that had been stolen from the drawing room of Mr and Mrs Wilson's Norfolk House in Chiswick Mall over a year before. He remembered Mrs Wilson's description of the picture and the engraving he had seen at one of the art dealers.

He also felt certain that something was wrong, terribly wrong. According to their theory, this painting had been taken as a trial run for the theft of the Caryatid. A buyer had been found for the picture before it was stolen from the walls of the house by the Thames. After the burglary the painting would be delivered in secret to the purchaser and it would never be seen in public again. But the theft had taken place over a year ago. And the painting was not hiding away in a rich man's mansion. She was on public display in the centre of window of one of London's great auction houses. This Turner was not hiding her light under a bushel. She was flaunting herself in the heart of the city. Was their theory wrong? Was their whole approach to the Caryatid a terrible mistake? Should they abandon their theories and go back to the beginning?

Looking closely at the information in the window, Powerscourt saw that the painting was due to go under the hammer as part of a sale of Old Masters at eleven o'clock the following morning. Should he stop the sale? Should he call for Inspector Kingsley and have the painting taken into police custody? He thought there could be a terrible court battle about the provenance of the picture. Suddenly he saw Mrs Wilson, an old lady with white hair in the witness box being slowly tormented by a hostile barrister asking questions about when she began to lose her memory and was she absolutely sure of the date the painting was taken. Mrs Wilson should be saved from that. He resolved to watch the proceedings through to the end. There must be a seller. There had to be a buyer. And there had to be an owner to whom the balance of the price would be paid after the auction house's commission.

Powerscourt hurried inside and was shortly closeted with a Mr Rupert Fitzwilliam, a confident young man with a flamboyant waistcoat, a director of the firm and the man going to conduct the auction. And here he received his second major shock of the day.

'You do mean the Turner in the window, Lord Powerscourt? It's just that we've got another one, Dido preparing her pyre in Carthage, also for sale. The *August Riverside* is very beautiful, don't you think?'

'I beg your pardon, Mr Fitzwilliam. Did you say *August Riverside*? I mean, is the painting, the Turner, called *August Riverside*?'

'Why, yes, that's its name. It's on all the paperwork we've received. There's nothing wrong, is there?'

Powerscourt had to decide on the spot whether to make a fuss, to claim that the title was wrong. He was sure that this was actually *Mortlake Terrace, Summer's Evening*. The police record of the theft had included a rather laboured description of the picture. He resolved, as before, to play a waiting game and see what happened to the painting the next day.

'Of course,' said Powerscourt with a smile, 'I was mistaken. I thought it was called something else. Forgive me.'

'Don't worry, Lord Powerscourt. Are you going to bid for it tomorrow?'

Fitzwilliam inspected his visitor carefully as if he could tell by the cut of the suit if the man had sufficient funds to meet the asking price.

'I'm not sure,' Powerscourt laughed. 'I shall certainly come, mind you.'

'You are an investigator, are you not, Lord Powerscourt, currently looking into the disappearance of the British Museum Caryatid? Your name is well known in these parts. There isn't anything wrong with the painting, is there?'

'I'm sure there's not, Mr Fitzwilliam. Could I ask who the vendor is, and what price the picture is expected to fetch?'

'You may be surprised to learn that all I know of the vendor is that the work is described in our brochure as the property of a gentleman. Sometimes people don't want the bidders to know exactly who the owner is. There might be thieves about who would learn where to break in and steal. You may also be interested to learn that the sale has been arranged in a great hurry. We were only instructed last week.'

'Indeed. How very interesting. And the price?'

'Sorry, Lord Powerscourt. I forgot to answer that part of your question. I did the valuation myself and I could be wrong, of course. It's surprising how often we are wrong in questions of cost. But I can tell you, privately, that the reserve is eight thousand guineas and we expect the winning bid will be well over ten thousand guineas.'

The auction room at Linfords was nearly full. There were over forty-five people present for the morning sale. The porters and attendants bustled about, bringing paintings in and out as if they were vergers in some great church or cathedral. Looking around, Powerscourt thought the

Caryatid inquiry was pretty well represented. Inspector Kingsley was there, flanked by a young constable with a fresh notebook and a battered pen. John Hudson of the *New York Times* was also present, with an older notebook and a newer pen. Lady Lucy was by his side. Johnny Fitzgerald had returned to Warwickshire. Powerscourt wondered how many of those present were regulars. He remembered a veteran auctioneer telling him of one pair of old ladies who never missed a sale, always sitting demurely at the back and keeping their hands very close to their persons so nobody could think they were trying to put in a bid. There were a number of art dealers here from the famous houses, no doubt, eyes trained to spot a bargain at the far side of a saleroom.

Rupert Fitzwilliam strode into the room as the clock struck eleven. He was wearing his dark blue suit with a plain white shirt and a pale grey tie. If the porters were the vergers in this cathedral auction room, Powerscourt thought, Fitzwilliam must be the dean, possibly the Bishop. He addressed his congregation as if they were old friends, nodding from time to time to show it was time to take one picture off the display easel and put another one on. He warmed up with a couple of early Constables and a Benjamin West. By the time he reached a late Joshua Reynolds, he was in full flow, playing his audience as carefully as a great comedian in the music halls. Nods, raised hands, an upright umbrella, a lifted hat revealed how the prices were rising. Lady Lucy had confessed to Powerscourt over breakfast that she found bidding at auction so exciting she could hardly stop herself. Once her hand went up, she said, she found it impossible to bring it down. Francis was to ensure that her fingers did not move this morning.

At a quarter to twelve it was the turn of the Turner, the last item on the catalogue.

'And now, ladies and gentlemen—' Rupert Fitzwilliam had lowered his voice to a dramatic whisper '—we have the finest painting of the morning, if not of the month, if not, even, of the year, *August Riverside*. I can say without hesitation that this is the finest Turner I have ever had the pleasure to handle. Shall we start the bidding at five thousand guineas?'

Three hands went up simultaneously.

'Five thousand.'

A top hat was raised in the front row.

'Thank you, sir, at five thousand five hundred.'

A rolled auction brochure went up from the back row.

'I'm obliged to you, sir. Six thousand guineas.'

A pen this time, belonging to a very tall man stretching his legs in the front row.

'I'm grateful, six thousand five hundred. Six thousand five hundred guineas.'

'What do you think it will go for, Francis,' Lady Lucy whispered, holding her hands together very tightly, 'eight, ten, eleven?'

'Keep counting, my love. I'm sure it'll go beyond that.' The top hat was back.

'Seven thousand, seven, thank you, sir.'

Back came the rolled brochure. The price shot up to 9,500 guineas in a series of rapid exchanges that only lasted a couple of seconds. Then a new player entered the ring. A folded copy of *The Times* in the second row raised the stakes yet further.

'Ten thousand guineas, I'm grateful to you, sir.'

Powerscourt wondered if the rise to five figures would force some of the bidders out of the contest. They might have decided to go up to the high nine thousands and no further. The brochure kept on going.

'Ten thousand five hundred guineas with you, sir, thank you.' Rupert Fitzwilliam seemed to be growing calmer as the prices went higher. His eyes roamed across his auction room, looking for movement. He raised an eyebrow to the man with the pen and the long legs in the front row. The pen shook its head.

'Ten thousand five hundred to the gentleman in the back row.'

The Times wasn't giving up after just one round in the ring.

'Eleven thousand. I'm in your debt, sir.'

There was a pause. The man with the top hat was having a hasty conference with the man beside him, as if seeking further instructions. He held a hand up as if asking for an adjournment. John Hudson was writing furiously in his notebook. Inspector Kingsley was looking closely at the man with the top hat, as if he suspected him of some criminal activity. Lady Lucy was holding Powerscourt's arm very tightly.

The brochure went up again. 'Eleven thousand five hundred guineas with the gentleman in the back row.' Top Hat shook his head furiously and glowered at his neighbour, who seemed to have turned the bidding off.

'Twelve thousand guineas, twelve.' *The Times* was just getting into his stride.

'Twelve thousand five hundred.' The brochure sent the ball back over the net at once.

'Thirteen thousand, thirteen.' *The Times* was moving from lawn tennis to ping-pong, firing off his replies faster and faster. Powerscourt thought this was a really dangerous moment for both bidders. They could get so caught up in the auction that the will to win would conquer common sense and previously agreed ceilings.

'Fourteen thousand, thank you, sir.' The brochure was still in business, jumping the price up by a thousand rather than the usual five hundred. Rupert Fitzwilliam's good manners were unperturbed by the bidding frenzy in his auction room.

'And five hundred.' *The Times* was aloft once more. The thousand pound increase hadn't worked.

'Fifteen thousand.' The brochure wasn't giving up yet.

'Fifteen thousand five hundred.' *The Times* returned fire immediately. There was a pause. Everybody in the room turned to look at the man with the brochure. He was now writing something on the front page and shook his head at the auctioneer.

'At fifteen thousand five hundred guineas, fifteen thousand five hundred, with you, sir.' Rupert Fitzwilliam nodded to the gentleman with the newspaper as if they were old friends.

'Are there any more bids, ladies and gentlemen?' Powerscourt thought this was like the *Jane Eyre* moment in the wedding service when the vicar asks if anyone present has just cause or impediment as to why these two people should not be bound together in the bonds of holy matrimony. Fitzwilliam looked around very slowly,

'Going.' He raised his gavel with his left hand.

'Going.' There was a hush in the room now. The union of the Turner and *The Times* was almost complete.

'*August Riverside*, by Joseph Mallord William Turner, with you sir, for fifteen thousand five hundred guineas, gone!'

He banged his gavel twice and began collecting his papers. The pen and the rolled brochure went up to *The*

Times to congratulate him. The top hat made a hasty departure through the back exit. The auction was over.

Fifteen minutes later Powerscourt and the Inspector were closeted with Rupert Fitzwilliam in his office. He looked carefully at his visitors. Inspector Kingsley introduced himself.

'So there is something wrong with the painting then. Otherwise why are you gentlemen here?'

'There's nothing wrong with the actual painting, if that's what you mean,' said Powerscourt. 'We have no reason to think it's not genuine.'

'It's more a question of where it came from,' Inspector Kingsley put in, 'and where it's going, if you follow me.'

'I see,' said Rupert Fitzwilliam. 'I did look up our details on the vendor, actually. The Turner was offered by a small antique dealer in Burford. I presume he was acting for somebody else.'

'Did you say Burford? Not Burford Antiques by any chance?'

'Why, that is absolutely correct, Lord Powerscourt. There are two such shops in the town, but Blakeways is where it came from.'

'And what about the purchaser?' Inspector Kingsley was looking at Rupert Fitzwilliam as if he wanted to arrest him on the spot.

Fitzwilliam laughed. 'The final battle was between the biggest art dealers in London. The rolled-up brochure was from Andersons and *The Times* spoke for Houranis. I'm sure they were both acting for private buyers who wanted to remain anonymous. I'd be very surprised if the Turner isn't sold on within the week.'

Powerscourt arranged to meet George Blakeway in the

back room of the Mermaid in Burford at six o'clock the day after the auction. For some reason Blakeway didn't want to meet at the antique shop. You could see what he must have been like as an auctioneer, Powerscourt said to himself, as Blakeway strode into the bar ten minutes late. More flamboyant than Rupert Fitzwilliam, possibly not so polite. He was smartly dressed in a plain blue suit with a white shirt and well-polished black boots. He had a cheerful air as if he was friends with all the world.

'Sorry I'm late,' he said, 'got delayed in Oxford.' He went to the bar and collected a couple of drinks. 'How can I help you, Lord Powerscourt? You said on the phone that it was a matter of some importance.'

'As it happens, Mr Blakeway, there are a couple of things I'd like to ask you about. My sister-in-law, who's married to a Greek businessman, is thinking of sending her sons to the Hellenic College.' Please forgive me, Lucy, he said inwardly to his wife, suddenly converted into a sister-in-law, it's all in a good cause. 'I'd welcome your opinion of the place.'

'I'd be delighted to help,' said Blakeway, 'and the other thing?'

'That has to do with your antique shop here in Burford.'

'It's not my antique shop any more, Lord Powerscourt. I sold the place three months ago.'

'But I looked in there recently, and the young man told me you weren't there but that you popped over to see them at the weekend. At least, I think that's what he said.'

'I never told Skinny Simon I'd sold the place. His mother is the biggest gossip in the county. Might as well have put it on the front page of *Jackson's Oxford Journal*.'

Powerscourt wondered if the man was lying. If he was, he was pretty convincing. But if all he had heard about Blakeway was even half true, he'd had years of practice. Even so, if it was three months ago that he sold the antique business, then he could have nothing to do with *Mortlake Terrace* or *August Riverside* coming to the auctioneers. Or could he?

'Really, Mr Blakeway? I presume you popped in to see if the new man had made any changes to the place?'

'Absolutely, Lord Powerscourt. How clever of you to have worked that one out.'

'And has he?'

'That's the curious thing. The fellow said he wanted to spruce the place up a bit, make a bit more noise on the High Street, those were his very words. All he seems to have done is to sack the cleaning woman. The shop has now got more dust lying about than the storerooms at the Ashmolean.'

'That's a pity,' said Powerscourt, still wondering if the man was telling the truth. 'Tell me about the Hellenic College, Mr Blakeway. My sister-in-law said she'd seen you teaching there when she went to look at the school.'

'We were doing Byron with the senior class,' said Blakeway. 'The College is always keen to emphasize his links with the struggle for Greek freedom.'

'He died fighting for it, if I remember right,' said Powerscourt.

'Well, in a manner of speaking. He wasn't actually killed in battle, though I'm sure he would have preferred that. He caught a fever and that was the end of him.'

'Anyway, tell me about the Hellenic College. Would you recommend it?'

George Blakeway took a draught of his beer and stared at Powerscourt for a moment. 'I don't find that an easy question to answer, oddly enough.'

'Why not?'

'Well, let me put it like this. If you wanted your children to be brought up in an English tradition, the Hellenic is not the place for you. If you want them to be brought up in a very particular Greek fashion, then it might be. The people who run the place – I wouldn't describe them as fanatics, that would be going too far – but they are very pro Greek, evangelists for Greek culture and Greek rights and all that sort of thing. They think Greece is special because of all that Homer and the historians and the playwrights and people like bloody Socrates droning on in Athens over two thousand years ago. I'm not sure it makes any difference nowadays whether your long distant ancestors were discussing Plato's cave or the best way to kill a deer with a bow and arrow. I suspect some of the Greek teachers over in the College might even believe in the ancient Greek gods rather more than in English Christianity but I'm not sure.'

'You sound as if you don't altogether approve of the standards of the place,' said Powerscourt.

'Don't get me wrong, Lord Powerscourt, I'm as big a fan of Sophocles and Lord Byron as the next man. And some things they are very good at, science and mathematics and that sort of stuff is taken very seriously, much more so than it would be at an English school.'

'Good to know that the spirit of Euclid and Archimedes lives on in the Chilterns,' said Powerscourt.

'Quite so. And the children are all very keen to learn, even when it comes to performing the rituals of ancient Athens, that's always an advantage. So on the whole I would advise your sister-in-law to send her children there as long as she is sure she wants them to have a very Greek education.'

'Thank you very much, Mr Blakeway.' Powerscourt was wondering how on earth he could ask about Blakeway's past. He didn't think a straight question along the lines of 'Weren't you in Wormwood Scrubs for eighteen months?' would go down very well. And it would certainly imply that he knew rather more about the man's previous activities than he was letting on. 'Do you enjoy teaching? Have you done it before your current spell at the Hellenic?'

'I've done all sorts of things in my time, Lord Powerscourt, art dealing, auctioneer, antiques, I've dabbled in them all. And now, if you will forgive me, I must go. I have to be on call at the College this evening. If you will excuse me.'

Blakeway departed, shaking hands as he left. Powerscourt wondered if the man was telling the truth. And one other thing struck him. The Headmaster had told Lady Lucy that Blakeway had been hired on the express recommendation of Tristram Stanhope, Head of Greek and Roman Antiquities at the British Museum and consultant to the College. But Blakeway hadn't mentioned his links to Stanhope at all. How significant was that?

Word spread fast around the cafés and the bars and the brothels of the port of Brindisi. Captain Dimitri, captain of the circus ship, The *Isles of Greece*, was back. People never tired of telling each other and any strangers who could be persuaded to listen the tale of the package that fell into the sea. Some said it contained cannon, others held that it was a consignment of marble for a sculptor on the neighbouring island of Levkas, one or two maintained that the broken image was a statue of the risen Christ destined for the church further up the coast. Nobody, not even small and curious boys, had managed to dive down deep enough to discover what it really was. *The Isles of Greece* was back too, the lion still mangy, the monkeys querulous, the jugglers and the clown still aboard.

But the Captain had company on this, his return journey. Four young Greek Orthodox monks from the monastery on the island of Kythnos were with him now. They had no obvious circus talent, they could not cross the ship on a high wire or play the fool with the children in the audience. They were serious. They had brought their very own icon with them, of a sad and mournful Christ who looked too young to be taking on the sins of the world. They would take him to the end of the pier and kneel in prayer as the sun set across the bay. People wondered who was in charge. Were the monks holding Dimitri and *The Isles of Greece* prisoner? Were they going to take over the vessel for a pilgrimage to some sacred spot in the islands? Or had the Captain recruited the monks to act as cover for some spectacular, if unspecified, act of piracy?

This time, the telegraph boys noted sadly, the Captain wasn't waiting for a message from their office. Whatever he was doing there, he seemed to know the appointed hour. The man who owned the bar believed that they would wake up one morning and find the mooring empty and *The Isles of Greece* a small dot on the distant horizon. But when, or with whom, the appointed hour was, the Captain kept to himself.

21

August Riverside, with its delicate sunshine and the curve of the Thames, was now gracing the window of Houranis, the art dealers, in New Bond Street. Sylvester Hourani, the third member of his family to become Managing Director of the firm, showed Powerscourt and Inspector Kingsley into his boardroom, the walls hung with portraits of earlier Houranis and their families.

'Rupert Fitzwilliam said you would be coming my way,' he said with a smile, ushering Powerscourt into a chair by a coffee table laden with the latest art magazines. 'He thinks you suspect all is not well on *August Riverside*. Is he right?'

'Well,' said Powerscourt, 'I do have some concerns. And I will tell you precisely what they are since anything suspicious or illegal probably took place before you were involved with the picture. My first problem is with the name. I think this painting is not called *August Riverside*, but *Mortlake Terrace, Summer's Evening*. *Mortlake Terrace, Summer's Evening* was stolen from a property on Chiswick Mall called Norfolk House over a year ago. What do you say to that, Mr Hourani?'

'Well, I don't know, I've never heard of such a thing. As far as we knew when we bid for it, the painting was called *August Riverside*. Perhaps you'd better take that up with Linfords. It was their auction after all.'

'Very well,' said Powerscourt. 'We shall have to conduct further inquiries. I have another problem, Mr Hourani. Can you tell me where *August Riverside* is going?'

'I can, indeed I can. I received permission to tell you that only this morning. Rupert said you were bound to ask. The painting is going to the United States, Lord Powerscourt. I am going to take it there myself the day after tomorrow. We were acting at the auction for an American firm called Knoedler, Alfred Knoedler, who have a high reputation for Old Masters at Old Masters prices. They, in turn, are acting for one of America's great collections, the Huntington Library in California, built, endowed and stuffed to the rafters with railway money. Henry Huntington, the founder, is so wealthy that he feels sure that if it is known that his library is interested in a work, the price will rise automatically and I dare say he is right. This is not the first time we have acted for him through Knoedler. He must keep them in profit, he buys such a lot through them.'

Inspector Kingsley looked like a man who has just solved a mathematical problem in his bath. It was the mention of a possible departure the following day that spurred him into action.

'You may be going to the United States the day after tomorrow, Mr Hourani,' he announced, 'I'm afraid the painting will be staying here. I'm arresting the picture called *August Riverside* or *Mortlake Terrace*. It will remain in police custody pending further considerations.'

'You can't, you can't do that,' Hourani spluttered. 'The

tickets are booked and everything. I have one dinner appointment at the captain's table, for heaven's sake!'

'The painting stays here. And so do you, Mr Hourani. For the moment you are going nowhere. Count yourself lucky you're not being arrested as well.'

'On what grounds?'

'Receipt of stolen goods. We believe the painting was taken over eighteen months ago. The theft was reported to the police. Until we have further information I must ask you to remain in London until further notice.'

It was the mention of the report to the police that sent Powerscourt's brain working in a totally different direction. 'Inspector, I've just thought of something,' he said, the words tumbling out very fast, 'this could be the reason why the name has changed. The theft was reported to the police at the time. Customs departments, the people who grant export licences, police authorities, art dealers and experts all over the Western world will have been told of the theft of *Mortlake Terrace, Summer's Evening*. They will have been told to watch out for her. They will have been asked to notify the authorities in their own country if they see the painting or hear any trace of her. They will not have been asked to look out for *August Riverside*. That could sail through without anybody taking any notice at all. So the whole purpose of the auction may have been just that, to change the painting's name. Maybe our American friend was worried about being in receipt of stolen goods. So he organized this charade instead. What do you think?'

'I think that's very plausible, my lord,' said Inspector Kingsley. 'But why wait for so long? Why didn't he do it before?'

'I don't know. Maybe he thought the warning ran out

after a year. Maybe it had to be renewed. Maybe there were circumstances in his own affairs that caused the delay. I'm sure we can find out.'

'For now,' said Kingsley, 'I'm going to take the painting away. My sergeant is going to organize a parade of experts to inspect it. I shall look into the question of the renewal of the theft notification.'

'And I,' said Powerscourt cheerfully, 'shall get in touch immediately with the *New York Times* European art correspondent and ask him to launch some enquiries in that city.'

Sylvester Hourani watched sadly as *August Riverside* or *Mortlake Terrace, Summer's Evening* was removed from his window and his bank account and taken into police custody. Powerscourt wondered where Inspector Kingsley was going to keep her. If only, he said to himself, if only she could share a cell with the Caryatid.

'We've found him! We've found Lucas Ringer!' Inspector Davies's voice was breaking up on the telephone line from Wales. Inspector Kingsley, fiddling with his pen in the little office he shared with two other inspectors, was delighted that the lost undertaker had been located.

'Where did you find him?' he asked.

'I'm in Aberystwyth. The local police found him sleeping rough near the seafront. You'll never guess what's happened.'

'Why don't you tell me?'

'Friend Ringer has turned the rules of police procedure upside down. Most people can't wait to get out of a police cell once they've been inside it. Lucas doesn't want to leave. He says the prison cell is the only place in the whole of Wales where he feels safe.'

'And are you going to let him stay there, Inspector Davies?'

'I've offered him a bargain. If he agrees to talk, to tell us everything that was going on before, he can stay in the cell for the time being.'

'Well done.'

'I've been thinking about this, mind you. In my opinion Ringer will say more to somebody he doesn't know than he will to somebody he does. I don't live in the same town but I'm not that far away. I think he suspects that anything he says to me will, sooner or later, get passed round the community. His granny or his auntie will be spreading the news within the week. Word gets round fast in Wales. People talk. So I think it would be best, certainly best for your investigation, if you came to talk to the man yourself.'

'The fact that I'm a policeman won't matter? He won't think that I would tell you and word would get out that way?'

'I don't think so. Once you're in plain clothes he won't necessarily think of you as a policeman at all. Aberystwyth is quite bracing at this time of year, my friend. A blast of sea air will do you good, "blast" being the operative word.'

'Very well, Inspector Davies. I'll pack my best bucket and spade and be with you tomorrow.'

Lucas Ringer looked like a man who had spent too many days and nights sleeping rough. He had shaved badly with a borrowed razor and spots of blood were all over his left cheek. The police had taken away his clothes and lent him some others which had been made for a much larger man so they hung off his frame. And, as Inspector

Kingsley soon discovered, it was more than his body that had been affected. His brain was not what it had been either.

'They kicked him to death, you know,' were his first words to Inspector Kingsley in the little interview room in Aberystwyth police station the following afternoon.

'I know,' said Inspector Kingsley, desperately trying to work out how to handle this crucial witness who might be able to open the whole case up.

'Cigarette burns too. On his arms.'

'Indeed,' Inspector Kingsley replied. One route to follow was the obvious one. Play the policeman – *Look here, you'll be in real trouble if you don't answer my questions, do you want me to throw the book at you, I could have you locked up for a long time*. Inspector Kingsley didn't think that would work. Something softer, something gentler was required. He had plenty of experience of the first route and a little of the second. He would just have to work it out as he went along.

'Do you remember leaving home?' Inspector Kingsley asked in his mildest voice. 'Could you tell me why?'

'I was frightened.' Lucas Ringer stared hard at the policeman from London. 'Didn't want to get kicked to death, I suppose.'

'Well, nobody's going to kick you to death in here, you know that. Nobody knows you're here for a start. Inspector Davies and the local men haven't said a word to anybody.'

'One day he was alive all day. That evening he was gone. No one knows how long it took to send him from one state to the other.'

'What do you think Carwyn would say to you now, what advice do you think he would give you?'

There was a long pause. 'Don't know, I'm sure.'

'Well, I'm quite sure of one thing, Mr Ringer. He would want you to help us catch the people who killed your friend. Once they're out of the way you won't have to worry about being kicked to death any more. But we don't need to think about that just at the moment. Is there anything we can do to help you just now?'

'I'm frightened, see. Very frightened.'

'I can quite understand that. I'd be frightened too if I were in your shoes.' Inspector Kingsley wondered if that had been a mistake as soon as he finished saying it.

'I've asked this before, but I don't think they knew I was serious. Can I stay in my cell for a while? I feel safe here, you see.'

'Of course you can. Don't worry about that. It'll be fine, just fine.'

Inspector Kingsley wondered suddenly if the under-taker was hungry. Certainly he looked as though he hadn't had a square meal for some days.

'Tell me, Mr Ringer, would you like something to eat? You must be hungry, surely, after all you've been through. Could I order some sandwiches for you from the canteen? Some tea perhaps?'

Lucas Ringer nodded emphatically. 'Ham?' he said. 'Do you think they have ham sandwiches? They've always been my favourite. Sometimes I have ham sandwiches for my lunch every day of the week.'

Inspector Kingsley departed to the front desk to be told the canteen would send them up directly.

'We're temporarily out of caviar and champagne, mind you,' the sergeant on duty told him, 'we hope to get fresh supplies next week.'

Ringer devoured one pair of sandwiches, then another.

293

He finished a cup of tea and asked for a refill. The Inspector thought he began to look a little better. It was proving to be a most unusual interview.

'What I'm going to do, Mr Ringer, is to tell you the little I know about what was going on. Then I would like you to fill in the gaps in my knowledge if you will.'

The undertaker gave a reluctant nod, but it was a nod, none the less.

'Some strangers came, I don't know how many. They were based either in one of the caves or at a great barn out on the Crickhowell Road. Neighbours heard a lot of banging in the night. You were asked by somebody, I don't know who, to make an enormous coffin, much bigger than normal. The schoolteacher came up with the cover story about how it was going to send a statue to America. Something, we don't know what, it might have been anything, was placed inside the coffin and it was sent off to Bristol.'

'That's good,' said Lucas Ringer, tucking into the last pair of ham sandwiches, 'there's some things I know about and some I don't. I don't know anything definite about the strangers, it was all rumour and gossip. Some people said the people were foreign, but I'm not sure. I do know about the coffin. A man came from London to order that. At least he said he'd come from London. He gave me the dimensions of the thing. When it was finished, I was to drive it out to that big barn on the Crickhowell Road and wait while they put something inside it. Then I had to drive it back to my place and wait for the transport to Bristol.'

'What sort of man was he? Well spoken? Did he sound like a Londoner? What sort of age, would you say?'

'He looked about forty years old. He sounded like a

professional man, rather like yourself, Inspector. His clothes were ordinary, as far as I remember. Dark blue suit, plain tie. He left me an address in London to write to if there were any complications. That was the address I gave to Carwyn Jones. I don't know what part of London it was. But don't you see?'

Lucas Ringer's eyes took on that hunted look again. 'If they came to kill Carwyn for what he knew, then why shouldn't they come to kill me too? I know even more than he did.'

'And the two men who came down to see Carwyn after he sent that letter? What can you remember about them?'

'They were thugs, basically,' Lucas Ringer said. 'They made me feel uneasy, just looking at them.'

'And you have no idea what was in Carwyn Jones's letter?'

'Not a clue.'

Inspector Kingsley thought that he had information now to banish most of the terrors that haunted the undertaker. If Ringer knew that Carwyn had been trying to blackmail the man from London, then he would surely feel safer. Always assuming he, Ringer, hadn't been trying a bit of blackmail too. But there was one thought and one thought only uppermost in Inspector Kingsley's mind. If he could get Ringer to swear in the witness box at the Old Bailey that the twins in the dock were the same people as those who had come to see Carwyn Jones on his last night alive, the twins would surely hang. Inspector Ferguson's problem with the silent witnesses of Deptford would be solved. He couldn't work out, for the moment, whether a very frightened Ringer would be more likely to identify them than a Ringer who was just a little bit scared. He resolved to think about the matter overnight.

'You've been very helpful, Mr Ringer. I think you have had enough for one day. I'd like to come back in the morning and we could have another talk. Is there anything else you can tell me before I go? Anything more about the man from London perhaps?'

'I don't think so, my mind has got confused. There is one thing, though. I think he was bald, the bloke from London, but I'm not sure. I could be wrong.'

Lady Lucy Powerscourt was opening the mail from the afternoon post in the drawing room in Markham Square. Her husband was reading a long account of the search for the Caryatid in the *Morning Post*.

'Look, Francis,' she said, 'they've sent us a whole lot more information, the Hellenic College people. We've got details of the staff and where they come from, and a page of school news. This will interest you, my love. The new Erechtheion building will be officially opened on Saturday evening – that's two days from now – by Dr Tristram Stanhope, Head of Greek and Roman Antiquities at the British Museum, and Classical Consultant to the Hellenic College. "Unfortunately," the news goes on, "there will not be enough room for us to welcome parents and visitors on this important day, but we are sure you will wish us well on the happy occasion." What do you think of that?'

'Did you see the new building at all when you were there, Lucy? Is it very enclosed, perhaps?'

'That's the curious thing. The new Erechtheion is at the end of a long glade, a broad stretch of grass that runs between the trees up towards the Parthenon. You could put loads of people in there, I'm sure.'

'Maybe they haven't got enough chairs, Lucy.'

'You can't be serious. The people in that big house up the road must have heaps and heaps of chairs. They often have concerts and things like that by the side of the lake.'

'Do they say what time the opening is going to be?'

Lady Lucy checked the news sheet on her lap. 'Eight o'clock in the evening. It's going to be quite dark. How odd, to open a new place when most people won't be able to see it.'

Powerscourt strode downstairs to send an urgent message to Warwickshire.

Inspector Kingsley thought he was seeing quite enough of the country's penal establishments. Aberystwyth police station the day before yesterday, one of London's most notorious prisons today. His second interview with Lucas Ringer had been uneventful and yielded nothing apart from another round of ham sandwiches. He had left a set of recommendations with Inspector Davies.

'The only thing that matters is that Ringer should be able to identify the Twins in court. Whatever we have to do to make him fit for that, we must do it. If he's happy staying in the police station, so be it. If he wants to go home with a police guard, that's fine. If he wants to go to a bloody hotel, the Met will pay. Let's just hope we can keep him on track.'

The land surrounding Wormwood Scrubs Prison had once been the favourite place in London for duelling. The building itself, he had been told by the Governor on a previous visit, was constructed entirely by prison labour. There were two reasons for his visit today. He was going to see the convict he had sent there eighteen months ago, in a bid to raise the man's spirits and, possibly, to save him from suicide. The other reason concerned the three men who had been sent to prison in recent years for fraud and other related crimes in London's art world. Inspector Kingsley felt sure that at least one of them must have been incarcerated here in the Scrubs. He had sent a list of names to the Governor's office on his return from Wales.

'Easton, Kennedy, Blakeway,' the Governor began, 'they sound like a firm of solicitors, don't they? Now then, I've had my people look them up and ask around about what we remember of these characters. We only had two of them, the records say that Easton was sent to Pentonville. I've written to my opposite number there to ask for any news.'

'So what of Blakeway, Governor? Nicholas George Blakeway, former auctioneer and fraudster?'

'Blakeway was an interesting character, Inspector. He seemed to fit into the prison routine from the day he arrived. Some people do. Perhaps he'd been to boarding school. He was rather an expert at cards. Most of the inmates refused to play poker with him after a while so he taught them whist instead. I remember him telling me that the criminal mind, for some unknown reason, had a natural ability to remember all the cards that have been played so far.'

'Did he make friends with anybody in particular during his time here?'

'I think you could have said he was friends with everybody and nobody at the same time. He got on well with most people but he didn't get close to anybody.'

'I see,' said Inspector Kingsley. 'What about the other man, Michael Moloney Kennedy?'

'Ah, Kennedy. The man with his hand in the till. The

inmates knew he had been called Trustworthy Kennedy the day he arrived. He was one of the strangest prisoners I've ever seen. From the day he came through the doors, he was miserable as sin. He used to rent out his services as a financial consultant with some success. Odd how the prisoners rate a man as better qualified if he's actually been convicted for theft. But he was very unhappy at the beginning. Then, after three or four months in here, he cheered up. He got a letter in the post, Michael Moloney Kennedy, and after that he was as cheerful as the lark until the day he left.'

'Do you know what was in the letter?'

The Governor laughed. 'We only found out after he'd been released. Clever of him to have kept the good news to himself for so long. Some distant relation had died and left him a great deal of money. He would never need to work again apparently.'

'Lucky man,' Inspector Kingsley said, wondering if Kennedy's retirement might have included the theft of a Caryatid. 'I presume he didn't make any special friends when he was here?'

'He spent the last fifteen months of his time here not making any friends at all. I'm sorry I can't be more helpful to you.'

'Well,' said Inspector Kingsley, 'at least we know what happened to those two here. Who knows what the news from Pentonville may be?'

John Hudson arrived in Markham Square at twenty past eight the following morning.

'I've seen him!' he panted to Powerscourt. 'He's in Paris!'

'Seen who, in heaven's name?'

'Michael Moloney Kennedy, that's who. He was at an auction.'

'Was he indeed. You'd better come in and have some breakfast. Have you just arrived back from Paris?'

'I have and I'm starving,' said Hudson, sitting down with a slice of buttered toast. 'I've not been home yet. The auction was at Drouot's. They were selling a lot of Post-Impressionists. The auctioneer must have known him from some previous event as he kept referring to him as Monsieur Kennedy, *le monsieur Anglais*. That's how I came to realize he was our man, he was the right age.'

'What was he buying?' asked Lady Lucy, sending out for more tea.

'Cézannes. He bought three of them. That was what I talked to him about. I asked him if he was building up a collection of the man. He told me that he owned eight of them already and now he would be into double figures. When he got to twenty he was going to open a Cézanne gallery. So I asked if I could write an article about his plans for the *New York Times*. American visitors to Paris and London are always keen to go to see the latest thing.'

Powerscourt realized that if Hudson hadn't been home yet he couldn't have seen his request for information about the American railway magnate. That would have to wait.

John Hudson took a large gulp of fresh tea and carried on. 'Well, Mr Kennedy asked me if I could wait until his plans were further advanced. He thought the public-ity would be more useful to him just before his gallery opened. If I published now, he said, people would have forgotten my story by the time it opened. He's probably right.'

'So what happened then?'

'I gave him my card,' John Hudson said, making short work of a pair of coddled eggs, 'and he said he would get in touch the next time he came to London. He said he always stays at the Ritz.'

22

The young reporter on the Brindisi newspaper hired by Powerscourt to report back on any further sightings of *The Isles of Greece* was a conscientious fellow. His immediate superior, the chief reporter and sub-editor on the *Puglia Messenger*, thought he would go far. Antonio Paravicini bought himself a second-hand bicycle with his very generous retainer. The chief sub-editor disapproved on principle of all modern devices, but he noted with gratitude that tyro journalist Antonio seemed able to report on more and more stories every week.

He had laid down his lines shortly after Powerscourt and Johnny Fitzgerald left the Hotel Mazzini with the owner of the bar on the quays and with the stationmaster in the square. Any fresh packages for the ship or fresh sightings of her would be reported to him on his next visit. If it seemed urgent, a message would be left for him at the newspaper office. Even with this proviso business never moved very quickly in the port or the freight department of Brindisi. It was a couple of days after the departure of *The Isles of Greece* before Antonio learnt of her absence and the strange addition to the crew of the four Greek Orthodox monks, praying nightly to their sad icon at the end of the pier. The ancient guardian of incoming and outgoing freight at the station told him that a package had certainly arrived, and had been delivered to the circus vessel. No, he couldn't remember what it was, the old man told young Antonio. Of course it was only a short time ago, but nobody could expect a fellow to remember every bloody object that passed through his hands, could they? Even a drink, even many drinks in the taverna in the square, could not bring forth the memories of what it might have been.

Antonio had been improving his English in an evening class at his former school but he decided to write his telegram in Italian and ask his old teacher to translate it. The missive cost a quarter of the money left in Powerscourt's original gift. It arrived in Markham Square at lunchtime: '*Isles of Greece* back in port with four young Orthodox monks. Package delivered from station. Left Brindisi a few days ago. Thought to be going to Athens via Corinth Canal. Might be in Athens now. Regards. Antonio Paravicini.'

An urgent message brought Inspector Kingsley to Markham Square just before three o'clock. Lady Lucy thought he looked tired as he took his seat in the chair by the fire. She remembered being told of his dislike of murder inquiries and the three in a row he had completed before the start of this one.

'*The Isles of Greece* is on the move again,' Powerscourt told him. 'She's picked up a package, though our man doesn't tell us what it was. The fact that it came as freight rather than through the postal service suggests it was something big. And she's heading for Athens through the Corinth Canal. With four Greek Orthodox monks on board to keep the lion company. Maybe they'll convert the monkeys.'

'Do you think there's another bloody Caryatid on board,' asked the Inspector, 'surely not?'

'God knows,' said Powerscourt cheerfully, 'maybe Zeus knows, that's his part of the world after all, but he's not telling. And we have news of Dr Stanhope of the British Museum. You remember we discovered he was linked with the Hellenic College in Amersham? Well, Lucy here has been to check the place out. She was posing as a possible parent.'

'Tell me more,' said Inspector Kingsley.

'Well,' said Lady Lucy, 'it's all very interesting. To get there you have to go through the grounds of that big house, packed with replicas of ancient statues, ancient temples, ancient obelisks. There's a pantheon and a Parthenon sitting there quite happily. The actual school seems to be very well run, but very Greek, very keen on teaching Greek customs and culture, all that sort of thing. I saw a couple of classrooms, one of them where the senior boys were reading aloud from Byron's *Childe Harold*. And this is the interesting bit, Inspector. They were reading the passages where the poet is very rude about Lord Elgin for stealing the Marbles. Byron thought they should go home to Greece. And you'll never guess who the teacher was.'

'I won't even try, Lady Powerscourt. Please tell me.'

'Why, it was Mr Blakeway, Nicholas George Blakeway, the man who was sent to prison for his crimes.'

'I was going to tell you about his time in jail,' said the Inspector. 'The Governor of the Scrubs filled me in. Blakeway fitted in very well, apparently. He taught a lot of convicts to play whist. They refused to play poker with him, presumably because he won all their matches or their cigarettes or whatever they were playing for.'

'There's more to do with our friend Mr Blakeway and the Hellenic College, Inspector.' Lady Lucy was well into her stride now. 'Dr Tristram Stanhope recommended him for the job there. Really. They sent us a lot of information about the school yesterday. They have just finished a new building, a replica of the Erechtheion, a temple on the Acropolis in Athens, the temple, as you well know, that was originally home to the British Museum Caryatid. The new building's being declared open tomorrow evening. There's no room for parents apparently, which I think is rather odd, none of them being invited to the ceremony. Have they got something they wish to hide? Anyway, Francis and I were going to see if we could watch from the shadows. Maybe Dr Stanhope will appear, dressed as Pericles for his Funeral Speech or ranting away like Demosthenes with his pebbles on the seashore.'

Before Inspector Kingsley could comment, Powerscourt cut in. He told the Inspector about his trip to the Cotswolds and his meeting with Blakeway. 'He told me that he'd sold Burford Antiques three months ago. I've just realized I forgot to ask him for the name of the man who bought it.'

'Did you believe him when he told you he'd sold it?' Inspector Kingsley sounded as if he wouldn't have believed a word of it himself.

'I don't know,' Powerscourt replied. 'He's a very plausible fellow.'

'I too have some news,' said Inspector Kingsley. 'You won't be surprised to hear that it concerns Dr Tristram

Stanhope. You remember I said earlier that our financial people were looking into all the key personnel at the British Museum? That's how we found out about Kostas's enormous savings account. Our financial wizard thinks that Dr Stanhope has recently received a very large sum of money, thousands and thousands of pounds. It hasn't gone directly into his account, naturally, but into some trust fund we can't at present open. Smaller lumps of money, hundreds at a time, have been transferred from this fund into his regular account. Even that was hard to get into. The Commissioner had to write to the chairman of the bank, threatening a major investigation of all the directors, before they agreed.'

Powerscourt jumped up from the sofa and began walking up and down the room. 'I presume you have at present no idea where this money came from?'

'None at all. All the same, if a relative had died, or some colleague had left you a packet in his will, you wouldn't go to such lengths to conceal it, would you?'

'But if some version of the Caryatid has been sold, possibly to our friend Lincoln Mitchell by the Hudson River in upstate New York, for example, you might receive heaps of cash for your part in the affair, might you not?'

'That's right. And there's another thing that has just occurred to me. You mentioned Amersham just now, Lady Powerscourt. I've just remembered. When I put young Constable Smithson onto the freight records at Paddington, he mentioned that a couple came from Amersham. I'm sure of it. I'll send him up to Amersham station the moment I get back. We should hear his report tomorrow.'

'Could I ask you a question, Inspector?'

'Of course, Lady Powerscourt. Fire ahead.'

'It was the mention of Mr Blakeway that did it,' she said. 'Isn't he one of the three people who went to prison and might be linked to the shades of the prison-house mentioned by old Sokratis in his wanderings?'

'That's right.'

'Suppose you think of this case like a long piece of string,' Lady Lucy went on. 'At one end you have the three men who went to prison and possibly Dr Stanhope. The poor Mr Ragg and the Caryatid are in the middle. At the other end are the horrible Twins who went to Wales to kill the schoolteacher and may have pushed the porter under the train.'

'That's right, Lucy,' Powerscourt said, wondering where his wife was going.

'I think this idea comes from remembering the bit about the prison-house. Inspector, I presume your colleague in Deptford, Inspector Ferguson I think he's called, knows who the Twins' master and controller is, the man who gives them their orders?'

'He most certainly does.'

'Why then, don't you see? Maybe the master and controller's been in prison at the same time as one of the other three, Blakeway, Easton and Kennedy? It's the same question you're asking already but looked at from the other end, if you see what I mean.'

'I do, indeed I do. An excellent suggestion, Lady Powerscourt. I shall get onto it right away.'

'There's one thing that's always puzzled me about this case, especially with this new information about Stanhope's money.' The master of the house was still pacing up and down his drawing room.

'You could just about envisage Stanhope having a hand

in planning the theft, though I can't see him knowing the contacts to produce the actual thieves. But connections with the Twins and their various murders? Surely not. And you can easily imagine the Twins or their controller going round the place murdering people. But it's hard to think of them stealing the Caryatid. I doubt if the Twins have even heard of the British Museum.'

'When we've answered that question, my lord, we'll have solved the mystery. I must get back and set my men to work. Perhaps we could meet again after lunch tomorrow? I should have something to report by then. Perhaps you and Lady Powerscourt would care to think about whether you would like me and some of my men to accompany you to Amersham tomorrow? It could be a prudent move to have reinforcements on hand.'

That evening Powerscourt read Keats's poem about seeing the Elgin Marbles for the first time. He read again Lord Byron's poetic diatribe about Elgin's theft of the Marbles.

He woke up shortly before four o'clock in the morning. He levered himself slowly out of bed and tiptoed over to the chair by the window. He peered slowly out through a crack in the curtains. Markham Square was silent. Even the leaves on the trees were still. Only the Markham cat, a battered and bedraggled beast from regular fights on the King's Road, fed occasionally with milk from the Powerscourt kitchen by the Powerscourt twins, was on the prowl, checking that her enemies were not at large on this night. Behind him he could hear Lady Lucy's breathing, slow and regular, like a well-made clock.

Powerscourt had just been visited by one of the most extraordinary dreams of his life. He wanted to fix it in his mind before it disappeared between now and the dawn, lost for ever in the secret filing cabinets of his brain. In his dream he was sitting by the ground-floor window of one of the Nash terrace houses in Great Russell Street, the young John Nash's very first architectural commission, long before he went on to astonish the world with the great sweep of Regent Street and the improbable fantasies of the Brighton Pavilion. There was a noise outside, or a variety of different noises, coming closer by the minute. Then he saw them, the advance guard of a mighty army from many nations and of many different colours. In the vanguard was a phalanx of Homeric warriors from ancient Greece, dressed in the armour they wore to fight against the Trojans. They looked as though they had stepped out of one of the vases on display in the building up the street. Powerscourt thought he could recognize Achilles from the glory of his breastplate and the wily Odysseus, relying this time on a frontal attack rather than the ruse of the Wooden Horse. Every now and then one of these heroes would utter a fearful war cry and wave a spear towards their target, which, Powerscourt realized, could only be the British Museum. Behind the ancient Greeks in his dream marched a cohort of Roman legionaries with a trumpet call to make the blood run cold. But it was the people behind them who were the principal components of this invading army. They came in loincloths and in tunics, some wearing flowing robes and others clad in skimpy drawers, their bodies heavily oiled and glistening in the street lights. They came with primitive armour and leather shields. They came with spears and assegais and swords long and short, with axes and hammers and knobkerries that could smash a man's skull, with sharp daggers and early bows and arrows. Looking out of his window Powerscourt saw that they stretched back along Great Russell Street into Southampton Row and presumably down Holborn to the river at the Victoria Embankment. Perhaps the motley army had come by boat, primitive canoes and coracles nestling along the banks of the Thames, early sailing boats tied up by Waterloo Bridge. All these different tribes were singing their battle hymns as they marched, some stamping their feet and raising their weapons in defiance at the enemy. And the enemy, Powerscourt, realized once the vanguard had reached their destination, was the pillared and porticoed front of the British Museum itself. Only when he watched what happened when the warriors climbed the steps and smashed down the great doors did he realize what was going on. Not long after their entry he saw some of the Greeks come out, waving sections of early Greek pottery and sculpture in the air and yelling cries of victory, closely followed by the legionaries, arms laden with ancient Roman coins and jewels and the heads of their emperors. This was the revenge of the subject peoples of the British Museum. Looking at the disparate mob of many colours and of many nations behind the Romans, Powerscourt knew now who they were. These were the descendants of the Hittites, the Assyrians, the Canaanites, the Phoenicians, the Egyptians, the Sumerians, the Chaldonians, the Sudanese, the Amorites, ancient civilizations all, their cultures plundered and ransacked centuries before to glorify the British Museum and titillate bored Londoners on wet weekday afternoons. Each and every tribe had a room or an area in the museum devoted to their statues, the ornaments of their temples, the adornments of their rulers, the likenesses of their fearful gods. These armies of the night had come out of a troubled and turbulent present to rescue their past as a bulwark and safeguard against the uncertainties of the future. Soon the great halls of the museum would be emptied of everything that could be carried away. Stolen the day before yesterday, stolen back today.

Powerscourt had found the sweat dripping down his temples when he woke.

The Isles of Greece had to wait a couple of hours before she was allowed to enter the Corinth Canal and cross from one side of Greece to the other. Captain Dimitri himself took the helm as the circus ship inched her way very carefully down the four miles of the canal. The lion had shown absolutely no interest in the engineering marvel and had fallen asleep. The monkeys were pointing hysterically upwards at the 300-foot wall between the water at the bottom and the rough ground at the top. The monks were praying, staring straight ahead. The youngest monk was the brother of Kostas and Stavros. His superiors had not yet told him that one brother was dead and the other missing. Brother Andreas was part of the Orthodox community of St John the Divine on the Greek island of Kythnos, close to Patmos in the Cyclades. Andreas had waited in vain for *The Isles of Greece* to call at his island weeks before. Now, perhaps in atonement for his earlier vigil and the non-arrival of the ship, he and three of his fellow monks had been chosen to accompany *The Isles of Greece* on its voyage to the Greek capital.

Behind them, way to their left, stood the ancient site of Delphi, home to noxious vapours and ambivalent prophecies. Way up to the north Mount Olympus still stood, its gods silent now, their power impotent in the age of machines. On their right, to the south, lay Mycenae with its Lion Gate and the beehive tombs, and further south yet, the ancient city of Sparta, victorious over Athena's city in the thirty years of the Peloponnesian War. At the far end of the canal the sea was open to the little island of Aegina and the port of Piraeus, now virtually a part of Athens. The railway container was lashed to the mast so it could not be washed overboard in a storm.

Lord Francis Powerscourt had consulted his friends in the Foreign Office when he received the message from the young reporter Antonio. He discovered that the Ambassador had been one year behind him in his college at Cambridge, a man famed for rowing both for his college and the university. As he composed his message, Powerscourt wondered if some splendid oar, adorned with the names of all the crew, was now sitting on a wall in the Ambassador's office. 'Ship arriving soon called *The Isles of Greece*,' his message began. 'May contain Caryatid or Caryatid-related objects. Please keep watch for any local reception or celebrations.' He signed it Powerscourt and added the Trinity Hall Boat Club watchword, named after the college motto, 'Our powers are crescent.'

The sun was setting in a ball of blazing orange behind the Parthenon. Shafts of golden light were lighting up the building, a half-sized replica of the one on the Acropolis in Athens. Powerscourt and Lady Lucy were lying on a rug just behind the top of a little hill by the Hellenic College in Amersham. They had booked a room for the night at the King's Arms in the town. They could see the main entrance to the school below their position. In front of them was the long glade that led up to the newly completed Erechtheion. The porch where the Caryatids would have lived was covered with a large gold cloth, gold being one of the colours of Athena. Inspector Kingsley and his men were not far away. The Inspector had given Powerscourt a whistle to blow if he needed assistance. 'Pretend you're some ancient warrior,' he had suggested to Powerscourt, 'calling for help in your time of trouble.'

Powerscourt had a pair of German binoculars, Lady Lucy had her finest opera glasses. Powerscourt also had a pistol in his right-hand pocket.

'God knows what's going to happen, Lucy,' he whispered. 'I still don't understand why no parents are allowed in.'

'We should know fairly soon,' said Lady Lucy, squeezing her husband's hand.

Eight o'clock, the hour mentioned in the literature as the start time for the ceremony, came and went. There was a rumble of noise from the Hellenic College, and the sound of horses neighing from the direction of the stable block. Powerscourt wondered if they wanted more darkness before they started. At a quarter past eight four young men, dressed in Greek-style chitons, simple linen tunics that hung down to the knee, carrying burning torches, marched very slowly across the grass to the Erechtheion and stood to attention at the four corners of the building. Just in front, clad in long white robes, were a couple of musicians, one with a lyre who might have been Apollo and one with pipes who might have been Pan. They began to play a haunting tune, standing in front of the temple, facing the College. Somewhere behind them, concealed on the other side of the Erechtheion, a drum sounded a rhythmic beat, like a call to arms.

The young men held their blazing brands very high and very straight.

Then the procession began. In front, making their way slowly and deliberately out of the front of the College, was a group of elder men bearing olive branches in robes of dark blue, another of Athena's colours, heading for the Erechtheion. Lady Lucy poked her husband in the ribs. 'This lot are the staff, Francis,' she whispered. 'That's the Headmaster in front. Two behind is Mr Blakeway, the man from Burford.' The soft pipes played again. A girl of about sixteen was the next member of the procession. She was leading a reluctant heifer with a garland round her neck.

> Who are these coming to the sacrifice?
> To what green altar, O mysterious priest,
> Lead'st thou that heifer lowing at the skies,
> And all her silken flanks with garlands
>   drest?

Then came four horsemen, naked apart from a cloak thrown loosely over their shoulders, young men of about eighteen years, Amersham's answer to the cavalry that rode across the field at Marathon. The drum beat on, slightly faster now. There was a rattle from the ground. Powerscourt and Lady Lucy could not see what caused it. Then a chariot emerged, obviously home-made, with two riders, one of whom got on and off repeatedly as it trotted slowly towards the shrouded temple. It was dark. The lyre and the pipe sounded more insistent now.

'My God, Lucy,' Powerscourt whispered, although there was little chance of their voices being heard above the music and the crying of the heifer and the neighing of the horses, repeatedly restrained by their riders from

314

galloping towards their goal. 'This is the Parthenon frieze in the British Museum come to life, my love. This procession is marble in Bloomsbury. It's real here in Amersham. This is the great procession of the Panathenaica, the greatest festival in Athens to their goddess Athena. It's meant to happen in the summer, I think. Maybe Stanhope has decided to move it.'

'What are they going to do with that heifer?' asked Lady Lucy, who hated bloodshed.

'God knows.'

Four pairs of young men with torches came out next. They moved ahead to place themselves between the marchers. There were long shadows on the grass now, one or two of the horses bright on one side and dark on the other. A strange cart, pulled by a pair of oxen, came next. In the middle of the cart Powerscourt and Lady Lucy could see a tall shape like a ship, with a great slew of material draped across the mast.

'My God, Lucy.' Powerscourt was pulling very hard at the grass. 'That's the *peplos*, a new cloth for the goddess on top of the ship. The point of the festival is to bring a new *peplos* to Athena. The women spend months weaving it. These people are leaving nothing to chance.'

Twenty-four young girls, some of them the team brought by Artemis Metaxas from London, came next, carrying baskets. This was the reason for Artemis's weekend trips to the Hellenic College. The girls she brought had helped to weave the *peplos*. Now they were making up the numbers of maidens, an important part of the great parade. Then came another pair of musicians. The top of the procession had reached the Erechtheion now and began to line up in rows in front of it, facing the porch of the Caryatids. Powerscourt remembered how the procession was in two separate streams on the Parthenon frieze, the two joining together shortly before the finale. The music was beating faster now. A last charioteer brought up the rear, shuffling anxiously on his feet as if he felt he might fall off at any moment. Powerscourt thought all the inhabitants of the Hellenic College must be on parade now.

> What little town by river or sea-shore,
> Or mountain-built with peaceful citadel,
> Is emptied of this folk, this pious morn?
> And, little town, thy streets for evermore
> Will silent be; and not a soul to tell
> Why thou art desolate, can e'er return.

It was completely dark now, the torches shining more powerfully than before. A gust of wind blew over the watchers towards the charioteers and the musicians. Powerscourt hoped it wasn't going to rain.

The musicians fell silent. The drum beat on. The procession was over. All those taking part were now lined up in front of the temple. The heifer, Lady Lucy noted, seemed to have disappeared, led away to have its throat cut in more peaceful surroundings, or just put out to pasture. The torches were all around the front and the near side of the Erechtheion so that the new building and the porch, still covered in its cloth, were bathed in flickering light. The charioteers were hopping from foot to foot. The horsemen were holding back their steeds. The drum stopped. There was a moment of complete silence. Then the *salpinx*, the Greek trumpet, whose noise was described by the ancient playwright Aeschylus as shattering, sounded from inside the temple. The leader of the men at the front of the procession stepped forward and took hold of the rope holding the cloth over the porch. When the *salpinx* stopped, the drummer started up again, his beats loud and insistent. The Headmaster pulled on the rope. The cloth fell away. Leaning forward, Powerscourt saw that space was there on the temple porch for six maidens, just like the original, but only one was in place. At one end of the line stood a single Caryatid, her long gown falling down below her waist, her face proud and haughty. She looked at the crowd as if they were riff-raff outside her palace gates. At the other end stood Dr Tristram Stanhope in a very ornate robe with vine leaves in his hair.

'Is that the real Caryatid, Francis?' murmured Lady Lucy.

'Heaven knows,' her husband replied, 'but that's certainly the real Stanhope.'

'I begin to sing of Pallas Athena,' Tristram Stanhope began, 'the dread Protectress of the city, who with Ares looks after matters of war, the plundering of cities, the battle cry and the fray.'

'That's a Homeric hymn to Athena, my love,' Powerscourt whispered. 'They don't think Homer actually wrote it, but it's bloody old.'

'It is She who protects the people,' Stanhope went on, 'wherever they might come or go. Hail, Goddess, and give us good spirits and blessed favour!'

The little audience stayed silent, uncertain if they were in church or a pagan temple. Stanhope raised his voice once more. 'Day and night, eternally, in even the loneliest hours, Hear my prayer . . .'

'God help us, Lucy, here's another of those bloody hymns. Some of them go on for ever. We could be here all night.'

'. . . and grant us an abundant peace, fulfilment, good health. Make prosperous the hour, grey-eyed One, inventor of Art, The object of the people's ceaseless prayers – Athena My Queen!'

23

Tristram Stanhope bowed to the statue as if she were Athena herself. He strode off back to the College. His followers returned in the same order they had come. The procession was over. Only the four young men with torches stayed in their places by the sides of the building. Shadows and shafts of light played over the surface of the Erechtheion. The Caryatid had found a new home in the Chiltern hills. Now it was for Powerscourt and Inspector Kingsley to determine how permanent that new home should be.

They met in a back room of the King's Arms, Inspector Kingsley looking preoccupied, Lady Lucy pensive, Powerscourt writing down the order of the procession in his notebook. 'Well, my lord,' Inspector Kingsley began, 'I don't know what news you have to report but mine is pretty serious. The Twins are in town. God knows how many other criminals from Deptford are at large here in Amersham this evening.'

'What were they doing?' asked Lady Lucy.

'They were watching the entrance to the College, presumably to make sure there were no unwanted visitors.

Like yourselves. It's just as well they didn't go looking in the grounds around the College, my lady.'

Lady Lucy shuddered. Powerscourt carried on scribbling.

'There's more,' the Inspector went on. 'Young Smithson, the constable who's been looking into the traffic in railway containers, reports a number of them passing through Amersham. The dates suggest they may coincide with other developments in the case. It's not conclusive, of course, but is certainly suspicious.'

Powerscourt looked up, as though he had just returned from a long journey.

'We saw the Caryatid, Inspector. Let me correct that. We saw *a* Caryatid. God only knows if it is the real one or a fake. You will recall that the ceremony at the school a couple of hours ago was to mark the completion of the Hellenic College Erechtheion, a temple dedicated to Athena. The real one, like the building here, is close to the Parthenon. There was a ceremony, like the one described on the Parthenon frieze: maidens with baskets, musicians, a trumpeter, animals meant for sacrifice, horsemen, city elders, a charioteer or two. They could have all walked out of the Acropolis in Athens nearly two and a half thousand years ago. This, however, is the key point. The porch of the Caryatids, one part of the building, was covered with a cloth until the climax of the proceedings. When it was revealed, there was a Caryatid, looking remarkably like the British Museum one in the photographs. There too was Dr Tristram Stanhope at the other end of the porch, ranting away with some Homeric poetry.'

'Do you think my men should go and seize it now?' said the Inspector.

'I think it might be better to leave her till the morning,'

Powerscourt replied. 'Heaven only knows what they're all getting up to down there now. Bacchanalian orgy? Dionysian revels? Anything could be happening.'

'Pardon me, Inspector,' said Lady Lucy. 'Isn't this the first time you have seen a link between the Twins and, presumably, their horrid boss in Deptford, and Dr Stanhope and the Hellenic College?'

'It is,' said Inspector Kingsley. There was a pause. Lady Lucy and the policeman looked at Powerscourt who seemed to be wrestling with some impossible question in his mind. Through the walls they could hear the sound of singing in the public bar. Outside the town clock struck ten.

'Let me make a proposal,' Powerscourt said finally. 'If either of you don't like it, I will drop it.'

They both nodded.

'I was thinking just now about the difference between success and victory.'

'Success and victory?' Inspector Kingsley sounded incredulous.

'Sorry if that sounded rather grand. Let me explain,' said Powerscourt, now pacing up and down the room. 'Victory in this case would mean the arrests of the Twins, their keeper, Dr Stanhope and whoever the link is between those two parties. I suggest we refer to him as the missing link from now on. All of them would be tried and convicted for their various crimes.' Powerscourt stopped under a hunting print where the hounds were just about to tear a cornered fox to pieces.

'And success?' Lady Lucy spoke very quietly.

'Success for me—' Powerscourt was on the move once again '—is not the same as success for the good Inspector here. Success for me is the return of the Caryatid. That,

321

after all, is what I was asked to do by the British Museum. This is how I propose to try for success. It should not rule out, and might even contribute to, a measure of victory.'

The public bar was now singing 'Jerusalem'. Powerscourt thought it more pleasant than the music of the lyre and the pipes and the incantations from a world that passed away so long ago.

'I propose to call on Dr Stanhope tomorrow morning. I believe you have a record of his London address, Inspector. I shall, of course, try the College first. I rather fancy he will have spent the night here in Amersham. I shall tell him he has forty-eight hours to return the real Caryatid to the British Museum.'

'And what will you say if he laughs in your face, my lord?'

'We have quite a lot we can throw at him, when you think about it. The presence of the Caryatid at the ceremony here this evening, the presence of the Twins, the progress of the railway containers, the large amounts of money floating through his various bank accounts, the fact that he could have organized the original theft more easily than anybody else. I shall have thought of a whole lot more by the morning. But there is one area where I'm sure I need your permission, Inspector.'

'What would that be, pray?'

'I propose saying to the fellow that cooperation would mean not that the police would leave him alone, but that any cooperation could be helpful to his case in the future. It wouldn't be anything specific, there would be no guarantees, just the knowledge that to help would be more profitable than retreating behind a barrage of lies and lawyers.'

'Permission granted.'

Powerscourt smiled. 'Thank you, Inspector, thank you very much.'

'What makes you think this plan might work, Francis?' Lady Lucy was looking worried.

'Vanity. The man is very vain. That could be his undoing.'

'Give it a try, my lord, give it a try. Now, if you will forgive me, I must go and organize my men to seize this Caryatid first thing tomorrow. If there are revels tonight, they may all still be asleep at half past seven in the morning.'

The Isles of Greece docked at Piraeus later that evening. The four monks were in the prow, peering towards the port. Nobody would have expected a welcoming party at that time of night, but there was a force of about twenty more monks, all of them young. They sang the Greek national anthem, rather out of tune and with some words missed out, as they untied the container from the mast and placed it on the back of a cart. The package and the young men set out for the heart of Athens. It was ten minutes short of midnight.

Inspector Kingsley took five men with him on his mission to capture the Caryatid. Dawn was breaking over Amersham. A couple of foxes were making their way home across the fields at the back of the Erechtheion. The birds were staking out their early morning positions in the high trees. The curtain that had shielded the statue during the procession the evening before had been pulled back again to keep the contents of the porch invisible. Sergeant Burke, the Inspector's right-hand man, gave it a great pull. The porch was empty. The Caryatid had risen.

24

The policemen rushed to inspect the interior of the temple. They looked round the back. One enterprising constable ran at full speed to the Parthenon to see if she had travelled there in the night. It too was empty. Inspector Kingsley rushed back to the King's Arms to tell Powerscourt before he set out on his success or victory mission to Dr Tristram Stanhope.

The porter on duty at the Hellenic College was not expecting visitors at nine o'clock on a Sunday morning. His jacket buttons were undone and his tie was in his pocket.

'Beg pardon, my lord,' he said to Powerscourt after the introductions were made, 'perhaps you would like to wait in here. I'll tell Dr Stanhope you've come to see him, my lord.'

Powerscourt found himself in the chair opposite the Headmaster's desk in the Headmaster's study. He realized that Lucy must have sat in this very chair a couple of days before. Breakfast was in full swing at the Hellenic College with the noise of crockery and the young voices coming through the walls. Powerscourt suddenly thought of the contrast between the innocence of the young and the crimes of their elders that swirled round the school – theft, murder, fraud. Now he was going to try a form of blackmail. Suddenly he remembered the words of his brother-in-law during a previous case: 'pressure, Francis, pressure, a much nicer word than blackmail'.

Dr Tristram Stanhope came in and sat down in the Headmaster's chair. He was wearing a dark blue blazer with brass buttons and a hint at naval connections with a pale yellow cravat under a white silk shirt.

'Good morning, Powerscourt. Welcome to the Hellenic College. I was not expecting you, I must say. To what do I owe the pleasure of this unexpected visit?'

'I've come about the Caryatid,' said Powerscourt pleasantly.

'What of the Caryatid? There are no Caryatids here.'

'I know there are no Caryatids here now, or not in the Erechtheion anyway. Inspector Kingsley told me about that earlier this morning. The police came to take her away, you see.'

Stanhope looked shocked and rather alarmed at the mention of the police but he stuck to his guns.

'I don't understand, Powerscourt. Why this talk of Caryatids?'

'Because there was one here last night. It could have been the one stolen from the British Museum, or it could have been a copy, or it could even have been a copy of a copy.' Powerscourt found his brain was reeling at the thought of multiple copies of the statue, forming up in columns in his mind and then dissolving. 'But there was a Caryatid, of the same size and the same general features as the one stolen from the British Museum where you work, Dr Stanhope.'

'What nonsense, man. You're out of your wits. There are no Caryatids here.'

'You know perfectly well you're wrong about that. You see, I was here last night. Lady Lucy and I saw the unveiling of the statue and your recital of the hymns to Athena. I had some German binoculars. I had a very clear view.'

Tristram Stanhope stared very hard at Powerscourt. Then he looked out of the window as if the cavalry or the charioteer from the previous evening might ride past to save him. Powerscourt carried on.

'That's what I came to talk to you about the Caryatid. I want to make a suggestion.'

'Look here, you've got hold of the wrong end of the stick. This is a Hellenic College. It's devoted to ancient Greece and ancient Athens. We have a replica of the Parthenon not two hundred yards from where we are sitting now, for heaven's sake. What could be more natural than we should build a life-size copy of the Erechtheion to sit with it, as they sit together on the Acropolis? The Headmaster and the Board of Governors agreed immediately when I suggested it. And what could be more natural than engaging a local sculptor to produce a copy of the Caryatid? I have no idea what your suggestion is, but I make no apologies for my behaviour or that of the College.'

Powerscourt had to admit that Stanhope's brain worked extremely fast. He seemed to have cooked up this story in a matter of seconds.

'My suggestion is quite simple, Dr Stanhope. That Caryatid yesterday did not look to me to have been created by some local sculptor here in Amersham. Either it was a copy, or it was the real thing. If it was a copy you must know where the original is. In either case I am suggesting that you return the original to the British Museum within forty-eight hours. By nine o'clock on Tuesday morning, to be precise.'

'This is ridiculous. You're mad, Powerscourt, quite mad.'

After years of experience as an investigator Powerscourt was well used to people calling him mad. He now believed that it was a sure sign that he was on the right course.

'I am not mad, I assure you. There are certain matters where the police are very anxious to talk to you. There are your financial affairs for a start. There are a number of lines of inquiry under way in the case of the missing Caryatid where you will be a suspect, or, quite possibly, taken into custody. You would not expect me to give you details of these inquiries before the authorities are ready to make their move, but time is not on your side.'

'And what happens if I tell you to go to hell?'

'Under present circumstances, Dr Stanhope, I think you are much more likely to end up in hell than I am. However, I am empowered by the Inspector in charge to say that cooperation would be helpful to your case in the future. There are a number of factors I think you should consider. The first is that I do not think you would welcome a posse of policemen marching into the British Museum and taking you into custody in the most visible way possible. Nor would you welcome detailed reports of your arrest appearing in the quality newspapers the following day. I do not think you would welcome the Inspector and I going to see Theophilus Ragg in private and telling him the full nature of our suspicions. I do not think he would fire you on the spot, but you might be asked to take leave of absence until the matter was cleared up. We would do the same with the Caryatid Committee. Your position there would have a question mark over it, to say the least.'

'This is monstrous, Powerscourt. This is blackmail.'

'It is not blackmail. You could call it pressure, if you like, but you will not find a sympathetic hearing from the Metropolitan Police if you go to them babbling about blackmail. You do not have to decide about this offer right now, Dr Stanhope. You have until Tuesday morning. I shall be at the King's Arms hotel in the town, if you wish to speak further. Or you can ask any of the policemen who will soon be swarming all over the place to take you to Inspector Kingsley. Talking to him is as good as talking to me.'

Powerscourt rose to go. Stanhope waved him back to his chair.

'I tell you now, Powerscourt. You are out of your mind. I have no intention of doing as you suggest. You can take that back to your policemen friends. You can all go to hell!'

'I shall await your decision, Dr Stanhope. You have until Tuesday morning. There is one other matter you should take into consideration. Rumour can often move in a more deadly fashion than the truth. Especially as rumour doesn't have to be true. I do not move a lot in what is called fashionable society, but I have a number of friends and a great many relations who do. Grand and aspiring hostesses might think twice about inviting a man said to have assisted in theft from one of our great national institutions and, furthermore, to have connections with people who commit murder as others might swat a fly. I wish you a very good morning. I can see myself out, thank you.'

Every priest in every pulpit of the Greek Orthodox Church in Athens and the surrounding areas mentioned the procession in their Sunday sermons. At four o'clock that afternoon, the worshippers were told, the Archbishop would lead a mighty multitude of the faithful to the heart of the city. They would be bringing with them an object worthy of veneration from all Athenians and all Greeks in the greater Greek diaspora. The congregations thought that a new relic must have been discovered, a fragment of a long dead saint perhaps, or some remnant of one of the heroes of the War of Independence against the Turks.

In the vanguard were four monks, solemn in their black outfits. Then came a small platoon of military veterans, still wearing their uniforms, still marching in step, their medals pinned to their breasts. Behind them rode half a dozen troopers from the cavalry division of the regiment assigned to ceremonial duties in the capital. Behind the horses was another monk, carrying a huge silver cross in front of the Archbishop himself. To his left was the Metropolitan of Salamis and Megara, to his right the Metropolitan of Piraeus. After the episcopal heavy artillery marched one of the two choirs taking part in the procession.

> We knew thee of old,
> Oh divinely restored
> By the lights of thine eyes
> And the light of thy sword

The Greek national anthem was written by a poet from Zakynthos during the fight for freedom. It was to punctuate today's procession from the first choir at the front to the second choir at the rear. But it was the contents of the float behind the singers that captivated the crowd. Four monks were pulling it. Standing erect in the centre was a Caryatid, flanked by two huge priests in case she fell over. The Church of today, founded some nineteen hundred years ago, was bringing home a statue created four hundred years before the birth of Jesus, a Christian city welcoming a marble maiden from the pagan times. Behind the float was a throng of about fifty priests and monks, waving to the crowds as they went by. Then a body that grew larger with every moment of the procession. People left their houses and whatever they were doing to fall in behind the clergy. Some of those travelling on the buses leapt off and joined the march. The tail of the gathering swelled from fifty to a hundred to two hundred to five hundred. It went on growing all the way to their final destination.

> From the graves of our slain
> Shall thy valour prevail
> As we greet thee again
> Hail, Liberty! Hail!

The British Ambassador, the man who had rowed for Cambridge and for his old college, was standing in the shadow of the Parthenon. He could hear the noise but he could not yet see the procession. Down there, mingling with the crowd, was *The Times* correspondent, Marcus Fielding, whose wife was Greek and whose family antennae had reported the call to arms from the city churches that morning. Fielding had arranged to meet the Ambassador. Whatever was going on, whatever the point

of the festivities, his wife had assured him, it would be
sure to pass or to finish at the Acropolis.

> Long time didst thou dwell
> With the people that mourn
> Awaiting some voice
> That would bid thee return

The procession was to take the Caryatid on a journey
round some of the most sacred sites of fifth-century BC
Athens as if they were the Stations of the Cross. They
paused at the Ceramicus by the Dipylon Gate just outside
the Acropolis where many famous Athenians were buried – the lawgiver Solon, and Pericles the statesman who
was responsible for the Parthenon. They moved on to the
site of a shrine to Demeter and Kore on the route of the
Panathenaica just below the Acropolis. The Archbishop
bowed his head in silent prayer. The choirs stopped singing until they moved off. The taxi drivers were now hooting their horns continuously as the Caryatid continued
on her journey. People were leaning out of their windows
and cheering as she went past. Flowers now littered the
feet of the marchers.

> Ah, slow broke that day
> And no man dared call
> For the shadow of tyranny
> Lay over all:

The Ambassador was on tiptoe now, peering down at
the procession. The Caryatid was not yet visible. They
took over ten minutes to pass through the Propylaea,
literally the gate building to the Acropolis, and, as the

331

man from *The Times* reminded the Ambassador, the model for the Brandenburg Gate in Berlin. In ancient times only Athenian citizens were allowed through this gate; strangers and the unclean were not permitted in Athens's holy of holies. There was a cheer from the sightseers visiting the Acropolis when the monks and the huge silver cross led the crowd onto the sacred soil. The few Americans present thought about the wine they had drunk at lunchtime and wondered if they had been transported back in time.

> And we saw thee sad eyed
> Thy tears on thy cheeks,
> While thy raiment was dyed
> In the blood of the Greeks.

When they reached the Parthenon the procession fell into ranks in front of the building. The Archbishop climbed to the top of the steps and looked down on his people. He raised a hand aloft for silence.

'My fellow Athenians,' he began, 'my fellow Greeks, what a joy it is to welcome you here this afternoon. I thank you all for coming and I thank all those, alive or dead, who are with us here in spirit on this great day. For all eternity, my friends, today will be known as the Day of Return, the Day our Caryatid came home. She lived here in ancient times, she has stood next to this great building, our Parthenon, when it was a Roman Catholic church, she has stood here when it was a mosque, she has stood here when it was used as an armoury and a Venetian shell ripped the heart out of the Parthenon in the bad times of the Ottomans. She was seized, in an act of international piracy, by the wicked pirate Elgin and carried off to the cold climate and the colder religion of England. Today she has come home. Today, very soon now, we shall lift her back in the place where she belongs. One of our great scholars, a professor of theology at the university here no less, suggested to me that we should welcome the statue home with a Hail Mary. I thought long and hard, but I said no. We in the Church do not claim the Caryatid as one of our own. That would be to deny her origins and the culture she came from. The men who put her on her porch knew of the gods who lived on Olympus, often driven by whim and pique and ridiculous conflicts with their fellows, they knew of the gods who dwelt in the woods and the streams, they were always aware of those hard taskmasters, Fate and Necessity, who could call, unexpected and unannounced, at any door at any time. But she is still ours, the Caryatid. We embrace her as an example of the spirit of Greece, the essence of the Hellenes and one who will dwell happily with us in our new freedom.'

The Archbishop made the sign of the Cross and returned to his station. The choirs picked up the National Anthem again.

> Yet behold now thy sons
> With impetuous breath
> Go forth to the fight
> Seeking Freedom or Death.

The great crowd, now a couple of thousand strong, moved across to the Erechtheion. A screen was erected outside it to hide the work necessary to place the Caryatid securely on her porch. As the restoration went on, the two choirs spread out, holding hands right round the

333

audience. Everyone was encouraged to sing the last verse. They sang it twice.

> From the graves of our slain
> Shall thy valour prevail
> As we greet thee again
> Hail, Liberty! Hail!

A great blue cloak, large enough to adorn a giant, was now fluttering above the porch. A set of steps was placed next to it for the Archbishop. He mounted very slowly. As he tugged it aside he shouted to the assembled multitude: 'Caryatid of the Erechtheion porch, Caryatid of the Acropolis—' he waved his right hand very slowly round the ruined buildings still standing on the High City '—Caryatid of Athena, Caryatid of Athens—' the Archbishop raised his arms to his Christian God in the heavens above '—Caryatid of Greece, Welcome home!'

25

There were twenty-four hours left before the Caryatid might be returned to the British Museum. The Powerscourt telephone rang shortly after eight o'clock that morning.

'Powerscourt? Good morning to you. Kingsley here. I've just had some great news. We've found Easton, the man you described as the missing link between Stanhope and Deptford. I've just had a note from the Governor of Pentonville, complete with the last address they have for him. The local police confirm that a man answering to that name is still there.'

'Well done, Inspector. Good news indeed. Where is the fellow?'

'He's in Maidstone, my lord. A villa in the better part of town, houses set back from the road, you know the sort of thing, Holland House, Riverside Drive. And that's not all. The Governor tells me that he befriended Carver Wilkins during his days in prison. Carver was locked up in Pentonville at the same time. Carver Wilkins is the criminal boss of Deptford and controller of the Twins, as you know. They became, if you'll pardon the expression, as thick as thieves in Pentonville, forever plotting the crimes they would commit once they left the jail. The Governor is sure they kept in touch after they were released. Carver Wilkins was let out a fortnight after Easton.'

'So what are your plans, Inspector? Are you going to interrupt the man's peace down there by the river in Maidstone?'

'I most certainly am, my lord. I just need to talk to our money man here at the Yard so he can begin inquiries immediately into the Easton bank accounts. Then my Sergeant and I are going to Kent. I've asked the local police to pick him up and hold him in a cell. I've suggested they give him a pretty hard time. The Governor told me that Easton was a frightful coward, always worried about being beaten up in the jail. He only calmed down when Carver Wilkins was able to give him some protection. With any luck he'll be ready to talk by the time we get there.'

Robert Burke, Inspector Kingsley's sergeant, was reading through all his notes on the case so far as their train pulled out of Charing Cross. Inspector Kingsley was staring out of the window as the suburbs of London sped away. This case is going to end very soon, he said to himself. It might even end this week. It could not end early enough for the Inspector. He had made up his mind now. The Affair of the Missing Caryatid would be his last case. His resignation note was already written, waiting in a drawer at home. He wondered how he could conduct the interview with William Tyndale Easton to close the case even quicker.

'You still haven't given me a proper answer to my question, Francis.' Lady Lucy Powerscourt was hardly ever really cross with her husband. But when he failed to give you a proper answer to an important question for almost a whole day, it was inevitable that there should be a certain fraying of the edges in a wife's temper.

'What question is that, my love?'

'You know perfectly what the question is, Francis. It's perfectly simple. Do you think the Caryatid will be returned to the British Museum tomorrow morning?'

'Ah, the Caryatid. Perhaps a Caryatid, who knows, Lucy. I have to confess that I have not given you an answer because I don't know. I'm not sure. I'm not at all sure. Last night I felt certain that she would be back where she belongs in Great Russell Street tomorrow morning. This morning I am in two minds all over again. I am beginning to feel superstitious about the matter, that if don't express an opinion, she will reappear, and that if I do, she won't. You see my difficulty?'

'I do, of course I do. Why didn't you say so? But really, Francis, I know you fairly well by now. We have been married for a while. I'm sure you must have a view, one way or the other.'

Powerscourt sighed and picked up his hat. 'Very well. I am going to Amersham to root about in the outhouses and the neighbouring buildings of the Hellenic College.'

He was halfway out of the front door now. 'But let me tell you, Lucy, if you twisted my arm right up my back and asked me for my thoughts on the possible return of the statue, I would say yes, I think it will be returned. But I would not offer an opinion on whether it will be the real thing or a copy. I wouldn't bet a single farthing on that, one way or the other.'

William Tyndale Easton was sitting on a plain prison chair in front of a plain prison table. He was wearing a tweed jacket and a pair of brown trousers. His hair looked as if it had not been combed properly that morning and there was a small cut on his left cheek. The Maidstone police had arrived before he had completed his toilette. On the other side of the table were Sergeant Burke, looking serious, and Inspector Kingsley, who had conducted a long inspection of the prisoner, including a slow walk right round Easton's chair. He knew that his first question could determine the shape of the whole interview.

'Looking forward to going back, are you?'

There was a long pause. 'I don't know what you mean.' Easton sounded hesitant.

'You know perfectly well what I mean. You've been there before after all, haven't you?'

'Been where, please, Inspector? You're confusing me.'

A more sensible prisoner would have told me to go to hell, or words to that effect, Christopher Kingsley said to himself. Easton was looking frightened now.

'It was Pentonville last time, wasn't it? God knows where it'll be this time. His Majesty has a large number of places where he can park his criminals. You remember what prison's like? The food? The lack of privacy? The beatings-up? The queues where you can be kicked and punched for a quarter of an hour at a time? The dark places at the end of a passageway where a knife or a fist or a boot might be waiting for you? I'm sure you remember them well.'

Easton looked at the Inspector with pleading eyes. He said nothing. Kingsley wondered how many times he had been assaulted in Pentonville before Carver Wilkins gave him protection. The Inspector took a deep breath. He felt suddenly like a man about to jump off the edge of a cliff into the river below and is not sure he will survive.

'Come, come,' he began, 'we don't need to go into details at this stage. We just need to know how they worked, the links between you and Carver Wilkins and Dr Tristram Stanhope. That's all.'

A part of the Inspector's brain was expecting an instant denial. But that was not the response he got.

'What do you mean, the links between us?'

'You know perfectly well what I mean. I should remind you of some of the crimes connected with the affair of which I speak: robbery, blackmail, extortion, murder. You can work out the length of prison sentence those crimes carry.' The Inspector paused and placed his hands round his neck. 'Or, indeed, the length of the drop.'

'I didn't know anything about any murders. I didn't know there had been any. You've got to believe me, Inspector, please.'

'We'll see about that. We know perfectly well how the links worked but it would be good to hear it in your own words.'

Easton looked desperately at his interrogators as if a very long stare might make them disappear. 'This is how it worked,' he whispered. 'God help me and my family if Carver Wilkins ever finds out that I told you.'

Scylla and Charybdis, Sergeant Burke, who had liked the ancient myths at school, said to himself. Scylla is here with my Inspector threatening him with the rope, Charybdis lurks in Deptford with broken bones and cigarette burns from the Twins.

'Stanhope had the ideas. I worked them out. Carver Wilkins organized the criminals.'

'Could you give us an example of how it worked in practice?'

There was another pause, then a great sigh, as if from

a man who realizes that he has no choice but to put more cards on the table.

Inspector Kingsley took another deep breath and prepared for another jump.

'How about the Caryatid?' he asked. 'The Caryatid from the British Museum?'

'I didn't have much to do with that, Inspector. Dr Stanhope told Carver how to bribe the Greek porters and when they should steal it during the fire alarm. I don't even know where they took it.'

'Really? Really?' was the Inspector's reply. 'So what precisely was your role in the affair?'

'I went to America for them. I'd been to New York once before to sort out the Turner before that all got stuck. I fixed up the sale of one of those Caryatids to that rich American fellow. His people bought me a very lavish dinner in New York. It must have been the most expensive meal I've ever had. Caviar, langoustines, champagne.'

'We don't want to know the bloody menu, thank you very much.' Inspector Kingsley felt an overpowering urge to ask William Easton if he had travelled first class across the Atlantic. There was a knock at the door. A sergeant with a giant moustache handed a note to the Inspector. 'Thank you,' said Kingsley, taking out his spectacles to read it. 'No reply for the moment, thank you.'

Looking at his watch, Sergeant Burke noted that it was exactly half past eleven. He wondered if the time of the note's arrival was not a coincidence.

'This note provides more interesting information about your position, Mr Easton. It tells me that you have a great deal of money in your main bank account. How much of that came from the American sale?'

Easton was trying to shrink, to turn himself into a

smaller, almost invisible, Easton. 'I don't know. I have no idea.'

'Don't be ridiculous,' snapped the Inspector. 'Let me remind you of the more sinister aspect of these crimes, the blackmail, the murders. Do you want to be named in those indictments?'

'It was a great deal of money. But then the man Mitchell is a very wealthy fellow. He's a millionaire many times over.'

'How much?'

'He had a town house in New York, you know. And a place out at the Hamptons where the millionaires have those parties. And one up near West Point.'

'I don't care if he owns all of Fifth Avenue and the Statue of Liberty.' Kingsley was getting cross now. 'How much?'

'Well, there was rather a row about the price.'

'For God's sake, man. I don't care if he gave you an updated version of the Sermon on the Mount. How much?'

'Over a hundred thousand dollars.'

'How much more than a hundred thousand dollars? And don't give me any more nonsense or you'll be back in Pentonville before lunch and you may never come out again.'

'A hundred and twenty-five thousand.'

'Well, well,' said the Inspector, 'it's easy to see where your bank balance came from.'

Inspector Kingsley had a sudden picture of the Twins, prowling round Maidstone looking for their prey. He thought Carver Wilkins would not hesitate to issue a termination order on William Tyndale Easton if he knew what he had told the police. He remembered Lucas

Ringer, still holed up in his Aberystwyth hotel, the only man who could give firm evidence against the Twins, and even then, as the Inspector knew well, a clever barrister could plant doubt in the mind of the jury because the witness had seen the Twins in the pub, but that did not mean that they had committed the crime.

Easton began to shake slightly, as if he had the beginnings of a fever. 'Please, Inspector, I don't think I should say any more now. I think I've said far too much already.'

'Nonsense, man,' growled Inspector Kingsley, but his mind was racing as he looked at his prisoner. The man was now rocking slowly from side to side in his chair. If he carried on with more warnings of immediate imprisonment and threats of the rope, Easton might suffer a complete collapse. The Inspector had heard of colleagues in the past who had carried on too long with their interrogations so that the prisoners went to pieces and were unable to give evidence. Easton had given them invaluable information. Better, surely, to keep that intact than to humiliate and terrify him any further.

'I've got other business to attend to,' Inspector Kingsley said harshly. 'I'm having you kept inside overnight. Don't argue or you'll be back in Pentonville. We'll be here again tomorrow.'

Dear Lord Powerscourt, (the letter was from John Hudson, European art critic of the *New York Times*)

Please forgive the haste. I am about to set out for an exhibition in Florence. I have, as you requested, been making enquiries about Mr Huntington, the railway king who bought the Turner. I have been in touch with my friend Franklin, who has been talking to the politics and the business departments on the paper. They are entranced and fascinated by this story, the politics and business people. They want to buy you a very expensive dinner the next time you are in New York.

Powerscourt smiled. He had never been to New York. Lady Lucy had been trying to persuade him to go for years.

Myron Guthrie, (the letter continued) the chief politics man, has worked in London for some time. He says the principal thing to remember about Huntington at this time is that he is in the middle of a process that very few British people understand. The phenomenon is particularly American. Ever since the days of John D. Rockefeller and his control of the oil business, captains of industry have tried to buy out or ruin their main competitors. Then they have a monopoly. They can control the prices. They can, in effect, charge whatever they like. For years now these people have been known as robber barons.

Powerscourt thought they were a long way from an oil painting hanging on the walls of Norfolk House on Chiswick Mall.

When politicians opposed to big money feel things may have got out of hand they call for the Congress or a committee or a subcommittee of Congress to investigate the tycoon. These investigations are very thorough, far worse than the Inquisition apparently. Specialists from the Department of Justice go through the books. They check everything. They begin, according to their critics, with a presumption of guilt rather than innocence.

Eighteen months ago, just before the Turner walked off the walls, Henry Huntington of the Huntington Library and his railways and all his affairs were put under investigation. It's still going on. Nothing, according to my colleagues on the *New York Times*, would have given these investigators greater joy than to find that their victim had been importing or trying to import stolen works of art. It could have finished his whole career. So, they suspect the reason for the delay in bringing the painting across was simply Huntington delaying the transfer in case it damaged his business. They suspect the thieves in London may have got fed up waiting for their money and invented the change of name. For once the painting had a different name, not on any blacklist in the New York Police Department or any of the great galleries, the problem would have gone away.

I hope this is useful,

In haste,

Yours sincerely,

John Hudson

Lady Lucy Powerscourt was having a last supper the evening before the Caryatid might reappear at the British Museum. Johnny Fitzgerald was still on manoeuvres in Warwickshire, but her husband and Inspector Kingsley were present at the feast. The Powerscourt fishmonger on Sloane Street provided some excellent oysters, the

Powerscourt butcher on the King's Road sent some delicious lamb and the Powerscourt cellars contributed a bottle of Batard Montrachet and a couple of Charmes Chambertin.

Powerscourt passed on the details of John Hudson's letter about events in New York. He was thrilled with the news from Maidstone. 'Congratulations, Inspector,' he cried, pouring him a large glass of white wine, 'you've cracked the case wide open! Excellent news!'

'Well done, Inspector, well done indeed,' echoed Lady Lucy.

'We have some more interesting news too,' said Powerscourt, 'though not as germane to the case as yours. I heard this afternoon from the British Ambassador in Athens. A Caryatid, a fairly authentic-looking Caryatid in his words, has been put back in her place on the Acropolis by the Archbishop of Athens and a couple of Metropolitans. The Greek military guarded her all night apparently.'

'Heavens above,' cried Inspector Kingsley, 'how many of the bloody things are there? Do you have any idea, my lord?'

'Before we start counting Caryatids,' said Lady Lucy, 'could you clear up something more important? There have been two murders in this case, two dead men, two families who have lost loved ones. Do you know why they were killed?'

'I've thought a lot about that, Lucy,' said her husband, 'we know how Kostas and Carwyn Jones died, of course. We're not sure why. But the evidence from the people in Wales suggests they were killed because they tried to blackmail Carver Wilkins. He had paid the two brothers pretty well, from what we know of the Kostas's bank account, for stealing the Caryatid and replacing it with a fake. And he sent money to Lucas Ringer to pay Carwyn Jones for concocting the story about the statue. But they both had a bad dose of the Oliver Twists – they asked for more. Carver knew that if either of them started talking he'd be in trouble. He couldn't take the risk. So he sent in the Twins, once to the tube station and once to Wales. God knows what happened to Kostas's brother. We may never know, but we presume he's dead too.'

'How terrible,' said Lady Lucy.

'I agree,' said Inspector Kingsley. 'It is terrible.' He didn't refer to his decision to leave the Metropolitan Police because of another two or three murders. 'There are other questions we need to clear up. Perhaps you could return to the number of Caryatids, my lord?'

'Before I answer that,' said Powerscourt, polishing off the last of the oysters, 'let me ask you a question. Do you think the Caryatid, or perhaps a Caryatid, will be restored to the British Museum tomorrow morning?'

The Inspector stared into his wine as if the answer lay in a tiny commune in the Cote de Beaune. 'No, I don't,' he said finally. 'I don't think it will come back tomorrow. I don't think the people who took it have any left. The cupboard is bare. All the copies and the original have been accounted for. Or do you think there are enough Caryatids floating around for one of them to get to Great Russell Street? I have, by the way, ordered a very light surveillance of the museum during the night. I very much doubt if the people who bring her back, if they do, will be the same ones who took her in the first place. Better to let her come home, I say. I come back to my question, my lord. How many of the damned things do you think there are?'

346

Powerscourt paused and stared down at his plate. He picked up a single pea and held it aloft between the thumb and forefinger of his right hand.

'One,' he said, 'sent to Greece, but fell into the sea on the way. Maybe there was an ancient curse over that harbour in Brindisi.' He dropped the pea into the palm of his left hand and picked up another one.

'Two, and this statue in a way is the key to the whole affair, this one is sent to upstate New York in a giant coffin where I think it now resides in the millionaire's art gallery. Maybe the fellow could be persuaded to return it once he knows the circumstances, or he may claim that he bought it in good faith from friend Easton.' A second pea was transferred to his left hand. A third took its place.

'Three, there is now a Caryatid back in Athens, cherished by the Greek Orthodox clergy and the population of Athens. I should say there is a chance of that being the real one, but—' another pea was transferred, another taken up '—I cannot be sure.'

'Four—' Powerscourt waved this particular pea around for some time as if some new thought had just struck him '—there was a Caryatid at the Hellenic College in Amersham the other evening. Maybe that will be the one to go back to the British Museum tomorrow morning, if it does go back. If not, God help us—' a fifth pea was pressed into service '—there might be five of them. You see, it is virtually impossible to know how many Caryatids there are. There's one vital fact that has been staring us in the face all the way through this investigation and we haven't noticed it. I only thought about it for the first time a moment ago.'

'What's that?' said Lady Lucy.

'Simply this,' replied her husband. 'The thieves had

made a copy of the statue before the theft. They replaced the real Caryatid with their own version.'

'So?' Inspector Kingsley sounded puzzled.

'So, they could have made three or even four copies before the theft. Don't you see? They might have only needed to make one more copy after the event, the one over in Wales with the enormous coffin.'

'God bless my soul,' said Inspector Kingsley, 'I see what you mean. Just going back to Amersham for a moment, I hadn't realized that the one at the Hellenic College could be the one going back to the museum, but of course you're right. Tell me, my lord, why did you say that the one going to America was the key to the whole affair?'

'Well,' said Powerscourt, 'it depends on what or who you think the driving force behind the whole thing was. It depends if you think Byron is more important than Mammon for the participants. And we cannot forget the question of the relationship between the three players, Carver Wilkins, William Tyndale Easton and the good, or bad, Dr Tristram Stanhope.'

'When you talk about Byron, Francis—' the memory of the young men reciting *Childe Harold* had stayed with Lady Lucy '—do you mean that one motive for stealing the Caryatid might have been to send her back to the Acropolis where she came from? So the one in Athens is probably the real one?'

'Exactly so,' said Powerscourt. 'On that assumption, the principal player would be Stanhope. Carver Wilkins probably thinks the Acropolis is a nightclub in the West End, and Easton, from what we know of him, is unlikely to read Greek poetry in bed last thing at night. But Stanhope would be different.'

'Do you believe that, Francis?'

'As a matter of fact, I don't. I'd be very interested to hear what the Inspector thinks.'

The Inspector laughed. 'I've been too busy thinking about what I need to get out of Easton tomorrow to consider these grand questions, my lord. I have to say I agree with you, though, I don't believe Stanhope or Stanhope's beliefs and desires are the key factors. Money is at the root of this case. Once you take on board that our American cousin paid well over a hundred thousand dollars for his statue, the rest is obvious. Stanhope can do what he likes with the others once the dollars have arrived.'

'So do you think William Tyndale Easton is the most important member of the conspiracy?'

Lady Lucy's question hung in the air between her husband and the policeman for a moment. Kingsley waved to Powerscourt as if saying, you first.

'I don't know if I am right in my version of how this particular Holy Trinity worked. It's very easy to get these kinds of relationship wrong from the outside. I've been thinking for some time about Faust and Mephistopheles, and who is Faust and who is Mephistopheles in this case. I think Easton is Mephistopheles. Remember the time they spent together in the prison, thick as thieves as the Governor so aptly put it. Carver's knowledge of crime is restricted to protection rackets, burglary, intimidation, beating up your enemies. Easton widens his horizons. Art, Old Master art, fetches very large prices. The possibilities of making enormous sums, far greater than those possible in the poverty and squalor of Deptford, appeal to the gangland boss. Easton whets his appetite. But Easton has a problem. Everybody in the art world knows he has been sent to jail. He is a leper in Old Bond Street. But he finds his Faust in Stanhope. Stanhope is always in need of money with that lifestyle and those clothes. Easton knew Stanhope from his time in the art world before he went to prison. Mephistopheles Easton tells Stanhope that if he suggests the targets, Easton and his friends will provide the means of stealing them and selling them on. Nobody will know that Stanhope was involved at all. For Marlowe's Faust the attraction of twenty-four years with Mephistopheles as his servant was the wealth this connection would bring. Like the original Dr Faustus, Dr Stanhope did not care at first what happened to him after the twenty-four years. At least Faust had twenty-four years of visions of Helen of Troy and all those other delights. Stanhope looks as though he may be consigned to hell rather sooner.'

'Before Mephistopheles turns you into Christopher Marlowe, Francis, and an early death, appropriately enough, in Deptford, perhaps you could tell us how it worked, here in twentieth-century London rather than in sixteenth-century Germany?'

'Sorry, Lucy, I got rather carried away. The Turner was a dry run, a sort of exam. Stanhope proved that he could recommend thefts that would be both easy and profitable. Easton showed he could handle the subsequent selling of the painting. They weren't to know when they planned it that Huntington would be ensnared in the thickets of a Congressional investigation and the suspicious minds of the men from the Justice Department. That was just bad luck. But Carver Wilkins saw how much money he could make from a simple burglary. Now came the Caryatid. I'm sure Stanhope suggested it. Only he could have guessed how much you might get for a Caryatid from a rich American millionaire. Easton may have got a whisper about Lincoln Mitchell on his trip to New

York to discuss the Turner. The main reason for the theft of the Caryatid was the American money. The rest was camouflage, a chance for Stanhope to realize some of his ideals.'

The Inspector nodded. 'It could all have been the other way round, of course. Stanhope's love of Greece might have been the driving factor, but I'm not convinced. I read *Dr Faustus* at school, my lord. I remember the teacher telling us that Faust was like Icarus, the boy who flew too close to the sun and fell to earth. Maybe Stanhope is not only Stanhope Faust but Stanhope Icarus as well. There's another thing about Easton, by the way. He told me he was the man in the taxi at the Ritz, the one who took Ragg for a ride. Easton's as bald as a coot.'

'You don't think we are avoiding the real question, gentlemen?' Lady Lucy was refilling the glasses.

'Which is?' said the Inspector.

'Why, which is the real one?' Lady Lucy replied. 'The American Caryatid? The Athenian Caryatid? The Hellenic College Caryatid? The British Museum Caryatid, if there is one tomorrow?'

'I'm going to be very boring,' said her husband. 'I'm going to sound like a parent telling his children on Christmas Eve that they have to wait until the morning to find out what Santa Claus is going to bring them. We'll just have to wait and see. If a Caryatid comes back tomorrow, the museum experts will have a view, but that may take time. I believe that American academic who told the museum that the current one was not the original is still in Europe somewhere. Presumably Ragg can bring him back to London.'

'I've just thought of something, my lord.' The Inspector looked worried suddenly. 'Nobody at the museum knows the statue may come back tomorrow. It's going to take time for the different experts to have a view. We must make sure that no word leaks out to the newspapers that the Caryatid has returned, if it has. That would be a sensation. The only bigger sensation would be if it transpired a week later that the thing was a fake.'

'Well done, Inspector,' cried Powerscourt, 'you're absolutely right. One person in particular will have to be sat on. He might even try to go about saying he had secured her return. There are no prizes for guessing who I am talking about. Call him Icarus. Call him Dr Faustus. Call him Dr Tristram Stanhope.'

26

Nobody knows who was the first person to see the six Caryatids on their porch in Athens's new Erechtheion 2,300 years ago. Maybe the high-born young ladies broke with protocol and came out of seclusion to see what the sculptors had made of them. It was hard to tell who was the first to see the Caryatid that returned to the British Museum early on Tuesday morning. Inspector Kingsley's officers might have relaxed their vigil in the night hours, but they were about in force from six o'clock onwards. As Londoners began their journey to work, a young constable spotted what he thought was a packing case in the shadows at the side of the great loading bay at the back of the museum. Inspector Kingsley was summoned. Torches revealed that it was a battered railway container. The Inspector greeted it like a long lost friend.

'Just keep an eye on this thing, boys,' he said. 'I'm fairly sure there's a Caryatid inside. I'm going to see if we can get her into the building before it gets light.'

The staff of the museum, the curators and the librarians and the archivists began work at nine. The cleaners and the maintenance staff came much earlier. The Inspector found the Buildings Manager at his post just after a quarter past seven. Tom Harris took one look at the container and had it moved to a side room off the loading bay. He sent for a couple of porters.

'I'd like to open it now, Inspector, I really would, but I think it would be only fair to wait for Deputy Director Ragg before we open the box. He's had to take most of the strain, after all.'

The policeman and the Buildings Manager talked about football while they waited. There was a needle match between Tottenham Hotspur and Arsenal the following Saturday. Theophilus Ragg arrived just after eight o'clock with Powerscourt in tow.

'Thank you for waiting,' he said, 'thank you so much. Please carry on now. Let's see what's inside.'

The porters took their crowbars and inserted them very carefully at the top of the container. After a few minutes the top was off. Wrapped in many layers of cotton, lying on a series of blankets that held her in position, was a Caryatid. The Buildings Manager gestured to his porters to stand back out of the light.

'My God,' said Ragg quietly. 'She's come back. I never thought she would. I never thought I'd see this day. Thank God for his mercies.'

'Amen to that,' said the Inspector. Powerscourt was peering at the statue and realized he had absolutely no way of telling if she was real or a fake. Everybody waited for the Deputy Director to announce what was to happen next.

'If I could make a suggestion, Mr Deputy Director, the Inspector and I were discussing the possibility of this return only yesterday.' Powerscourt did not choose to mention that the Caryatid had only come back to the

British Museum because he had blackmailed the Head of Greek and Roman Antiquities into producing her. He wondered where Stanhope was now and how he would react. 'Forgive me if I am speaking out of turn,' he continued.

'Please, please,' said Ragg, 'this is such a shock. Any suggestions would be more than welcome. My mind is in such a whirl I can hardly think.'

'We wondered if it might not be prudent to keep the Caryatid under wraps for a little while. Not to tell anybody just yet that she has been returned. That will give the experts a window in which they can determine whether this is the real thing or not. Maybe that young American from Yale, Stephen Lambert Lodge, who pointed out that the original Caryatid had disappeared, could be brought back to London. I don't need to tell you, Mr Deputy Director, of the fuss there would be if you pronounced it real today and had to say it was a fake next Monday. The museum would be humiliated.'

'Quite so, quite so.' Ragg was on his knees now, feeling the Caryatid's face very gently with the tips of his fingers. 'I so hope this is the real thing. But you speak wisely, Powerscourt.' He turned and looked his Buildings Manager in the eye. 'Tom, you have heard this discussion. Could you arrange to have the statue kept here, out of sight, with the door locked at all times, and one of your porters permanently on duty near the entrance?'

Harris nodded. Ragg rose slowly to his feet. He seemed reluctant to leave the presence. Finally he led the little company out into the main body of the building.

'I had a letter from young Lambert Lodge only the other day, you know. It won't take him very long to get back. You'll never guess where he was.'

355

'Berlin?' said the Inspector.

'Vienna?' offered Powerscourt.

'Those are two good guesses,' said Ragg happily, 'but you're both wrong. He's in Athens.'

Powerscourt wondered if the American had been in the city two days before when he could have seen a different Caryatid carried in triumph through the streets of her native city and restored to her place on the Acropolis.

Dr Tristram Stanhope had disappeared. His staff at the British Museum sent word to all his London clubs but he was not there. His flat in St James's Square was empty. The lady who looked after him reported to the police that she had not seen her gentleman for several days. The Hellenic College in Amersham where Powerscourt had directed Inspector Kingsley's men said he had not been in the building since Sunday when he had been seen departing with two large suitcases.

'It is nearly midnight in Christopher Marlowe's *Faustus*,' Powerscourt said to Lady Lucy, 'the doctor has nearly come to the end of his twenty-four years with the power and the glory. Listen, the clock strikes eleven.

'"O Faustus, Now hast thou but one bare hour to live, And then thou must be damned perpetually! Stand still, you ever moving spheres of heaven, That time might cease and midnight never come."'

Inspector Kingsley spent six hours that day with William Tyndale Easton in the interview room at Maidstone police station. Sergeant Burke's record filled a notebook and a half. At the end he sent a message to Inspector Ferguson in Deptford. Carver Wilkins was arrested shortly after five o'clock. Two of the three principals were behind bars, the third still missing, his bones perhaps, like Faustus's, to be discovered strewn across a stage.

The Inspector felt cheerful when he went to report his news to Powerscourt and Lady Lucy.

'It just remains to find the wretched Stanhope,' said Inspector Kingsley. 'Do either of you have any idea where he may have gone?'

'To hell,' said Powerscourt cheerfully, 'straight to hell, like Dr Faustus. The clock strikes twelve.

'"It strikes, it strikes! Now, body, turn to air Or Lucifer will bear thee quick to hell! Oh soul, be changed into small water drops And fall into the ocean, ne'er to be found . . . I'll burn my books! Oh Mephistopheles."'

'Do be serious, Francis, for heaven's sake. That's quite enough *Dr Faustus* for one day. I believe, Inspector, that Dr Stanhope has family in the West Country. Taunton perhaps?'

'I tell you what worries me,' said Kingsley. 'These ladies he has affairs with, would they be so besotted that they would hide him away somewhere?'

There was a knock at the door. Rhys, the Powerscourt butler, coughed in his usual way as he entered the room.

'Telephone,' he said, as if he had only just encountered the instrument, 'it's for you, Inspector. Perhaps you would like to take it in my lordship's study. This way, please.'

'Nobody's rung the Inspector here before, have they? I do hope nothing's wrong,' said Lady Lucy.

'It's probably routine,' said Powerscourt, 'some minor matter that needs to be cleared up this evening.'

But when Inspector Kingsley came back into the room it was clear that this was no routine matter. His face was dark and he was wringing his hands.

'Damn, damn, damn!' he said.

Powerscourt and Lady Lucy waited to hear the news.

'It's Lucas Ringer,' he announced. 'The undertaker. Holed up in his seafront hotel in Aberystwyth.'

'What of him?' said Powerscourt.

'He's dead!'

'He can't be.'

'He is.'

'Was it natural causes?' Powerscourt knew only too well why the Inspector was devastated. They might have Carver Wilkins and Easton behind bars but the people who had, so far as they knew, committed the murders, were the Twins. And the only witness prepared to give evidence against them in court was Lucas Ringer, now the late Lucas Ringer, gone to meet his maker by the sea in the middle of Wales.

'How did he die?' asked Powerscourt.

'His heart gave out. The local doctor thought he might have been suffocated but the hotel staff swore blind that nobody else had gone into the hotel yesterday evening. So the verdict looks like accidental death.'

'In which case,' said Powerscourt, 'unless we come up with a plan, the Twins will be left at large, able to continue intimidating witnesses and killing off their adversaries. I would not wish to end this case in these circumstances. I couldn't live with myself if I did.'

Powerscourt began walking up and down his drawing room, running his hands through his hair.

'You don't have anything else you could arrest the Twins for, Inspector?' Lady Lucy was worried about any plans her husband might cook up on his progress up and down the carpet.

'Believe me, Lady Powerscourt, Inspector Ferguson, the

man on the ground in Deptford, has been trying to arrest those two for years now. Nobody from Deptford would dare appear in court to give evidence against them. The last person to threaten to speak out in front of a judge and jury can just about get around in a wheelchair. He'll never walk again.'

'Dear me,' said Lady Lucy, 'I wish there was something I could suggest.'

'How about this?' Powerscourt had returned and resumed his seat by the fire. 'I can't say it's my favourite of all the plans I've ever dreamt up, but I think it would work.'

'How would it work, my lord?' asked the Inspector.

'Well,' Powerscourt replied, 'we can't obviously suggest that we ask someone to get killed by the Twins in front of witnesses just so the Twins can be brought into court. But suppose they were observed just about to assault somebody? Suppose the watchers were not going to be intimidated by any threats and will appear in court whatever happens? We just need the right piece of bait.'

Lady Lucy turned pale.

'Did you have something in mind, my lord?'

'As a matter of fact, I do, Inspector. I'm the bait. Sorry, Lucy, I don't think it's dangerous at all. Consider where we are now. You reported that the Twins had been seen in Amersham the other evening. I have noticed a couple of unsavoury-looking characters knocking about the square here recently. And I have also noticed a number of police officers who seem to be stationed discreetly round this house twenty-four hours a day. The two events may be related, I do not know. And I don't think I want to know if you have put those officers here, Inspector.'

'You're not suggesting we arrange some sort of

showdown in broad daylight in Markham Square, are you, my lord?'

'Certainly not,' said Powerscourt. 'But suppose we change the venue. Suppose I go to our place in the country, Rokesley. Johnny Fitzgerald comes too. You, Inspector, and as many policemen as you can muster are concealed round the house. The bait goes for a walk. We hope the Twins have followed us there. Maybe you could work out how to tell them where we are going, Inspector. The Twins prepare to attack. You come out of your hiding places. Johnny and I are both armed in any case. You arrest the Twins. They appear in court with lots and lots of unimpeachable policemen as witnesses. They may not hang but they go down for a very long time. How's that?'

'It sounds very dangerous to me,' said the Inspector, reluctant to support the plan until he knew what Lady Lucy's reaction would be.

'Dangerous? Dangerous?' Lady Lucy cried. 'I'll say it's dangerous. You could get yourself killed!'

'I've been in more dangerous places before,' said Powerscourt, 'battles in India, that sort of thing.' He had realized suddenly that there had been a number of very dangerous encounters in his career which he had forgotten to mention to Lady Lucy.

'Well,' said Lady Lucy, who could tell from her husband's expression that his mind was made up. There was a loud creak from a floorboard in the hall. Lady Lucy realized that the Inspector had forgotten to close the door when he came back from his phone message. She heard a set of footsteps hurrying towards the upper floors but she saw nobody.

'We must get that floorboard fixed, Francis. That squeak goes right through my head.'

'Could I make a suggestion,' said the Inspector. 'We've all had a long day. Could I suggest that we consider this proposal overnight and reconvene in the morning? I think that would be sensible.'

'Good idea,' Powerscourt replied. 'Come to breakfast. We'll get some kippers.'

> Temperature one hundred and four. Fever so bad I can scarcely walk. Hope to return to town when better. Behave yourself. Beware of Greek maidens. Johnny.

Lady Lucy's face fell as she read the telegram from Warwickshire over breakfast the following morning. Johnny Fitzgerald would not be here to accompany Francis on any hare-brained expeditions. There was another, slightly more cheerful, telegram, announcing his imminent arrival at Rokesley Hall, from William Mackenzie, the tracker who had worked with her husband in India and in the Boer War. Mackenzie could follow man or beast across the most unpromising country without being detected.

Inspector Kingsley was devouring a couple of kippers. He thought he should approach the main question as circumspectly as he could. 'Lady Powerscourt, I wonder if you have had time to think about the matters we were discussing yesterday evening?'

Lady Lucy smiled. 'You should have been a diplomat, Inspector. I'm sure you'd have gone far.'

'Maybe it's not too late,' said the Inspector. 'In my new role as Ambassador, maybe I could ask for the answer?'

Lady Lucy looked at her husband. She hated the idea of Francis as live bait, as if he were to be thrown into the water to attract the sharks. She knew how sick she would feel until the affair was resolved and he was returned to Markham Square safe and sound. She could be in for the worst twenty-four hours of her life. But she knew what she married into. Francis had never attempted to pretend his work was not dangerous some of the time. She loved him. She was aware that if she asked him not to do it he would grant her request without complaint. But she couldn't. She couldn't have lived with herself. She smiled at Inspector Kingsley.

'My dear Inspector, you know perfectly well what my answer will be, I'm sure. If Francis wants to become a form of human bait, so be it. I will support him with all my powers.'

Inspector Kingsley bowed. 'Thank you so much, Lady Powerscourt, that can't have been an easy decision. We'll look after him, don't you fear.'

Powerscourt and Inspector Kingsley began discussing their plans. Thomas Powerscourt came in and helped himself to a couple of kippers. Lady Lucy decided on a mission to the shops. The house badly needed some new furniture, she decided. And, if she had time, she would lay her hands on the latest auction catalogues. These would not relieve the worry while Francis was away, but they might provide an element of distraction.

27

The great battle plans of history have the virtue of simplicity. The details of the Rokesley campaign were finalized in the Powerscourt dining room and further refined by Inspector Ferguson in Deptford. He was to tell Carver Wilkins's people, by an unconventional but reliable route, that Powerscourt, Inspector Kingsley, Dr Stanhope and William Tyndale Easton were planning to hold a conference in Rokesley Hall this weekend.

'That should flush the buggers out,' had been Inspector Ferguson's advice to Inspector Kingsley. 'Carver would probably like to knock off all four of them. Pity two of the visitors won't be able to make it, but never mind.' The Deptford police, he told his colleague, proposed to attend the event in person with a cast comprised of the Inspector, his sergeant and four constables used to a bit of a roughhouse, as Ferguson put it. 'Wouldn't miss it for worlds,' had been his parting shot, 'see you later in Northamptonshire. Tally ho!'

Powerscourt had insisted on one thing, that a couple of capable officers should be on duty at all times by the front and back doors to the house. In the event of a full frontal assault, they would be able to make an immediate arrest. He did not want any violence inside Rokesley Hall. Lady Lucy and the children, he felt, would never come again if there was blood on the floorboards. Instead he declared that the field of battle should lie between the gardens of his house and Southwick Wood a couple of miles away. There were clumps of trees along the way and an entire police force could be concealed in the wood itself, or in the adjoining area of the Short Wood, famed for its bluebells in the spring. Advance guard and advance notice of any arrivals would be provided by Mackenzie patrolling the only road between Oundle and the Hall. At four o'clock on Saturday afternoon and at eleven o'clock the next day Powerscourt would set out to walk from the house to the wood.

The policemen began arriving at two o'clock. Only the most observant noticed a small slim figure with a deerstalker hat saluting them as they drove past. Mackenzie was famous for the discretion of his observation posts. At half past two a cab with a couple of burly men in suits drove past and pulled up at the Shuckburgh Arms, the local pub near the Hall that backed onto the cricket pavilion and the cricket pitch. Mackenzie was about to depart to the Arms for a closer look at the visitors when another traveller arrived. This one carried a golf bag with the top section closed. He conferred briefly with Mackenzie and departed for Rokesley Church where, he told the Scotsman, there was a superb view of the surrounding countryside from the bell tower high above the nave and the bodies in the churchyard below. Mackenzie collected a Deptford constable from the back of the church and conducted a brief reconnaissance from the public bar.

'You're sure?' said Mackenzie, sipping a half of mild and bitter.

'Those two by the window? I'm positive,' said the policeman. 'We'd better get back to our posts. The curtain will be going up fairly soon.'

Five minutes later Mackenzie was with Powerscourt, staring out over the gardens and the tennis court. 'So,' Powerscourt said very quietly, 'the Twins are in the saloon. I don't suppose they'll start anything in there. Maybe I should walk past the windows and see what happens. You didn't see anybody else on your travels, William? No other unexpected visitors?'

'None at all,' replied Mackenzie, 'I've seen everything that goes up and down on that stretch of road.'

At ten to four Powerscourt checked he had his pistol in his pocket. He had grabbed it from its hiding place in his desk before he left Markham Square. Is this the end of the trail, he wondered, a trail that led from Great Russell Street to the harbour front in Brindisi and the millionaire's retreat in the Hudson Valley and the procession to the Acropolis itself? Is this where it ends? He wished Johnny Fitzgerald was with him.

Lady Lucy was pacing up and down her drawing room just like her husband did when detective thoughts were racing through his brain. All her children were out. She had indeed collected a number of auction catalogues on her trips round the shops of Sloane Avenue and the King's Road that morning. Eighteenth-century armoires and Georgian dining tables were not enough to anchor her thoughts in Markham Square. What was happening up there in Northamptonshire? Was Francis all right? Not for the first or the second or the third time she wished that Johnny Fitzgerald was by his side.

The clock in the hall was striking four as Powerscourt set off for his afternoon walk. In the woods and in the clumps of trees, in the dark recesses of the farm buildings and, in one case, high up in one of the great oaks of Southwick Wood, the policemen checked their watches and waited for their prey. The Inspectors fingered their whistles. One or two of the constables had armed themselves with fearful wooden clubs lying about on the ground. Powerscourt went past the pub very slowly. He set out on the footpath to the woods that led past the cricket pitch where he had scored a century in a village match three years before. He was in open ground now. He could hear nothing behind. He could see nothing suspicious in front. Way over to his left was Fotheringhay where Mary Queen of Scots had breathed her last. He hoped he wasn't going to join her this afternoon.

He was on the path between the hamlet of Southwick and the wood that bore its name when there was a shout behind him.

'You,' said the voice, 'you're Powerscourt, aren't you?'

He could see no point in denying it. He turned to face them. His hand was fumbling in his pocket. 'I am.'

'My brother and I here, we want a word.' The Twins drew closer. One brought out a pair of knuckledusters and put them on ostentatiously. The other lit a cigarette. They were only a couple of paces from his face now. Surely this was enough, thought Powerscourt. Where are the police? They should be coming now, running at full speed to arrest his opponents. They weren't here. Where was Mackenzie? For God's sake, where was Inspector Kingsley?

High up in the bell tower the traveller peered down his telescopic sight. He fiddled with it until he had the three people in the line of fire. He would have to wait till they were separated before he could pull the trigger. As things looked he could as easily hit Powerscourt as his assailants. Powerscourt pulled out his pistol. Before he could bring it level, the right boot of the twin with the knuckledusters sent it sailing into the grass by the side of the path.

'Time to get started,' said Robert, rubbing his hands together. Richard began waving his cigarette closer and closer to Powerscourt's face. Powerscourt was about to start running towards the woods when Robert kicked him in the leg so hard he fell over. The Twins moved in for the kill, boots at the ready.

The first shot caught Robert in the centre of his back. He crumpled forward and lay still. Almost immediately there was a second shot which took him in the head. Richard turned to see where the firing came from. The third shot caught him in the centre of the chest. He fell to the ground, pulling Powerscourt down with him until he lay on the ground with Richard's sixteen stone lying prone on top of him. As he fell, Powerscourt could see a line of policemen running at full speed towards him. Whistles were blowing in the wood. Another posse was advancing at full speed from the direction of the village and the pub. He was trapped beneath the weight and the blood of the dying twin who was making gurgling noises as the life ebbed from his body.

'My lord.' Inspector Kingsley and his Sergeant were pulling Powerscourt clear. 'Are you all right?'

'Just about,' said Powerscourt, dusting his jacket and realizing that he had blood all over his trousers. 'Where the hell have you been?'

'Sorry we're late. I think we waited too long before we moved in. I'm so sorry.'

Inspector Ferguson pronounced both the twins dead.

'Was the sharpshooter one of your officers, Inspector?' asked Powerscourt. 'Bloody good shot, whoever he was.'

'Neither Inspector Kingsley nor I have any idea who fired the shots, my lord. It's hard to tell where they came from. I suppose they must have come from somewhere in the village.'

The traveller with the golf bag had packed his kit away. He made his way very carefully down the winding stone stairway that led to the bell tower. By the front of the church he checked that the coast was clear. Then he made his way to the railway station by a back route.

'Well,' said Inspector Kingsley in the Rokesley drawing room, 'that was a close shave indeed. My apologies once again, my lord, for leaving it so late. But nobody in Deptford will be in fear of their lives any more. They'll be drinking your health down there once they hear the news.'

Powerscourt had recovered from his ordeal, back in his house, helped by a clean pair of trousers and two glasses of champagne. 'I still want to know who fired the shots,' he said to the Inspectors and their Sergeants.

'I think he may have been in the bell tower, whoever he was,' said Sergeant Burke, who rejoiced in a Quaker mother and a Presbyterian father, and was enjoying the first glass of champagne he had ever tasted. He had carried out a survey of the village. 'I've been up there,' he went on, 'I didn't see any traces of a gunman, but the line of sight from up there goes straight to the twins' position when they were shot. It's the height. You can see for miles from up there.'

'Where is Mackenzie?' Powerscourt asked suddenly. 'He may have the key to the mystery.'

But William Mackenzie had not been found. He seemed

to have disappeared and the waters had closed over him as surely as if he had been spirited up to heaven. On his way back to London Powerscourt decided that Mackenzie must have fired the shots and vanished in case one of the many policemen decided to charge him with murder.

The traveller with the golf bag reached home in the early evening. He saw that a couple of policemen were still on duty by his front door so he headed for the back entrance.

'And who might you be with that bag?' asked the third policeman on guard at Markham Square.

'I'm terribly sorry, Officer. I live here.'

'You do?'

'My name is Thomas Powerscourt,' the traveller announced, 'I have lived here for years.'

'Beg pardon, I'm sure, sir. You go straight in now. Don't venture out this evening unless you have to.'

The constable resumed his guard duty. He did not mention the meeting in his evening report. Thomas passed his mother on the stairs. He replaced the contents of the golf bag and changed his clothes before supper. Thomas Powerscourt had heard about the terrible risks his father was proposing to take. His had been the footsteps disappearing up the stairs with the creaking floorboard. He knew how his mother would worry. If Johnny Fitzgerald had been in attendance, Thomas would have stayed in London. As it was, the time had come for the eldest son to replace his father's oldest companion in arms. Time for youth to take up the baton.

Four days after the events at Rokesley, Stephen Lambert Lodge, the American academic from Yale, returned to the British Museum. He made a detailed inspection of the restored Caryatid and said that he could not be sure if she was the real thing or not. There were certain imperfections in the marble, he said, that he had not noticed on his previous inspection. He was so sorry he could not be definite. The day after that, Dr Andrew Cronan, Director of the British Museum, returned from his travels and took command of his kingdom once again. And the morning after that, Powerscourt was invited to Number Ten Downing Street for a meeting with the Prime Minister. The only other guest was to be Dr Cronan.

'Do you think you will solve the last mystery now, my love?' asked Lady Lucy, half an hour before her husband had to set off.

'I think there are two last mysteries, myself. If you mean will we learn which one is the real Caryatid, then I hope so, Lucy, I really do. Maybe the Director has some special knowledge.'

'And your other mystery, Francis?'

'Why, I should have thought that was obvious. Who fired the shots that saved my life from Rokesley Church? I was going to write to Mackenzie but I have thought better of it. I feel almost certain that he was the gunman, but that he's reluctant to admit it in case somebody brings charges against him.'

Lady Lucy smiled. 'Well, that's all right then.'

The Prime Minister was late for the meeting in the upstairs drawing room at Ten Downing Street. Dr Cronan entertained Powerscourt with stories about his adventures in Mesopotomia and the villainous camel drivers he had met. 'Far worse than London cabbies, far worse,' had been his verdict. 'The sense of direction of a bat and the morals of the seraglio.'

The Prime Minister's hair had turned white since Powerscourt had last met him. He was quick to offer congratulations. 'I am told, Lord Powerscourt, that you have performed another act of valiant service to your country. As if we were not deeply in your debt already. Without you, I am told, we would not have the Caryatid back at all.'

Powerscout did not say that the statue had been returned thanks to an act that could only be described as blackmail, and that the last drama in the affair had been ended by an act that could easily be classed as murder.

'It was nothing, I assure you,' he murmured.

'There is, however, one thing the Director and I feel that you should be aware of. He and I are the only two people in the country who are in on the secret. I know I can count on your discretion.'

'Of course,' said Powerscourt. What on earth was coming next? The Prime Minister coughed, as if playing for time. He looked briefly at Cronan.

'The Caryatid that was stolen from the British Museum was not the real one,' he began. 'She was not the one brought back to this country by Lord Elgin.'

'God bless my soul. Am I allowed to ask why?'

'You may, of course you may. Some time before the *Mona Lisa* was stolen, Dr Cronan came to see me, very concerned about the thefts of works of art and the attacks on valuable exhibits in museums across Europe and America. In a world populated by more and more mad men, he said, he felt that leaving some of these invaluable works on show is too risky. Dr Cronan suggested we make a substitution of the Caryatid for a trial period of six months. Six weeks later the Leonardo walked off the walls in the Louvre.'

'So where is the real one, Prime Minister?'

'The real one is in a deep vault underneath the Cabinet Office. There are one or two other valuables down there.'

'Correct me if I am wrong, Prime Minister, but are all the Caryatids I have been chasing recently fakes? The one in America? The one that fell into the sea in Brindisi? The one that was carried up to the Acropolis the other day? The one at the Hellenic College? The one sent back to the museum? Are they all, every single last one of them, copies of the copy made to replace the original?'

'I'm afraid so, Lord Powerscourt. That is correct.'

'And what will you say to the Greeks? What will you tell the people of Athens?'

'That is in hand,' the Prime Minister replied. 'I have personally informed the Greek authorities that the Caryatid now on the Acropolis is not the real one.'

'And what did they say?'

'They complained a great deal, of course, like the tiresome and emotional people they are,' said the Prime Minister wearily. 'They jumped up and down and shouted a lot. They are going to blame perfidious Albion, Greece raped of her glories once by Lord Elgin, now deceived by the treacherous British. Don't trust the English, I said to them, even when they come bearing gifts.'

'I see,' said Powerscourt. 'How soon are you going to put the real one back on her plinth?'

'Dr Cronan?' said the Prime Minister.

'Well,' said the Director of the British Museum, 'well, for the moment, with the *Mona Lisa* still missing and so on, I think we'll leave the real Caryatid in her vault underneath the Cabinet Office. Just for now, anyway. Better safe than sorry, don't you think?'

Powerscourt was going to take Lady Lucy out to dinner that evening to celebrate the end of the case. 'I feel slightly cheated, you know,' he said, on his return from Downing Street, 'all that effort for a fake.'

'Nobody knew it was a fake, Francis. Even that poor man Ragg didn't know, did he?'

'No, he didn't. It doesn't really matter which one was sent back to the British Museum, does it? They were all copies, or copies of copies, heaven help us all. That young American, Lodge, deserves a medal, don't you think?'

'Why do you say that, Francis?'

'Well, he was right way back at the start of this affair when he told Ragg that the Caryatid on display wasn't the real thing. And he was right at the very end when he told Ragg that the one that came back wasn't the real thing either. They should give him a medal.'

'Perhaps they will, though that would mean admitting they were wrong at the start.'

'Who knows? Do you realize, Lucy, how much I have been thinking about the ancient Greeks since the start of this case? I began reading Pericles' Funeral Speech on the train to Italy, the one where he talks about the Athenians who died in the battle having the whole earth as their memorial. The end of the speech – I was reading it in bed last night – is very downbeat and very moving. Maybe it's a fitting close to the death of an Elgin Marble. Pericles sings the praises of those who died for the honour of Athens and have the whole earth as their memorial. It's the high point and the epitaph for Athens's glory.'

Powerscourt went over to a table by the fireplace

and opened a well-thumbed copy of Thucydides' *The Peloponnesian War*.

'"Such then were these men and the glory they brought their city. For the time being our offerings to the dead have been made and for the future their children will be supported at the public expense by the city until they come of age. This is the crown and prize which she offers, both to the dead and their children, for the ordeals they have faced. Where the rewards of valour are the greatest, there you will find also the best and bravest spirits among the people. And now, when you have mourned for your dear ones, you must depart."'

There was a ring at the front door. Rhys the butler showed Inspector Kingsley into the drawing room.

'I've left the parcel in the hall,' he said. 'I don't see that we need to hang on to it any more. Anyway, I have some news.'

Powerscourt felt desperately sorry that he was not allowed to tell his colleague the truth about the Caryatids.

'What is that, Inspector?'

'I've done it at last. I've handed in my resignation. It will become effective at the end of the month. The Commissioner has been very good about it, I must say.'

'Congratulations on becoming a civilian, or being about to become a civilian,' said Lady Lucy. 'What are you going to do now?'

'I'm going to write a book,' said the Inspector. 'It's going to be about a policeman and I've already had promising talks with a publisher about it.'

'What sort of policeman?' asked Powerscourt. 'Constable? Sergeant? Inspector? Commissioner?'

'I'm sure you won't be surprised to hear that it's going to be an Inspector, my lord. He's going to be like Conrad's

Lord Jim. He makes one terrible mistake and gets away with it. Then he has to seek redemption and salvation on the streets of London and in a showdown on Hackney Marshes.'

'Splendid,' said Lady Lucy. 'We look forward to reading it.'

Half an hour later Powerscourt parked the Silver Ghost outside Norfolk House on Chiswick Mall. He picked up the parcel, still in its layers of wrapping paper. He had warned Mrs Wilson that he would be dropping by. He happened to be in the neighbourhood, his note said.

Powerscourt left his parcel in the hall as the maid showed him into the huge room with the view out over the river.

'Lord Powerscourt, how nice to see you again,' said Mrs Wilson. She seemed to have shrunk since Powerscourt last saw her. The white hair was, if anything, even whiter than before. 'You look tired. Have you been working too hard? I'll order some tea. That should set you up.'

'That's very kind, Mrs Wilson. How have you been yourself? Keeping well?' Powerscourt remembered that Mrs Wilson's husband, Horace, had died a few months after the theft.

'I can't complain, Lord Powerscourt. The eyesight is going some of the time and my memory isn't what it was. I was trying to remember, after I got your note, how long it was since you called the first time. Do you know, I couldn't put a date on it at all. I know it happened, of course, but it could have been last month or last year for all I can recall now.'

The tea arrived. The blank space was still there above the fireplace, the picture hooks still in place on the wall.

'I'm sure your memory is fine, Mrs Wilson. Don't worry about it. Now then, I've brought you a present, a sort of present anyway. Would you like to see it now?'

Mrs Wilson sounded young again as she thought of presents and happy birthdays long ago. 'Yes, please, Lord Powerscourt. How very exciting!'

He brought the parcel in from the hall. It measured about three feet high by four feet across.

'That looks very impressive, Lord Powerscourt. Could you be very kind and open it up for me?'

Armed with his penknife, Powerscourt untied the string and put the brown paper into the waste basket. The painting was the wrong way round, the back facing the lady of the house.

'Oh, Lord Powerscourt, I'm so thrilled! Have you brought me a new painting to replace the one we lost? How very kind!'

Powerscourt smiled. 'I'm afraid I haven't brought you a picture to replace the one you lost, Mrs Wilson,' he said, turning it round very slowly. 'I've brought back the one that was stolen. This is Turner's *Mortlake Terrace, Summer's Evening*. It's come home for you to enjoy it again.'

Mrs Wilson stared at the painting. She shook her head very slowly. She began to cry.

'I don't believe it,' she sobbed into Powerscourt's shoulder. 'I've dreamt of this moment for so long. It can't be true, it can't be.'

Powerscourt held the old lady very tight. 'It's true all right,' he murmured, 'your Turner is back. It's home again. I'm so pleased.'

Mrs Wilson pulled back. 'I'm sorry. I can't go on crying into your nice jacket,' she said. 'Could you do me a favour, Lord Powerscourt? I'd be so grateful.'

'Of course. What is it?'

'Could you hang the picture back on the wall where it was before? The hooks are still there, you see.'

Very carefully Powerscourt put the painting back where it belonged. Mrs Wilson poured herself another cup of tea.

'Just think,' she said, 'I'll be able to look at it last thing at night. I'll be able to look at it first thing in the morning. Horace will be so pleased. I'm sure he can see it too, wherever he is.'

Powerscourt felt a great wave of happiness. He was glad he had decided to bring the painting back in person.

Fifteen minutes later the sun came out as he was navigating his way along Chiswick Mall towards Hammersmith Bridge. The light sparkled on the waters of the Thames. On the far side, the light, Turner's light, Turner's glory, glittered and shone on the river by William Moffatt's house in Mortlake Terrace.